HER HEART BEAT LIKE A TRIPHAMMER

Would it be right and proper to tell Brian she loved him? Weren't the words, "I love you," supposed to be spoken by the man first?

Regina sighed softly as she lay with her arms around Brian, gazing past his resting head toward the far-away glitter of the stars.

"What is it, Regina?" he asked huskily.

"I was just thinking that I will never be able to wear a sapphire now."

He stroked a forefinger across her lips. "And why not, pray?"

"Because it would change color if I did, since I am no longer chaste."

"If there is any consistency in the romance industry, it's Patricia Matthews's historical romances." —L.A. *Daily News*

"Patricia Matthews is a consummate storyteller who brings history alive. She writes wonderful, sensual stories."
—*Romantic Times*

"Bold romance and peerless adventure spring naturally from the pen of Patricia Matthews." —*Bestsellers*

"Patricia Matthews is an author I've read and enjoyed for years." —Janelle Taylor

Sapphire

Patricia Matthews

WORLDWIDE®

TORONTO • NEW YORK • LONDON • PARIS
AMSTERDAM • STOCKHOLM • HAMBURG
ATHENS • MILAN • TOKYO • SYDNEY

SAPPHIRE

A Worldwide Library Book/September 1989

ISBN 0-373-97111-7

Sapphire

PROLOGUE
1880

IT WAS 4:00 A.M., and the East End of London was almost deserted. The night was cold and damp, and fog hung in the narrow streets, causing the light from the gas lamps to diffuse in soft halos.

A lone woman hurried along Whitechapel High Street, a tattered shawl around her bent shoulders providing poor protection against the chill.

Adelaide Paxton was weary from her hard night's labor as a charwoman for Slostrum's, one of London's most prestigious gem dealers. She was looking forward to the comparative warmth of her small flat, and a hot, restorative cup of tea.

Although forty years old, Adelaide looked sixty; she was a mouse of a woman, small, thin and stooped, her pale features pinched with misfortune and years of hard labor. Her brown, gray-streaked hair was bound up in a scarf, and her long, heavy skirts brushed the cobblestones as she walked.

The district, known as the Evil Quarter Mile, abounded with cutpurses and thieves, some of whom would slit a throat for a shilling or less; yet Adelaide had no choice but to frequent it. It was the only area in which she could afford to live. Still, despite the rough neighborhood, she had never been accosted: she was recognized as one of the East End's own, with a poor purse hardly worth stealing.

Only a few blocks from her building now, Adelaide's footsteps quickened in anticipation of shelter and nourishment.

But just as she passed the dark entrance of a narrow alley, she heard a strange, mewling sound. Her step slowed, and she turned back, peering into the alley. The sound came again. A cat? No, it had been the sound of a baby crying! Could it be, she wondered? Adelaide knew that it was not unusual for some poor, unfortunate woman, without a husband or a means of caring for a child, to abandon an infant.

The cry came again, from deep in the recesses of the alley. After a moment's hesitation, Adelaide drew a deep breath, squared her shoulders and ventured into the darkness. She had to feel her way along by keeping one hand on the moisture-slick surface of the building on her right. She shuddered at the sound of scurrying rats disturbed by her passing. Once she stumbled and almost fell to her knees. She would have turned back, but the cry came again, this time very near. Bending over, she felt blindly toward the ground before her. One hand struck a wooden box and the cry came again, a plaintive wail. There was no lid on the box and Adelaide felt carefully inside. She brushed against human flesh, and she sucked in her breath as a tiny hand clutched her fingers.

Tenderly she picked the small creature up, cuddling it in her arms as she clucked to it gently. She made her way out of the dark alley into the spill of light on the street. There she gazed down at the infant. Two huge eyes looked up from a small, white face as the child drew in a shuddering sob of a breath. It could not be over a few weeks old at the most, and the blanket it had been wrapped in had come loose. The baby was naked.

What kind of heartless woman could leave a baby in a dark alleyway, unclothed? It, she glanced down, was female—she could have died from exposure before anyone had found her. Carefully Adelaide wrapped the little girl back in the blanket, held her against her breast and glanced around to see that she was unobserved. Without any further hesitation, she began to hurry toward her flat.

Her small flat was in the basement beneath an ancient building. It consisted of one small room, but it did have the advantage of an outside entrance. Once inside, with the door closed and bolted behind her, Adelaide lit a lamp and pulled back the curtain of the tiny alcove that served as her sleeping quarters. She placed the little girl on the narrow bed and stood gazing down at her. The baby began to wail again.

Poor little tyke!

Adelaide had been married once, to Robert Paxton. Both she and Robert had wanted children badly, but they had never been blessed. Robert had died of the smallpox five years ago, leaving her destitute; and Adelaide knew then that she would never have children of her own. She was doomed to live out her life in solitude, or so she had believed.

Now it appeared that the fates had relented and had given her a daughter; not the fruit of her womb, but she knew in that moment that she would fight to the death to keep the child.

Adelaide clasped her hands together and looked toward the ceiling. "Thank you, sweet Jesus!"

The sound of her voice intensified the baby's cries. Bending down, Adelaide extended her finger, and the baby seized it with determination.

"There, there, little one," Adelaide murmured. "You're safe now, warm and safe."

The baby fumbled the finger into her mouth and tried to suckle.

"Of course! I must be daft! You must be starving, poor thing."

She felt at a loss. There was no milk in her flat, and what food there was was not suitable for a baby not yet weaned. In the end she soaked a piece of thin cloth in water, filled it with sugar and made a sugar teat.

The baby took to it eagerly, suckling on the teat while Adelaide held it in her mouth. She made two more, and the baby finally settled into a peaceful slumber.

Adelaide looked down at the child, remembering the fierce determination on the tiny face as the baby had seized upon the sugar teat, her blue eyes intent. She was going to be strong willed, of that there was no doubt.

Adelaide felt a welling of love and tears stung her eyes. She extended a careworn hand and tenderly caressed the child's head, which showed a few wisps of fine, black hair.

"Regina," she said softly. "That is your name henceforth, little one. Regina Paxton." She leaned down to plant a kiss on the baby's forehead, and the child stirred, whimpering faintly.

CHAPTER ONE

ON A LATE SPRING afternoon in 1899, a tall, handsome young woman hurried along Commercial Street in London's East End. She walked with a vigorous stride and carried a bag of fresh produce.

Regina Paxton had dawdled at the market too long, admiring the fresh fruit and vegetables, harbingers of spring. The highly polished fruit always reminded her of jewels and stirred her to flights of imagination: the apples as red as rubies, the grapes as green as emeralds, and the peaches as pink as pearls.

She laughed at herself as she hurried along; her mother would be waking soon and would be needing her supper before going to her job at Slostrum's.

Regina had grown into a striking woman. She carried herself with a grace that caught the eye, but it was her coloring that one first noticed: the heavy mass of rich, black hair; the deep blue eyes; the pale but glowing skin, the hue of rich cream.

Thinking of her mother brought another thought to mind. It was time she was taking on the responsibilities of an adult. She must find a paying position. At present, the only work Adelaide allowed her to do was the household chores, including the cooking. She had been performing these duties since she was eleven, over her mother's protests.

"You should have a chance to be a child first," Adelaide had often said. "A chance to play and enjoy yourself, not grow old before your time with drudgery."

"You work hard, Mother, harder than any woman should," Regina had responded. "It's the least I can do to help out. You shouldn't have to do the household chores after working all night as a charwoman."

Regina could have added that she didn't much enjoy the company of other children, or playing children's games. Perhaps she wasn't normal, but she felt years older than her contemporaries. She had been a serious child from the beginning. It wasn't that she didn't enjoy herself, but she found her pleasure in other ways—in books, in her flights of imagination, in the love of color, such as those of the fruits she had just bought in the market. Regina loved color and had once thought that she might become an artist. She abandoned that notion when it became apparent that she had absolutely no talent in that direction.

Regina had recognized, quite early in her life, that she was different from the other children. Perhaps it was because she was a foundling. Adelaide had told her, as soon as the girl was old enough to understand the circumstances under which Adelaide had found her.

Regina could not have loved Adelaide more had the woman been her natural mother. True, there were times when Regina wondered what her natural mother looked like, who she was, and what had driven her to abandon a child in such a manner; yet she was never plagued long by such thoughts.

She already knew that to rail against the fates was futile; and one of the first lessons she had learned was that the world was not always fair. A look at Adelaide told her that. Adelaide was a good, kind person, a fine mother, and yet she had to work as a charwoman—hard, demeaning work, about which Regina had never heard her complain. Adelaide deserved more, and Regina was determined that she would provide a better life for her as soon as she was old enough to do so.

Now she turned down a side street toward their building. When Regina was ten, they had been able to move to better living quarters in a better neighborhood. Although it was still a poor area, crime was not as rampant as in the old district. One reason was probably the proximity of the Commercial Street Police Station a few blocks away. Most of the people abiding here were honest and hardworking.

Their flat was small, but it had three rooms, so that they each had separate sleeping quarters. It was on the third floor, which made it difficult for Adelaide who had to climb the three flights of stairs after a hard night's labor; yet there were compensations. There was a corner room with two windows, providing light and air on hot summer nights. From the windows there was a good view of the street below and Regina spent many pleasant hours there, a book in her lap, occasionally looking up from her reading to study the mass of people on the street going about their business.

Adelaide was already up, making a pot of tea. She turned around, her worn face breaking into a fond smile. "Hello, dear."

"I'm sorry I'm late, Mother," Regina said breathlessly, hurrying to the cupboard with her purchases. "As usual, I dallied at the market too long. Here, you sit down while I make the tea." She took the pot.

Adelaide acquiesced meekly. Once she would have complained that she was not that helpless, but no longer. Regina loved doing for her, and Adelaide loved being spoiled. Her heart swelled with love as she watched her daughter bustle about the small kitchen. She never thought of Regina as adopted; it seemed that the girl was truly of her own flesh and blood.

Regina came with a cup of steaming tea. "I'll make supper now. Are you hungry, Mother?"

"Not really," Adelaide said with a sigh, sipping at the aromatic tea.

"You have to eat, Mother," Regina said reprovingly. "As hard as you work, you need sustenance."

As Regina began preparing the meal she turned to her mother, asking "Has anything new happened at Slostrum's?"

"Well, let me think." Slostrum's had grown as the years had passed, now employing some twenty people, and had prospered mightily. At least Adelaide no longer had to clean the building by herself. The firm had hired three more charwomen, placing Adelaide in charge of them. Yet it seemed to her that she worked even harder, seeing to it that her charges did their work properly, often doing i' over herself.

She brightened. "Oh, yes, Maggie Reardon left her job yesterday."

"Maggie Reardon?" Regina glanced back over her shoulder. "That's one of the women who cleans and polishes the new gems?" At her mother's nod, she said, "Was she discharged?"

"Oh, no, you know Mr. Slostrum would never discharge anybody, unless she was terribly derelict in her duties. Maggie is getting wed and moving out of London with her new husband."

Regina turned back to her cooking, her thoughts suddenly spinning with a plan.

Behind her, Adelaide was saying, "And the firm is going to have a standing exhibit of new gems on Saturday. It is open to the public and Mr. Slostrum said I was welcome, if I'd like to attend. Would you care to go, Regina?"

Regina whirled around, her face alight. "Oh, Mother, could I?" She had visited the jewelry firm only rarely, but each time she went, she had been mesmerized by each display, fascinated by the fire, color and beauty of the stones. And by their great wealth; she was not reluctant to admit that to herself. Early on, she had understood the difference between the stations of the rich and the poor, and she had determined that she would one day be wealthy enough to sweep into a place like Slostrum's and buy anything her heart desired. Once she had confessed this dream to Adelaide, and Adelaide, in a rare display of anger, had slapped Regina stingingly across the cheek.

"Don't fill your head with such dreams, child! It can only bring you heartbreak and grief. We are born to a certain station in this life, and few can rise above it."

Regina had had the good sense to keep quiet and had not mentioned her dream since, yet her determination burned all the fiercer.

Now Adelaide said indulgently, "Of course you can go if you wish, dear."

Adelaide, watching the girl covertly as she put the finishing touches to their dinner, knew what was going through Regina's mind. Although they had not talked about it since that one time when when she had regrettably lost her temper, Adelaide was well aware that Regina still retained her dream of rising above her station. Her heart ached for the girl. She knew that a visit to the gem exhibit would only reinforce that dream, yet how could she deny her? Regina had so little pleasure in her life, and if she enjoyed the jewelry displays, what real harm could the visit do? The reality of life would soon be forced upon her, crushing any dreams she might have, causing her to realize their futility. Naturally this would cause her some heartache, but Regina was a sensible girl and would make the necessary adjustments.

When Regina had placed their supper upon the table and settled herself in her seat across from Adelaide, she said, "Has the firm employed someone to replace Maggie Reardon?"

"Not that I know of." Adelaide took a bite of food and chewed it before she said, "They're particular who they employ. Why do you ask, Regina?"

Regina said casually, "Oh, I was just curious." Then she leaned forward and said in a rush, "Do you suppose Mr. Slostrum would employ me, Mother?"

"You!" Adelaide reared back in astonishment. "Why would you want the job?"

"I am more than old enough to find employment, Mother. It is time I assumed some of the burden of supporting us!"

Hurt, Adelaide said, "Are you wanting for anything? If so, tell me."

There were many things Regina wanted, but she knew better than to mention them. Instead she said quickly, "Of course not, Mother. You provide well for us."

"Well, then?"

"Mother, I can't stay home and keep house forever. You can't expect me to do that, now can you?"

With a feeling of dismay, Adelaide realized that she expected just that. For some time, she had accepted that Regina was a grown woman, but so far she had successfully managed to ignore the consequences. It could only mean that Regina would leave her, either through marriage or to a place of employment, and then once again she would be left alone. But Adelaide knew that she could not expect the girl to stay with her indefinitely. It would not be fair to her.

Still, she seized on the first excuse she could think of. "But dear, you don't know the first thing about polishing and cleaning gems."

"I can learn, can't I? It can't be all that difficult. It's not some unusual trade that requires arduous training. I met Maggie Reardon once, remember? She didn't seem to me to be the brightest woman in the world...."

"Regina, that's not a nice thing to say about anyone!"

Regina made a dismissive gesture. "Oh, I didn't mean that she's not a nice person, but you know that what I said is true."

"Regina," Adelaide said sternly. "I worry about you sometimes. You're too blunt spoken. Even telling the truth, at the wrong time, can get you into trouble."

"Then you admit that it *is* the truth?"

Adelaide had to smile. "Yes, I must confess that Maggie is a little . . . well, slow."

"Then if she could learn how to perform the tasks required of her, I can as well."

Adelaide admitted reluctantly, "Yes, I'm sure you could. But is it what you want?"

"Yes!" Regina said, leaning forward eagerly. "I would dearly love to work with gems. Would you talk to Mr. Slostrum for me?"

"I can do that much, I suppose," Adelaide said with a sigh. "But I cannot promise anything, dear. After all, I am only a charwoman."

"But you're one of his oldest employees, Mother. I'm sure that Mr. Slostrum values your opinion," Regina said with the confidence of youth.

SLOSTRUM'S held a well-attended standing exhibit once a year to display their choice pieces. Over the years, the company had become one of the most prominent jewelry firms in London, drawing the trade of the gentry. Regina had heard that even members of the royal family had patronized the establishment from time to time.

Still, she was astounded as she and Adelaide approached the building. Carriages were drawn up for blocks, and elegantly attired men and women were entering in a steady stream. The building had three stories, all occupied by the firm. The top two floors were taken up by offices, and by the artisans employed by the firm. Regina knew that only the very best gem cutters and jewelry makers worked there, and that some of the pieces they made were the envy of the industry.

The whole of the first floor was given over to the cases displaying single gems, as well as necklaces, bracelets, rings, tiaras—every possible piece one could desire.

Adelaide's step slowed as they neared the entrance. "Oh, my!" she exclaimed. "Look at all the fine dresses on the ladies! Alongside them we look dowdy. I look what I am, a plain charwoman."

Regina was not intimidated. They were wearing their best garments, and while it was true that they were not elegant, nothing was going to stop her from observing the dazzling display of gems firsthand. "Nonsense," she said briskly, taking Adelaide's arm in a firm grip. "You look fine. We both look fine. Besides, there are so many people here we won't be noticed. Now come along."

Holding tightly to Adelaide's arm, she maneuvered them through the throng and into the building. The store was indeed crowded, with knots of people standing before each display case. To one side was a long table set with refreshments—tiny sandwiches and cakes, tea and bottles of champagne.

Regina soon lost Adelaide in the crowd as she wormed her way up to the forefront of the first group of people around a display case. People were exclaiming over the diamond tiara on display in a round glass case set on top of the counter. The many-faceted diamonds glittered like stars under the light cast by the candelabra that sat alongside it. Behind the counter stood the salesclerks, resplendent in morning coats, and as haughty as royalty. Regina ignored them and lost herself in a study of the diamonds.

After a bit she moved on, ignoring the crowd as much as possible, stopping before a number of exhibits and studying them at length. She examined diamonds and pearls, rubies and sapphires, garnets and emeralds.

And then her breath left her in a rush, and she thought her heart had stopped beating as she came to a full stop before one case. Inside, bedded in white satin, rested a single stone of great size. Propped up against it was a hand-lettered sign: star sapphire. The stone had been cut *en cabochon*, a phrase Regina was to learn meant "cut with a flat bottom and a rounded top, in order to emphasize the star quality." The color was a deep blue, and yet the light striking the stone from all sides seemed to create a number of rays of blinding white that radiated outward from the core. She could well understand why the gem was called a star sapphire; it seemed to capture and hold the light within, like a distant star.

Regina stood for a long while, utterly entranced. It was the most beautiful thing she had ever seen. It possessed a beauty that was almost mesmerizing.

In that moment, Regina resolved that someday, in some way, she would possess such a stone. She knew, without being told in so many words, that star sapphires were rare, and, therefore, terribly expensive.

A chilly voice jarred her out of her reverie, "Madam, would you please be so kind as to move along? You are blocking others."

Regina glanced across the counter into the supercilious countenance of one of the clerks. A mischievous impulse came to mind. How would he react if she asked, in an equally haughty tone, the price of the sapphire? But she knew that she hadn't fooled him for an instant. His icy, contemptuous stare told her that he probably knew to the pence how much money she had in her reticule.

With a toss of her head, she moved on down the line, stopping at the other displays in turn. But no matter how beautiful the other gems were, none aroused in her the fascination she felt for the huge sapphire. When she reached the rear of the store, she was thinking of working her way back up to a position before the sapphire again when her attention was caught by a rich, melodious voice. "Look here, my good fellow, I insist on seeing Andrew Slostrum!"

Not too far away stood a giant of a man, with flaming red hair and a luxurious red beard. Young, broad of shoulder, with a leonine head, he was dressed in faded clothing and he carried a scuffed canvas bag in his right hand. His clothing and great stature made him stand out among the impeccably dressed men and women; and his resonant voice was attracting many disapproving stares, all of which he ignored.

The clerk behind the counter looked harried. "Sir, Mr. Slostrum is very busy. As you can see, we are having a showing today."

"He will see me. Tell him Brian Macbride is here. By the saints, I'll see him before I leave."

A distinguished-looking man of some fifty years pushed his way through the throng to Brian Macbride's side. With a crown of thick white hair and a florid face, he was clad in a morning coat like the clerks. Regina recognized him as Andrew Slostrum.

"For God's sake, Brian, lower your voice, will you?" Slostrum said in a low voice. "You're attracting attention."

"Andrew!" The big man swung around, teeth flashing whitely in the red thatch as he grinned. "It's glad I am to see you. As for attracting attention, I'm accustomed to that."

"I'm sure you are," Slostrum muttered, "but it's my exhibition and I want to attract attention to the stones, not to Brian Macbride."

Macbride chuckled. "Maybe you should let me take over from these proper boyos." He swept an arm around to indicate the clerks. "They look like they're presiding at a wake. I could sell some pieces for you. At the very least, I would stir things up."

"Indeed. That's what you're doing already. Now what do you want, Brian?"

The big man looked wounded. "It's been . . . what . . . two years since we've seen each other and that's all the greeting I get?"

"Brian..." Slostrum sighed in exasperation. "I am holding an exhibition here. This is not the time to renew old acquaintances."

"I have something for you." Brian Macbride slapped the canvas bag in his hand. "I'm after thinking your eyes will pop out of your skull when you see what I have for you, Andrew."

"It will have to wait, Brian. Monday morning, perhaps?"

Macbride shook his head. "Can't wait, old friend. If you can't see me today, I'll just have to go somewhere else."

"Your purse is flat, I assume?"

Macbride laughed, unoffended. "Isn't it always?"

Slostrum nodded resignedly, "Indeed. All right, you wild Irishman. Go upstairs to my office. There is a bottle of whiskey. I'm sure you can make yourself at home with that. I must make another circuit of the room, then I shall be up, and perhaps we can do some business."

"Sure, and we'll do business, my friend." Again Macbride patted the bag. "When you see what I have."

With a nod, Slostrum turned away. As he did so, Macbride's gaze met Regina's and lingered. His eyes were a startling pale blue-green, like aquamarine. His face was grave as he studied her; and even from that distance, she could feel the vitality emanating from him in waves. She felt herself flush. He smiled faintly, saluted her with a flip of his hand, and turned away toward the stairs leading to the next floor.

At a touch of her elbow, Regina faced around to see Adelaide. "Where have you been, Regina? I've been looking all over for you."

"I've been looking at the displays." Regina motioned with her head toward the big man climbing the stairs. "Do you know that man, Mother? His name is Brian Macbride."

Adelaide gazed at the receding back of the large man, then back at Regina. "The name means nothing to me. Why do you ask?"

"Merely curious," Regina said with a shrug. "He seems so . . . well, out of place here. He had something in a bag, and he told Mr. Slostrum that he wished to do business with him."

"He probably has some gems to sell. Some very odd people come here to sell gemstones. Regina, I spoke to Mr. Slostrum about the position."

"And what did he say?" Regina asked eagerly.

"He said he would think about it. Dear, don't get your hopes up now . . ."

A voice from behind Regina interrupted the conversation. "Mrs. Paxton, is this the girl you told me about?"

"Yes, sir, my daughter, Regina." As Regina turned, Adelaide added, "Regina, this is my employer, Mr. Slostrum."

Regina said primly, "How do you do, sir?"

"Not too well, I'm afraid," he said grumpily. "These exhibitions are wearing on the nerves."

All the while, his deep-set black eyes were studying Regina intently. Then he said abruptly, "Want to work here, do you?"

"Yes, sir. I should like that very much."

"No experience, your mother said."

"That is true, Mr. Slostrum, but I am quick and willing to learn."

"I have found your mother most trustworthy and hardworking. I trust you are the same?"

"I would hope so, sir. But that is not for me to say."

"Indeed. Most modest of you. Very well. You must understand that as an apprentice, so to speak, I cannot pay you much at first, only a few shillings a day until you prove your worth?"

"Oh, I understand that, sir."

"Indeed. Very well, then," he said gruffly. "You may start Monday morning. Seven o'clock."

CHAPTER TWO

BRIAN MACBRIDE quickly found a glass and the bottle of whiskey Andrew Slostrum had mentioned. He poured a generous amount of the liquor into the glass and, with a sigh, sat down in the chair before Slostrum's desk, tucking the canvas bag carefully between his feet. He downed half of the whiskey in a single gulp, welcoming the warmth that flowed down his gullet.

By the saints, he was bone tired!

The ship he had taken from Africa had just docked that morning, and he had gone directly to Slostrum's. He'd really had no choice in the matter; Slostrum's guess about the state of his purse was more accurate than the man realized—there wasn't enough left in it to pay for a night's lodging.

But that would be taken care of once Slostrum had a good look at the contents of the bag. At twenty-seven, Brian was accustomed to being without funds for long periods. As a gem hunter, roaming the far reaches of the world, the periods between good finds were often long. This time he had really hit it big.

Of course, he had been lucky to escape with his life. It was a risky business, hunting for diamonds in South Africa. After Cecil Rhodes and Barney Barnato, two British adventurers, had struck it rich in the diamond fields of the area, they had formed the De Beers Consolidated Mines. They now controlled the flow of diamonds to every country in the world. It meant they also controlled the prices. But to maintain this monopoly, they had to guard their fields very carefully; the guards patrolling the district were not averse to shooting any man rash enough to try to sneak diamonds out of the fields.

Brian was accustomed to venturing into dangerous territory. Almost any country rich in gems was also zealous in protecting its preserves. This time a guard patrol had spotted him as he was leaving a South African streambed with a number of diamonds. Luckily the horse he had been riding was swift, and the guards had been terrible shots.

He raked his long fingers through his beard; it itched annoyingly. He never shaved when he was out adventuring, but once back in civilization he longed for an unshaven countenance and new, expensive clothes. He should realize enough profits here today to see him through six months of leisure and sport, with enough left over to finance the next expedition.

Macbride grinned to himself, thinking of his father, wondering, not for the first time, what the old man would think of his elder son's life. He would probably consider him a wastrel, an idler. Daniel Macbride had been a man of the earth, scratching at the thin soil of Ireland, earning only enough for a bare existence as he suffered through one potato famine after another. But despite the poverty, the backbreaking toil and hardship, he had believed until the day of his death in the virtue of hard labor.

On his seventeenth birthday, Brian had asked his father, "Da, why do you do it? You hump your back, you starve one year, make a few pounds the next, but never enough for much more than an extra pint or two, and maybe a pair of new shoes. Why?"

Daniel Macbride's faded brown eyes had taken on a blank look. "'Tis a foolish question you're asking, laddie buck. Life is hard for a poor man. 'Tis the Lord's will."

"I hardly think the Lord, in all His wisdom, decreed that a man must be poor to get to Heaven. Just because your life has been spent that way doesn't mean that it must be so. By all the saints, I'm not going to labor my life away cultivating the poor soil of Ireland so that I can fall into a pauper's grave at the end. Somehow I don't think the Lord would wish that fate upon me. There has to be more to life than that!"

"Don't blather such foolishness, boy! And don't be after blaspheming the Lord!" His father's hand had lashed out and clouted Brian alongside the head so hard that his ears rang. "I have raised three children, including you, you insolent whelp, all by the hard work of me own hands. I'll be thanking you to remember that!"

"And it's not been the best of life for us, Da. Many's the night we've gone to bed with empty bellies." Never before had he dared to talk to his father in such a manner, but his anger drove Brian past caution.

His father's face went dark red. "I have done me best for you."

"Your best hasn't been good enough, Da."

Daniel Macbride made a fist and took an angry stride. Forewarned this time, Brian managed to duck away from the blow. Slightly ashamed of himself—his father was a good, decent man and didn't deserve such abuse—Brian held up his hands. "I'm sorry I am, Da. I have no call to say such things to you."

Brian left home a few weeks later and had not returned until five years ago, when his father had died of a heart attack while working in the fields. Brian attended the wake and the funeral, said farewell to his mother and siblings, and had not been back to Ireland since. He kept in touch with his mother by post, sending her money when he made a strike, and he would return to Ireland for the last time for her funeral. . . .

His musings were interrupted as the door swung open, and Andrew Slostrum came in, looking harried. "Well, Brian, I hope this is important."

"Aye, that it is," Brian began cheerfully, "as you'll soon see."

Slostrum sat down behind his desk with a weary sigh. "Such an impetuous fellow you are, Brian. It seems you always arrive at a bad time."

"Sure, and you should be flattered, Andrew, that I usually come to you first. And don't I always bring good quality to you?"

"No, not always," Slostrum said in a grumbling voice. "Once you came with opals of poor quality. I lost money on them, Brian."

Brian gestured airily. "My apologies for that. I confess I wasn't a good judge of opals at that time. But this will more than make up for it."

"Indeed. We shall see. Show me what you have, and let's get on with it. I have to return to the floor shortly."

Picking up the bag between his feet, Brian opened it and dumped the contents onto the broad expanse of Slostrum's desk. There were roughly fifty uncut diamonds of varying sizes.

Slostrum's breath left him in a rush. "Diamonds! Where did you get...? No." He held up a staying hand. "I don't want to know."

Brian grinned faintly. "Never occurred to me that you would. But they're fine goods; you can see that for yourself."

Slostrum was poking a long forefinger delicately at the gems. "You know the problem with diamonds, Brian," he said almost absently. "With the tight monopoly De Beers exercises, they could come down on me hard if they learn that I have diamonds that are unaccounted for. They could refuse to let me attend a sight for years, perhaps longer. Or they could bar me for good."

Brian was lounging back in his chair, one long leg crossed over the other. He gestured dismissively. "Come now, Andrew. With the volume of your business, you can sell those a few at a time without the corporation ever being the wiser."

"Indeed. Perhaps, perhaps not."

With a pair of tweezers, Slostrum picked up the diamonds one at a time and examined them. Then, from his desk drawer he took a set of hardness points—small metal tubes containing cylinders of a mineral of a known hardness that was ground to a point at one end and cemented into the tube. He selected one, picked up a diamond and carefully scratched the hard end across the stone, making a minute scratch. Then he wiped the test surface with a soft cloth and peered at the area closely through a loupe.

Although his features showed no reaction, Brian knew that Slostrum was satisfied.

The jeweler leaned back and gazed across his desk at Brian. "What is your estimate of their worth?"

Brian knew from past experience and from the narrow-eyed expression on Slostrum's face, that the man was ready to bargain. With an equally grave expression, Brian said, "I'm sure we won't have any trouble arriving at a price agreeable to both of us. I've always found you to be a fair man, Andrew...."

REGINA WAS STANDING before the star sapphire taking a last, lingering look when Adelaide found her.

"Come along, Regina. We must leave before we wear out our welcome. We are not customers you must remember, but are here only on Mr. Slostrum's sufferance."

Regina still held back, indicating the star sapphire with a nod of her head. "Isn't that a beautiful object, Mother?"

"Of course it is, as well it should be, considering the price. You would likely swoon if you knew how dear it is." Adelaide took a firm grip on Regina's arm. "Now let us take leave."

Regina went along docilely now, still dazzled by the gems she had seen, particularly the star sapphire. Her mind and her senses were overwhelmed.

Once outside, away from the press of the crowd, she said dreamily, "Someday I am going to have a jewel like that for my very own."

Adelaide stopped short. "What?"

"I said, I'm going to have a star sapphire like that someday."

"Don't talk such nonsense, child!" Adelaide said sharply. "Haven't I warned you before? You're going to have to put those extravagant dreams out of your head, Regina. Perhaps it is a mistake for you to work at Slostrum's, seeing precious stones every day, gems forever beyond your reach."

Feeling a tug of alarm, Regina said quickly, "Mother, wouldn't it be better for me to be around them, so that I will no longer need to dream about them?"

Adelaide nodded thoughtfully. "Perhaps you are right. Perhaps their beauty and power will wear thin if you work with gemstones every day. I devoutly hope so, at any rate."

Regina knew better; she knew in her heart that the glowing stones would always intrigue her, but she did not voice the thought. Instead she said, "Mother, didn't you ever have dreams when you were younger?"

Adelaide looked startled and thought hard for a moment before answering. Her voice was tart as she said, "Certainly I had my dreams, child. You think I *wanted* to be a charwoman? But that was when I was much younger, before I married Robert. Then when he died, I realized that my dreams were a waste of time and only made me unhappy. I had to get on with my life and be practical. But I do have one dream still, Regina." She smiled now and hugged the girl to her. "My dream now is for you. I want you to have a good life. My dream is for you to marry a fine man, have children and be happy."

Regina felt tears mist her eyes, and she felt a great outpouring of love for this woman who had devoted her life to raising her. Impulsively she opened her arms and embraced Adelaide.

"I thank you for that, Mother," she whispered passionately. "I could not have asked for a finer mother, and if I'm often a trial to you, I am sorry for that."

"Why, I..." Adelaide, at a loss for words, fought back a wave of emotion. How she loved this girl! She freed herself, and noticing the amused glances of passersby, she said brusquely, "What people must think of us, hugging out here on the street! Come, we must get home."

She set off at a brisk pace. Regina followed more slowly, her thoughts chaotic. She had never given a great deal of thought to love and marriage, yet she knew, in a deep part of her mind, that she would likely experience both one day. But someday was not now; all that was for the future.

There were more important things to think about at the present. She realized, in a spurt of awareness as sudden and as bright as a sunburst, that today marked a turning point in her life. She knew that, contrary to what Adelaide had said, she would never lose her dreams, her sense of wonder. To do so, it seemed to her, would mean that her life would lose most of its meaning. Even more important, despite what she had told Adelaide, she knew that she would never lose her fascination with gems. Somehow they would be an important part of her life from this day forward.

ON MONDAY MORNING, Regina arrived at Slostrum's a half hour early and had to wait impatiently for someone to show up to admit her to the premises. The first person to appear was one of the clerks.

"Who are you, and what do you want here?" he demanded rudely.

Unintimidated, Regina said, "I'm Regina Paxton, and I have been employed to work here. Mr. Slostrum said to report at seven o'clock."

"Well, I know nothing about that, and it's not seven yet," he said dourly. "You'll have to wait until Mr. Slostrum gets here."

He unlocked the door and Regina followed him inside. The clerk scowled at her. "You will wait outside."

"Why should I, since I'll be working here?" she said tartly.

He looked undecided for a moment, then gestured. "All right, you can wait inside, but stay out of the way."

While he began to prepare the store for its opening, Regina wandered around. To her disappointment, the case holding the star sapphire was not in evidence.

"Where is the star sapphire I saw on Saturday? Has it been sold?" she finally asked the clerk.

"No, young woman, the star is in the vault, where it is always kept, except during a showing or when a customer wishes to view it," he said. "It is far too valuable to keep on the floor."

Regina was nettled at his arrogant manner, and a sharp retort was on the tip of her tongue when a key sounded in the lock and Andrew Slostrum entered briskly. He smiled broadly at the sight of her. Taking out his pocket watch, he unsnapped the case and looked at it pointedly. "You are very prompt, young lady. I like that in an employee."

"It works no hardship on me, sir. I always rise early to prepare our breakfast. Mother gets home from work around five in the morning. She needs a hot meal and is too weary to prepare it for herself."

Slostrum looked vaguely uncomfortable. "Indeed. A fine woman, your mother. Did you know that I offered her a better position than charwoman when our business began to expand?"

"No, sir, I didn't know that," Regina said in surprise.

"I was beginning to employ women then to clean and polish rough gemstones, and offered to so employ Mrs. Paxton. But she refused, saying that she was accustomed to being a charwoman and didn't want to change. Of course, in the end, her decision was probably for the best. For her, I mean," he amended hastily. "When we finally took over the entire building, I had to hire additional charwomen, and I placed her in charge. Thus, she earns more money than I could possibly pay the people doing the job you will be doing, my dear."

"She has great respect for you, sir."

"And I her. Indeed. In fact, I shall be eternally grateful to her. She sees to it that my establishment is sparkling clean at all times, so much so that the gentry, and occasionally royalty, are not loath to patronize my firm."

He turned at the sound of voices as the door opened to admit several more employees, among them two women. Slostrum motioned them over and introduced them to Regina one by one.

There were five men—two clerks, two gem cutters and a jewelry designer. The two women, Jane Worthington and Elizabeth Cranston, were cleaners and polishers. The elder, Jane, was a jolly, apple-cheeked woman whom Regina liked immediately. Elizabeth was about forty, dour, and uncommunicative.

"Jane will be your mentor, Regina," Slostrum said. "She has worked for me for six years and knows everything there is to know about cleaning gemstones."

As Regina accompanied the two women upstairs, Jane said cheerfully, "Ain't all that much to know about cleaning stones, ducks. It's hard, tedious work, but most times it's something like cleaning pier glass."

"Sometimes I'd just as soon be a charwoman," said Elizabeth with a twist of bitterness.

Jane laughed. "Don't pay any heed to her, Regina. Elizabeth is an old sourpuss, even if she ain't so old."

"My mother works as a charwoman here." Regina had decided that she might as well get that fact out in the open, since she well knew that most people looked down upon charwomen.

Jane looked at her. "You're Adelaide's daughter! I thought the name Paxton was familiar, but I didn't make the connection. Adelaide is a fine woman, Regina. You should be proud of her." She smiled. "We always make a great mess when we clean and polish the gemstones. But when we come in the next morning, everything is as clean as can be."

"I *am* proud of my mother. Mr. Slostrum just revealed to me that he once offered to let her clean and polish gemstones, instead of being a charwoman, but she turned the offer down."

"A wise decision, if you want my opinion," Elizabeth said glumly. "Many more years of squinting at the stones, and I'll likely go blind. And we have to be careful not to scratch or shatter the stones. Should we do so, their cost would likely come out of our pay."

"Now, Elizabeth, wherever did you get such an idea?" Jane exclaimed. "Mr. Slostrum never docks our wages."

"We haven't damaged any stones, that's why."

"Maggie did, not too long ago. A rough diamond came in, and while she was cleaning it, it squirted out of her hands and fell to the floor, cleaving it right in two. 'Course, it was probably flawed, and nobody had noticed. Anyway, Elizabeth, she didn't have to pay for it."

"We don't know that for sure. She left soon after, you notice."

"Of her own accord. To be wed."

"We don't know that for sure, either."

Jane clucked, shaking her head as they emerged at the top of the stairs into a huge, loftlike room. Except for several small, partitioned-off cubicles in the rear, the room was one large, open area, filled with long tables.

"This is it, Regina. Those walled-off rooms in the back are for the cutters and the jewelry makers." Leading the way to one of the long tables, Jane placed her reticule on the bench. "And this, ducks, is where we work. I'll fetch the cleaning materials," she added, moving toward the back of the room.

Regina noticed that there were only a few high, narrow windows in the room. They provided little light, although they were sparkling clean. But as she sat down alongside Elizabeth, a man came through the room, lighting the gas lamps suspended overhead, and soon the area was bright.

"It appears that there is sufficient work light," Regina commented to the woman beside her.

"It's not enough," Elizabeth grumbled, "as you'll soon see. It's close work, what we do."

Jane returned with two boxes, which she proceeded to empty onto the table: soft polishing rags; small brushes; two empty water pails: and long strips of worn felt. "I must fill the pails with warm, soapy water," she said. "We use that to clean away the dust and dirt before we start to polish."

Regina saw Mr. Slostrum enter the room. He was carrying a scruffy canvas bag that looked like the one the red-bearded Irishman had been carrying on Saturday. Slostrum came directly to their table. Opening the bag, he began removing the contents, spreading them out on the strips of felt.

"These diamonds just came in, ladies, and need getting ready for the cutters."

Regina stared at the stones placed before her. These were diamonds? They looked like a scattering of simple stones of no value whatsoever.

With a wave of his hand, Slostrum turned and went back downstairs.

Regina leaned down for a closer look at the stones. "These certainly aren't what I imagined diamonds would look like," she said dubiously.

Jane, sitting down beside her, laughed. "These are rough stones, ducks, actually called crystals at this stage. We have to clean them up, then sort them according to size, color and clarity. Color is quite important. 'Course, color can't really be decided until they have been cleaned and polished a little. Here, let me show you." With her forefinger, she separated two of the larger stones from the others. "Most of them are white, colorless, perhaps with a tinge of yellow or gray. Like these two." She turned to Elizabeth. "Fetch some warm, soapy water while I explain things to Regina."

Regina leaned down to study the pair shown. Through the debris—clay and other dirt particles that clung to them—she could see the white, clear color; one had a touch of yellow.

"Richly colored stones called 'fancies' in the trade, are quite rare, and dearly prized," Jane informed her. "Fancy colors include golden yellow, blue, green, pink and amber. The best yellows are 'canary color.' Other colors are sometimes found, but they are even more rare. I don't see much color in these." Her quick fingers were swiftly moving the diamonds around. "Oh, here's a pair of blues. And here's good color."

She held the stone up for Regina's inspection. Through the crust of dirt she could see a bit of greenish-yellow.

"As I said, true color can't really be decided until we've cleaned them properly. The shape and size, we can pretty well figure out now. But clarity will have to wait until they're cleaned."

Regina leaned back. "What do you mean, clarity?"

Jane smiled. "That's what you're here to learn, ducks. It refers to flaws or spots in gemstones. Most gemstones contain tiny bits of other minerals, which, I understand, were formed in them at the time of crystal growth. The more flaws, the less valuable the gems. After they're cleaned, we find the flaws by using a magnifying glass. What they call a 'perfect' diamond is one with very few flaws, clouds, cracks or carbon spots. A perfect gem is very, very rare, Regina. In all the time I have worked here, I've only come across about a half-dozen perfects. Finding one of those, ducks, is a cause for celebration. By the way, I'm talking about diamonds here, only 'cause that's what we're about to work on. But most of what I've told you pretty well applies to all gemstones."

Regina expelled her breath with a sigh. "Good heavens, this is all much more complicated than I thought! There's much more involved than just cleaning the stones, isn't there?"

Jane nodded. "Much more. The most important thing we do is grade the gemstones. 'Course, they're graded again later. They don't trust a mere female to do it just right. But it starts here with us. Some people have a knack for grading, some don't. I'm pretty good at it, while Elizabeth, here—" she grinned up at Elizabeth, who had just returned with a pail of water "—she has never learned. She wouldn't know a perfect from a pebble. As for you, ducks, time will tell the tale."

"Who wants to know one diamond from another?" Elizabeth said with a sniff.

"I do, and perhaps Regina will, as well," Jane said.

"I want to learn everything I can," Regina added.

"Well, this part requires little but hard work." Jane picked up one of the larger diamonds, dipped it into the pail of water, sloshed it around and then proceeded to scrub it with one of the brushes. The encrustations began to slough off. After a bit, Jane took a soft rag and rubbed the stone, then held it up for inspection.

Regina examined the diamond. It was clean now, and while still dull in appearance, it looked less like a common pebble.

"I think this batch will clean up fairly easily," Jane said. "But some are harder, much harder. It pretty much depends on where the stones come from. We have to soak the more difficult ones in acid, which is about the only way to dissolve the overlay material.

"That can be done in two days. One is to soak the gemstones in an acid bath for a week or so. The second way is quicker, and is known as an acid boil. But this can be dangerous, both to you and the stone. Mr. Slostrum never lets us use a quick boil unless nothing else has worked.

"But even the straight acid bath can be harmful to you, so a word of advice. Never forget this. Always put the water in first, then add the acid crystals. Even a small amount of water poured directly onto the crystals can cause them to explode and splatter, and I don't need to tell you what acid can do to your skin.

"We use a wide-mouthed jar with a watertight cover. Fill it about half full with tepid water, then add the acid crystals, stirring the mixture with a wooden stick. You need to stir until some of the crystals lie on the bottom of the jar. Then you place the gemstones into the acid mixture, close the cover on the jar and gently shake the sealed jar for a bit. You do this once or twice a day for about a week. At the end of that time, all the encrustation should be gone."

Regina shook her head ruefully. "It is quite a procedure."

"Not really. I have you pegged for a clever girl. You'll soon catch on."

Regina took a brush from the table, picked up a diamond, dipped it into the soapy water and began to scrub. She felt a thrill of delight and accomplishment when the encrustations started to flake away.

At the sound of heavy footsteps on the stairs, she glanced up just as the head and shoulders of a man showed above the level of the floor. As he came on up the steps, Regina realized that it was the red-bearded man she had seen on Saturday. It took her a moment to be certain, for the beard was gone, his hair was trimmed and he wore new clothing. But there was no mistaking the size and build of him, nor his booming voice as he came toward the table where she was sitting. "Andrew said my goods were in here being cleaned. I'd like a peek at what they look like all tidied up."

He bent to examine their work, his large hands supporting his weight on the table. As had been the case on Saturday, Regina could sense his enormous vitality. For the first time in her life, she admitted that she found a man very attractive.

Then he looked up from his position across the table, and she found herself the focus of those startling blue-green eyes. His gaze was unsettling, and Regina had to exert all of her willpower to keep from looking away.

"You!" He leveled a finger at her.

Despite herself, Regina gave a little jump. "Sir?"

"I'm thinking I've seen you before. Aye, that I have. You were on the floor this Saturday past."

"I was, yes. That's when Mr. Slostrum employed me."

"You're new at this? Then you be careful with my diamonds, my fair colleen."

Emboldened, Regina said, "If I'm not mistaken, these diamonds are no longer yours, sir. You sold them to Mr. Slostrum, did you not?"

For just a moment, he scowled blackly; then he laughed heartily. "Aye, lass, that I did. But I'll always think of them as mine, since I found them. Of course, I've thought many times that diamonds, and other gemstones as well, never belong to any one person. It's the people, whoever possesses the gem at any particular time, who belong to the gem, not the other way around." He laughed again. "By all the saints, 'tis a wise thing I'm saying, do you not agree?"

Regina could not help but respond to his statement, for she recognized this man as a kindred soul, touched as she was by the compelling magic of gemstones.

"It sounds both wise and true," she said softly, feeling suddenly shy at speaking so openly to this stranger.

The big man's expression changed to one of seriousness as he stared at her, seeming to study her face. Then his eyes crinkled as he grinned, showing strong, white teeth. "Aye, so it's gem struck you are, woman. I should have seen it sooner. Well, I'm afraid there's no hope for you, then. No hope at all. Once you're gem struck, it usually lasts forever. Perhaps if you burned a candle to Mary, she might save you, but it's doubtful."

Regina, knowing that he was teasing her, felt the hot flush of annoyance, stung by the fact that her honest remark was being taken so lightly. "Perhaps it's a blessing," she said tartly. "After all, I would think that Mr. Slostrum must also be 'gem struck,' as you put it, and he seems to be doing well enough."

She was spared Brian's reply by the arrival of one of the clerks from downstairs, who informed Brian that Mr. Slostrum wanted to see him in his office.

Before turning to follow the clerk, Brian made a deep bow in Regina's direction. "I did not mean to offend you, lass, or to make sport of you. I like a woman of spirit. We shall be meeting again, I'm thinking.''

Nodding to the other two women, who had been watching the exchange with considerable interest, Brian strode away, leaving Regina with red cheeks and confused feelings.

CHAPTER THREE

As THE WEEKS and months passed, Regina grew increasingly familiar with the workings of the gem business. Far from being bored, she found it endlessly fascinating. She had quickly become adept at cleaning and polishing gems and was able to judge the quality of a stone with a single glance.

"You have the knack, ducks," Jane had said admiringly as she watched Regina work. "I don't think I've ever seen anyone, man or woman, who caught on as quick as you did. You're a natural, you are."

"Thank you, Jane," Regina said with a flush of pride. "I value your judgment."

Apparently Andrew Slostrum had also been keeping a close watch on her progress, because at the end of the first month he raised her wages to equal Jane's. He had also paid her a very high compliment, which Regina often relived in her mind: "My dear Regina, sometimes I surprise myself with my wise decisions. One of the wisest I have ever made, I have come to believe, is in employing you. You will, I venture, become one of my most valued employees."

Regina had felt herself flushing. "Thank you, Mr. Slostrum. I shall try to live up to your good opinion," she had answered.

"If, of course, you don't decide to wed and leave me," he had added with a twinkle in his eye. "You are a very pretty young woman. Indeed."

Adelaide, when told of Slostrum's praise, had been very pleased and proud, her early reservations forgotten. She did say with some concern, "I don't think you should become so engrossed in your job that you neglect to keep an eye open for a husband, girl. Marriage is the proper state for a young woman."

In Regina's opinion, the work wasn't really hard; at least they weren't at it for hours on end. When there were no roughs in, and all the gemstones on hand had been cleaned and graded, there was some idle time. Usually Jane and Elizabeth used the leisure time to gossip and stroll outside. Andrew Slostrum was surprisingly tolerant for an employer of his day; and as long as an employee was caught up in his or her work, they could use the free time pretty much as they pleased. Often Regina chose not to accompany the other two women, but remained behind to observe the artisans at work. At first they were annoyed at her standing about, pestering them with questions, but as soon as they learned that her questions were intelligent and not empty-headed nonsense, their attitudes changed. Before long, she was fast friends with all the artisans, and she absorbed everything they shared with her about their craft.

She learned the most from the chief gem cutter, Giles Dupree, a Frenchman. He had been a cutter for forty years, and now at sixty-five, he was gray and gnarled, nearsighted from so many years spent cutting gems; yet his hand was as steady as a rock.

One day, as she silently watched, Giles sliced a groove into a large diamond, then placed a steel cutting blade into the groove and tapped it with a wooden mallet. The diamond split cleanly.

"This is called cleaving," he explained. "This splits the diamond along its grain, like a piece of wood. 'Course, you have to know exactly where and how the grain runs. Actually gem cutting is a general term. A cutter not only cuts the diamond, or any gem, but we saw, turn it and do most of the fine polishing."

"Have you ever ruined a diamond?" she asked.

"Never," he said with his twisted grin. "Not once in all the years."

Another time she watched him sit at a strange-looking contraption as he cut and carved a rough chunk of jade. The machine was attached to a wooden platform. There was a wooden spindle tapered down from several inches thickness at one end to approximately two inches at the other, which was fitted into a greased socket. On the thick end, a metal blade was attached, with a hood covering it and with a tub beneath the spindle to hold water and grit. The center part of the spindle was looped with a leather strap, the ends leading down to a pair of wooden boards used as foot pedals.

Giles held the piece of jade in one hand under the lower edge of the blade. The other hand was filled with loose grit, which he held pressed against the side of the blade. Then he pushed the foot pedals alternately, causing the blade to spin back and forth. The saw worked with astonishing speed and accuracy, considering its rickety nature.

"What in the world is that object?" Regina asked.

Giles grinned up at her. "It's called a Chinese circular mud saw. The Chinese invented it many years ago. Today there are modern devices for sawing gems, but this one is just as efficient, and I still use it. Let the young lads use the new methods; I'll stick with the tried-and-true."

Giles was quite garrulous, and he found a rapt audience in Regina. He knew well the lore of gems, and he told her many fascinating tales. She learned that diamonds had been traded in India four centuries before the birth of Christ, and that mystical powers were attributed to gems. For instance, Buddhists believed that a person's soul had to be purified before joining the "universal soul" or karma, and the steps in this process involved incarnations as animals, plants and gemstones. It was this process that gave birth to the notion that gems have life, a belief that had persisted for centuries.

"And the belief still exists in some cultures," Giles told her. "Even the Greek philosopher Plato attributed life to gems, and considered diamonds the noblest."

Diamonds, according to Giles, were once considered strong medicine, with their properties of hardness, dispersion and brilliancy. It was believed that the powder of white, flawless diamonds would, if ingested, grant good health, potency and long life. "On the other hand," Giles said with his twisted grin, "flawed diamonds would have the opposite effect. In fact, many believed that powder made from flawed diamonds was a deadly poison, and the deaths of many prominent rulers of the world were blamed on just such a powder.''

A great many other mystical powers were attributed to diamonds. He told Regina that if put in the mouth, a diamond could cause the teeth to fall out; if touched to certain parts of the body, it could cause incurable illnesses. On the other hand, diamonds were said to repel demons and phantoms, ward off evil magic and, carried into battle, they supposedly gave a warrior courage, virtue and invincibility.

Even in the beginning, fabulous diamonds, according to Giles, symbolized wealth and power and were regarded as emblems of rank and status. Most importantly, diamonds, and other precious stones to a lesser degree, represented easily portable wealth.

''That still holds true today,'' Giles told her, ''and likely will until the end of time. The monetary value of gems, most especially diamonds, may fluctuate, but never so much as currency. The value of currency in any one particular country may become worthless, but a man with a pouchful of diamonds will still be a wealthy man.''

But Regina was most intrigued by what Giles told her about sapphires. Since ancient times, the sapphire had been the birth gem for September, and Adelaide had found her, Regina, only a few days old, in September. So the sapphire was her birthstone! Giles also told her that the gem had long been known as a symbol of wisdom. ''*The Bible* tells us that the Ten Commandments were carved on sapphire, but the so-called experts now claim that the blue stone referred to in the Good Book was probably lapis lazuli,'' he said. ''Let them believe what they wish. I firmly believe that the Commandments were carved on sapphire.''

Because of its association with wisdom and purity, the sapphire was often used in ecclesiastical rings. It was also believed that wearing a sapphire ring guaranteed chastity; a sapphire that changed color was supposed to indicate that a woman had been unfaithful to her husband.

Regina mentioned the star sapphire she had seen on the Saturday she had attended the exhibition. ''It was the most beautiful thing I have ever seen.''

Giles nodded, smiling. ''Yes, it is a beautiful gem. A Kashmir star sapphire. They have the most fabulous color of all sapphires, although many of them have foggy inclusions. Sapphires tend to be clearer, with less extraneous material inside than either rubies or emeralds, but it is rare indeed to find a gemstone of any size without any inclusions at all. Inclusions give character to a stone. Only diamonds, of all the precious stones, are expected to be perfect, absolutely flawless, although very few of them actually are.''

Giles was an endless source of information. Regina learned how to evaluate gems—the standards by which the price of a gem was measured. She learned that the hardness and rarity of the gem was of primary consideration. Hardness meant durability and rarity was a factor, since much of the gem's value was derived from its scarcity. Color was also of paramount importance and could make the difference between ten pounds and ten thousand pounds per carat in some gems. Brilliance also affected the value, especially in colorless gems.

Brilliance was the effect produced by the return of light from the gem to the eye and thus, Giles informed her, was most often good or bad because of proper cutting.

Clarity, or freedom from flaws, had much to do with the value of a gemstone. Beauty, of course, was the most important criterion of all to a buyer, but beauty was almost totally subjective. It was truly in the eye of the beholder. This accounted for the fact that the selling price of a great gem could vary so widely from buyer to buyer.

"One aspect of gem value that many people overlook," Giles told her, "is the fact that gems can so easily be carried. A person can close his fist around a diamond, for instance, worth thousands of pounds. Only a gem can be enclosed in such a small space. A fortune in gold and silver, no matter what the price at any given time, cannot be carried about in your pocket. However, many a fortune has been saved because its owner was able to carry gems away on his person in times of danger."

One person at the firm did not immediately warm up to Regina. The company employed only one jewelry maker, Peter Mondrain, who, like Giles, was in his sixties. The Dutch jewelry maker and designer was world famous for the pieces he produced. His work was painstakingly slow, but when he completed a piece, whatever it might be, it was a marvel to see, and always sold for a fabulous price. Slostrum had hired him away from a Dutch jewelry firm several years ago, paid him a princely salary, and apparently Mondrain was well worth the price.

Mondrain was a cold, distant and arrogant man. From what Regina could gather, he had no family, no wife and children; his work was his whole life. His cubicle in the rear of the room was the only one with a closed door, which he often kept locked. Regina longed to watch him at work, but when she broached the subject to him, she received a cold stare.

"My dear young lady, I am very good at my trade, and I need privacy when I practice it. I certainly do not need a woman observing me."

Jane, who had overheard the exchange, laughed aloud when Mondrain had strode out of hearing. "Oh, he's a strange one, ducks, is our Mr. Mondrain. To him, we're peasants. As far as he's concerned, we don't even exist."

"I don't know why he should care if I watch him at work," Regina said angrily. "I can be as quiet as a mouse."

"I don't know why you would want to watch, anyway."

"I'm fascinated by everything connected with the jewelry business."

"Well, it ain't as if you'll ever become a jewelry designer. Not a woman. Nor become a cutter, either, although I notice you're always hanging around old Giles."

"Just because women have never done those things doesn't mean they never will! Besides, I've been told that the firm of Fabergé in Russia uses women designers."

"Oh, Russia." Jane dismissed the comment with a gesture. "Who knows what happens over there?"

"Women are obtaining employment they've never had before. Clerical jobs, secretarial positions."

"That's as may be, ducks, but it will never happen here in the jewelry trade. Jewels is a man's business, always has been, always will be. Sure they hire some of us for scut work, 'cause they don't have to pay us as much as a man, but as for the fine work, never!" Jane grinned mockingly. "The only way a woman gets close to the fine pieces is having the money to buy and wear them."

"I thought you liked to work here."

"I like it well enough, better than I would at some places," Jane said with a shrug. "But it's just a job, Regina, not a life, as you seem to look upon it. You're young and pretty. You should be thinking about a man and marriage, not gemstones."

"Why does everyone keep saying that!" Regina said angrily. "My mother, you. You both seem to think that's all there is in life."

"For a woman, it is," Jane said wryly. "I only wish to God I had a spouse. If I did, you wouldn't see me working here."

THIS CONVERSATION took place during their lunch hour about a year after Regina had come to work at Slostrum's. They were caught up on their work, and Regina, too restless to remain inside, went out into the streets. As usual when she had time to spare, she gravitated to the open-air markets. It was autumn now, and there were very few fresh vegetables. The only fruits to be found were pears and apples. She bought a basket of the fruit and started back toward Slostrum's, munching on a tart apple.

"It's Miss Paxton, is it not?" asked a deep voice beside her.

Regina glanced up with a start. It was the red-headed Irishman, Brian Macbride. The first thing she noticed was that the beard had grown back. His eyes were as startlingly green as she remembered, and they held a rakish, devil-may-care glint.

"And you're Brian Macbride, the diamond man."

"Diamond?" He looked blank for a moment. "Oh, I see." He threw back his head and bellowed laughter, drawing the attention of people passing by. "Not diamonds exclusively, lass. I'm a gem hunter. Any kind, anyplace, as long as they may fetch a tidy sum. Right now, I am about to sail for Australia, in search of sapphires. A new field has been discovered there. Or so I've heard."

"Sapphires? Sapphires are my favorite gemstones." She took a bite of the apple and started on along the street.

Brian Macbride fell into step alongside her. "Are they now? Sure, and it wouldn't be because the sapphire is your birthstone, now would it?"

"It might be." She glanced up at him with sparkling eyes. He was so *big*, towering over her. "Are you interested in the legends concerning gems, Mr. Macbride?"

"I make it my affair to know all there is to know about the gemstones I look for, the truth, the half-truths and the myths."

"Would you like an apple?" She held out the basket of fruit.

"I would indeed." He selected an apple from the basket and took an enormous bite out of it with strong, white teeth.

"Tell me, Mr. Macbride, how long have you been a gem hunter?"

"Well, let's see.... I left home at seventeen. I'm now past twenty-seven. That makes it ten years, according to my calculations."

"And you've never done anything else?"

"Never had an urge to do anything else. I'm as happy as a flea on a dog when I'm off looking for gems."

"And do you always find them, Mr. Macbride?"

"Sooner or later."

"Let's see, it's been almost a year since I saw you last at Slostrum's. Where have you been gem hunting all that time?"

His red eyebrows climbed. "Nowhere, Miss Paxton. Nowhere at all. I have been spending the proceeds from the diamonds I sold Andrew."

"You mean, the money is all gone?" She came to an abrupt stop, staring at him in shock.

"Not quite," he said cheerfully. "I have enough left to finance my trip to Australia. I usually try to keep enough aside to finance my next expedition. Sometimes I fail, but I try."

"But those diamonds! They must have been worth a fortune."

"Aye." He shrugged massive shoulders. "A small fortune, that is true."

"And you've been idling away since then, doing nothing but spending?"

"That about tells the tale."

"What a waste, a terrible waste! Why didn't you do something with the money?"

He gave her a puzzled look. "But I did. I enjoyed myself to the fullest."

"Spending it, instead of investing it in something worthwhile," she said scathingly.

"What is the sense of making money if not to spend?" They were abreast of a tea shop. Brian gestured. "The apple was delicious, lass. I thank you. But now I'd like a cuppa. Would you care to join me?"

Regina hesitated. She scarcely knew this man, but he was fascinating; clearly he knew much about gems. He might be a source of valuable information. "I shall be pleased to accept your kind invitation, Mr. Macbride," she said regally.

He winced. "Brian, please, Regina. Since I have shared your fruit and you're having a cuppa with me, I think we can be less formal."

Inside the tea shop, which was not crowded, they found a table and soon were served tea, bread and butter and cakes.

Regina wasn't hungry after the apple, so she contented herself with the tea while Brian ate as if it was the first meal he'd had that day. Watching him, she was sure that he had a great appetite for life as well, and lived it with much gusto.

Catching his amused glance on her, she said hurriedly, "You say you're going to Australia just on a rumor of a sapphire find. Suppose it is nothing but a rumor?"

He said negligently, "Rumors of gem finds are more often true than not. The only difficulty is, the finds are generally several months old before the news reaches London. So by the time I get there, it being a long sea voyage, all the stones may already be gobbled up.''

''So then what would you do, since you will have spent all your money to finance the trip to Australia for nothing?''

''Oh, I doubt that it will be for nothing.'' He took a sip of tea and munched on a cake. ''There are always a few gemstones to be found, enough to pay my expenses.''

''Such as?'' she said challengingly.

''Well, for one thing, there is coral to be found, true black coral, along the Great Barrier Reef in Australia. Coral is far from being as valuable as sapphire, but black coral is rare, difficult to find. Once it was found aplenty in the Persian Gulf, but that source has been exhausted.''

Not bothering to hide her interest, Regina leaned forward. ''But coral is found under the sea, is it not?''

''Aye, lass, that it is.''

''How do you recover coral? It's not like scooping diamonds from dry streambeds, or digging into the earth.''

''That it is not, at all.'' He gave her an amused glance. ''So you do know something about gem hunting, eh?''

Not to be put off, she continued, ''How do you recover coral?''

'''Tis not easy. You go fishing for it.''

''Fishing?''

''Aye. You take a boat out over the reef. You drop a heavy crosspiece of wood overboard, with a strong net attached. Then you wait for a favorable

wind to fill your sails and drag the net along behind you. If you are lucky, you eventually come
across a coral outcrop on the reef. Again, if you are
fortunate, the net snags a whole tree of coral and
uproots it, which would be a good haul. But at least
you should snag one or more of the branches from
the coral tree and bring that up. You keep sailing
back and forth until you have the amount that you
think will make it worth your while.''

''It sounds like not only hard work, but very
much hit-or-miss.''

''That it is, Regina.'' He gave a careless shrug.

''It also strikes me that being a gem hunter is a
precarious means of earning a living.''

''All too true. Rich one day, poor the next.'' He
grinned crookedly. ''But it's all one grand adventure. To me, it's the only life. It has zest, and best
of all, you're your own man, beholden to no one.''

''At least you're fortunate to have someone like
Mr. Slostrum to buy your gemstones.''

''Aye, I am indeed. But it wasn't always so.''

She stared at him with some interest. ''Who did
you sell to, then?''

''To this one and that one. And it was a sly
business, believe me. Not all gem traders are as
honest as Andrew. When I first began, I was
robbed blind by some of the shrewder, craftier
traders, but I learned. There are tricks to buying
and selling gems, much as any other trade.''

''Such as what, Brian?''

''Well, let me see.'' He cocked his head in
thought, then smiled broadly. ''For one thing, it
took me a while to learn to read a gem buyer.''

'' 'Read'?''

"Yes. Sure, and they dearly love to barter. You have to learn when they reach their highest bid, so that you won't be accepting a lower offer. When you know a man well enough, you learn to 'read' the signs that give him away. I well remember one gem buyer I did business with early on. I was green as Killarney grass in those days. This particular buyer was located in Amsterdam, a Dutchman by the name of Van Helm. He was connected with a respectable firm of gem dealers. I sold him a number of gems before realizing that I got stung."

"You mean he cheated you?"

"Not at all. He got the better of me in the deal. It's not cheating, Regina, if a man makes an offer and you're stupid enough to accept it. Anyway, I soon caught on to a little habit Van Helm had. He always wore a cap with a tinted glass bill, like many casino dealers wear. To protect his eyes, I'd reckon. A gem dealer gets poor eyesight after many years in the trade, squinting all day through a loupe and the like.

"Now I noticed that Van Helm always made low bids to start, upping them a bit each time I spurned his offer. He would stand behind the counter, with my goods spread out before him, poking at them with a pen as he made an offer. Each time he did so, he would give a slight, clockwise tug at his cap. It soon dawned on me that he had made his final offer when the center of the peak of his cap returned in perfect alignment with his nose. I knew then that he would go no higher. After that, I always got the last guilder out of him!" Brian threw back his head and laughed heartily.

"Seems to me that's a strange way to conduct business."

"'Tis a strange business, lass, the gem business."

"Well, if I'm ever in a position to buy gemstones, I won't go through all those shenanigans."

"Shenanigans, is it?" he said amusedly. "Do you plan on going into the gem business?"

The idea startled her, and she was silent for a bit. She hadn't consciously thought along those lines, but the concept appealed to her. Certainly she was fascinated by every aspect of the jewelry business, and she didn't want to spend the rest of her life cleaning and sorting gems.

As the silence grew, Brian laughed again. "By all the saints, I'm after thinking you *do* have such plans!"

She wasn't about to tell him that it had not actually occurred to her until now. Instead she said with a show of defiance, "Is the idea so farfetched?"

"Farfetched? Indeed it is. You're but a lass, and you're earning a pittance doing scut work at Slostrum's."

"I don't intend to do that forever!"

"Perhaps not, but the point is, do you have any idea of the kind of financing you would need to start a gem business? Even as a simple trader, you would need money to buy gems. And no woman would ever succeed as a gem trader. No one would deal with you. The only way you could get into the business would be to *own* a jewelry firm, and you could never attain the money necessary for that. No, Regina, 'tis impossible.''

''Nothing is impossible,'' she said stoutly.

His amusement did not abate. ''I much admire your spirit, but the obstacles before you are staggering, so staggering as to blunt that strong spirit.''

''We shall see.''

''That we shall. Well...'' He took out his pocket watch and glanced at it. ''I must be off. My ship sails in the morning, and I have business affairs to settle yet this day.'' He looked across the table at her, his face crinkling in a smile. ''It has been a great pleasure seeing you again, Regina Paxton.'' He got to his feet.

''How long will you be away, Brian?''

''I'll not be knowing,'' he said with a shrug. ''As I mentioned, it's a lengthy voyage, and I have no way of knowing how long it will take to find enough goods to make it worth my while. At least a year, perhaps even more.''

Strangely she felt a tug of disappointment. Although this was only the third time she had seen this man, she liked him, and liked his company.

He smiled down at her. ''Will you be missing me?''

She felt a flush mount to her cheeks. ''I hardly know you, sir! You are impudent!''

''Am I, now? I think not.'' He turned grave. ''I shall be looking forward to seeing you on my return. Will you still be at Slostrum's?''

''I fully intend to be.''

''Then I shall bid you farewell, Regina, until my return.''

He bowed slightly and, turning away, swung off without another word.

Regina watched until his tall figure was out of sight, feeling a strange sense of loss. Then with a start, she got to her feet and also hurried away. She had been gone from work much too long.

CHAPTER FOUR

REGINA DID NOT SEE Brian Macbride again for nearly two years.

They were a busy two years for her, and by the end of that time Regina had become a truly respected and valued employee at Slostrum's.

A few changes had taken place at the firm. Elizabeth Cranston was gone, but Jane Worthington remained, along with two new women Andrew Slostrum had employed to work as cleaners and graders.

By now Regina was quite familiar with most aspects of the business and spent half her time away from the sorting tables. She often helped Giles in his cutting room; in fact, on her solemn word that Andrew Slostrum would never know, Giles had allowed her to cleave some of the less valuable stones. The first time she had tried it, she had approached the stone with a steady hand and an expert eye, and the stone cleaved cleanly.

Giles shook his head. "You are a wonder, girl," he said. "You are born to it. Of course," he added with his hoarse laugh, "I have never before seen a woman cleave a gemstone."

And Regina had been able to work another miracle—she had broken through to Peter Mondrain. It had taken some time, but he had finally unbent and allowed her to watch him at work. She knew his position was the heart of any jewelry firm. Much of the money that Slostrum's made came from the pieces that Mondrain produced in his small cubicle. The firm sold single gems, of course, but the big profit was in the mounted pieces.

The designing of jewelry took great artistry, and Mondrain was truly an artist. Regina was entranced as she watched him at work.

When he got to know Regina better, Mondrain relaxed his reserve and talked to her, explaining what he was doing. In time she came to see that he was starved for companionship, for someone with whom he could share the delights of his craftsmanship.

Mondrain told her about his long apprenticeship with other jewelry designers and work masters in Holland. "Most designers," he said in his stilted English, "are born to the trade. By that I mean it's passed down from father to son. I did not have such a background. My father was a cheese maker." He grimaced with contempt. "I grew up around the stench of cheese. To this day I cannot eat the stuff. Just the odor is enough to roil my stomach and spoil my digestion. I went to the city as soon as I could and began learning my trade. It took me a long time to rise to where I am today," he said with strong pride.

Regina nodded. "I can easily see why you would be proud of your accomplishments. You have never had a family of your own, Mr. Mondrain?"

He became distant, his glance moving away. "I have never had the time. My work absorbs all of my energies. An artist must make sacrifices."

Regina said nothing to this, yet she had to wonder if she could devote all her time and energy to a trade or a business to the sacrifice of a husband and children. Would it be worth it? She had to laugh at herself—scarcely past twenty-two and she was worrying about something that could be years in the future!

In spite of the thaw in his attitude toward Regina, Mondrain would not let her touch any of the pieces he was making. But she was content to observe. Regina was intrigued with the process of drawing designs for proposed pieces and then making the models for them. At home, after work, she often sat over drawing paper, thinking out designs of her own. The first few she drew disappointed her, but she kept at it, growing more inventive and surer of hand with practice.

Finally she drew one that satisfied her. With some trepidation, she took it to Mondrain.

He took the sheet of paper gingerly. "What is this, Regina?"

"Just look at it, please," she implored. "But be honest. Tell me exactly what you think."

Frowning with concentration he studied the sketched design of a crown. Finally he looked up at her; he wore the distant expression she so disliked.

"You are intending to become a jewelry designer now?" he asked in a dry, cool voice.

"Oh, no. I would never dare." Yet even as she spoke the words, Regina knew that she was not telling the whole truth. If she became good enough, she would dearly love to design jewelry. "It's just something I have been tinkering with."

"Tinkering is an apt expression," he said in the same dry voice. "In the first place, there is a very limited market for crowns. Only royalty wear crowns, my dear. And even if there was a purchaser for such a piece, there are many things wrong with your design...."

Regina let her breath go with a soft sigh as she leaned over the design on the table, and Mondrain painstakingly pointed out where she had gone wrong—precisely what she had hoped he would do.

Two weeks later, she came to Mondrain again with a design, this time for a ladies' brooch.

Mondrain looked at her with raised eyebrows and said, "Tinkering again?"

She nodded mutely.

He examined the new sketch closely. The delicate brooch was designed in the shape of a star. A narrow band of gold formed the outline, and this band was set with rose diamonds. In the center of the piece was a large stone, also surrounded with small diamonds.

He looked up at her. "And how is the large stone to be anchored?"

"At the points where the arms of the star indent. See, here, here, here, here and here!"

He said thoughtfully, "Yes, it could work."

"Well?" she said impatiently. "What do you think?"

He took on a stern expression. "It is an improvement over the other, true, but it is very simple and not the fashion. See, this is what the ladies are buying."

He indicated a partially completed pendant. It was circular in shape, made of chased green gold, with a border that was set with twelve brilliant diamonds and four large rubies. Regina knew that the unfinished center of the ornate pendant was to hold a small photograph of the husband of one of Slostrum's wealthier clients.

"But styles are changing," Regina said. "Clothing, hairstyles, they always change."

Mondrain said coldly, "And you think you are the arbiter of style? You have drawn two amateurish designs and you think you can dictate fashion?"

Regina felt crushed. He was right. She was arrogant and impatient and ignorant. "I'm sorry, Mr. Mondrain. I did not mean to be presumptuous. You are right, of course."

He smiled slightly and shook his head. "Ah, Regina, you are so impetuous! You rush at life headlong. To be a designer takes much study, much patience. However, I must say that your design is not bad. It would make a very pretty piece, with a large stone in the center. A cabochon ruby, for example, would be quite striking."

"Sapphire."

He looked at her without comprehension. "Sapphire?"

"Yes, a star sapphire in the center of the star."

He was already shaking his head. "No, no, a sapphire does not fit with a star. It must be a ruby."

"But the firm has a star sapphire. It has been for sale ever since I first came to work here. If it is set into a brooch like this, it will sell."

"Not so. A sapphire is not suitable. It must be a ruby. The star sapphire will sell in time. It needs only a purchaser with the desire and enough money." He picked up her sketch. "I shall show this to Mr. Slostrum. If he agrees I should make it, you shall receive credit for the design, never fear." He smiled. "And you shall be allowed your signature on the piece."

"Signature?"

"Yes, all designers or work masters stamp their signatures, or their marks, on the finished work. Look here."

He picked up a pair of men's cuff links he had just completed. The gold cuff links were made in the form of dumbbells and were set with rose diamonds. Mondrain turned them over and pointed to what looked like scratches on the gold. Looking more closely, Regina made out two letters: *P M*.

"My initials. That's what designers use to identify their work. Shall we stamp your piece, *if* it's made, *R P*?"

She clapped her hands in delight. "Oh, yes!"

THE NEXT MORNING was wet and cold, and Regina was hurrying as she neared Slostrum's, her head ducked down beneath a parasol.

As she stepped into the entryway of the building, she collided with someone and would have fallen if her arm hadn't been caught in strong hands.

She folded the parasol and stared into the concerned face of a young man of her own age. "I'm sorry," he said. "I should have warned you that I was here, but you came in so unexpectedly."

Regina shook her head. "The apology should be mine. I should have been looking where I was going."

The young man was slender and dark, with black hair and deep brown eyes set in a narrow face. He was a stranger to her.

Regina seized the initiative. "I'm Regina Paxton. I work here."

"I'm Eugene Leacock, and I *hope* to work here."

Regina looked at him in surprise. "Oh? Doing what?"

"I...well, I hope to become an apprentice." Eugene shifted uncomfortably. "I want to become a gem cutter. At least that's my father's ambition for me, and I go along with it. I'm to apprentice to some fellow here by the name of Giles Dupree."

"You're going to work with Giles?"

"That's what I was told."

Just then, another person came into the alcove before the door, shedding water from a shining slicker. It was Andrew Slostrum. "Why are you standing out here in the wet, Regina?" he demanded. "You have a key, do you not?"

Without waiting for a reply, Slostrum took his own key out of his pocket and opened the door. He stood back for Regina to precede him, then frowned as Eugene followed her in. "Who are you, young man?"

"Eugene Leacock, sir. I was supposed to report for work today. Apprentice gem cutter."

"Indeed. I remember now. Go on up to the third floor, young man. Giles should already be on the premises."

As Eugene started off with a sidelong glance at Regina, she said, "Mr. Slostrum, I didn't know you were employing an apprentice gem cutter."

"My dear young lady," he said severely, "I do not ordinarily consult with my employees when I consider hiring someone."

Abashed, Regina said, "I'm sorry. I know it isn't my business."

"Indeed." He sighed. "I should not have spoken so sharply. Giles is growing old. Before too many years have passed, he will become too infirm, his touch unsure, to entrust with valuable gemstones. He is well aware of this fact, although he is loath to admit it."

"Perhaps you don't know, Mr. Slostrum, but I have been working with him . . ."

"Oh, I know. I make it my business to know what takes place within my firm."

"Then has he told you that I have what he called the 'touch'?"

"He has mentioned it, yes."

"Then why can't I become his apprentice?"

Slostrum started to smile, then became grave. "Regina," he said heavily, "a woman does not become a cleaver, a cutter. It is simply not done."

"But why can't there be a first time?"

"My customers would not trust the work of a woman cutter. My dear Regina, why on earth would you wish to do such a thing? It is dry, dusty, hard work, and no matter if you do have the 'touch,' years of apprenticeship are required. It will be at least five years before that young man is a fully qualified gem cutter."

Regina knew that it was hopeless to argue further. By this time, the well-dressed clerks had all arrived and were busy removing the counters and putting out the display cases for the special gems.

She was struck by an inspiration. "If not a cutter's apprentice, Mr. Slostrum, how about transferring me down here to the salesroom?"

He gave her an incredulous stare. "Use you as a *sales*clerk?"

"Why not?"

"Regina, all jewelry clerks are men. It is traditional!"

"Then I think it is time traditions were changed! From what I have observed, many women purchase jewelry. And most of the men who buy have their wives, or their mistresses, with them. It would seem logical to me that a woman would be better able to sell to other women. Especially since your clerks are so snooty—" her glance swept around the store "—that they are offensive."

Slostrum's gaze followed hers, and he said with astonishment, "They are?"

For a moment, Regina feared that she may have gone too far. After all, it was probably natural for the clerks to be contemptuous with her, but did that mean they also adopted the same manner toward the customers? Somehow she had the strong feeling that they did.

Slostrum was looking thoughtful. "Use a woman as a salesclerk? As you say, many of my buyers are women . . . No!" He shook his head. "It is too radical. It could only result in turning away customers."

"You can't know until you try it."

"By trying it, I will lose trade. No, Regina, be happy with what you are doing. I am content with your work, and so should you be content."

He turned away with a gesture of dismissal, and she knew that further debate was futile—at least this time. But she had planted the seed in his mind; perhaps it would bear fruit in the future.

She went on up to the third floor, and to work.

EUGENE LEACOCK proved to be a diligent worker and, according to Giles, he had an aptitude for cutting gems. "In time," Giles told Regina, "he may do passable work."

For Regina, Eugene's presence at the firm was a breath of fresh air. After he had settled in and overcome his shyness, he became a good friend. He was the only person on the third floor close to her own age, and she found him good company. In addition, she discovered that he shared her enthusiasm for gemstones. They took to eating their noon meal together, which they both usually brought from home. On nice days they ate outside in a small park up the street, and talked endlessly about the jewelry business.

Eugene was well educated for a young man of his circumstances and time. "My father owns a bookstore," he explained. "And while I didn't receive much formal schooling, he made me a confirmed reader. During the slack hours at the store, he taught me as well as if I had proper schooling."

Regina also loved to read, and the only schooling she had received had been from the books she read and what little instruction Adelaide had been capable of giving her. The difficulty was in getting books; they were very expensive.

When she, somewhat abashedly, explained this to Eugene, he said, "I can help you there. We sell both new and old books, mostly old. You tell me what books you want and I shall lend them to you. When you have finished with them, I'll return them to my father's store."

Regina clapped her hands together. "You, having been around books all your life, are far better able to select what I should read. Why don't you pick them for me, Eugene?"

"I shall be happy to, Regina."

She learned that there was not a great deal of money to be made from a bookstore: for that reason, Eugene's father had insisted that he learn a trade. It was a well-known fact that a gem cutter earned better-than-average money.

"I didn't know if I would like it," Eugene said. "I love books, and I thought I would rather be a bookseller like my father. But now that I am here, I find that I enjoy it. How did you come to work here, Regina? It seems to me that your position here is most unusual."

"My mother works here, as a charwoman." As was her habit, she looked directly at him when she divulged this information. When he showed no reaction, she went on, "She brought me here to a gem exhibition three years ago, and I fell in love with gemstones. One of the gem sorters had quit, and there was an opening, so I got the job. And there *are* other women working here, you know."

"Yes, but they do scut work," he said with a shrug. "They're not qualified to do anything else."

Provoked, she said, "That's not a very nice thing to say, Eugene."

"You know what I mean. You're capable of much more than that. And Giles has told me that you could even be a cutter; you have the talent for it."

"The talent, yes, but it's not a job for women," she said tartly. "Or so I have been told in no uncertain terms."

"Yes, I know. It's the tradition, and tradition is hard to overcome."

"Tradition!" She made a sound of disgust. "Did you ever notice that it's almost always men who talk about flaunting tradition when they don't want to do something?"

He held both hands up before his face in mock self-defense. "It's not my doing, Regina. For you, I'd flaunt tradition any day," he said with sudden seriousness. "Regina, I would like to take you to the theater next week. There's a Shakespearean festival at Stratford. We could go up on the train...."

"Eugene..." She cocked her head to one side, her eyes holding his. "Are you courting me?"

"I...uh..." He blushed a bright red and lost all power of speech.

"Because if you are," she said softly, "you would be wasting your time. I have no intention of getting married for some years yet. I have much to do before that event takes place."

He finally met her gaze. "No, Regina, I'm not courting you, although I think highly of you. But I cannot support a wife on the money I am making at present, and according to Giles, I can look forward to several years as an apprentice."

"Good." She nodded. "Under those conditions I would be most happy to accompany you to Stratford this weekend."

SLOSTRUM'S was about to hold the firm's annual exhibition, and the pace was hectic. The ground floor had to be spic and span, and the gems and jewelry pieces had to be tastefully arranged. All the workers on the third floor were pressed into service the Friday before the event.

At the end of the day, Andrew Slostrum sought out Regina where she was polishing the glass on the last exhibition case. He looked harried. "Regina, one of my clerks quit this morning in an imagined huff over something or other, and John Roland just went home desperately ill. He will not be able to work the exhibition tomorrow. That means I only have two clerks. I can fill in part of the time, but I have other things that will require my attention."

Regina just stared at him, but her heart began to beat faster.

"And I thought—" He broke off, his gaze sliding away. Then he squared his shoulders, looking at her resolutely. "I'm finding this difficult to say, Regina, but would you . . . you told me weeks ago that you would like an opportunity to sell?"

"If you're asking me to work as a salesclerk tomorrow, the answer is yes!" she said breathlessly. "I would dearly love to!"

"Some people are going to be shocked, I know, and I may lose a few customers. Do you think you can do the job?"

"I know that I can," she said steadily.

"Indeed. Then I'm going to give you the opportunity. Probably to my everlasting regret."

Regina was euphoric for the little time left before the store closed; but on the way home, doubts set in. What if she was wrong? What if she failed? And what if Mr. Slostrum was right? What if her presence behind the counters alienated too many customers?

At home she confided in Adelaide. "But now that I finally have a chance to prove myself, I'm scared to death, Mother!"

Adelaide's first instinct was to shake the silly girl. She would be entering a man's world, something that was just not done; but the mingled hope and fear on Regina's face dissuaded her. She took the girl into her arms, hiding her face against her shoulder so that Regina couldn't see her expression as she lied. "You have no need to be afraid, dear Regina. You will do very well indeed, I just know you will!"

Regina stood back, looking into Adelaide's face, smiling faintly. "I know you're just saying that to bolster my courage, Mother. You don't believe anything of the sort." She reached to gently touch Adelaide's cheek. "But thank you, anyway."

She was worried about the older woman. Over the past year, Adelaide's health had deteriorated. She had lost some weight, and she was always tired. Regina had tried to convince her to stop working, for she was earning enough now to support them.

But all of her arguments fell on deaf ears. Adelaide had shaken her head and said, "I have worked all my life, Regina. I wouldn't know what to do with myself without a job to go to."

THE NEXT MORNING, Regina put on her best dress, a demure gray garment with a white collar and cuffs, and went to work with high hopes. She was the first clerk on the floor, and she established herself behind the counter on the south side of the room. The star sapphire lay nestled in its bed of white satin on the counter before her.

The other two clerks soon arrived, wearing their morning suits; both gave her a look of disdain and did not speak to her.

Andrew Slostrum was the next to arrive, and he came directly across the room to her. "Good morning, Regina. I may have spoken too brusquely yesterday. These exhibitions always present so many problems and I become irritable. I'm sure you will do fine."

"I'm grateful for your confidence, Mr. Slostrum," she said quietly. "I shall certainly do my best."

"Indeed." With a nod, he turned away.

By midmorning the store was a mass of people, and Regina became too busy to worry. She did notice a few looks of surprise, but to the best of her knowledge no customer stalked out in outrage at the sight of a female clerk.

In fact, one well-dressed woman, already heavily bejeweled, leaned over to speak to her in a confidential whisper, "I am delighted to see a woman serving as clerk, my dear. Now I would like to see a good string of pearls. I've grown jaded with diamonds. It seems that *everyone* wears diamonds these days!''

It was an easy sale, and Regina's first. After draping several different strings of pearls around the woman's neck she finally made her selection and paid the asking price without protest.

As the woman left with her purchase, Regina glanced around to see Andrew Slostrum observing her. ''You handled that very well, Regina,'' he said with a nod of approval. ''And contrary to my fears, no one has objected too strenuously to your presence. A few men have grumbled, but that has been the extent of it.''

Regina could scarcely contain her delight.

It wasn't until the end of the day that she encountered a problem—one that she had certainly not anticipated.

A slight, elegantly attired woman had entered the showroom alone. She was well into her seventies and appeared quite frail. Regina had been busy with a customer, and when she was finished, she glanced up to see the woman standing before the case enclosing the star sapphire.

She felt a sudden stirring of dismay. Was this woman interested in the sapphire? The gem had almost become a fixture at Slostrum's, at least in Regina's mind. The possibility that it might be purchased was unthinkable! Of course, she knew that such thoughts were treasonable as far as the firm was concerned. The sapphire was certainly for sale, and the firm had invested a large sum of money and a great deal of time in it.

She moved down the counter, across from the old woman, who was indeed quite frail.

She looked up at Regina and asked in a thin, cranky voice, "Is this sapphire for sale?"

"Of course, madam," Regina said, almost having to force the words out. "Everything on display is for sale."

"I see no price attached."

"Madam, it is a very expensive gem. Perhaps madam would care to look at something less expensive?"

"My dear young woman, if I had wanted to look at pearls or emeralds, I would have said so, would I not? This is not for myself. Unless you are blind, you will see that I am not wearing any jewels. I personally think jewels are a waste of money."

"It is for a relative, then?"

"It is indeed. It is for my daughter. She married a blackguard and my husband disowned her. Now my dear husband is deceased, and I shall follow him soon...."

"Oh, I'm sure not, madam," Regina said hastily.

"You're sure not?" The old woman glared. "You are a physician?"

"No, of course not." Regina knew that she was making a mess of things, but she couldn't seem to help herself.

"Then do not venture an opinion as to something you know nothing of!" the woman snapped. "At any rate, my daughter is finally leaving her husband and coming home. I wanted to have a gift for her. Many years ago she saw a star sapphire and expressed a wish for one. Now will you please tell me the price of this one?''

''It's sixty thousand pounds, madam,'' Regina heard herself saying. She glanced around quickly, fearful that she had been overheard. She had quoted a price ten thousand pounds over what Mr. Slostrum was asking for the sapphire. If he discovered her action, she would be discharged on the spot. The old woman said something, but such was Regina's inner turmoil that she did not hear. ''What did you say, madam?''

''I said I will take it.''

Dazed, Regina could only stare at the woman for a long moment. An urge to laugh seized her, and it was all she could do to keep a straight face. She had tried to the best of her ability to discourage the woman, but she had bought the sapphire anyway! It occurred to Regina that she might have inadvertently stumbled upon a selling technique that would be of value to her in the future.

Arousing herself, she caught Mr. Slostrum's eye across the room and beckoned to him.

As Andrew Slostrum took the old woman into his office to complete the sale, Regina watched them. Then she turned to look at the empty case that had held the star sapphire. Oh, well, she thought, her spirits rising. There would surely be other star sapphires in her life.

A short time later, Slostrum ushered the old woman out of the store and came directly to Regina.

''Regina, you are a marvel! You have just become a permanent salesclerk, with a substantial rise in salary. But I do not understand one thing. You sold the sapphire for ten thousand more than the asking price. How did you manage that?''

Regina knew that she couldn't tell the whole truth—she would undoubtedly be discharged.

''I . . . I didn't realize,'' she stammered. ''I quoted the wrong price, and when I realized my error, she had already accepted it.''

''Indeed?'' Slostrum arched an eyebrow in amusement. ''Well, please be more careful in the future. But I must congratulate you again. I do believe you will be an asset here on the floor.''

CHAPTER FIVE

WITHIN SIX MONTHS, Regina had proved herself an unqualified success at selling jewelry. There had been some resistance at first from a number of the male customers, it was true, but Slostrum's had gained far more than it had lost. Wealthy women who spent money on jewelry heard about the female clerk at Slostrum's and became customers. Andrew Slostrum was more than pleased and was not hesitant to tell Regina so.

The design that she had drawn for Mondrain had also been turned into a splendid piece and had sold for a handsome price the third day it was on display. Mondrain had given Regina credit for the design, and Slostrum had congratulated her.

"I would be more than pleased if you could provide Mondrain with more such designs. Indeed." He laughed ruefully. "Of course, I should probably be gravely concerned—you may well take over the operation of the entire firm in time."

"I doubt that will ever happen, Mr. Slostrum. A woman taking your place?" She smiled as she said it to take the sting out of the touch of sarcasm, yet, it may have been at that very moment that her dream was born.

The three male clerks resented her presence and didn't try to hide it. Their resentment deepened when her sales record soon outpaced theirs. The other women working in the firm also resented her promotion, even Jane. Outside of Mr. Slostrum, it seemed that the only people who applauded her success was Giles, Mondrain and Eugene Leacock.

Eugene, in fact, was delighted with the turn of events. "I think you deserved the change, Regina, and I'm happy for you." He smiled shyly. "Perhaps you will be selling gems that I have cleaved, cut and shaped."

"I'm sure that will happen, Eugene, and before too long. Giles tells me that you have the 'touch.' You only need more experience."

Eugene smiled wryly. "But with Master Giles, 'more' can mean years."

Regina and Eugene had been out together twice since their excursion to Stratford-upon-Avon, which Regina had enjoyed immensely. Although he had never put his feelings in to words, she was quite sure that Eugene was falling in love with her. It saddened her, for she knew that she could never return his love in full. She had grown quite fond of him, and enjoyed his company, yet she felt only sisterly feelings toward him.

The one person who had really disappointed her was Adelaide. On the day she had returned from the exhibition, she had been bubbling with happiness as she'd announced, "Mother, I am now a full-time salesclerk! Mr. Slostrum is pleased with me!"

Adelaide stared at her in dismay. "You are now to be a salesclerk? I thought it was just for today?"

"I thought you would be pleased for me, Mother. It's a great opportunity."

"It's not . . . not womanly, Regina. Just today would do no harm, but . . . Well, I thought you would only work at the firm until you found a man and got married."

"Mother, I have no interest in getting married now. I've only recently turned twenty-two."

"Already an old maid," Adelaide said in a grumbling voice.

Regina had to smile. "I hardly think that is true."

"You probably never will be wed now," Adelaide said darkly. "No man will have a woman for his wife who has worked at a man's job."

Regina sighed in exasperation. "Mother, it's no more a man's job than it is a woman's. In fact, many more women will no doubt come in to buy gems, now that a woman can serve them."

"Yes, married women with wealthy husbands."

Regina had to laugh. "Mother, I love you."

"And I love you, too, girl."

SIX MONTHS AFTER Regina became a salesclerk at Slostrum's, Adelaide came home after a hard night's work burning up with fever. As she entered their flat, she was relieved to find that Regina was just stirring in her bedroom. Adelaide slipped quietly into her own room, undressed and got into bed.

She soon heard Regina leave her bedroom and she tried to compose herself as she waited for Regina's knock. She tried to make her voice strong as she called out, "Come in, dear."

Regina opened the door and entered. "Mother, you're already in bed!" she said on a note of surprise. "Is anything wrong?"

"I'm just a bit more tired than usual this morning."

Regina frowned, concerned. "Should I send for a doctor?"

"No, no. I'll be fine, Regina. Just tired."

"What would you like for breakfast?"

"I'm not hungry this morning."

"Perhaps I'd better stay home from work today and tend to you."

"No, I don't want you doing that. I'll be perfectly fine after a good rest. Now you run along to work like a good girl." She smiled with an effort. "You wouldn't want to disappoint Mr. Slostrum after all the faith he's placed in you."

"All right," Regina said uncertainly, "if you're sure."

"I'm sure, dear."

After Regina left, Adelaide drifted into a fevered sleep. She dreamed of Robert calling to her over a vast chasm of time and distance. She dreamed of hearing a baby crying in a dark alley, and of walking down the endless alley forever, never finding the wailing child.

She awoke to find a wet cloth on her forehead and a concerned Regina hovering over her. "Mother, you're burning up with fever! You're very ill. I should never have left you alone!"

"I shall be all right." Adelaide struggled to sit up. "I must get ready to go to work."

Gently Regina pushed her back down. "You're not going anywhere, Mother. I've sent our neighbor's son, Tom, for the doctor. He should be here soon.''

''I don't need a doctor,'' Adelaide said weakly. ''The expense, we can't afford it.''

''Your health is far more important than any expense, Mother.''

The doctor, a middle-aged, fussy man, arrived a few minutes later and closeted himself with Adelaide. Regina made a pot of tea and sat drinking it nervously.

The doctor was grave of face when he came out of Adelaide's bedroom. ''Your mother is very ill, Miss Paxton.''

Regina sat up in alarm. ''What is wrong with her, Doctor?''

''She has contracted pneumonia. Her lungs are badly congested.''

''But she will be all right?''

The doctor sighed. ''What can I say? Very little is yet known about pneumonia. We can only see that she gets plenty of rest, keep her warm, and hope. There is no medication that I can give her. If she were younger, stronger, but at her age and in her weakened condition...'' The doctor shrugged expressively, his face dolorous.

THREE DAYS LATER, Adelaide died in her sleep.

Regina had nursed her mother and watched helplessly as the fever consumed Adelaide.

Now Regina was filled with a feeling of utter desolation as she stared down at Adelaide's waxen face. The only family she had ever known was gone. She began to weep, racking spasms of grief that caused her body to shudder painfully.

At last, drained and quiet, she arose from where she had been kneeling beside Adelaide's bed. She was going to be alone now; it was a fact that she was going to have to face. She must go on with her life. She would miss Adelaide dreadfully, and for a long time, yet she could hear her mother saying, "You're a strong girl, Regina. You can manage very well on your own... until you find a husband."

Regina smiled wanly to herself and said aloud, "Yes, Mother, I shall manage. You taught me to be self-reliant. I am grateful to you for that."

Two hours later, tidying up the flat as she prepared to receive her mother's mourners, she came across something that astounded her.

She found two documents in a drawer in Adelaide's bedroom. The first was a simple, one-page will, leaving all of her worldly goods to her daughter, Regina. No mention was made of the fact Regina had been found abandoned in a noxious alley.

There was nothing unusual about finding a will, of course. But the second item was quite unbelievable. It was a bankbook, listing deposits in a joint account in the names of Adelaide and Regina Paxton. Regina's amazement mounted as she looked at the total. Over the past twenty years, her mother had accumulated five thousand pounds!

Regina stared at the figures in a daze. How could she have saved that much money? And when had she put Regina's name on the account? Vaguely Regina recalled that several years ago, Adelaide had asked her to sign some papers—"Just a bit of business," she had said—and Regina had done so without questioning her mother. Regina knew that Adelaide had been frugal, but never once had she breathed a word about all the money she had saved.

At any rate, there was her name on the bank-book, Adelaide's last gift to her. It was a small fortune! At least it seemed so to Regina. The question now was, what would she do with it?

In the end she decided not to touch the money for the time being. She had the unsettling feeling that it would serve some good purpose in the not-too-distant future.

A MONTH AFTER Adelaide's death, Regina was at work behind the counter, rearranging some gem trays in a more attractive fashion, when she heard a familiar voice.

Glancing up, she saw a big man in tattered clothes talking to one of the clerks across the room. It wasn't until she saw the flaming red beard that she realized the man was Brian Macbride.

In that instant he turned around, and his blue-green eyes blazed in recognition. He came across the room toward her. As he drew near her, she was shocked by his appearance. He had lost weight, his face was gaunt and his clothes were shabby. And she noticed, with a feeling of dismay, that he limped slightly. But there was still an air of blazing vitality about him.

He stopped across the counter from her. "Sure, and it's Regina Paxton."

"It is, sir," she said demurely, her heart beating strongly.

"Working as a salesclerk?" he said in astonishment.

"And doing very well at it, thank you, sir."

A slow smile lit up his face. "I'm sure you are, Regina Paxton. I'm after thinking you would do very well at anything you might set your mind to. I have a strong feeling that I may have underestimated you."

"It's been a long time, Brian. I was beginning to think that something had happened to you. You don't look too well."

"Something did happen to me, lass," he said dourly. "I would like to tell you about it, but 'tis a long tale. Perhaps over lunch? I must see Andrew first."

"I would like to have lunch with you, Brian, and hear your story."

He smiled again before moving toward the stairs leading up to Andrew Slostrum's office.

THEY HAD THEIR noonday meal at an eating establishment around the corner from the firm. Brian seemed strangely subdued after his meeting with Andrew Slostrum, and said little as they walked together to the building. After they were seated in a booth in the rear, the barmaid came over for their order.

"Would you care for a drink, Regina?" Brian asked.

"No, thank you."

"Well, I would. Bring me a large Irish whiskey, would you, lass?"

After the barmaid had gone for his drink, Brian sighed and massaged his face wearily, then smiled with an apparent effort. "So what has happened to you, Regina, since I last saw you?"

"Well, several things. For one, the promotion to salesclerk."

"How did that come about?"

She hesitated briefly, then told him the story about how she had sold the star sapphire for more than the asking price.

Brian threw back his head and laughed, and it seemed to relax him. "Andrew mentioned that you were clever, and that you sold more than anyone else in the store."

"Please don't tell him about the sapphire."

"Wouldn't dream of it."

The barmaid came with his whiskey, and they ordered their meal—steak-and-kidney pie.

"One of the things that happened has been very difficult for me to accept," Regina said. "My mother died."

"Ah, lass, it's sorry I am." He reached across the table and squeezed her hand. It was the first time he had ever touched her, and a current of warmth flowed through her.

"I miss her terribly. It's only been a month. She wasn't my natural mother, you know. I was a foundling. She found me thrown away like a rag doll in an alley," she said in a burst of candor, although she immediately wondered why she had revealed the truth. It was the first time she had told anyone the real story.

"Ah, an orphan, is it?" Brian finished off the last of his whiskey.

"But I could not have loved her more if she had been my natural mother."

"I'm sorry for your troubles, Regina."

She made a dismissive gesture and studied him intently. "Enough about me. I'm curious about you. You have been gone for so long. Did you find your sapphire field in Australia?"

He shook his head. "I did not. It was not a good field and was played out by the time I arrived. If I recall correctly, I think I mentioned that possibility to you."

"Yes, you did. But you also mentioned that if all else failed, you would work the Great Barrier Reef for black coral."

"That I did. Or tried to do." His face was like a thundercloud. "But the Great Barrier Reef does not have the black coral it once had, and gem hunters are fighting over what's left like starving dogs over a bone. And they are blackguards, one and all. Armed to the teeth and dangerous as jackals. I was shot, my boat stolen from me and I was left to drown in the sea."

"How horrible!" she exclaimed. "What happened?"

"No bunch of boyos like that can finish off Brian Macbride," he said grimly. "Of course, I had a stroke of luck. I found a bit of driftwood to cling to and managed to make it to shore, more dead than alive. I had two bullets in me. One in my arm and another had shattered my knee. The knee got infected during the time before I was found unconscious on the shore and taken to a doctor. The sawbones lived up to his name and told me he would have to remove the leg above the knee. I told him I wouldn't have it and swore by all the saints that I would kill him if he sawed off my leg. He told me that if he didn't cut it off, I'd die. I said I'd rather be dead than live as a one-legged man.''

"Oh, Brian!" Without thinking, she reached across the table and touched his hand. "And then what happened?"

He grinned slightly. "Well, obviously he was wrong. I'm still alive. It took me a long while to recover, and I reckon I'll always limp. But otherwise I'm still in one piece."

"So that's why it took you so long to return."

"There's more to it than that. I didn't have a shilling to my name, so I had to work and scrape together enough money to pay for my passage back to England. By the saints, it's not easy for a man with a bad leg to get work. Some of the jobs I had were little more than drudge work. It took me over a year to get the passage money together." He leaned back with a sigh. "But finally, I'm here."

Their food came, and they were silent for some time as they ate.

Brian began to talk again after a few bites. "But that's not all my troubles. I landed back in London with hardly enough money for a night's lodgings. That's why I came to see Andrew this morning."

"And what did Mr. Slostrum say?"

"He said no." Brian was glum. "In a way, I suppose I can't blame him. He's not in the business of financing wild-arsed gem hunters, if you'd pardon the expression. But I have to get backing somewhere!" He slammed his palm down onto the table. "I'll go mad if I have to slave away at some job. Even if I did, it would take me years to save enough to go on another hunt."

Privately Regina thought it might be beneficial for this wild Irishman to settle into the tedium of regular employment for a while. Idly she said, "Did you have someplace in mind, Brian?"

He became still, squinting at her suspiciously. Then he shrugged and muttered, "What does it matter?"

"What?"

"I do have something in mind, yes. In Sydney I came across an old friend, another gem hunter. He was dying. But before he died, he told me of a place in Kashmir where sapphires and rubies lay on the ground for the picking, like pebbles. He even drew me a map of the place."

Regina felt her heart begin to beat faster. "Kashmir? I've heard of it, but I'm not sure . . ."

"The Vale of Kashmir. Halfway across the world. It's a part of India."

"If the gemstones are in such abundance and so easy to find as your friend claims, why didn't *he* come back with some?"

"That was the first thing that occurred to me, so I asked him that very question. He told me that he was waylaid by bandits before he could get out of the country with his stones. He was lucky to escape with his life. He had it in mind to go back, then he fell ill."

Regina, scarcely listening now, was thinking hard as she finished her meal. "Brian . . . how much would be required to finance this expedition?" She looked at him intently.

"Quite a bit." He snorted softly. "Right now, ten pounds would be more than I could raise."

"But how much would it take?"

He looked thoughtful. "I could manage on two thousand pounds, perhaps." He stared at her. "Why do you ask?"

Regina's thoughts were racing. "Suppose I was to supply the funds you need?"

"You!" He reared back in surprise. "Where did you get that much money?"

"An inheritance from my mother," she said coolly.

He was shaking his head. "No, lass. I couldn't take your money. This is a risky enterprise. You could lose every shilling."

"On the other hand, I could earn more from my investment than I could hope to gain anywhere else. Besides, it's my decision to make, isn't it?"

His eyes began to gleam. "You would really finance me?"

"I would. If the terms are right."

"What terms?" he asked with a canny look.

"Since I shall be providing all the necessary funds, I believe that I am entitled to fifty percent of the proceeds."

"Fifty percent!" He pretended to be scandalized. "The funds may be yours, but the risk will all be mine, and this will be a very risky venture. The minute I enter the Kashmir, my life will be in danger. No, seventy percent for me, thirty for you. That's after your investment has been paid back, of course," he added virtuously.

"No, Brian. Fifty-fifty. *After* I have been paid back."

He looked at her with some amusement. "I see why you are so successful. You drive a hard bargain, woman." He was silent for a long while, deep in thought, as Regina waited. Finally he looked up. "If matters were normal with me . . . but they are not. All right, agreed!"

He reached across the table to take her hand, and they shook solemnly.

Without letting go of his hand, Regina said, "I have one additional condition, however."

"I'm after thinking you're taking a large risk, Regina Paxton. What assurance do you have that I won't take your money and simply disappear . . ." He blinked. "What did you say about a condition?"

"I will accompany you on the expedition. That way, you cannot simply disappear, can you?"

He gaped at her, stunned. "You! *You* accompany me? You must be daft to even suggest such a thing."

"That is the way it must be," she said quietly, "or we have no bargain."

"No! By the saints, I would not dream of taking a woman along on such an expedition. Even if the peril was less, I would not do such a thing. I cannot devote even a small part of my time to seeing to a lady's welfare."

"That is gallant of you, Brian," she said dryly. "But I am fully capable of taking care of myself, and of doing my full share of whatever is to be done."

"Again, I say no!" He thumped his fist on the table.

"Then we have no bargain. Either I go with you, or you do not get financing from me."

"So be it." His green eyes blazed with anger. "If I cannot get financing elsewhere, then I will not go."

Before she could say anything else, he was on his feet and striding out of the pub. She sat where she was, staring after him, musing. Actually her reason for wanting to go on the expedition had little to do with keeping an eye on her investment. It was the thought of finding a star sapphire like the one she had first seen at Slostrum's, of picking it up from the ground with her own hands—that lay behind her desire to accompany him.

Of course, she could not tell Brian that; she dared not tell him since she knew it would only serve to infuriate him further.

CHAPTER SIX

TWO WEEKS PASSED with no word from Brian, and Regina regretfully assumed that she would never hear from him again.

Then one afternoon, she glanced up from her position behind the counter and saw him standing just inside the door, glaring at her. His hands were on his hips, his feet set wide apart. Catching her glance, his scowl darkened, and he came toward her, limping slightly.

"All right, wench," he said in a growling voice. "We have a bargain, if you are still agreeable."

Suddenly giddy with delight, she said, "Oh, Brian, I'm so glad!"

"I will probably live to regret it. In fact, I *know* I will!" He relaxed a trifle. "But I must confess that I've tried everywhere else, with no success. You're my last resort."

"You won't regret it, Brian! I swear you won't!" She reached across the counter to clasp his hand in both of hers.

Staring into her sparkling eyes, seeing the childlike delight on her lovely face, Brian suddenly realized that no matter what happened, he would not regret his decision. He had never imagined taking a woman with him on a gem hunt; but then he had never known a woman quite like this one.

Of course, it certainly would not do to let her know that. Sternly he said, "We have a great many preparations to make before we can depart."

"Just tell me what to do, and I'll do my share. I shall withdraw the money tomorrow."

"Not all at once, foolish woman. We only need a few hundred pounds to begin with, to purchase clothing and other necessities."

"Whatever you say, Brian."

"What about your job here, and Andrew?"

"Why, I shall resign, of course. I'll tell him today."

"Perhaps you shouldn't be telling him the real reason."

"Why not?"

"Well..." His glance slid away. "I think it might be best."

"You want me to lie? No, I shall tell him the truth. He is entitled to that."

"I should have known that's what you would say." In reality, he was afraid that Slostrum would try to change Regina's mind.

And that was precisely what Andrew Slostrum did try to do that evening after the store closed and Regina informed him of her plans.

"My dear Regina, you must be mad!" he said in shock. "Aside from the fact that I don't wish to lose you because I believe you have a bright future here, it is absolute insanity to go chasing halfway across the world with that wild man!"

"It's what I want to do, Mr. Slostrum. It's what I *have* to do. I can't really explain it any more clearly than that. I am sorry to leave you so suddenly."

He waved a hand. "That is unimportant, Regina. It is your welfare that concerns me. A woman going on such an expedition is unthinkable. And to go off with Brian Macbride! The man is an adventurer, a freebooter."

"Are you saying that he is dishonest?"

"No, he is honest. At least within the boundaries of his rather strange concept of honesty. But the man courts danger, Regina. He thrives on it. What I'm saying is, he is not the sort of man to see to the welfare of a woman."

"I will have to take my chances."

"Indeed? Nothing I can say will dissuade you?"

"I'm sorry, sir, but no."

In the end, he lost his temper. "I thought you were beginning to show maturity, Regina. Instead you are still a foolish young girl. You are a bloody idiot, to be truthful! Adelaide would have been ashamed of you."

Regina flinched, and then her own anger surfaced. "Sir, that is unfair! Mother might not have approved, but I am doing nothing shameful. She taught me to be independent, and she would have at least wished me Godspeed."

"Indeed? Well, you may not expect me to do the same. If you are fortunate enough to survive this mad expedition and return penniless, do not expect me to show pity!" With a final glare, he stormed off.

However, of the three people she cared most about at Slostrum's, at least two wished her well.

Giles's faded eyes twinkled. "Off to Kashmir, is it? In search of your star sapphire?"

Regina was taken aback. "How did you know?"

"For Lord's sake, young woman, you think I am dense? Kashmir is well-known for its rubies and sapphires, and what is it that you have prattled on about since you've been here? Have you forgotten that you told me you intend to possess a star sapphire someday?"

"Don't tell anyone, especially Brian. They would all think me even more foolish."

Giles shrugged his bony shoulders. "I shall tell no one, most of all your Brian Macbride. I don't even know the man to speak to. I wish you good fortune on your search."

"Thank you, Giles." Impulsively she kissed him on the cheek and laughed when he flushed a dark red.

Eugene Leacock was also pleased for her. "I envy you, Regina. I would give anything to be able to go on such an expedition."

Regina cocked her head at him, smiling wickedly. "You don't think it's unwomanly of me?"

He looked surprised. "Why should I think that? I think a woman has as much right as a man, if she will not be a burden," he said stoutly. "And I don't believe for a moment that you will be."

"You're about the only one who doesn't seem to think so," she said in a dry voice. "And that includes Mr. Macbride. He would never let me accompany him if I was not financing the expedition."

"Well then, he is wrong. With your knowledge and feel for gemstones, I am confident you will be an asset. And I have a strong feeling that you will come back a rich woman."

Regina experienced a rush of feeling for this young man who seemed to have an understanding beyond his years. "Well, if a miracle does happen and I come back with a good find, I may open a jewelry store of my own, and if that ever happens, I will have need of a gem cutter. So work hard while I'm gone, and learn all you can from Giles."

"I would be most happy to work for you, Regina."

Peter Mondrain was far from pleased by her revelation. "I thought you might be different, Regina. I thought you might overcome the female weakness for rash actions, actions based on emotion instead of logic. It appears that I am in error."

"My decision is not based on emotion!"

"No?" He raised a supercilious eyebrow. "You're undoubtedly swooning over this adventurer, Macbride, and anxious to journey off alone with him."

Regina felt her face flush. "It is insulting of you to imply, sir, that I am entering into a liaison with Mr. Macbride! This is strictly a business arrangement."

"Is it now?" He sneered openly. "I do not believe you. I should have realized that no woman is capable of resisting a charming rogue. I should never have allowed your signature on the piece."

"Why not?" she said hotly. "It was my design!"

"Without my tutelage, you would never have achieved a usable design."

"I shall be forever grateful to you for what you have taught me, Mr. Mondrain, but I—"

He cut her off with a gesture. "I do not wish your gratitude, Miss Paxton." He turned back to his worktable, dismissing her.

THE NEXT MORNING, Regina met Brian at her bank and withdrew the amount of money they would need to get started. In spite of her firm denial to Mondrain, Regina had to wonder if she *was* falling in love with Brian. If she was, being alone with him for so long on the expedition would complicate matters considerably. He was a charming and handsome man, she was forced to admit, and there was no denying that she felt a physical attraction toward him. This was something that she had not bargained for, and for the first time, she wondered if she was indeed being very foolish.

Brian was certainly in an exuberant mood, and if he took any notice of her creeping doubts, she saw no evidence of it. During lunch, he never stopped talking long enough to look closely at her. He was outlining their plans.

She studied him closely as he talked. When he had come into Slostrum's the day before, he had been clean shaven; this morning red stubble was evident. Apparently he was letting his beard grow back. Regina examined him closely, waiting for some sign of her true feelings for the man before her. But the trouble was, she decided, she didn't quite know what symptoms she would be experiencing if she was falling in love. Heart palpitations? Giddiness? Cold sweats? She felt none of these things.

Well, in any case, she was committed now and she was not about to back away from the expedition. If they made a respectable find, there should be enough money to launch herself into the kind of life she wanted. And there was always the possibility, however remote, of finding a star sapphire. . . .

A sudden and startling thought struck her. Was Peter Mondrain in love with her? How could he be, a man more than old enough to be her father? But then in a sudden flash of insight, she knew that age, as such, was no barrier. It would certainly explain his harsh words to her yesterday. She stared down into her teacup, mulling over the idea.

Regina had misjudged Brian; he was well aware that she was distracted this morning and had put it down to her having second thoughts about the expedition, and her investment.

It was for that very reason that he was prattling on at such a great rate, talking extravagantly of the wonders of the trip; it would be a disaster for him if she backed out now. When she had first broached the idea of accompanying him, Brian had been outraged, actually insulted. Gem hunting was a man's business; women had no place in it. He liked the lass. Bloody hell, why not admit it? He was utterly charmed by her, even if she was a mite more strong-minded than he would have liked.

Handsome, charming, virile—and well aware of these traits—Brian Macbride had never had trouble attracting women, but he divided his life into two separate compartments. When he was flush with money and ready to enjoy himself—that was the time for women. But when he was on a gem hunt, no women were allowed to be part of that life.

Until now.

He was breaking one of his cardinal rules, and he was somewhat baffled as to the reason. Oh, he had been without funds and unable to talk anyone else into financing him, and Regina had offered a solution. Yet he was astute enough to realize that there was more to it than that. He had been flat of purse before and had managed.

Now he was finding himself actually looking forward with anticipation to having Regina with him.

All the while these disturbing thoughts were running through his mind, he was talking, "I'm thinking you'll like the Vale of Kashmir, Regina. I have never been there, but I have heard on good authority that it is one of the most beautiful places on this earth."

"Brian..." Regina's sudden smile was mischievous. "What happened to all the bandits? The great danger I'm liable to be in?"

Brian had the grace to look embarrassed. "Aye, they are there, so I'm told, but I hope we can slip in and out, and manage to avoid them."

Still smiling, she leaned across the table. "You're afraid that I may be having second thoughts, that I may withdraw my financing, aren't you?"

"The thought has crossed my mind, yes. You seem so . . . well, distracted this morning. There is something on your mind."

"Yes, there is, but it is not second thoughts about the expedition. I am firmly committed to that and am, in fact, looking forward to it. Actually I have no choice but to forge ahead now."

"Then what is troubling you, Regina?"

"The reactions I received from Mr. Slostrum, and another man at the firm. Peter Mondrain, the jewelry designer." With some misgivings, she told him of the harsh words spoken to her by the two men, sure that Brian would wholeheartedly agree with them.

He surprised her. "Their reactions were predictable. It is a man's world, Regina, especially the jewelry business. It was exactly my own reaction."

That didn't entirely explain Mondrain's harshness, since he had been willing to accept her jewelry design. She stared at Brian with a skeptical smile. "You speak as if you no longer feel that way."

"Oh, I'm reconciled to our joint venture," he said with a shrug. Be damned if he was going to tell her more than that. "I needed the money, you offered it, with your condition, and I had little choice but to accept."

"Oh, I don't know. You could have taken a job," she said dryly.

"Don't be saying such a thing," he said with a mock shudder, "even in jest."

"So I'm the lesser of two evils, is that it?"

"If you wish to put it that way."

"All right, Brian, since you appear to be saddled with me . . ." She leaned back. "Tell me what I can do to help."

"No need for you to do a thing," he said quickly. "I'll do what needs doing, most of it. I'll give you a list of clothing you'll be needing. Also, you'll have to get some papers in order. That'll keep you busy.''

''Oh, no, you can't shuffle me off so easily. I fully intend to do my share.''

''And what might that be, exactly?'' he asked, all innocence.

''Why, I don't know.... One thing I can do. We have to book passage on a ship, don't we? I can handle that.''

''Lass, what do you know about ships?''

''What is there to know? After all, since I'm paying for our passage, I should have a say in what kind of ship we sail on. According to you, much of the trip will be uncomfortable at best, so at least the sea voyage should be as comfortable as possible. Left to you, I may end up sleeping in a hammock in some smelly hold.''

He gazed at her indulgently. What harm would it do to let her look for a ship? It would keep her busy, out of his way, and the final decision would be his, anyway. He said, ''Since, as you say, the money is yours, go ahead. But don't look for anything too expensive.''

THE NEXT TWO WEEKS were busy ones for Regina, and for Brian, too, she supposed, since she seldom saw him. First, she was occupied purchasing the items on the list he had given her. They included sturdy clothing, a blanket bedroll, and the minimum of toilet necessities she would require.

She made several purchases not on Brian's list. She went into a men's clothing store and ordered a complete outfit for a man. To the astounded clerk, she said, "This is for my brother. He has been ill for a long time and needs new clothing."

Recovering from his astonishment, the clerk said, "Do you know his sizes, ma'am?"

"They are for my younger brother. He is about my size. I shall try them on."

Finally she was ready to look for a ship bound for Bombay. She went down to the London docks in search of a ship soon to embark for India.

The dock area was abustle with ships from all over the world, loading and unloading cargo. It was a rough area, and many of the dockworkers eyed her suspiciously—a well-dressed lady, especially one unaccompanied, was out of place here. But no one accosted her, and she soon overcame her apprehension and strode freely around.

She loved the many smells—spices; fruits from exotic ports; tea and coffee—and the boisterous shouts of the busy workmen; even the profanities soon ceased to bother her.

The vast majority of the vessels were steamships, but here and there she saw the graceful rigging of a sleek, racy clipper. She would have loved a voyage on such a ship, but the day of the clipper was past, made obsolete by steam. Even if they could book passage, it would be impractical, she knew well. Sailing vessels were much slower, even the ones augmented by steam engines, and since the Suez Canal had been opened in 1869, the route to India had been cut almost in half—for steamships. The canal could not accommodate sailing ships, and thus they had to sail around the Cape of Good Hope.

No, they would have to be content with a steamer; not so romantic, perhaps, but far more practical. After all, this was definitely not a pleasure cruise.

To her dismay, she discovered that her task was not going to be easy. From the harbormaster's office, she learned the names of the ships bound for India and China; most of them carried only cargo, with no passenger accommodations.

Narrowing her search to the ships that carried passengers and made a stop at Bombay, Regina went from ship to ship. Each carried only a limited number of passengers, and the first few she investigated were already fully booked.

Finally she found a ship bound for Bombay with a cargo of trade goods to be exchanged for Indian tea. The tea trade, she had read, was well past its heyday, yet there was still a strong market among the British. Learning that the captain was on board, Regina walked along the docks to the *Galatea*. It was a stubby, ungainly-looking vessel, with paint peeling in unsightly scabs from the sides. She hesitated about going on board, wondering what sort of accommodations it had to offer.

But in the end, seeing no alternative, she dodged the seamen and longshoremen trudging up and down the gangplank. Up on deck, she asked the first sailor she saw for an audience with the captain.

The grizzled seaman eyed her dubiously. "What business do you have with Cap, Miss?"

She looked him directly in the eye and said imperiously, "I shall state my business to your captain, and to no other."

"Very well, Miss. Come along with me."

Regina followed the seaman along the deck, which was strewn with crates of cargo. She noticed that the deck was in no better condition than the outside of the ship, and for the first time she recognized the unpleasant stench of oil.

She was escorted below decks and along a dim passageway, which also smelled of oil. She began to have real doubts about the ship; it certainly carried no aura of romance on the high seas.

At the end of the passageway, the sailor knocked on a door, and a gruff voice from within said, "Come."

The sailor opened the door and motioned Regina inside. The captain's cabin was cramped—a bunk against one wall, two chairs bolted to the deck and a small desk and bookcases against the bulkhead. A heavyset man with a grizzled beard turned away from the desk, scowling. "Yes? What is it?"

"Lady here wants to speak with you, Cap."

"Visitors ain't allowed on board the *Galatea*."

"I'm not a visitor. My name is Regina Paxton."

"I'm Captain Elias Parker, master of this vessel." He squinted at her, eyes as dark and shiny as buttons. The portion of his whiskered face that she could see was as dark and weather creased as old leather. "If your name's 'sposed to mean something to me, it don't."

"Of course it doesn't, Captain Parker. I'm here to see about booking two cabins for passage to Bombay."

"Why come to me?" he said dourly. "Cabin bookings are handled by our office on the wharf."

"Yes, I know that, but I have no intention of booking cabins until I can get a look at them, and your agent told me he would be busy elsewhere today."

"Two cabins, you say?"

"Yes, for myself and a Mr. Brian Macbride."

His squint grew suspicious. "A relative?"

"No, a business associate. Mr. Macbride and I are journeying to India on business."

He grunted. "Well, you appear respectable enough." He raised his voice a little. "Benbo, show the lady the passenger cabins."

The sailor, apparently still lingering outside in the passageway, appeared in the doorway. "Aye, Cap."

Regina followed the sailor back down the passageway until they had almost reached the other end. He stopped at the door, opened it and stood back for her to enter.

Regina went in slowly. The cabin was tiny, with a square porthole that would at least offer some light and fresh air—when the weather was calm enough to open it. There was a bunk beneath the porthole, two chairs and a chest of drawers, all pegged to the decking. She remembered reading an account by Charles Dickens, writing of his crossing the Atlantic on one of the earlier passenger liners; he had written that the cabin was so tiny that his luggage would barely fit into it. But she supposed they should consider themselves lucky; she had read somewhere that passengers on the earlier ships to the East Indies had to buy their own furnishings for their cabins, in addition to paying a steep fare.

Regina had learned from the booking agent that the round-trip fare for one to Bombay on the *Galatea* was four hundred pounds. This seemed reasonable to her; she had questioned other agents as to their fares, which varied widely from line to line, and four hundred pounds was in the middle of the range.

She thanked the sailor and made her way off the ship and to the agent's office, where she purchased two round-trip fares to Bombay.

BRIAN WAS LESS THAN pleased when she told him what she had done. "You booked two cabins on your own, without consulting me? Don't I even have a say?"

"Brian, I checked every shipping line with vessels bound for India over the next three weeks," she said patiently. "These were the last two cabins left, unless you'd care to wait for several more weeks. I didn't think you wanted to do that."

"And you've already paid the fares?"

"I had to, to be sure we'd have the cabins."

"How much?"

"Eight hundred pounds for both, round-trip."

"Well, it's a fair enough price," he said in a grumbling voice. And the next day he was gracious enough to tell her, "I inspected the *Galatea* and our cabins, and they will do. You did fine, Regina. The captain seems a right bloody bastard, but from talking to the men on the docks, I'm told he's a respected skipper. There is one thing...he tells me they have moved the sailing date up. They leave in three days."

"Oh!" she said, dismayed. "Is that going to cause a problem, Brian?"

"It shouldn't. I have made most of the necessary purchases. How about you?"

She nodded. "I've bought everything on the list you gave me." She thought of telling him about the men's clothing she had bought, but decided to keep quiet.

"All your papers are in order?"

"That is taken care of, as well."

"Then I think we're as ready as we'll ever be."

THREE DAYS LATER, Regina stood alongside Brian at the railing of the *Galatea* as the steamer slipped her moorings and began to ease out into the Thames. It was March, and the morning was chilly. A heavy fog blanketed the ground, and very little of London could be seen as they inched along. Foghorns sounded on every side, like mournful mammoths lost and calling to their mates.

Brian's big hand clasped hers on the railing, and she looked up into his face.

Smiling faintly, he said, "So far, everything is going smooth as silk. Let's hope it continues that way."

Regina had to wonder, as London slid past, if she would ever see England again. She felt a moment of panic, which she hid as well as she could behind a tremulous smile.

CHAPTER SEVEN

REGINA'S FIRST FEW DAYS at sea were not pleasant. Just after leaving London, the *Galatea* ran into rough weather, and Regina, on board a ship for the first time fell prey to seasickness.

It was a disgusting, demeaning business, and for the first two days she spent a great deal of her time vomiting into a basin. To make matters worse, Brian was not affected at all and attempted to tend her with unfailing, and unbearable, cheerfulness.

A portion of her mind was disturbed that anyone should see her in such a condition, and yet another part of her had to admit that physically she felt too awful to worry about such matters.

On the third day, although the rough weather had not abated, she felt considerably better and ventured to the dining room for the evening meal. The dining room had been planned for rough seas—the tables and benches were pegged down, bottles and glasses were set in racks along the walls. But even so, Regina was amazed when she saw a leg of mutton fly off the table and strike a gentleman on the head, rendering him unconscious, and a steak-and-kidney pie jump off the table and splatter all over Brian's shirtfront. It had been enough to kill Regina's awakening appetite, but Brian had laughed heartily.

Regina looked at him unhappily. "This is awful! But it doesn't seem to bother you, Brian."

He shrugged. "You get used to it. Sure, and you'll be fine when you get your sea legs."

At the time, Regina doubted that she would ever feel really well or comfortable again. But the next day, the sea was calm, and she felt almost like her old self.

Feeling like a prisoner released, Regina went topside for the first time since they had left London, carrying with her some maps of India and Kashmir, and some reading material about the areas.

It was a perfect day; sunny and clear. Looking at the sparkling sea and inhaling the fresh salt breeze, Regina felt her spirits lift. The wake of the ship, white and fresh, stretched out behind them, and a lone sea gull soared overhead. Most of the other paying passengers were also taking advantage of the sun and good weather, and several of them nodded to her in a friendly fashion as they paced the deck.

Regina, still feeling uneasy about walking on a moving surface, and still a bit weak from her bout with mal de mer, decided to look only for a place to sit. She finally found an empty bench by the railing on the afterdeck, where she made herself comfortable.

It was a pleasant spot, except for one thing—the chicken coops were located across from her. The chickens, she understood, had been brought along to provide eggs and fresh meat for the passengers. During the storm, the coops had been covered to keep the chickens from drowning; now the coops were uncovered, and feed had been scattered along the deck. Sticking their heads out through the slats of the cages, the chickens pecked at the grain and voiced their approval with loud clucking and cackling. The odor was rather strong, but Regina thought it a small penalty to pay to be out in the fresh air and sunshine.

She studied the maps first, trying to figure out exactly what their route would be from Bombay. Then she began to browse through the books she had bought—one a guidebook, the other a short history of India.

She gave a start as a voice said, "Good morn to you, Regina."

Glancing up, she saw Brian looming over her.

Smiling, he said, "It's happy I am to see you hale enough to take the air."

"I'm happy as well. I was beginning to feel like a prisoner."

He gazed out at the coastline, a brown haze in the distance. "That's the coast of Portugal over there," he said with a wave of his hand. His red beard had almost grown back to its full luxuriance. "Some time tomorrow we should steam past Gibraltar and on into the Mediterranean."

"Brian . . . I'm curious about something." She held up the book she had been reading.

"And what might that be, lass?"

He sat down on the bench beside her. Somehow in the close proximity of the ship, she seemed more aware of his physical presence, his sheer size.

"Well, you warned me about danger, about brigands, but from what I've been reading, India seems quite civilized. If the country is under our colonial rule, how can it be teeming with bandits?''

"You know what my old Da used to say? He said that reading books corrupts the morals and the mind." He took the book from her.

She said tartly, "And is that what *you* say?"

"No, no, of course not," he said irritably.

"You still haven't answered my question, Brian!"

"I may have exaggerated matters a wee bit," he said with an infuriating grin.

"So that I would not insist on accompanying you?"

"Probably true. But I wasn't being wholly misleading. Where there is the possibility of riches, there are always thieves and brigands. You will find them at every gem field in the world, and I doubt that Kashmir will be any different."

She shook her head in exasperation. "You are a rogue, Brian Macbride."

"But a charming rogue, you must admit."

She had to laugh. "Why should I admit to something like that? Your opinion of yourself is high enough as it is."

"Ah, well." He spread his hands. "It has been my experience that if a man doesn't hold himself in high regard, no one else will, either."

"Brian..." She became serious. "Are you sorry that I came along?"

"Not so far," he said judiciously. "In fact, I'm rather enjoying your company. But when we get to India, to Kashmir...aye, there matters will be different!"

"How so?"

"For one thing, you're mistaken about Kashmir. It is not under direct British rule. It has its own government, and it's rather rigid. Here..." He swept a hand around. "You are living in comparative comfort. But once in Kashmir, we will be in rugged terrain, camping out, and among a strange people who will look upon you askance. The female of the species is not highly prized in India, and a foreign woman is even more scorned. Have no doubt about that. And when we find our goods, speed and secrecy will be necessary, if we are to escape with our hides intact."

"And you think I'm capable of neither?"

He shrugged. "We shall see. But I must be candid, Regina. The women of my experience have not been known for those particular talents."

"Perhaps you just haven't known the right women."

"Perhaps." He looked skeptical.

"I can be as speedy and secretive as you, you great lummox!" she retorted, then frowned in thought. "Secretive? Why should we be so secretive?"

"Because we shall have two sets of enemies, lass. Those who would rob us of our goods, and those who would clap us in irons for making off with a few of their stones."

"Brian...." She looked directly into his eyes. "We will be stealing the gemstones, won't we?"

"I wouldn't put it in such strong terms," he said blandly. "I'm after thinking that the good Lord is responsible for the making of gemstones. Therefore, they properly belong to those who find them. No country has the right to claim exclusive ownership. To take the stones from a person would be stealing, but from a country, no. Not to my way of thinking.''

''I have been stupid! It never occurred to me, but no matter how you describe it, we will be stealing. We could end up in prison!''

''''Tis certainly a possibility, but I fully intend to see to it that that does not happen. Brian Macbride does not take kindly to prison.''

''Those diamonds you sold to Mr. Slostrum, how did you get them?''

''I picked them up off the ground, like many men have before me. De Beers claims a monopoly on diamond production in South Africa. *They* tell a gem merchant how many he can buy every year, and only from them. To my way of thinking, that is not right and proper.''

''I'm beginning to realize, Brian, that you have a strong tendency to rationalize.''

''Look at it this way, lass. The good Lord put the stones there for everybody. Look at the California gold rush of '49. Men went in there and took out the gold, and no one thought the worse of them for it. Who can it harm if we take a few gemstones out of Kashmir? Not the people. If they found them, they would get a mere pittance for them, or the government would simply seize them without issuing any payment of any kind. Most common people there, except for the bandits or the greedy buckos, have no idea of the gems' value, anyway. We are as entitled as anyone else.''

Perhaps he was right. Who would they be hurting, in actual fact? Regina realized that *she* was now rationalizing. Adelaide had taught her to be honest in all things, yet it seemed to her that Brian was right. Perhaps someday governments would more clearly define the rights to anything of value in or on the land, but as of now it appeared to be finders, keepers.

Brian was speaking, and Regina saw that he was staring at her with some amusement. "What did you say?" she asked.

"I said, if you're having conscience pangs, you can get off the ship at the first port we reach and sail back to England."

"Oh, no, you're not getting rid of me so easily, Brian Macbride," she said quickly. "The land where the sapphires are located . . . is it private property, or does it belong to the government?"

"Why, I'm thinking it would belong to the government, if it belongs to anybody. Certainly not to the people, who are either farmers or goat herders, in the main—and the area in which we'll be searching is good for neither." He cocked an eyebrow at her. "Does that satisfy your Victorian morality?"

"Don't patronize me, Brian!" she said in annoyance. "I'm going through with the expedition no matter what."

"Now that's the spirit I like to see, lass." He applauded softly.

Before she could frame a retort, Regina realized that someone had stopped before them, and she gazed up into the whiskered face of Captain Parker. He doffed his cap. "Miss Paxton, Mr. Macbride. Good day to you."

"Good day, Captain." She noticed that the captain was carrying a sextant.

Brian nodded. "Captain."

"And it is a fine day. I'll wager you are happy to be above decks finally." The captain seemed in unusually good spirits. Noticing the direction of Regina's glance, he hefted the sextant. "I am about to take a sighting of the sun. Then I can post the latitude and the longitude, an estimate of our progress, as well as our present position. Have you joined our pool yet, Mr. Macbride?"

"What pool is that, Captain?" Regina asked.

Smiling, Captain Parker said, "Passengers like to wager on the precise time we shall arrive in Bombay, Miss Paxton. The one coming the closest to our arrival time wins the pool. The sum is usually quite considerable."

Brian perked up. "I hadn't heard anything about such a wager."

"The foul weather, sir, has kept all below decks and there has been little interest until now. But my steward tells me that several passengers have made inquiries today. A sheet is now being posted in the salon."

Brian stood, stretching. "Then I think I shall wander down and register for the pool. When the results of your sightings are posted, I shall employ all my seamanship skills to make my estimate of our arrival time."

The captain nodded and marched off.

Brian gazed down at Regina, grinning. "Would you like for me to make a wager for you, lass?"

"No, thank you. I don't think you should, either. We have a better use for our money."

"My good woman, 'tis not good for a man to spend all his time at serious matters," he said with false pomposity. "A little relaxation is good for the circulation and keeps a man alert."

"I'm sure," she said in a dry voice.

"Besides, there is always a good chance that I may win. You heard the captain. The pool will be considerable."

"Then get on with your foolishness and leave me to my reading."

"Sure, and it's sorry I am for you, Miss Paxton. Always so bloody serious!"

When his back was turned, she allowed her face to relax in a smile. In some ways, he was as irresponsible as a child, and yet his shenanigans did lighten her spirits. She was sure that he was fully capable when it came to the matter of gem hunting.

At least she hoped so; otherwise they faced disaster. With a shrug, she opened the history of India and resumed reading.

THE WEATHER REMAINED clear, the seas calm, as they plowed through the Mediterranean toward the Suez Canal. Regina realized that it grew steadily hotter the farther they traveled. The afternoon sun was fierce. Sailcloth was stretched across several portions of the deck so that the passengers, especially the ladies, could still take advantage of the fresh air with the benefit of shade.

She had learned that the *Galatea* carried about thirty paying passengers, and now that most of them had recovered from mal de mer, they crowded the deck. Many of them seemed inordinately curious about Regina and Brian, especially once they learned that they occupied separate cabins and were not married. She and Brian had invented a story to explain their voyage to India: they had been acquaintances for years, but their presence on board the ship was more or less coincidence; Regina was on her way to Bombay to visit relatives, and Brian was on a business trip, looking for Indian art objects to purchase.

Regina soon realized that Captain Parker must have gossiped to the effect that it was Regina who had booked passage for the both of them. The probing questions of some of the women hinted that they knew as much. Regina parried the questions as best she could and kept to herself as much as was possible, considering the confined space of the ship. She quickly gained the reputation of being antisocial and was left alone, which suited her just fine.

Early one morning, they reached Port Said and the entrance of the Suez Canal. Regina had read about the impressive ceremony, presided over by the French Empress Eugenié, which had been held at the official opening of the canal on November 17, 1869. The age of the steamship, combined with the opening of the canal, had marked the beginning of the end for sailing ships. The canal shortened the trip from England to China by almost two thousand miles, but the narrow, shoal-strewn passage could not be used by ships of sail, and most of China's tea was now carried to England by steamships.

Regina and Brian stood at the railing as they entered the first lock of the canal. Apparently the arrival of a new ship was still enough of a novelty that it attracted the local residents. Both banks were lined with dark-skinned people, mostly men and children. The men were turbaned and wore flowing robes.

"Muslims," Brian said. "They're not very friendly to the British, or so has been my experience. As a matter of fact, get a good look at them, Regina. They're much like many of the people we'll be seeing in India."

"From what I have read, there are actually four predominant religious sects in India. Muslims, Hindus, Buddhists and the English, of course, are Christians."

"Again, what you have read of India does not apply to Kashmir! Eighty percent or more of the people there are Muslims. And about the only British you'll see will be on holiday, on the houseboats on the lakes. And most of the natives of India *and* Kashmir consider all whites to be foreign devils."

"Perhaps they have a right to consider us that, Brian. We, especially, since we're coming to take their gems."

He grunted. "You're after starting on that again, are you?"

She smiled. "Not really."

"Bloody hell, that's a relief."

They fell silent as the *Galatea* made its way slowly from lock to lock. The sun's rays were powerful; even the wide-brimmed hat Regina wore provided little protection and it seemed to her that it grew hotter and more humid with each mile they traveled.

With her handkerchief, she wiped the perspiration from her forehead. "Good heavens, it's hot here!"

He laughed. "It's partly the humidity. The closer we get to India, the hotter and more humid it will become."

"Wouldn't it have been better to make the expedition during a cooler time of the year?"

He shook his head. "No, for two reasons. Most importantly, I want to get to the area my friend mapped out for me as soon as possible, before someone else stumbles onto the gem field. And we need to get in and out before monsoon season, which starts in June and lasts into September. Travel is almost impossible during the monsoon season. But it will be cool in Kashmir, due to the high altitude."

"Well, I certainly hope so. This heat is unbearable."

"That's why I put summer clothes on the list. It will get worse before it gets better, believe me."

BRIAN'S PREDICTION proved accurate. When they finally passed through the canal and entered the Indian Ocean, where the air was very still, the heat was almost stifling. Then they encountered what Brian told her was the Southeast Trades, cooling winds that blew all day, dulling the heat of the sun.

By the time the city of Bombay came into view and they had tied off at the docks, it was deathly still and hot again. Brian had not won the pool, missing their arrival time by over twelve hours, which prompted Regina to comment, "Your seamanship skills are not of the best, Brian."

"Sure, and a man can't be best at everything," he said airily.

As they disembarked, Regina decided that the smell was even worse than the heat. It was comprised of many odors—rotting fruit, spices, tea, perspiring humanity and offal. The press of humanity was terrible. Regina and Brian were immediately besieged by filthy urchins, their hands held out, crying, *"Rupees, memsahib!"*

"Ignore them," Brian growled. "If you give even one of the poor buggers a coin, we'll be besieged by the others."

There were other beggars, adults—armless, legless, blind and diseased—all so pitiful that it was all Regina could do to keep from weeping.

Yet others along the wharf were well dressed and prosperous looking. The style of dress varied widely; she saw people in western clothing, others in saris and robes. To Regina's astonishment, she saw a number of dark, comely young women with flashing rubies attached to their foreheads; a few wore rubies in the sides of their nostrils.

Noting her surprise, Brian chuckled. "Aye, a ruby is a beauty mark here, a sign of high caste and wealth."

She heard several languages spoken, all impossible to understand, except here and there a word or a phrase spoken in English.

To her consternation, she soon learned that they were to see very little of Bombay. The moment their luggage was removed from the ship, Brian hired a carriage to take them directly to the railroad station.

"But, Brian," she protested, "aren't we even going to spend the night here? We need a night's rest!"

"What have we been doing but resting on the ship? We have to move fast now that we're here." He grinned. "After we find our goods, *then* we can rest, and the better for it, I'll wager."

Two hours later, they were on a train to Delhi, which was approximately a twenty-hour trip.

It was dark when they left the outskirts of Bombay, and Regina was disappointed that she wouldn't be able to view the countryside.

"We're not here on a pleasure excursion, woman," Brian said in a grumbling voice. "We are on business."

"I can't understand why we can't combine a little sight-seeing with our business. I'd like to see some of the country."

"I'm thinking you'll get your fill of the country, lass, by the time we leave here. Right now, there's only one thing on my mind. The place on my map showing the location of our goods. That's all *you* should be thinking about, as well."

CHAPTER EIGHT

REGINA WAS ALMOST ASLEEP; her body ached from days of riding, and the change in altitude. She held on to the pommel of the saddle with both hands, but she didn't realize that Brian's mule, directly in front of her, had stopped until her animal bumped into it.

She looked up as Brian flung out a hand and shouted, "There it is, lass! The Vale of Kashmir!"

She looked past him and gasped aloud. They were at nine thousand feet, just having reached the top of Banihal Pass. The panorama spread out below them was breathtaking. The valley was verdant, with green fields of rice, and flowering plum and apple trees. In the distance she could see the majestic, snowcapped peaks of the Karakoram Range, towering several thousand feet higher than their own vantage point.

Regina, gazing upward at the huge spires of rock, felt an awe and exhilaration that was almost mystical. "I've never seen anything like it!" she exclaimed. "They look almost close enough to reach out and touch."

"Actually the peaks are more than eighty miles distant." Brian shifted, getting more comfortable in his saddle. "Some people call the Vale of Kashmir 'Happy Valley,' others 'The Venice of the

East.' But all agree that it is one of the most beautiful spots in the world. In ancient days, it was simply called 'Paradise.'"

"I can well understand why." She squinted at him suspiciously. "You seem to know an awful lot about this place, considering that you have supposedly never been here."

"No, never. I swear. But before we left London, I read everything about Kashmir that I could find. I believe in being fully prepared, on any expedition."

"And you laughed at me for my reading!"

"Just having a little sport with you, lass. We had better move along. We have a ways to go. It's some seventy miles to the capital, Srinagar, and the map belonging to my friend shows that the dry riverbed where he found the stones is in the foothills, at least three days' ride beyond Srinagar."

He dug his heels into the sides of the mule, which with a complaining bray, resumed its slow, plodding gait. With a groan, Regina followed suit. Brian was in his element here, taking great pleasure from "roughing it." But for Regina, who had never been astride a mule before, it was pure torture. Brian had assured her that she would become accustomed to it in time; but she had yet to do so and her body ached all over. It hadn't helped that they had been sleeping out at night since leaving Jammu. And sleeping on the ground, she found, was not conducive to rest, particularly if one was already sore and aching from riding a mule all day.

At least it was considerably cooler here, as Brian had promised. During their first few days in India, the long train rides had been hot, the air in the cars almost suffocating. To further add to her discomfort, the food had kept her stomach in a constant state of turmoil. Indian food was hot and heavily spiced; usually they ate curries made with chicken, lamb or fish. Even Indian tea was not served plain, but was perfumed with saffron, and had almonds and cardamom floating in it. Brian had told her that the curries were actually milder than most Indian dishes. "And you should be grateful for the tea. Whether you like it or not, it's supposed to be good for upset stomachs."

What had made everything even more infuriating to Regina was the fact that Brian thrived on the food, eating heartily. Even the heat didn't seem to bother him.

The railroad had ended at Jammu, where Brian had purchased three mules—two to ride and one to carry their supplies.

The first day of riding, in skirts, had been almost intolerable for Regina. Awakening on the second morning, stiff and sore, she had waited until Brian went to start a fire to cook their breakfast, then quickly changed into the boy's clothing she had bought. Her original idea had been to disguise herself, certain that she would attract less attention if the people thought she was a man—or a boy—but now she was glad she had brought the clothing for another reason. Riding a mule wearing trousers was bound to be more comfortable.

She had the trousers, man's shirt and boots on, her hair bound up and hidden under a large cap, when Brian looked around. Regina held her breath, certain that he would be furious.

He had stared at her without any expression at all for a few moments, then threw back his head and laughed uproariously, hands on hips.

"I don't think it's funny at all!" she said indignantly.

After a little while, he had finally gotten his laughter under control. "I don't think it's funny, either. It was more a surprise than anything else. What made you think of dressing like a man?"

"I just thought I'd attract less attention if I was thought to be a male."

He nodded. "It's right you are about that. Why did you keep it a secret from me?"

"I was afraid you wouldn't approve."

"Oh, I approve. I approve wholeheartedly," he said, smiling broadly.

"You do?" she said in astonishment.

"I do indeed. You have a head on you, Regina. It will be much better for us if people take you for a man, although I doubt it will be a man they take you for, but a boy, a bonny boy!"

Now they made their way down the twisting mountain road. The air was fragrant with the scent of wild briar roses, and a small stream rushed down the mountainside along the road. The air at this altitude was marvelously clear, and the sky was the deep blue of the finest sapphire.

Soon they would be finding their own sapphires, perhaps even a star sapphire. Regina's spirits lifted, and her aches and pains were forgotten.

She realized with a start of surprise that she was actually enjoying herself. The valley below had to be one of the most beautiful spots in the world, and no matter what happened with their gem hunting, she was fortunate to be here.

Brian had told her that if anyone should inquire as to the reason for their visit to Kashmir, they should say that they had come to buy shawls. Kashmir had once been famous for its shawls, but apparently shawl making had declined after a famine had decimated the population, killing off many of the craftsmen. However, some of the artisans remained, weaving shawls of the finest quality from the pashmina wool that came from the small Ladakhi goats. Brian said that the "royal" shawls were so fine that they could be passed through a ring, and that they sold for many thousands of rupees.

They met very few people as they rode down the steep mountain road. Those that they did pass were natives, and Regina called out, "Brian?"

He turned in the saddle. "Yes, lass?"

"Why aren't we seeing any British?"

"As I told you, the British do not really rule Kashmir, except in an advisory capacity to the Maharaja. The British do come here in the summer to holiday on the lakes. It might be a little early yet, but I'm sure we'll see a number of them abiding royally on the houseboats."

"Houseboats?"

"There are two lakes close by Srinagar, Dal Lake and Nagin. They abound with houseboats, which people on holiday may rent for a period of time. Very colorful, I understand. You'll see when we pass by."

THEY MADE CAMP that night halfway down the mountain, but they were still at a high altitude, and the night was cool when the sun disappeared behind the distant mountains. Brian made a fire by the rushing stream, and Regina cooked their meal—a dish of lamb stew, with as little spice as she could manage. She had found that it took much longer for water to boil at this altitude, therefore, meals took longer to prepare. The night was redolent with the scent of cooking meat and the odor of the Kashmir pines surrounding them.

Immediately after the meal, Brian, stating that he was weary, rolled up in his blankets while Regina washed their few utensils and put them away. She was also tired, but she lay awake for a long time after she had crawled into her blankets, staring up at the night sky, which was strewn with stars.

Her thoughts were of Brian, lying asleep only a few feet away—troubling thoughts. In London, as they prepared for the expedition, she had been too busy to give much thought to the fact that she would be alone with a man of Brian's charm and physical attraction for such a long period of time. On board the *Galatea* she had often found herself thinking about the possible aspects of their relationship, and she had been at a loss to predict her reaction should he make advances toward her.

Somewhat to her surprise—and possibly her chagrin—his behavior had been perfectly proper at all times. Didn't he find her attractive? She had to smile to herself at the question. And yet it was a reasonable speculation. Without being vain, she knew that she was above average in looks and was attractive to men. And Brian, she was fairly certain, was a man who liked women.

Of course, he had mentioned that he divided his life into separate parts—business and pleasure. Apparently he never mixed the two.

What would happen after their gem hunt was concluded, especially if it was as successful as they hoped? Would he then turn to her as a woman? And if he did, how would she respond?

She was of two minds about it. She was a grown woman now, still untouched by physical love, and yet she had often wondered how it would be. More to the point at the moment, how would it be with Brian?

She tossed restlessly, feeling unduly warm and uncomfortable at the thought. A woman would be foolish to hope for a permanent relationship with a wild man like Brian Macbride. But then hadn't she been telling herself that she was not ready for an emotional relationship, and least of all marriage? From what she had observed of most marriages, the man was dominant; it was the accepted, the expected thing, by both sexes. She didn't know if she wanted to be dominated by a man; certainly not at this time in her life.

She smiled at herself again. It could well be that she was worrying over a problem that didn't even exist—Brian might not be attracted to her at all.

Strangely disturbed by such a thought, she tossed and turned for some time before she finally fell into a troubled sleep.

REGINA WAS MISTAKEN about Brian on two counts—he was not asleep, and he was more than attracted to her.

He lay in his blankets, feigning sleep, and listening to Regina toss and turn, wondering what was troubling her. Every night since they had left Jammu, she had been so tired that she had fallen asleep the moment she was in her blankets.

Brian was strongly impelled to ask her what was bothering her. To be truthful, he longed to move over to her and take her into his arms. Yet he knew that he would not. As hard as it was to admit to himself, he was afraid of being rebuffed. Imagine Brian Macbride feeling such reservations! Bloody hell, he had sailed through life, taking women where he found them, with never a thought of rejection—and never finding it, either.

Regina Paxton was different, in several ways. Oh, she attracted him right enough. By the saints, she did! From the very first moment, he had wanted to make her his; but he knew instinctively that she was several steps above the women he had bedded so easily in the past.

She was more intelligent than most of the women he had known, or at least she *used* what intelligence she possessed. Regina was also passionately interested in gems, a trait that he had never found in a woman before, except for the wealthy ones who were only interested in them as decorations.

Beyond anything else, he was impressed by the way she had behaved on the trip so far. She had been seasick the first few days on the *Galatea*, but that was usual for landlubbers, male or female, their first time on a ship in rough seas. And she had been weakened by the heat and discomfort of the trains, yet he couldn't really fault her for that. Once on the trail, on muleback, she had suffered much physical discomfort, but she had not complained; and now it appeared that she was becoming hardened to it. He had been afraid that she was going to be a burden on the expedition, but clearly that would not be the case. Brian had to admire her for her fortitude.

But aside from how much he was drawn to her, how much he liked and admired her, he was afraid that he was falling in love with her. That was a new experience for him, and one that he wasn't sure he was happy with.

He turned his face toward her. She was quiet and still now; she was asleep. No, it would be better to keep his distance, as difficult as he feared that might be.

He squirmed about, trying to find a softer spot on the hard ground, and attempted to push all troubling thoughts out of his mind as he courted sleep.

THEY APPROACHED THE TOWN of Srinagar down a broad, tree-lined avenue. On each side of the road peasants worked in the fields. Regina noticed that most of the men wore only two garments: an upper cloak made of rough, brown-colored sacking and a pair of voluminous knickerbockers. Most of them wore turbans on their heads and open sandals on their feet.

Here and there she saw men working stripped to the waist; their torsos were covered with scars. Finally Regina remarked on this to Brian.

"That's because they wear portable heaters under their overcoats in winter, and burning charcoal spills out and burns the body. The heater, called a *kangri*, is a small wicker basket with a metal pan to hold the burning charcoal."

The Jhelum River flowed on their left as they rode along. Hundreds of brown houses, like little boxes, lined the river. They had painted shutters and inlaid arches over the small windows. Vividly dyed skeins of wool hung from doorways. But the most colorful feature of all was the flowers growing on top of the tiny buildings. The roofs were made of earth, and now in spring a profusion of bright flowers bloomed on each. In many doorways, old men wearing turbans idled away the time, smoking hookahs.

On the outskirts of town, Brian guided his mule onto a side road to the left. "I want to avoid the center of town. I don't want to call attention to ourselves any more than necessary."

But they still passed through a commercial area as they rode along the river, which was spanned by a bridge every so often. It was a region of many shops, the fronts of which were shrouded from the bright sun by narrow, colored awnings. Men in fur caps and women in dark-colored robes and flashing jewelry strolled along the streets. Stalls displayed a great number of items for sale: furs; embroidered leather or fabrics; carved woodwork; shawls; carpets; and even displays of precious stones.

Regina wanted to linger and examine the gemstones, but Brian refused. "That would only serve to draw attention to us. Most of what you'd see are semiprecious stones, anyway. No sapphires, lass, no rubies.''

Soon they were riding along the shore of a beautiful lake that was crowded by houseboats of all sizes. Great plane trees grew at intervals along its shore.

''Houseboats have long been popular with the people here,'' Brian commented, ''but when one of the rulers, I forget which one, forbade Europeans to own property in Kashmir, the houseboat really began to flourish. The Brits own most of them, and they summer here, as I told you. Do you see the small boats, the ones that look like the punts we have back in England?'' He indicated the many small boats moving back and forth. They were only large enough to accommodate about four people; most of them had canopies of plaited straw, from which silk curtains hung. ''The Kashmir name for them is *shikara*. The Brits call them the 'gondolas of Kashmir.' Peddlers row out to the houseboats, selling food, fresh produce in season, as well as fresh flowers and various artworks.''

Regina noticed many floating gardens, and water beds of lotus flowers. Kingfishers darted here and there, their azure wings beating the air, which was fragrant with many scents. Regina inhaled deeply and thought that she had never seen or smelled anything so beautiful.

She noticed that Brian consulted his map on occasion, always choosing a time when they were unobserved.

''Brian, you've never told me exactly where we're going.''

"According to my friend's map, it's still several days' ride. The field he found lies northeast, in the foothills, in an old riverbed coming down out of the mountains. You know," he said musingly, "sapphires and rubies were found here in abundance over two hundred years ago, or so history has it. They evidently formed in the mountains and washed down to lower altitudes over the years. That's why they're called alluvial deposits, or alluvial stones, moved by water and found in streambeds. According to legend, they were plentiful back then. But I'm thinking the pickings are leaner now."

"I wonder why this particular field has lain undiscovered for so long?"

"Again, according to my friend, it's in a relatively isolated area."

"How long has it been since your friend made his find?"

"Well over a year." She could hear the hesitancy in his voice.

"That's a long time, Brian. How can we know that someone hasn't stumbled onto them?"

"We don't," he said curtly.

He drummed his heels against the mule's flanks and rode on ahead, cutting off further conversation.

IT WAS MIDAFTERNOON three days later when Brian suddenly drew his mule to a halt and said excitedly, "By the saints, I think we're here, Regina!"

Regina rode up alongside him. "How can you be so sure?"

They had been climbing all day, the mules picking their way daintily where they had little if any trail. Except for a goatherd tending his flock, they had seen no one all day.

Brian slid down from the mule, and kneeling, spread his map against a boulder. It was the first good look Regina had had of his precious map; and now that she finally saw it, she was little wiser. It was a terrain map that made absolutely no sense to her, with almost indecipherable handwriting scribbled here and there.

"Oh, no doubt at all." In his excitement, Brian's brogue thickened. "See those two peaks?" He jabbed a forefinger at something on the map. "Like a woman's two breasts, Joshua said." He grinned slyly at her, then turned to point up at the mountains. There were two peaks, still capped with snow, that did faintly resemble a woman's breasts. "And a rise of land, with a tall tree growing slantwise atop it, and another dead and splintered one. Struck by lightning at some time, I'm thinking."

"If you say so," she said dubiously.

"I do say so!" He clapped his hands together with a sound like a pistol shot. "Don't be tarrying; let's go!"

Instead of mounting, he started up the steep slope on foot, leading his mount, as well as the pack mule. Regina followed, but she soon fell behind as his long legs covered the ground in giant strides. His limp was scarcely noticeable now, except when he was quite weary.

When she reached the top, panting in the thin air, Brian was standing with his feet planted wide apart, hands on his hips. They were on a small plateau, flat as a table, but a few yards ahead of where they stood, the ground plunged steeply down again.

"There! There it is, Regina!" He swept a hand around in a grandiose gesture. "Just like Joshua said it would be."

As she gazed down, Regina experienced a rush of disappointment. All she could see was a deep gulch, with a dark, sandy bottom, strewn with large and small rocks.

She didn't bother to hide her disappointment. "It doesn't look like much to me."

Brian laughed. "Bloody hell, what did you expect? Elysium Fields, strewn with precious stones?"

"Well, I . . ."

"Look!" He interrupted her, pointing up the gully. "See that great boulder up there?"

About three hundred yards up the dry riverbed a huge boulder lay across the gully, like a stopper in a bottle.

"Just like Joshua said. Sometime in the days of long ago, a landslide came down the mountain, stopping up the streambed, diverting the water. Everything is just like he told me. This is it!" he said jubilantly.

Regina was squinting down at the streambed, hoping to catch a gleam of sunlight off gemstones, but it was too far to see; and the sun was sinking behind the mountaintops, throwing the gulch into shadow. "Are we going to search today, or make camp and wait until morning?" she asked.

"Now, lass, now. We don't want to waste any time. But first, there's something we must do."

He turned to the pack mule and unslung a canvas sack. Opening the sack on the ground, he took out a revolver and a leather holster, which he strapped around his waist. "This is a .45 revolver, made by Samuel Colt in America."

"You're going about armed?" she asked in alarm.

"Aye, that I am. Not only me, but you as well, Regina."

"Me!" She backed a step in horror. "I've never fired a gun in my life."

"I calculated as much," he said, grinning. "But you're going to learn, right now. At least learn how to dry fire one." From the sack he took another revolver, a smaller, shorter one, hefting it in his hand. "This is a Smith and Wesson .38. It doesn't have the firepower of my Colt, but it's lighter, has less kick and I'm after hoping you'll never have to use it."

"Brian, I'm not going to carry around a gun," she said obstinately.

"Regina..." He sighed. "There could be danger here. I know it looks peaceful enough now, but precious stones draw thieves, as I've already told you. A discovery of gems seems to send out some kind of mystic message. Now don't balk me on this. You've done very well so far. It's proud of you I am. Don't make me regret it this late. As my old mother used to say, a grain of caution saves stitches."

"Oh, all right!" she said in exasperation. "But won't the sound of gunfire draw attention to us?"

"There'll be no gunfire to hear."

She frowned. "I'm afraid I don't understand."

"There's no time to turn you into a sharp-shooter, so we'll have to settle for less. The pistol is empty now, but you'll be carrying it loaded. See, the cartridges go in here." He showed her how to flip the cylinder out. He took several cartridges from his coat pocket, showed her how to load them, then unloaded the revolver again. "Now! You hold the weapon in both hands like this, raise it to aim and gently squeeze the trigger." He squeezed the trigger and the hammer came down with a dry clicking sound on the empty cylinder.

"Try it." He handed her the revolver, butt first.

Regina took it gingerly. It gave her a queer feeling, holding a weapon in her hands for the first time, a weapon capable of killing someone. She raised it, aiming down the barrel at a tree stump halfway down the slope. She squeezed the trigger and flinched as the hammer came down.

"No, Regina, no! Don't flinch away. If the thing was loaded and you were shooting at an enemy, the barrel would have jumped, throwing your aim way off. If you ever do fire it loaded, you're going to have to expect some recoil. Here, let's try it this way."

He took the revolver from her, stepped behind her, put his arms around her and placed the gun in her hands again. His big hands gently cradling hers, he raised the weapon to her level of sight.

"Put your finger in the trigger guard. Now squeeze, don't jerk. Gentle does it, Regina. Gentle as a virgin's kiss."

Immediately, of course, her mind jumped to other matters. What did he mean by that remark? Did it hold some hidden message? And the nearness of him, pressed against her back, smelling not unpleasantly of sweat and mule, was terribly distracting.

"Regina!" he said crossly. "That was no better. Concentrate."

She willed herself to concentrate on the revolver in her hands. She aimed down the barrel and slowly pulled back on the trigger. This time she didn't flinch, and he made a sound of approval. "Better, much better."

They kept at it until Regina's finger was tired from squeezing the trigger; and all the while he stood behind her, the touch of his body against hers a stimulant agitating her senses.

Finally, he stepped back. "That's enough for today. We'll practice again tomorrow. Right now, I want to get down there and inspect the riverbed before it gets too dark."

"Brian, I don't see what good this is going to do me, without actually firing the weapon."

"You'll become familiar with it, and you'll get used to carrying it on your person. It's hoping I am that you'll never have to fire it. I'm praying that the threat of it will be enough to frighten away any buckos who brace us."

"But what if they don't frighten? What then?"

"Leave the firing to me," he said sternly. "As a last resort, aim at the villain's chest and keep firing. Hopefully you'll hit some vital spot before the gun's empty. If it comes down to that—" he shrugged fatalistically "—the game's probably up anyway. As me mother used to say, 'Katie, it's too late to bar the door, the horse has scampered.'" He brightened. "But let's not be borrowing trouble. We may never see hide nor hair of any brigands. Now . . . down we go, lass!"

He took her hand, and they started down the steep slope. Near the bottom, they both lost their footing and skidded the rest of the way on their backsides, laughing like children. They landed on the soft bottom of the riverbed with a thump.

They were up immediately. Although the sun was low in the sky, there was still sufficient light to see by. Regina ran on ahead, while Brian lagged behind, head down, his gaze raking the sand. Regina's step slowed after a bit, and she took her time then, scanning the ground before her feet. She walked all the way to the giant boulder that was blocking the dry river channel.

Nothing! There was nothing there!

Despair descended on her like a shroud. She turned and ran back toward Brian, calling, "Brian! There are no gemstones, nothing. Someone must have already found them. We came all this way for nothing!"

CHAPTER NINE

REGINA REALIZED that Brian was looking at her in amusement. "I fail to see anything humorous!" she said indignantly. "We've traveled all this way, spent all that money, and all for nothing!"

He fell serious. "You don't know that."

"But I've been all the way to the boulder, and I found nothing."

"For God's sake, woman, did you expect the stones to be laying about in plain sight?"

"Yes." She stared. "You said your friend picked them up off the ground."

"I may have exaggerated a wee bit," he said sheepishly. "Joshua did say that he picked up a few off the ground, but that could have been because a hard rain washed the sand away. He was here at the end of the monsoon season."

She felt renewed hope. "Then you think there are stones here?"

"Aye, that I do. I feel it in here." He gave his chest a mighty thump. "But we'll have to dig into the sand for them."

"Then let's get started!"

"Whoa now," he said, grinning. "And I thought I was anxious. It's grown late. Let's bring the animals down and set up camp. It's hungry I am. We'll get a good night's rest and be at it at first light in the morning."

They made camp next to the boulder blocking the river channel. Exploring, Brian found a small stream that flowed down out of the mountains on the other side of the boulder. Over the years, water rushing down the side of the ravine had partially eroded the earth, forming a corridor between the bank and the side of the boulder. It was filled with brush, through which Brian hacked a rough path. The ground on that side was mostly rock and not a good place for a camp. He tethered the mules there to graze and fetched a pail of water.

They had their evening meal and retired to their blankets early. The soft sand made a better bed than what Regina had been accustomed to over the past few days, yet she barely slept. Despite Brian's exuberant reassurances, she had strong doubts about finding any gemstones of consequence. She had already learned that Brian was an eternal optimist.

What if they didn't find anything? If she returned empty-handed, she would be poor again. Then what would she do? Could she to go to Mr. Slostrum, admit that she had made a foolish error and beg for her job back? She cringed at the very thought. As angry as Slostrum had been with her, she doubted very much that he would hire her back.

No, she would never beg. She would make do somehow. After all, it had been an enjoyable trip so far, one she would remember for the rest of her life—and she had known at the outset that the expedition was a gamble.

On that thought, she finally dropped off to sleep.

SHE WAS AWAKENED at dawn by Brian who was bustling around starting a fire. It was quite cold, and she was content to remain snug in her blankets for a moment.

Then the Irishman turned around and clapped his hands together. "Up, woman! You'll never find any stones in your blankets."

Regina waited until he turned his back, then got out of the blankets, shivering, and got into her clothes. She bent over the fire, hands outstretched, seeking warmth. Brian was already beginning to prepare the morning meal.

"I thought a pot of tea and some rice cakes would do us for breakfast," he said, disgustingly cheerful for so early in the morning. "I thought we'd get at it as soon as possible. Eh?"

"I certainly agree with that."

After a cup of steaming, heavily sugared tea and a cake, Regina's spirits picked up. Maybe the gloom of the night before was unwarranted.

"Now we will be using picks, shovels and wire mesh sieves, all of which I brought along," Brian said. "When you're poking around with the pick, Regina, don't go at it too hard. You might shatter the stones. I'm sure you remember that gemstones are often embedded in other rocks."

The sun was just rising over the eastern mountains, throwing a warm, golden glow on the riverbed as they started.

"I'll show you how to use the sieve," Brian said. The sieves were square, with wooden frames enclosing the wire mesh. Brian scooped up some of the sand and poured it into one of the sieves, which he then shook back and forth until all the sand had sifted through. He examined what was left on the mesh.

"Nothing here, only pebbles. Now the best way for us to do this is to work from both ends. You start from here, while I go down to the other end and work back toward you. We can cover the ground more quickly that way."

As Brian walked away, Regina poked tentatively into the sand with the pick. At first, digging only a few inches down, she uncovered nothing but more sand. Daring to go a little deeper, she struck something hard. Dropping the pick, she fell to her knees and dug down with her fingers. She uncovered a stone about the size of her fist. It was crusted with white, as Brian had warned. Regina carefully scraped away the crust, only to discover that it was only a rock, nothing more.

Disheartened, she tossed it aside. She remained on her knees now, gently probing the sand with the pick. When she had enough loosened, she sifted it through the sieve. The morning was warming up rapidly, and she could feel perspiration running down her sides beneath the man's shirt.

Doggedly she continued. Again the pick struck something, and again she dug down with her fingers. Her hopes deflated by her previous discovery, she scraped away the crust without much hope. And then suddenly a ray of sun struck the rock, and she saw a gleam of color.

With a cry, she was on her feet and she ran, stumbling in her haste, toward the other end of the ravine where Brian was digging into the sand.

"Brian," she cried, "I think I've found something!"

Reaching him, she held out the stone, cupped in both hands like an offering.

He took the stone from her, turning it over and over in his big hands. Then he took a small scraper from his pocket and gently peeled away the outer layer of white stone. It flaked away easily.

"By all the saints, lass, you have!" he said reverently. "It's a ruby, and it's a big one, too. This alone is going to be worth the trip."

He raised his arms above his head and shouted, a bellow of pure exuberance. Then he looped one arm around her shoulders and, holding the ruby aloft in the other hand, danced her around in the sand in a clumsy jig.

When he finally stopped, they were both breathless. He stood with one arm still draped around her shoulders, gazing down into her upturned face. Without warning, he bent his head and kissed her. After a brief moment of resistance, she gave way to the rich feeling of emotion that flooded her being, clinging to him fiercely, her fingers digging into his back.

He was the first to pull away, leaving her feeling bereft. His face was flushed above the beard, and he turned from her as though embarrassed. He shook the ruby in his hand. "This is a good omen, Regina, I know it is. We'll find a fortune here before we're done."

Infected by his enthusiasm, Regina said, "Then let's return to work." She started off, then whirled back to say mischievously, "It's your turn to find something now, bucko. Don't expect me to uncover everything."

He laughed. "Beginner's luck, lass. Don't worry. I'll find my share."

He stood looking after her as she hurried up the riverbed. Why had he kissed her? It had been done on a rise of enthusiasm at her find, yet he knew his action went beyond that. It was something he had been aching to do since they left London. But what had surprised and pleased him at the same time had been her warm, wholehearted response. It had to be an indication that she returned his feelings for her.

Whistling happily to himself, he went back to work.

Regina, who had reached her lucky spot in the riverbed, heard Brian whistling, and glanced back over her shoulder. Was he whistling because of her find, or because of the kiss? She shook her head ruefully and knelt in the sand, filling the sieve.

Shortly before noon, she unearthed another gemstone. It wasn't as large as the ruby, but enough of the outer covering had flaked away to show her that it was a sapphire.

She continued working. It had warmed up considerably, and she was perspiring freely. The pistol in the holster on her hip was an intolerable weight. She unbuckled the gun belt and started to lay it aside.

A bellow from Brian brought her head up. "No, you don't, woman! You keep that pistol strapped to your waist."

Did he have eyes in the top of his head? She glared along the riverbed at him. "It's foolish to be wearing it, Brian, and it makes it harder to work."

"It's not foolish at all. Now you keep it on. During the noon hour, I'll be giving you some more lessons."

For a brief moment, she was tempted to defy him. Who did he think he was, to order her around like that? Then with a heavy sigh, she strapped the gun belt on again.

By noon she had collected a few more stones, some of good size. And she was tired and hot. She stopped for a moment and leaned back on her hands, resting. Her gaze wandered idly along the riverbed to rest briefly on Brian who was busily at work, his head down. She glanced up at the ridge to her right, where they had stood when they first looked down into the streambed, and stiffened, a chill of fear going down her spine.

Had there been some movement up there? She squinted against the glare of the overhead sun and caught a glimpse of a turbaned head peeking over the rim of the plateau. It was too distant to make out any features, but there was definitely a man looking down on them. She shot a glance at Brian and saw that he was still working with his head down. Again she looked up at the edge of the plateau. The man, whoever he was, had slipped out of sight.

She got to her feet and hurried toward Brian. At the sound of her footsteps, he looked up alertly, then dropped his pick and came to meet her.

She stopped before him. "I saw someone. Up there." She pointed toward the plateau.

He raked the slope with his gaze. "You're positive?"

"I'm positive."

He loosened the Colt in its holster. "All right, you stay here. I'll go have a look. Stay right here now where I can keep an eye on you."

He went up the steep slope as nimbly as a goat. Near the top, he dropped down on all fours and slowly raised his head above the edge. As Regina watched, he got to his feet and stepped up onto the plateau. He sent one glance down at her, waved and then walked out of sight. He was gone only for a few moments before he reappeared, looking down again to check on her. He walked both ways along the length of the small plateau, then finally turned and came back down the slope.

He was breathing easily when he reached her. "Didn't see a soul...."

"But I saw someone, Brian, I swear I did!"

"Oh, I'm not after doubting you. It was probably no more than a passing goatherd, being curious. However, he may pass on the word that two foreign devils are digging away in the riverbed here, and that's bound to arouse some attention."

"So what do we do?"

He arched an eyebrow. "Why, we keep digging, of course, and keep a wary eye out. We've got a good find here, and no boys sneaking about are going to scare us off. Have you found any more stones?"

"A few. And you?"

"Quite a few good ones, rubies and sapphires, and we've hardly scratched the surface yet, in a manner of speaking."

"Have you found a star sapphire?"

He gave her a quizzical look. "Not yet. Of course, it's hard to be sure until the stones are cleaned. Still looking for your birthstone, eh? Stars would bring a good price, but they are rare, and that ruby you found is probably worth more than most stars.''

She looked off. ''I was just hoping we'd find one.''

''We may yet.'' He took her elbow. ''Now I'm hungry and thirsty, and it's past time for our noon meal. I also want to give you more shooting lessons. I think we'll use live ammunition this time. If any brigands are about, maybe the sound of gunfire will keep them away. From now on, Regina, always keep your pistol close at hand.''

After their meal, Brian set up a row of stones along the riverbank and had Regina stand about thirty feet back. ''For our purposes here, you should learn at close range, in case you ever have to fire at someone.''

She shuddered. ''I don't think I could, Brian. Not at a person.''

''Oh, I think you'll discover you can do more things than you ever thought possible, should the situation become desperate enough.'' He stepped aside, motioning to the line of rocks. ''Go ahead, fire at will,'' he said with a grin.

Regina gripped the revolver in both hands, raising it to eye level. She squinted her right eye and tried to line the sights up with one of the rocks.

''No, no, Regina, don't squint! That limits your vision. You don't want that.''

She opened her eyes wide, lined up the sights again and squeezed the trigger. The gunshot sounded like thunder rumbling in the narrow ravine, and the unexpected recoil was strong enough to send her reeling back a few steps. The stench of gunpowder brought the sting of tears to her eyes.

"Well, you came close, if the rock had been an elephant," he said dryly. "You flinched again and that threw your aim off."

"I didn't expect it to recoil like that."

"You'll get used to that. Now try again."

The second time, expecting it, the recoil wasn't quite so bad, but her aim wasn't much better. Brian kept her at it, reloading the gun when it was empty. She noticed that each time after she fired, he looked up at the ridges on both sides of the riverbed.

On the second round, she surprised herself—she hit the rock she aimed at. She felt a spurt of elation. "I hit it!" she shouted.

"That you did, Regina. Finally."

By the time the revolver was emptied the second time, she had hit her target once more.

Brian nodded. "Good. You're after getting the hang of it."

Without warning, he fell into a crouch, drew the Colt from the holster on his hip with a motion so fast that his hand was a blur, and fired rapidly at the line of rocks. Each shot went true, shattering the rocks. He fired five times and hit the target every time.

He straightened up, looked over at her with a sheepish smile, and began reloading the revolver.

Regina felt an unaccountable anger. "What was that all about?"

His glance held surprise. "Nothing at all. Just a little practice. That's the first time I've fired a gun in months."

"It wasn't just to prove how much better you are with a pistol than a mere woman?" she said acidly. "A little show of male vanity?"

"You malign me, lass," he said with a shrug. "I already know that I'm a better shot than you. In fact, I'm a better shot than most men, if it comes to that."

"I wouldn't say that was a talent to be proud of."

"Perhaps not, but it's a talent that is highly useful in my business."

All of a sudden, her anger was gone, leaving her puzzled. Over the past few days, it had seemed that she was often angry with him. "Have you ever killed a man, Brian?" she asked curiously.

"Never found it necessary. I've winged one or two, threatened a few others. That usually does it. Well . . ." He reholstered the loaded Colt, glancing at the slopes around them. "All that gunfire either scared off the brigands, or attracted a few. Time will tell. Shall we get back to work?"

As Regina started toward the spot where she had left her tools, Brian caught her arm. "No, we'll work close together from now on. Bring your tools and your goods up to the other end. We'll work back this way."

THEY WORKED HARD for three more days. By noon of the fourth day, they had raked every foot of the riverbed to a depth of several inches. They had collected a fair number of gemstones; by Regina's count, almost fifty stones of varying sizes. The majority were sapphires, with only a scattering of rubies. The first ruby she had found was by far the largest.

They stood together at the huge boulder, gazing back down the riverbed. "I'm thinking we should settle for what we have, lass," Brian said, finally breaking the silence. "We might find a few more if we dug deeper, but it would be hard work, and scarcely worth the risk. Every hour we linger only increases the possibility that we will be attacked by thieves."

"How much would you estimate the stones we've found are worth, Brian?"

"That's hard to say. But it's a good gathering, you can be sure of that. As I said before, the big ruby alone should be worth the trip."

"When shall we leave? This afternoon, or wait until morning?"

"We couldn't get very far today. I think we should get a good night's rest and start fresh in the morning."

"Then I'm going around to the stream behind the boulder and have a good wash. I'm completely grimy from the digging we've done."

He nodded. "Sounds like a splendid idea. You go first, then I'll follow."

Regina took a towel and a cake of soap, walked along the side of the great boulder and went a few yards up the stream where she began to disrobe. She hesitated for a moment over her undergarments, then removed them with a shrug. She was sure that Brian was too much of a gentleman to sneak up and spy on her nakedness. Of course, there was the goatherd, or whoever it was that she had seen three days ago, but there had been no sign of him since.

The water flowing over the stones was only a few inches deep, but there was a pool collected in an eddy in the rocks, about a foot deep and the size of a bathtub. Regina knew that the water, coming from melted snow, would be icy, but she longed to be clean.

Naked, she stepped to the edge of the shallow pool and dipped her toes in. The water was so cold that she shivered and uttered an involuntary cry. Gritting her teeth, she stepped into the pool and lowered herself into the water, the bar of soap clutched firmly in her hand.

She tried to ignore the numbing cold and began to apply the soap. Lathering herself all over, she finally completely immersed her body in the water; it was just deep enough to cover her. When she had rinsed away the soap, she was blue with cold. She snatched up the towel and began to dry herself, standing in a splash of sun. At least the sun provided heat. By the time she was dry, she had stopped shivering.

She stood for a few moments, her face upturned to the sun, before she began putting on her clothes. Just as she was strapping the pistol belt around her waist, she froze as a shout came from the other side of the boulder. It was followed by a rifle shot. She stood without moving, her ears straining. There were no more shots, but there was a babble of voices.

Had Brian been shot? If thieves had come upon Brian, did they know of her presence? Fear coursed through her as cold as the water she had just bathed in. Then apprehension for Brian pushed away her fear, and anger took its place.

Drawing the revolver, Regina made her way as quietly as possible to the boulder and carefully inched up and along the path Brian had made between the boulder and the bank. At the crest of the small rise, she hugged the stone and peered around it.

A feeling of relief almost made her weak—Brian was still alive. He stood with his hands raised above his head. Confronting him were three dark, turbaned men. One man aimed an ancient rifle at Brian. Insofar as Regina could ascertain, the other two men carried no guns, although each held a large knife with a curved blade.

As Regina watched, the man with the rifle motioned with it and spoke in a guttural voice. His words were incomprehensible to Regina, yet his meaning was unmistakable. He was motioning Brian back from the sack of gemstones, which sat at his feet.

Brian shook his head stubbornly. "Bloody hell, I will not. These are my goods!"

Regina was still puzzled as to why at least one of the thieves had not gone looking for her. If they knew about their presence here, they must also know of her existence. Had they, in spying on them, realized that she was a woman and thought that she posed no threat to them?

This thought only served to increase her anger. Gripping the revolver firmly in both hands, she stepped out into plain sight, calling out, "Here I am! I have a gun and I'm going to shoot if you don't leave right now!" She stifled an impulse to laugh aloud; she was certain that they couldn't understand a word she said.

Three heads swiveled in her direction, and they stood staring at her in wide-eyed astonishment.

She motioned with the revolver. "Go away! Leave us alone."

They remained frozen in place, gaping at her.

Regina aimed at the foot of the rifleman and squeezed off a shot. Her aim was fairly accurate—the bullet kicked up sand about two feet in front of the man. She had no stomach for killing him.

Brian used the diversion to spring into action. Drawing his own revolver, he covered the intervening space between himself and the man with the rifle. Before the rifleman could react, Brian brought his revolver down alongside the man's head. The rifleman cried out and slumped to his knees, dropping the rifle onto the sand. The big Irishman scooped it up and backed up a few steps.

He waved his revolver. "Now, buckos, take your fallen comrade and go!"

There was little doubt that the bandits caught his meaning. The two sheathed their knives in their belts and bent to help the third man to his feet. He was dazed, but he pointed to his rifle in Brian's hand and spoke rapidly in his language, clearly asking for it to be returned to him.

Brian shook his head, grinning savagely. "Oh, no, me bucko. You think I'm returning your weapon so you can later ambush us? I'm thinking you've forfeited all rights to it!"

He raised the rifle as if to fire it, and the two men turned with their companion, supporting him as they scrambled up the slope.

Regina waited, holding her breath until the three men were halfway up the bank. Then she rammed the pistol into the holster and ran down the rise toward Brian.

"Oh, Brian, when I heard the shot, I thought you had been killed!"

Without taking his gaze from the three men, Brian put an arm around her shoulders and pulled her against him. "It was close, lass. If you hadn't shown up when you did, they might very well have killed me."

The men had now disappeared from view. Brian heaved a sigh of relief and turned to Regina. "Well, they're gone."

"Do you think they will come back?"

"We're not waiting around to find out," he said grimly. "If we stay here, they could sneak back tonight, catch us asleep and slit our throats. We're moving out now."

THEY TRAVELED RAPIDLY down through the foothills, pushing the mules to their limit. Brian kept a constant watch on their back trail and the slopes around them.

They finally stopped just after sundown, making camp on the shore of a small lake. "I'm reasonably confident that they haven't followed us," he said. "Since I confiscated their only long-range weapon, they are probably afraid to attack us now."

"Are you certain of that?" she asked with a shiver.

"Reasonably certain, but there is always a chance that I'm wrong." He gave a short laugh. "I'm thinking I won't be getting much sleep this night."

He got busy unpacking the mules. "We'll leave them saddled, in the event that I am wrong and we have to take flight during the night. I'm afraid we'll have to eat a cold supper. It's better not to have a fire and attract undue attention. Here, Regina." He put the sack of gemstones by her feet. "Keep your eye on these. I'm going to take a bath in the lake. You had yours, now it's my turn."

"The water will be like ice, Brian, and no sun to warm you."

He laughed again, a warm sound in the darkness. "A cold bath should keep me awake. Now, keep your pistol to hand, and fire a warning shot should you hear anything."

REGINA COULD NOT SLEEP. It had been a long day and she was tired, but the events of the past few hours kept replaying in her mind. She had not really been frightened during the confrontation with the bandits but now, with time to reflect, she truly realized the danger she and Brian had been in. A delayed reaction set in as she lay shivering in her blankets.

The threat of the bandits had driven all thought of their find out of her mind. She should be on top of the world; they would be returning to London with a small fortune, if Brian's estimate of the gems's worth was correct, and she had no reason to doubt it since he had been a gem hunter for ten years. She would not have to go back to England a beggar seeking employment. She could open a jewelry firm of her own....

Regina sat up, startled, at that idea. Yet she knew, thinking back, that it was not the first time she had thought it. She remembered even mentioning the idea of her own firm to Brian back in London.

She lay back down, her thoughts racing a mile a minute as she examined the concept. Could she do it? Why couldn't she? She would have the resources necessary, and though she was young and still not too conversant with many aspects of the jewelry business, she could learn. She had already proven to herself that she had some talent as a jewelry designer; and she knew she was good as a salesclerk. Yes, she could do it. She *would* do it!

"Brian?" she said softly. "Are you awake?"

"Yes, Regina," he said instantly. "What is it?"

She started to speak, then fell silent. It had been her intention to speak of her plans to him, but something told her that this was not the time nor the place. And she already knew that he would not approve; he had told her as much back in London.

"Lass, you are frightened?"

"I suppose I am. A little," she said in a small voice.

"Sure, and every reason you should be. Most women would have fainted dead away at what happened today."

She heard a rustling sound, and before she quite realized what was happening, he had crossed the small space between them. Lifting the blanket, he slipped under and took her into his arms, pulling her close.

Startled, Regina attempted to draw away. "No, Brian . . ."

And then his mouth was on hers, warm and demanding, and all thought of resistance melted away as she felt her body respond; she wanted this as much as he did. She returned his kiss with ardor.

He rained kisses on her cheeks, her throat and then her mouth again. In a daze of vaulting pleasure and need, Regina stroked his hair and his beard. She had always thought that a man's beard would be prickly, but Brian's felt soft and warm against her skin.

Brian was exploring her body with his hands. They had both gotten into their blankets with their clothes on, in the event they were routed out during the night. Now, helping each other, they managed to divest themselves of their clothing.

All of Regina's reservations were swept away by the fever raging through her. She wanted only to be closer to Brian, to feel his warmth against her. Finally they were naked together. Brian did not hurry; his hands, surprisingly gentle for such a big man, caressed her. He seemed to know exactly where to touch her to further inflame her senses. His gentleness and skill were such that she forgot the fears engendered by her inexperience.

And then the moment came when he rose above her, his bulk blotting out the stars. At the moment of their joining, Regina felt a sharp pain; yet it was brief, gone almost before she felt it, and she was lost in the glory and the ecstasy of the entrance of his body into hers.

REGINA COULD FEEL her heart beating wildly in her chest. She lay with her head back, her arms around Brian. Past his resting head, she could see the glitter of the stars, and she realized that the outside world had been lost to her in her passion.

She laughed shakily. "So much for our keeping watch. Someone could easily have sneaked up without our ever knowing it and slit our throats."

"Sure, and it would have been worth it, love. Well worth it," he said huskily. Tenderly he caressed her cheek. "Do you not agree?"

"Yes, Brian." She squeezed his shoulder, her thoughts going off on a tangent.

Would it be right and proper to tell him that she loved him? She was suddenly aware that she did, and for the first time, the thought of love and marriage to this man appealed to her mightily. But weren't the words of love supposed to be spoken by the man first?

Again she laughed softly.

"What is it, Regina?"

"I was just thinking that I will never be able to wear a sapphire now."

He stroked a forefinger across her lips. "And why not, pray?"

"Because it would change color if I did, since I'm no longer chaste."

CHAPTER TEN

LONDON HAD SOMEHOW CHANGED. It appeared grayer, dingier, and the people on the streets seemed less friendly than Regina remembered.

It occurred to her that the difference might be in her. Could three months away from her homeland have wrought such a change? The life she had lived during that short period of time had been totally different from anything she had before experienced. She had seen exotic lands; she had been among strange, exotic people; she had come close to losing her life, and had instead emerged unscathed, with a fortune in gems. Or had the change in her come about because of her love for Brian Macbride, because of the relationship that had begun a month ago in Kashmir?

They had posed as man and wife on board the ship on the return voyage, which Regina thought was rather ironic since there had been no mention of marriage between them. Nor had she mentioned the idea of starting her own jewelry firm to Brian, although it was very much on her mind.

When they disembarked on the London docks, they took a carriage directly to the flat she and Adelaide had shared. Before they left, Regina had paid the rent for six months, wanting a place to return to.

As the carriage drew up before the building, Brian asked the driver to carry their luggage upstairs, and then to wait for them. Brian accompanied Regina to her flat, carrying the bag of gemstones.

"I'll have to leave the stones in your hands for a day or two, Regina. I must make contact with gem buyers, and calculate where we can make the best deal."

"Why not go directly to Mr. Slostrum?"

"From what you told me about his parting words to you, I'm thinking he might not be too hospitable to us."

Regina shook her head. "From what I know of Mr. Slostrum, he is a businessman first and would not let his personal feelings interfere in his dealings."

"Even if he is willing to deal with us, I doubt he would buy all our goods. It is simply too much for one buyer to handle."

"I'm not certain you're right, Brian," she said dubiously.

She took the bag of gems from him and stored them in the bottom drawer of her clothes bureau.

Brian looked concerned. "Sure, and I'm not too happy about leaving you alone with the goods, but I can't be lugging them around with me."

"They'll be safe here. I'll keep the door bolted and I won't go out until you return. And I'll keep the pistol with me at all times, since I now know how to use it." She smiled. "In the event a thief does try to get at them, I'll be prepared. But that hardly seems likely, since no one knows we have the stones."

"Thieves have an uncanny sense when it comes to sniffing out valuable goods, but I have no choice, it seems." He frowned. "But you say you won't be going out. I may not be back until tomorrow, or even later. How about food?"

Her smile grew impish. "I thought you might shop for me, while I take a bath. Shipboard facilities were hardly conducive to cleanliness."

He looked scandalized. "Shopping for food is a woman's chore. I know nothing about it!"

"Then it's time you learned, I should think," she said composedly.

"Sure, and it's something I have no wish to learn," he said in a grumbling voice. "But since it's in a good cause . . ."

"Before you go, there's something we haven't settled to my satisfaction."

He squinted at her in suspicion. "And what might that be?"

"I think you're wrong about not going to Mr. Slostrum with the stones. He may still resent me, but surely his anger has cooled and, as I said before, I certainly believe that he will not allow personal feelings to interfere with his business sense. Oh, you may be right that he can't, or won't, buy all our goods." She smiled to herself. She was sounding just like the man before her, referring to their find as "goods." She went on, "but they're of good quality, you said that yourself, so I'm sure he will be interested. I insist that we pay him a visit. I am your partner in this venture, Brian, so I am entitled to my say."

He studied her shrewdly. "I'm thinking it's not for purely business reasons that you want to go to

Andrew. You want to show him that his judgment was faulty. You want to gloat a little.''

She flushed darkly. ''That's not it at all!''

''Yes, it is, my little colleen. But there is no reason for you to feel embarrassed. There must be a little of the Irish in you. There's nothing wrong with a desire to get back at those who have slapped you down, nothing wrong at all. We Irish do it all the time.''

She had to laugh. ''All right, you Irish wild man. I confess. You're right. But I also think it's good business to go to Mr. Slostrum first.''

''I have no real objection, since we have nothing to lose,'' he said with a shrug. ''But to hedge our bets, I am still going to contact other potential buyers.''

The carriage driver came to drop two duffel bags onto the floor. ''That be the last, sir.''

''Fine, bucko. I'll be right down.'' Brian turned to Regina. ''I'll get your groceries, and then I'll be off. More than likely I will be back some time tomorrow. But if not, don't worry.''

''I still don't see why you can't stay here.''

''I need to get rid of this.'' He ran a hand through his beard. ''And my city clothes are stored in a trunk at the hotel where I usually stay in the city. I'll take a room there tonight, and perhaps tomorrow night.''

And it's *my* money you'll be after spending, bucko, Regina thought caustically. But she didn't voice her objection. Maybe he just wanted to be away from her for a few hours; after all, they had scarcely been out of each other's sight for three months. Still, another thought disturbed her. What if he was planning on visiting another woman in his absence? Regina was sure that he had any number of women available to him.

Then he swept her into his arms, and such traitorous thoughts vanished as the touch of his lips on hers brought that familiar tide of heat flowing in her veins.

When she finally pulled away, she combed her fingers through his beard. "I never thought I would say this, but I must confess to a sneaking fondness for that beard. I'll miss it."

"It will always grow back, darlin'."

"When you depart on another expedition, I suppose?"

"Sure, and that's the way of it." He kissed her again. "Well, I'm away now." After a few steps he turned back, grinning. "I'll not make an appointment with Andrew. We'll just drop in unexpected, surprise him. Would you like that, love?"

She smiled back and brought her hands together. "I'd like that very much, Brian."

IT WAS EARLY AFTERNOON two days later when they made their visit to Slostrum's. Insofar as Regina could ascertain, no changes had taken place at the firm. The same clerks gave them supercilious stares as she and Brian walked in. They did not deign to recognize her.

"Where is Andrew? In his office?" Brian asked one of the clerks.

"Yes, sir." As Brian started toward the stairs, the clerk called after him, "But you can't go up there! Mr. Slostrum does not wish to be disturbed."

Tightening his grip on Regina's arm, Brian strode on without pause. He winked at her. Accustomed to the beard as she was, he looked strange without it. At the top of the stairs, they headed for Slostrum's office. Brian knocked on the door, then pushed it open without waiting for an invitation.

Andrew Slostrum, behind his desk, reared back in astonishment as he recognized his two visitors. "Brian! And Regina!"

"Yes, Andrew, we have returned."

Regina nodded coolly. "How are you, Mr. Slostrum?"

"Indeed," Slostrum said stiffly. "If you have come to ask for your job back, Regina . . ."

"No need for that, Andrew," Brian said breezily. He placed the bag of stones he was carrying in the middle of Slostrum's desk. "Regina will never have to look for a lowly job like that one ever again. We hit the big strike!"

He opened the bag and took out several stones, unwrapping them one by one, but leaving them on their individual white papers. They had wrapped each stone separately in glossy white paper, then folded it, just so, into an outer paper. Each individually wrapped stone had been carefully packed into the carpetbag.

"I don't always do this," Brian had explained. "But this is the proper way to present stones to a buyer, even roughs, so I figured we might as well make the best presentation we can."

Slostrum's face took on an expression of awe, more expression than Regina had ever seen him show, and she felt vindicated.

"Indeed! You did very well, it seems."

"Better than it seems, Andrew. This is only half of our goods. Here." He picked up the cat's-eye ruby that Regina had found. "This alone should be worth twenty thousand pounds, at least."

Slostrum opened his desk drawer and took out his loupe and his "corn tongs" or tweezers. He carefully scrutinized the ruby. After a bit, he nodded. "It is a fine stone, Brian, but twenty thousand is a bit much . . ."

"Sure, and if you don't want it, there are other buyers interested," Brian said complacently.

Slostrum glanced up with a frown. "I did not say that I wasn't interested. You have contacted other buyers, Brian? And you say this isn't all of your stones?"

"Only half, aye. I thought all the goods would be too much for you to handle."

"Indeed. I have handled your business for some time, have I not? To our mutual satisfaction, I was given to understand."

"You have always been fair with me, Andrew, but circumstances are different this time. Why don't we see how it goes with this batch? If . . . If my partner and I—" indicating Regina with a sweep of his hand "—are satisfied, then we will decide if you are to be offered the rest of our goods." He sprawled back in one of the two chairs. "I'm thinking you may run out of funds before we're done."

Slostrum sat upright, an offended look on his face. "I doubt that very much, Brian."

"We shall see."

Regina took the other chair before the desk, realizing that they were about to get down to business. Brian turned his face toward her and winked. Regina felt a glow of pride and triumph; the wink was his way of telling her that she had been right to insist that they come to Andrew Slostrum.

AFTER TWO HOURS of dickering back and forth, they agreed on a price for the gemstones—a very satisfactory price, in Regina's estimation. Slostrum wanted to see the rest of their gems and Brian, after consulting with Regina in private, agreed.

"You go for them, Brian," she said. "I'd like to speak to my old friends here." She stole a glance at Slostrum. "If that is agreeable with you, Mr. Slostrum?"

"You most certainly have my permission, my dear," he said expansively. As Regina had surmised, his animosity toward her had vanished before the prospect of good business, and he was in an excellent mood.

As Regina started across the room on the third floor, Jane Worthington glanced up and saw her. The woman got to her feet with a broad smile. "Ducks! You're back!"

They met in the middle of the big room and embraced.

"How are things going, Jane?" Regina asked, pleased that the other woman had obviously forgiven her for becoming a salesclerk and then for leaving the company.

"No different," Jane said with a shrug. She eyed Regina keenly. "You came for your job back? I'm surprised Mr. Slostrum would take you back, as angry as he was. After you left, he raved like a bloody madman for days.''

Regina shook her head. "No, I'll not be returning, Jane." She couldn't keep from gloating a bit. "Brian and I, we made a big find, Jane. A fortune in stones!''

For just a moment, envy peeked out of Jane's faded eyes, and then she smiled without reservation. "I'm glad for you, ducks! I guess I always knew you wouldn't stay here forever. But why are you here now?''

"Just to talk a bit with old friends." She gave Jane's hand a squeeze. "I'm going back to speak to Giles.''

When Regina entered the cubicle, Giles and Eugene were bent over the worktable. Giles had his back to the door, and Eugene, glancing up, was the first one to see Regina.

His face split wide in a delighted grin. "Regina! You're back and you're all right.''

"More than all right, Eugene.''

Giles straightened up, turning, and Regina's heart ached at the sight of him; he had aged years, it seemed, since she had last seen him only a few short months ago.

His crooked grin was the same. "So you have returned, girl. And a triumphant return, I gather, from the rosy look of you.''

She nodded happily. "Yes, Giles, we made a good find.''

"Then I'm glad for you, Regina.''

She stooped to brush her lips across his grizzled cheek. Straightening up, she said, "And how is your apprentice doing, Giles?''

"He may make a gem cutter, if he lives long enough," he said in a grumpy voice. "He's too impatient, just like you. Wants to learn everything in a day."

"It's the impatient ones who get ahead in the world. Giles . . . I'm going to start my own jewelry firm."

"Doesn't surprise me in the least," he said simply.

"And I want you with me. I want you to be my gem cutter."

He was already shaking his head. "No, 'twould never do, girl. I'm too old. I'll finish out my days here."

"Please, Giles. I need you."

"Regina, I once told you that I had never destroyed a diamond. Well, a month ago, I did." He held up a gnarled hand, which shook slightly. "I'm not entirely stupid. I'm past my prime. Soon I'm going to have to find a corner by the fire and spend the remainder of my days there. But . . ." Smiling slightly now, he indicated Eugene with a nod of his head. "Take the lad. He will make a good cutter for you."

"I thought you just told me that it would take some time, that he was still learning?"

Giles had the grace to look abashed. "I was exaggerating a wee bit. Eugene is one of the natural ones. Oh, he's not as good as me, but then he likely never will be."

Regina looked at Eugene. "If I start my own house, would you like to work for me?"

"I would like nothing better, Regina!" he blurted, then turned a dark red. "If you would have me, that is."

"Well, I shall need a gem cutter, and if Giles says you'll do, that's good enough for me. It will probably take some time, Eugene. I'll let you know. Now I must go. I have some more business to transact with Mr. Slostrum, and I want to say hello to Mr. Mondrain first. It was good to see you both again."

As usual, Peter Mondrain's cubicle was locked. Regina hesitated for a moment. What kind of a welcome could she expect from him after the harsh words he had spoken to her? Maybe she should just forget it. Then she shook her head and knocked lightly on the door.

A key rattled in the lock, and the door opened a few inches, Mondrain's face appearing in the crack.

For a moment his face showed a startled expression. "Regina!" Then he became cold and aloof again.

"Hello, sir. May I come in for a minute?"

He stepped back, opening the door. Regina went in, wearing a strained smile.

"I assume that your adventurer friend left you stranded somewhere?"

Her anger surfaced. "You assume entirely wrong, Mr. Mondrain. My adventurer friend and I found a small fortune in rubies and sapphires in Kashmir." To her consternation, tears came to her eyes. "Why has your opinion of me changed so drastically, Mr. Mondrain? Once I thought we were friends."

His long face spasmed in some emotion Regina could not define. "My apologies, Regina. We were friends, and I hope we still are. It is just that I.... Often I am subject to moods that even I despise. Please forgive me."

He reached out for her hand, and Regina let him take it. It was the first time they had ever touched; his flesh was cold and dry. "Of course I forgive you, Mr. Mondrain. We are still friends, then?"

"I hope we shall always be friends, my dear, my very dear."

Flustered by the emotion in his voice, Regina stepped past him to his worktable. "What are you designing now, Mr. Mondrain?"

Her calculation proved correct—Mondrain was always happy to discuss his work with her, to the exclusion of everything else. For the next few minutes, she listened as he explained what he was working on—an intricate design of a locket for a duchess.

As he finished, she said casually, "I am thinking of starting my own jewelry firm. I shall need a good designer, a workmaster."

"I would be delighted to work for you, Regina."

She flashed him a look of astonishment. "You would? I probably can't pay you as much as you earn here."

He smiled slightly. "I see that you are surprised. It is true that Slostrum pays me well, but with him, gems are a business, a way to earn money. You, on the other hand, have a love and respect for gems, and I appreciate that, Regina."

"Mr. Mondrain..."

"Please." He held up a hand. "Call me Peter, Regina."

"Well, uh...Peter, at the moment, it's not much more than a thought, an idea. Many things must come to pass before I can start a business of my own. Aren't you concerned about my youth, my lack of experience?"

He smiled at her. "Men in their teens have conquered countries, and women younger than you have been queens."

"It's hardly the same thing, but I do think I can do it."

"I am sure you can."

"I'll let you know how my plans proceed."

Leaving Mondrain's cubicle, something occurred to Regina that gave her pause. Here she was, recruiting employees from Andrew Slostrum, the man who had been her benefactor in many ways. It was a rather underhanded way of paying him back. She knew that it was sometimes necessary to be ruthless to succeed in business, but still....

She shook her head sharply, remembering his harsh words when she had gone off with Brian—and she had earned every shilling that Slostrum had paid her. She needed people to work for her who trusted and respected her, in spite of her youth. Giles would still be here, so the loss of Eugene wouldn't be so severe, and Mr. Slostrum could always find a replacement for Peter Mondrain. She would sorely need a good designer and workmaster. But perhaps she was worrying unduly; she still had a long way to go before she could start her own jewelry firm.

Brian was already back in Slostrum's office when she entered. The second batch of gemstones had been emptied onto Slostrum's desk, and he was examining them with his loupe. At Regina's appearance, Brian turned his head and winked.

Slostrum leaned back, his face expressionless. "They appear to be fine stones."

"Fine, is it?" Brian chucked. "Sure, and they're great stones, Andrew, all of them."

For the next hour, they bargained, and finally reached an agreement on a price for all the stones. The final figure was more than Brian's estimate back in Kashmir—seventy-five thousand pounds! Regina felt giddy with triumph and delight. There should certainly be enough in her share to start her own business. Of course, they could begin in a much larger way if Brian would agree to become a full partner.

A few minutes later, they left the building with Slostrum's bank draft in hand. Brian managed to restrain his exuberance until they were out on the street. Then he waved the bank draft in the air, and seizing her by the arms, he twirled her, oblivious to the gawking passersby.

"How does it feel to be rich, lass?"

"It feels wonderful," she said, laughing at his foolishness.

"You know what I want to do right this minute?" He leaned close to whisper into her ear, "I want to make love to you, darlin'. We're due a grand celebration. And I want you to know that I appreciate your part in our find. Without you, it would never have happened. Sure, and in all my years of gem hunting, 'tis my grandest find of all!"

They hurried back to Regina's flat and made laughing, boisterous, triumphant love. Regina had never loved him more than in those moments, yet there was a strange feeling of melancholy to it, as though this was somehow farewell.

In the afterglow, lying breathless in the tangled sheets, Regina said, "Are you hungry, Brian?"

"Famished, love, famished!"

She got out of bed, put on her clothes, and began putting together a quick meal. Brian was sitting at the table, dressed, by the time she served the food.

He was still on a high, talking constantly. "With that much money, we won't have to go gem hunting for at least a year, perhaps two. We can do anything we want. I've never been to America, Regina. What would you think about taking first-class accommodations on one of those new luxury liners to New York?"

"No, Brian," she said quietly, looking at him directly.

"Aye, perhaps you are right. Sure, and we've had enough of sea voyaging for a bit. How about a villa for six months in the south of France? It is divine there, lass, a sight to melt even the hardest of hearts...."

"Brian," she said sharply, "stop babbling!"

"Babbling, is it?" He peered at her narrowly.

"You plan to idle away the time until the money is all gone?"

"Not idling, darlin'. Enjoying ourselves. That's what money is for. We worked hard for it, now it's time to enjoy it to the fullest."

"It would not be pleasurable to me, spending it all until I'm poor as a church mouse again."

"But that's the joy of it, you see." He spread his hands. "What's the joy in making a good find unless you're hungry, not knowing where your next meal is coming from?"

"No," she said with a vehement shake of her head. "I'm taking my share of the proceeds and starting my own jewelry firm."

"You still have that nagging at you, eh? I thought such foolishness had gone out of your head."

"It's not foolishness, Brian. It's what I want to do." She leaned across the table, her gaze clinging to his face. "When I talked of it before, you said I could never do such a thing without money. Well, now I have money."

"Aye, you have the money. But that's not the whole of it. You're but a lass, with only a wee bit of experience."

"I can employ people with experience. I have already spoken to two people. As for my being a woman, I think I have proven that I can do as well as a man in the gem business."

"Not to me. Sure, and it took a bit of financing and some hard work, but still and all, our find was a matter of luck. We might have found nothing at all. Running a jewelry business requires much more than luck. No, Regina, you would be foolish indeed if you continue on such a path."

"I was thinking..." She took a deep breath. "If you came in with me, if we became partners, we'd have more financing, we'd have the benefit of your experience, and I'd be willing for most people to think the firm is yours, since everyone I've talked to seems to think that people will only conduct business with a man.''

"You're asking me to go into business with you?'' He reared back in outrage. "To go to a store every day dressed like an undertaker, and sell stones to rich old biddies already so loaded down with jewels they can hardly waddle? You must be mad, woman!''

"I should think you would welcome the chance. You probably have more money in your share of our find than you'll ever have at one time again. You surely don't intend to waste your life away forever?''

"Wasting, is it?'' His eyes blazed like blue fire. "That's your word for it, woman. And to think that I was thinking of asking you to marry me! Well, now I can see what a mistake that would have been! You would try to domesticate me, and I don't domesticate easily. By all the saints, I don't!''

Her heart skipped a beat at the mention of marriage, and for just a moment she wavered, melting toward him, yearning for his touch.

Then he brought his fist down onto the table, rattling the dishes. "Now, woman, banish such foolishness from your head forever!''

"I will not, Brian Macbride. And what makes you think I would ever consider marrying such an insufferable clod? I was warned about you. You're nothing but an adventurer, an idler, a wastrel, a spendthrift. You will never make anything of your life. You're nothing more than a little boy. You'll never grow up.''

"Wastrel and little boy, is it?" he snarled, glowering. "How dare you, a slip of a girl with no more sense than a village idiot, call me names? I'll not stand for it."

He rose to his feet, leaning over the table, glaring at her in pure anger.

Regina also shot to her feet, her own rage icy. "I don't see how you could ever have thought of marrying me, since you have such a low opinion of me!"

"Since our opinions seem to match, I'm thinking there's only one thing to do."

"And what is that?"

"Go our separate ways, and never see each other again."

For an instant her heart gave a great lurch, and once again she almost weakened. Then her resolve hardened, and she leaned across the table until their faces were only inches apart. "That, Brian Macbride, is the most sensible thing you've said all day."

He blinked, drawing back a step, as though she had struck him. "Fine. I'll go direct to the bank and cash Andrew's draft and bring back your portion."

"No, you won't," she said grimly. "I'll go with you. I don't think I can trust you any longer."

"Sure, and now I'm a thief, is it?"

"You put the words to it, I didn't."

"Then let's be going. The sooner we part company, the better for it."

With exaggerated courtesy, he held the door open for her.

As she started through, Regina halted and faced him. Despite herself, she felt tears burn her eyes. "You said you had thought of asking me to marry you, yet you never once told me you loved me."

"And now you will never know, will you?"

CHAPTER ELEVEN

THE BREAK WITH BRIAN left Regina hurt and angry. How could he be so irresponsible, so thoughtless? He had said that he had considered asking her to marry him; didn't he realize that marriage involved a certain degree of responsibility? If he really cared for her, he would want to help build some kind of decent life for them, not expect her to lead the kind of hand-to-mouth existence he was so evidently used to.

She told herself that it was for the best. Certainly it was better to learn what kind of man he was now than to find out after they had formed a permanent liaison. Nevertheless it hurt—hurt terribly.

Determined to put the experience behind her, Regina immersed herself in the details of determining what would have to be done in order for her to open her own business. Her findings were not encouraging. She had not realized the number of jewelry firms that did business in London. The competition was fierce.

In the course of her investigation, she also discovered that many of the new firms that had gone into business during the past year had failed within a short time. Not only did the new businesses have difficulty in attracting customers, they had difficulty in purchasing stones. Most diamonds, the mainstay of the jewelry trade, had to be bought through De Beers, and that corporation was selective in choosing its customers. De Beers also kept its prices artificially high. As for other gemstones, the gem traders tended to gravitate toward the established firms. Regina realized that she was more fortunate than many people starting a business, because she had the necessary funds to carry her until she was established, providing, of course, that she *could* get established. In spite of the apparent obstacles—and no doubt a number of hidden ones—she was determined to go ahead with her plan.

And then she discovered that she was pregnant.

Now, in addition to being a woman in a man's business, she would also be an unmarried woman with a child. It was hardly a desirable image for a woman starting a new business.

She never once considered going to Brian and telling him that she was carrying his child. If she had her way, he would never know. She wouldn't marry him now, no matter what the circumstances!

Since returning to London, Regina had read everything she could find about the gem business. Much of the material also referred to the jewelry industry in the United States. That country was prosperous and the jewelry trade was growing, with New York the heart of the business. Of course, moving to New York would present a number of additional obstacles; she would be living in a new country, among strangers. But there would be one important plus; she could move there, claim to be a widow and have her child without stigma.

The more she pondered the situation, the more she came to believe that beginning her business in New York would be a wise move. In effect, she would be starting a new life, and that would probably be for the best.

Now she went back and reread the information referring to jewelry firms in New York. The largest and most famous was Tiffany's, which had been in business for over a half century.

Tiffany's had opened as a small firm. To Regina's surprise, she learned that Charles Lewis Tiffany, the founder, had first carried paste jewelry from Germany. He had never lied to his customers, but had told them that they were buying paste jewelry. Tiffany had borrowed money from his father to open a stationery store, gradually branching out into carrying Chinese bric-a-brac and other art items. After his paste diamonds sold well, he decided that it was time to begin selling real gems.

In 1848, Tiffany sent his partner to Paris. His visit coincided with the abrupt departure of Louis Phillippe and his queen, Amelie. They left Europe in such haste that they left behind the crown jewels. Tiffany's partner, John Young, managed to obtain some of the crown diamonds at a very low price from royalists who had nothing else to sell. This gave birth to the rumor that Tiffany got into the jewelry business by acting as a fence for the royal jewels. Apparently nothing was ever proven. At any rate, it was the beginning of the rise of Tiffany's to prominence in the jewelry business.

Charles Tiffany had died recently and his son, Louis, was now at the head of the firm.

Regina's spirits soared when she had finished the article. If Tiffany could make a smashing success after starting so small, and on borrowed money at that, then she certainly stood a chance. She no longer harbored any doubts about her course of action.

The next day, she met Eugene for lunch and told him of her plans.

"Go to the United States with you, Regina?" he said slowly. "I don't know. That would mean leaving England, my home and my father and mother. It is a drastic step."

She leaned forward excitedly. "But it would be a big chance for you, Eugene! I've already made up my mind. I am going, with or without you, but I would dearly love to have you with me. If I start my firm there and grow, you will grow with me. I realize that things aren't going to happen overnight. It will take some time and some doing. You can stay here and work, until I get set up. Then I'll send for you. I'll pay your passage, of course."

"I would like nothing better than to work for you, Regina." He caught fire. "But are you sure you want to employ me? Pay for my passage and all? I'm sure there are better gem cutters in New York, cutters who have long since served their apprenticeship."

"I would like to have someone I know and trust, Eugene. And I am sure that you will one day be considered one of the greatest cutters in the trade."

He flushed with pleasure. "I doubt that very much, but it's kind of you to say so. I will have to talk this over with my father. If he has no strong objections, I shall be happy to join you in America." .

Regina caught Peter Mondrain as he left the building after work that afternoon. He smiled slightly as he caught sight of her. "My dear Regina, how nice to see you."

"Could we talk for a bit?"

"But of course," he said with an arched eyebrow.

They walked together toward the small park. On the way, Mondrain said, "Today I gave Slostrum a month's notice. That should be about the right amount of time, do you not agree?"

"Oh, Peter," she said in dismay. "I wish you had waited."

"Why?" he said with a shrug. "Even if you are not ready for business by that time, it will not matter. I have worked at Slostrum's for ten years, steadily. So until the time that you require my services, I shall have a holiday. Also, my advice might be of some value, Regina. I have been connected with the jewelry business for many years, and I am knowledgeable in most aspects of it."

They reached the park and took a bench. "I'm sure your knowledge would be valuable, Peter, but I have decided to open my business in New York and not here," Regina announced immediately.

He looked surprised. "In the United States? Why did you make that decision? Not that it may not be a wise one, but it will present more difficulties than you would find here."

"Yes, I am well aware of the difficulties, at least some of them, but I have made up my mind. I am going."

"I visited New York once, a number of years ago. It struck me as raw, uncivilized. It may have improved, although I very much doubt that. On the other hand, there are many of the newly rich there, offering a strong market for expensive pieces. And your pounds will be worth considerably more in dollars. Regina—" He broke off, looking at her intently. "I would hazard a guess that there is something aside from business considerations behind your decision. Am I correct?"

She hesitated. Should she tell him the truth? If he went to America with her, he would find out in due course, anyway. In a low voice, she said, "Peter, I am going to have a child."

His face turned as cold as stone, and he seemed to gather himself as though to get to his feet. Regina was sure that he was about to stalk away, out of her life forever.

Then he relaxed, leaning back. Without looking at her, he said, "The Irishman, I presume?"

"Yes," she said in a small voice.

"The blackguard did not offer to marry you?"

"He doesn't know and I would never marry him."

"I see," he said in neutral voice.

"I'm not ashamed," she said, drawing herself up. "But there would naturally be a scandal if I remained here, and an unmarried mother would most certainly not be the proper image for a respectable businesswoman."

"Yes," he said thoughtfully. "A man can father a child out of wedlock, and while there might be some scandal, it would have little effect on his business life. But for a woman, it would be a definite hindrance."

"Then you see why I made the decision I did."

"Yes, I understand fully." He looked at her intently. "Regina, there is a way to remove the stigma. You could get married now, before it is too late. I will marry you."

She made a startled sound. "You would be willing to do that?"

"For you, I would," he said simply. "I realize you do not love me, so it would be a marriage of convenience only. You would have my name, and respectability." He became very intense. "You are very dear to me, Regina."

"That is very sweet of you, Peter." She placed her hand over his. "And I will always appreciate the offer, but no. It would not be fair to you."

"I believe I should be the judge of that," he said in a sharp tone.

"That is not the only reason. As you say, I don't love you, although I am fond of you...."

"Like a father?" he said wryly.

"Well, yes. I never knew my father, and you *are* like a father to me. But I will never marry a man without loving him, Peter. No, I made a mistake, and I do not intend to compound it further. I shall go to America and start life anew, if under an artifice."

"That is well and good, but it seems to me there is someone you are forgetting."

"Who?"

"Your child. It will be born and grow up under a cloud."

"I have made out well enough," she snapped.

"Perhaps. But do you wish your child to be so handicapped?"

"Insofar as anyone in America will know, except you, my baby will be legitimate."

"But someday you may wish the child to know the truth. It will naturally have questions concerning the father. What will you do then?"

"I'll face the problem when it arises. Peter... I do appreciate your concern, but nothing you can say will change my mind."

"Very well." He threw up his hands in defeat. "I felt that those were things I was duty bound to say. I suppose you no longer wish me to accompany you to New York?"

"Why not? I still need you, Peter."

"I thought perhaps it might be embarrassing, for both of us, after my proposal."

"I won't be embarrassed, and nor should you. Peter..." She touched his hand again. "I am deeply touched and honored by your offer. I'm only sorry that I cannot accept it."

THE NEXT FEW WEEKS were busy ones for Regina. She had a great many things to do—ship's passage to arrange; immigration papers to complete; the sale of the furniture and other items in the flat; and she had to shop for clothes.

Fortunately immigration posed no serious problem. The wave of immigration to the United States from Europe that had begun in the middle of the nineteenth century was still heavy; a million immigrants a year still crossed the Atlantic. The fact that she had funds and would not need to seek employment in New York meant that Regina received her immigration papers without difficulty.

She wanted to leave before her pregnancy became noticeable, and therefore, one of her priorities was a quick departure. With customary thoroughness, she went about purchasing passage. Most of the big liners plying the Atlantic left from Liverpool or Southampton, but one line did sail from London. The line was American owned, a company recently purchased by J. Pierpont Morgan, the American millionaire banker who was in the process of acquiring several steamship lines.

For several days, Regina worried over what kind of accommodations to book. By far the least expensive, of course, would be to travel steerage with the other immigrants; the fare would be about fifty American dollars. But she had heard many horror stories about the cramped lower decks, the terrible food and unsanitary conditions. Even if she were so inclined, she couldn't very well ask Mondrain to sail steerage.

The next was second class, which was considerably more expensive, and the best, of course, was first class, which would cost over five thousand American dollars for the two of them. It seemed that second class was the obvious choice.

Still, the idea of traveling first class was appealing. Wasn't she entitled to splurge just a little? To celebrate the fact of her pregnancy, she thought with a wry smile. Regina had never spent money foolishly in her life, thanks to Adelaide's lessons in thrift. Yet she knew that when she arrived in New

York, life was not going to be easy for a long time. She had to start doing the things that would have to be done before she could start up her own business; and she would have to weigh every dollar in that endeavor before spending it. At the same time she would be going through the various stages of pregnancy.

So wasn't she entitled to spend a little money on herself? But each time she reached that conclusion, she would think of what difference four thousand dollars would mean to the future.

Finally she discussed it with Peter Mondrain.

"I can relieve you of one worry, Regina," he said immediately. "I shall pay my own fare. I have always earned good money, and there has never been anyone to spend it on but myself. I will admit that although my life at Slostrum's may have appeared Spartan, I have often indulged myself in my private life. Not exactly a sybaritic existence, perhaps, but I have a love of good food, expensive wines, better than average living quarters, the theater and similar entertainments."

"And women?" Regina dared to ask.

He looked taken aback. "Yes, I must confess to that as well. I have not been a womanizer, but neither have I been celibate. But the point is, I can well afford to pay my own fare."

"But I feel that it's my responsibility, Peter. After all, if it wasn't for me, you wouldn't be going to America."

"Perhaps, perhaps not." His smile was brief. "I have toyed with the idea upon occasion. Good jewelry designers, I understand, are much in demand."

"Then once you arrive, you may desert me for a house that can pay you better."

"Do not fear, my dear," he said with a shake of his head. "Money does not really hold that much attraction for me. I shall be quite content to work for you, and watch your firm grow."

"I can only hope it does."

"I am confident that it will. In any event, I can well afford to pay my own fare."

She felt a sense of relief and was ashamed of herself. Was she going to become like Scrooge in Mr. Dickens's book, jubilant over saving a few pounds? "It's probably extravagant of me, thinking of going first class," she said.

"Not at all. First, you owe it to yourself. More importantly, you must make a good impression. That is always important in business. People who travel on cruise ships, except for steerage, of course, are often wealthy and as such, are potential jewelry buyers. Suppose you meet someone on board with whom you later do business? What would their impression be if you were traveling in anything but first class?"

THREE WEEKS LATER, Regina stood at the railing of the ship, Peter Mondrain by her side, as the gangplank was being drawn up. Smoke streamed up from the stacks, and two blasts on the ship's horn signaled their imminent departure.

People crowded the rail, waving farewell to relatives and friends on the docks. The air was filled with streamers and confetti, and most of the passengers held glasses of champagne.

Both Regina and Mondrain had a glass, and Mondrain had a half-empty magnum. Regina had already imbibed two glasses of the bubbly wine, and she was feeling light-headed and gay.

As the ship began to move, inching away from the docks, a great cheer went up, both from the passengers and the people on land. Mondrain turned to Regina, "Here's to your good fortune in America, Regina!"

"And to yours, as well," she shouted, the words lost in the roar of voices.

They clinked glasses and drank.

Regina, thinking of the unaccustomed champagne and the luxurious suite she had been shown to an hour ago, said under her breath, "You would be proud of me, Brian, should you see me now. Sure, and I'm spending money like there is no tomorrow!"

CHAPTER TWELVE

TRY AS HE MIGHT, Brian could not get Regina out of his mind. Despite how angry he was with her, he thought of her several times a day. Finally he decided that he had to see her. He certainly had no intention of changing his mind about becoming partners with her in the jewelry business, but there was no reason why they could not remain friends.

To his dismay, he found that she had vacated her flat, and the landlord either did not know her new address, or he refused to tell him.

At Slostrum's, he fared no better. Andrew Slostrum informed him curtly that he had no interest in Regina's whereabouts. "I understand that she's going into business for herself. Indeed! Not only is she foolish, but she is an unscrupulous female! She has lured my jewelry designer, Peter Mondrain, away from me. After all I have done for the girl, she does this to me."

As Brian left the shop, he heard his name called. "Mr. Macbride!"

He stopped, turning to see a gangly youth hurrying after him along the street. "Mr. Macbride, I heard you inquiring about Regina."

"Aye, that I was. Do you know where she is?"

"Yes, sir, she sailed for New York this past week. She is going there to start her own jewelry firm." The youth drew himself up proudly. "I am

Eugene Leacock, gem cutter apprentice. As soon as her business is open, I am to join her as a gem cutter."

"New York, is it?" Brian said, dazed by the news. "Thank you, lad."

Without another word, Brian turned and strode away. He was desolated and felt weighed down with a sense of great loss.

But as he walked on, anger drove out all other feelings. She was even more foolish than he had thought, going to a strange country in the hope of beginning a business. She would soon be destitute and back to work behind a jewelry counter, if she could find anyone in America as softhearted as Andrew and foolish enough to employ her.

Then his step slowed as he began to wonder why she had decided to start her business in New York instead of in London. Was it because he, Brian, was here, and she wanted to put as much distance between them as possible?

Well, if that was her reason, be damned to the woman! He had gotten along for almost thirty years without Regina Paxton, and by all the saints, he could continue to do so!

Determined to put her out of his mind henceforth, he stepped out briskly. He knew just the woman to take his mind off Regina.

WHEN REGINA HAD BEEN debating which ship to sail on, she had read a brochure that had stated: "Going Cunard is a state of grace."

The ship she was now on was a step below those

of the Cunard Line, but it still offered a state of luxury of which she had previously only dreamed.

She had enjoyed her voyage on the *Galatea*, but it had been nothing compared to this! Life on board the great liner was like living in a dreamworld; all worries and fears were forgotten, or at least pushed aside for the time being. The loss of Brian, her pregnancy, the new life awaiting her, were all a part of the real world, and the real world did not exist here. For the week, she, Mrs. Regina Paxton, widow, was determined to make the most of it.

Stewards were at her beck and call day or night, and could gratify almost every wish. The liner was steam heated and had indoor plumbing—a luxury few homes could boast of—provided by an apparatus that pumped salt water from the Atlantic. The ship's interior was lined with rosewood, holly and satinwood. The drawing rooms were lushly carpeted and furnished with plush armchairs and sofas. Ceilings were carved and gilded. Windows in the drawing rooms and the grand salon were decorated with stained-glass designs depicting the history of America. Highly polished mirrors hung everywhere. And electric lights, powered by the turbines, illuminated the ship as bright as day.

There was an ice room on board containing forty tons of ice, and as a result, the variety and quantity of food was amazing—green turtle soup; turkey in oyster sauce; boiled bass in hollandaise sauce; goose in champagne sauce. Fruits and vegetables remained fresh for the duration of the voyage. Desserts of almost every kind were available.

The food, Mondrain told Regina, matched the selections offered by New York's famous Delmonico Restaurant, where he had dined on his visit to the city.

Regina, used to a life of hard work and simple living, found that she took to the luxury like a cat to cream. Everything was new and surprising. It was a pure pleasure to lounge in a deck chair and simply motion to a deck steward when one wanted a refreshing drink, a blanket to ward against the chill, or a pillow. She loved the enforced idleness, although she knew that she would become bored and restless with that kind of life after a lengthy period of time. But now it was good to rest, to renew her strength and spirit for what she knew would be a busy, arduous time in New York while she tried to establish her business.

There was only one thing about the voyage that troubled her—the immigrants crowded below in steerage. They were never allowed on the upper decks under any circumstances. Sailors were posted at the top of the steps leading down, armed with clubs. Although she had never seen it happen, she knew that the clubs were to repel any of the steerage passengers should they try to invade first- and second-class territory.

From a few locations on the upper decks, Regina could see down onto the steerage deck. The immigrants were indeed packed in like animals, and they milled around, on good-weather days, like restless cattle. On the chilly days, they huddled together for warmth. And if the wind was just right, a noxious odor wafted up from the steerage deck. She understood that toilet facilities were inadequate, and that bathing facilities were non-existent. The only baths available to the steerage passengers were those taken from pails of water.

Regina, in view of what she enjoyed in first class, felt guilty about the difference in accommodations.

When she tried to explain this to Mondrain, he simply shrugged. "My dear Regina, why should you feel any guilt? Their plight is deplorable, certainly, but that is in no way your responsibility."

"But it is not right, Peter! Why should they have to suffer such hardships?"

He gave another shrug. "Two reasons, I would imagine. First, the ship owners have little concern for them. Secondly, they pay only fifty dollars for passage to America. If it was much more, enough so that better facilities could be provided, they could not afford it. After all—" he smiled his wintry smile and said with a certain cynicism "—they are going to America, the land of opportunity, in search of a better life, are they not? I very much doubt that one in fifty will find it, but that is not our concern."

THE MAJORITY of the first- and second-class passengers were Americans who had been in Europe either on business or on holiday. The six passengers sharing Regina and Mondrain's table at dinner were American. On the first night at sea, one seat remained vacant, and Regina was told that the man who was supposed to occupy it was suffering from mal de mer and was confined to his cabin. The other five consisted of two married couples returning from a holiday in Europe and a gentleman traveling on business.

Regina was eager for news of New York, but unfortunately none of the people at the table were from that city. However, they did tell her that the United States was riding a wave of prosperity. When told that she was emigrating to America with the intention of embarking in the jewelry business, they all agreed that the popularity of jewels was growing in that country.

"The nouveau riche," said one of the women with disdain. "New York is full of them. They are crude, vulgar and pushy, but they do buy jewelry by the cartloads, thinking, I suppose, that it makes them socially acceptable."

Regina didn't comment, yet she thought it strange that the remark came from a woman dressed in the height of fashion, complete with many jewels. If she and her husband, a farm implement manufacturer from the Middle West, represented Americans in general, Regina doubted that she'd come to like the American people. Yet the businessman was quiet and reserved, and the other couple, elderly and also quite wealthy, were warm and completely devoted to each other.

On their second night out, the missing passenger attended dinner, taking the vacant seat next to Regina. He was a slender man of thirty-five, with thick brown hair, brown eyes and a sensitive face. He was quiet, soft-spoken, and possessed an old-world courtliness. His name was William Logan.

After introductions were made, Regina turned to the man. "I'm sorry to hear of your illness, Mr. Logan. I can sympathize, since I had a bout of mal de mer not too long ago. But that was in a bad storm, and we have had calm weather."

His smile was wry. "I am one of those unfortunate people who get sick the minute they step on board a ship. I think I could get seasick in a bathtub. Frankly it is the bane of my life, since I must make the trip to Europe at least twice a year."

"And what is your line of business, Mr. Logan?" one of the men at the table asked.

"I am in the jewelry business. I buy for the firm of Tiffany's in New York. I have to attend diamond sights twice a year, and I also use the opportunity to purchase other gems in London and Amsterdam."

"You are in the jewelry business?" Regina clapped her hands together in delight. "So am I! At least I'm going to be."

Logan looked at her curiously. "How so, Mrs. Paxton? You're British, aren't you?"

"I am, yes. I am going to New York to establish my own firm."

His brown eyes widened with surprise, yet he didn't appear as shocked as most men were at such a concept. "As we say in the States, Mrs. Paxton, you have a hard row to hoe."

"I'm not sure that I know what that means, but I can guess. I have many obstacles to overcome, I well realize."

"Have you any experience in the jewelry business?"

"Yes, with Slostrum's in London."

He nodded. "I am familiar with Slostrum's, and I know Andrew Slostrum slightly."

Regina nodded toward Mondrain. "Mr. Mondrain designed for Slostrum's."

"I have heard of your work, sir, and from the pieces I have seen, your reputation is well deserved," he said leaning across Regina to speak to Mondrain.

"Thank you, Mr. Logan," Mondrain said distantly.

"Peter is going to design for me now," Regina said.

Logan nodded again. "At least you will be starting with the best. Design is very important in the jewelry business."

"What a remarkable coincidence meeting you, Mr. Logan!" Regina said. "I would dearly love to discuss the trade with you during the voyage. If you would be willing, that is. But perhaps you would be reluctant to pass on such knowledge to a possible competitor?"

Logan smiled slightly. "Surely you've heard our expression? Competition is the American way. Strong competition is supposed to keep firms on their mettle."

"But does Mr. Tiffany subscribe to that theory?"

"Charles Tiffany thrived on competition, and he always seemed to remain the leader. But Charles Tiffany died not too long ago."

"I know, I read about his death. He must be sorely missed," Regina said soberly.

"Well, the store's reputation and prestige is already well established. His son, Louis, is almost the opposite of his father in personality. Whereas Charles Tiffany lived a sober type of life, his son is somewhat flamboyant. It was, and is, the opinion of many in the trade that Charles Tiffany's way of life created a better atmosphere for the sale of luxury items than a more, shall we say, showy way of life. There is always a certain faction of the public that finds the sale of luxury items, such as diamonds, to be distasteful while poor people are starving. A dignified image seems to ameliorate their feelings.''

Regina looked at him shrewdly. ''Do I detect a certain note of disapproval toward the younger Tiffany?''

''Young Louis has not been running the firm long enough for me to make any sort of assessment of him. Although Charles naturally wanted him in the firm, Louis showed little interest in the business as a boy. I understand that he hated schoolwork, preferring to play with colored pebbles and bits of broken glass. His father allowed him to skip college and go to Paris, where he studied painting.

''He showed some talent as a painter, but he gave it up, deciding that his real bent was for designing and decoration. He came back to the States and formed the Tiffany Studios. Under his leadership, Tiffany Studios decorated many famous mansions and clubs, mostly in Oriental or Moorish style, always exciting and luxurious. His designs were not quite art nouveau, but often approached it. Louis Tiffany's greatest work is in stained glass. His work in that field has often been compared to Postimpressionist paintings.

''His firm was independent of Tiffany & Co., but he used the store as an outlet for many of his products, especially glassware. So Charles, although he couldn't get his son into the firm until after his death, did have him, in a manner of speaking, in the family business."

"So Louis is now at the head of Tiffany's?"

"Yes, and as I said, it is far too early to tell how the company will fare with him at the helm, but it is already clear that there will be some changes in the direction..."

A waiter interrupted Logan to take his dessert plate, and Regina took the opportunity to glance around. To her surprise, she saw that they were the only two left at the table; even Peter Mondrain had left. So engrossed had she been in what the jewelry buyer had been saying that she had not noticed that dinner was long finished.

"It would appear that we have talked the evening away, Mrs. Paxton," William Logan said with a smile.

"It would seem so, but it was all very interesting and I'd like to hear more."

"Well, we have several days yet." He moved his chair back, got to his feet and gave her a hand up. "They should be dancing in the ballroom by now. May I have the pleasure?"

"Why, I..." She was flustered, realizing for the first time that Will Logan was not only a very interesting man, but was also very attractive, in a quiet, understated way. "I must confess that I have had little practice at ballroom dancing, or any dancing, for that matter. Back in London, I had little time or inclination for socializing."

"Your husband does not care for the social life?"

Regina hesitated. "I am a widow, Mr. Logan."

"I'm sorry to hear that. It's always sad to lose someone you love."

Regina, feeling awkward with her lie, avoided his eyes. "Yes, of course that's true."

"And so you come alone, except for Mr. Mondrain, to a new country to begin a new life. I must say, I think it's very brave of you."

She smiled, relieved by the change of subject. It had suddenly dawned on her that if she should be asked how long she had been widowed, she would have a problem. If her supposed husband had died some time ago, he could not possibly be the father of her unborn child; and if he had died recently, she should be in mourning! It was true, the old saying, "Oh, what a tangled web we weave, when first we practice to deceive." She should have thought this through and worked out a detailed and plausible story before starting the trip.

But Will Logan seemed to have dropped the subject for the moment. "Although I'm a poor dancer myself, I think it's the proper thing to do on a pleasure cruise," he was saying.

"Then we should, by all means, try it."

The dancing was already underway when they reached the ballroom. A seven-piece orchestra on the stage at the end of the room was playing a sedate waltz. Light from the chandeliers overhead gleamed down on the powdered shoulders of the women, and glittered like fire off the many jewels they wore.

The men, in their formal attire and stiff white collars, looked dignified and affluent; the women, in their soft, flowing gowns and upswept hair, looked elegant and pampered.

Regina, gazing down at her own gown of pale blue silk ornamented with lace, was glad that she had decided to augment her wardrobe before taking the trip. The gown bared her shoulders and followed the curvature of her tightly corseted waist, then flowed softly to a bell-like fullness, accented by a slightly greater fullness at the rear, giving her the fashionable S-curve, which was considered so desirable. Beneath her gown, she wore a richly embroidered petticoat, which swished with enticing froufrou, embroidered silk stockings and kid shoes. Around her neck she wore a simple gold locket that had belonged to her mother, and on her finger was the plain gold band she had purchased to serve as her "widow's" disguise.

Will Logan, contrary to his disclaimer, was an excellent dancer; and after a few moments Regina lost her stiffness and began to follow his lead easily.

Then the orchestra swung into a lively polka. Regina held back. "Mr. Logan, I don't think I can dance the polka. I never have."

"Nonsense. It's time you learned." He took her into his arms again and swung her onto the floor. Laughing, she followed his lead.

She lost track of time as they danced. Now and then, they sat out a dance, and Logan fetched glasses of champagne for them. As the evening progressed, Regina became giddy from the dancing and the champagne—and with his nearness. For all his quiet manner, Will Logan was all male, and now that they were not talking business, he was full of fun and good humor.

Then the orchestra changed again, this time playing what Regina recognized as ragtime—a music that originated in America. It had started a few years ago and had only recently made its way across the Atlantic.

Once again, she protested that the music was too frenetic, too unfamiliar to her, but Logan would not heed her. He led her onto the floor and showed her the basic steps, and soon Regina fell into the swing of it, laughing out of pure delight. She did notice that at least half of the people stood on the sidelines, wearing disapproving frowns.

"Even though we Americans invented ragtime, many do not fully approve of it, considering it not quite proper and too racy," Logan said.

"I think it's wonderful music," Regina answered. "It's so joyous! I don't see how anyone could hear it and not *want* to dance, although I'm afraid I haven't quite caught on."

"You're doing fine, Mrs. Paxton, just fine."

They danced until Regina was exhausted, danced until the orchestra played the traditional last number of the evening, "Good Night, Ladies," at the stroke of twelve.

As they left the ballroom, Logan stopped and looked down at her. "Now I understand it's traditional for a gentleman to escort the lady for a few turns on deck. Shall we?"

"I'd like that. You seem to know what is traditional on board ship."

"If you mean, do I do this often, the answer is no. On my many trips back and forth across the

Atlantic, I have spent an evening like this on only three occasions that I can recall."

"And why is that, sir?"

"Because I have met only that many women with whom I would care to spend the evening in such a manner."

"Surely there must have been more than three!"

He smiled. "Perhaps I am too particular. Most of the women I became attracted to are either married or spoken for. Are you spoken for, Regina? May I call you by your first name? I feel as if we are old friends now. And you must call me Will."

Regina felt a flush of pleasure. It was so good to be here like this, with a man she could like and talk to; an attentive man who obviously was interested in her. "No, I am not spoken for, Will, and yes, you may call me by my given name."

Out on deck, the air was quite chilly, and Regina shivered involuntarily. Concerned, Will said, "Is it too chilly for you? Maybe we should go to your cabin for a wrap?"

"That would probably be a good idea."

They went down to the next deck below and along the passageway to Regina's cabin. At the door, Will held out his hand. "Your key, madam?"

She laughed and gave him her key. Just as the key rattled in the lock, the door to the adjacent cabin opened, and Peter Mondrain stood framed in the light coming from within. His eyes widened at the sight of Will opening Regina's door, and then his lips thinned in anger.

"We were going for a stroll on deck, Peter," Regina said quickly; too quickly, she realized. "It's quite chilly and we came down to fetch my wrap."

"I see," Mondrain said in an icy voice. Without another word, he turned on his heel and went back into his cabin, slamming the door.

Regina took an impulsive step toward his door, then changed her mind, her own temper stirring. He had no right to monitor her actions! She flushed slightly under Will's quizzical gaze, then went into her room. Will remained in the passageway while she found a wrap and threw it around her shoulders.

"Mr. Mondrain seemed somewhat disturbed," Will said tentatively, as they went back along the passageway.

"Well, he has no right to be. He is just an employee, or an employee-to-be," she said tautly. Then she softened her tone. "That was too harsh, perhaps. Peter is a dear friend, but that is *all* he is."

"That may be the way you think of him, but from the look he gave me, I'd say he was in love with you."

She was silent until they reached the promenade deck, wondering how much to confide in him. Then she said, "He has asked me to marry him."

"You turned him down, I gather? His age, perhaps?"

"That had something to do with it, true, but I don't love him. That's the real reason."

"Ah, well!" Will sighed dramatically. "I would imagine that a woman as beautiful as you has received many marriage proposals. I'm surprised that you have not remarried."

She was silent again, fearful that he would ask her how long she had been widowed. She wanted to see Will again, but what would he think when he learned that she was pregnant? Should she tell him, a man who was almost a total stranger, the truth?

Will gripped her arm lightly. "The men in London must be blind. Mark my words, Regina, you will be besieged by suitors in New York."

"You *are* a flatterer, Will Logan," she said with a nervous laugh. "Now tell me more about Tiffany and the company."

"What do you want to hear?"

"Anything and everything."

They strolled toward the bow in silence for a moment as Will arranged his thoughts. It was late and not many people were on deck. The air was cold but invigorating. Reaching the bow, they leaned on the railing. Salt spray stung their faces. Regina looked back over her shoulder. She could see the great funnels etched against the night; it was a stirring sight.

"One fact I find rather interesting," Will began. "Charles Tiffany's leadership of his company coincided almost exactly with your own Queen Victoria's reign of England. Both began in 1837. Your queen died in 1901. Charles Tiffany died in 1902."

"What does that signify?"

He gave a small shrug. "Nothing of any great importance, I suppose, but it strikes me as rather odd."

"Did Tiffany's really start as a stationery store, as I've read?"

"That is quite true. Charles and his partner, John Young, opened their Stationery and Dry Goods store on September 21, 1837, at 259 Broadway, opposite New York's city hall. Charles borrowed a thousand dollars from his father to start the store, and their receipts on opening day were the magnificent sum of five dollars, give or take a few cents, according to what story you hear."

"Then if Tiffany could become successful with a start like that, and only on a borrowed thousand dollars, I certainly should be able to make it."

"Of course, you have to take into consideration that he didn't start as a jeweler, but started by selling stationery and gifts. He got into jewelry gradually over the years. He also didn't have much competition until recently. There are a number of jewelry firms in New York now." He looked at her questioningly. "I hope I'm not being too personal, Regina, but what sort of financing do you have?"

She thought hard for a moment. Just how frank should she be with this virtual stranger? She had already confided quite a bit in him.

Will said quickly, "I'm sorry, I shouldn't have asked that. It's really none of my business."

"No, why shouldn't I tell you? I have over thirty thousand English pounds to invest."

He whistled softly. "Almost two hundred thousand dollars. That puts you in a strong financial position, but you also must consider that you may very well lose all of your inheritance."

"What makes you think the money is inherited?"

"Well, I just assumed that it came from your husband's estate," he said, taken aback. "You mean it doesn't?"

She shook her head. "It's money I earned myself. I did inherit a few thousand pounds when my mother died, but I invested that money to make what I now have."

"It must have been a wise investment."

"Well . . . most people wouldn't think so, but it turned out well in the end."

"May I ask what sort of an investment?"

Regina hesitated. How much should she tell this man? The champagne, the evening itself and the ease she felt with Will overcame her natural caution. As they strolled toward the other end of the ship, she found herself telling him about Brian Macbride, the expedition to Kashmir and the great find they had made.

Will shook his head. "That was a risky venture, but as they say, all's well that ends well. This Macbride, he sounds like quite a character."

"Oh, he is that!" Taking note of the enthusiasm in her voice, she said quickly, "He's a wild man, but he is a good gem hunter."

Will looked at her gravely. "He did well by you, that's evident. Do I detect romantic feelings toward him?"

Regina drew away. "You are being impertinent, Will!"

"You're right, I am. It's certainly none of my business."

She allowed him to take her arm again. "I suppose I am a little touchy where Mr. Macbride is concerned. We didn't part on the best of terms."

She suddenly felt tired. "Will, do you mind if I retire now? I find I'm exhausted."

"Of course, Regina," he said solicitously. "It is growing late."

He escorted her below and to her cabin. At the door, he took her hand and raised it to his lips; such a romantic gesture that Regina felt herself blushing with delight.

"I have had a most enjoyable evening, Regina. I am looking forward to seeing more of you during the rest of the voyage."

"And I you, Will. I fully intend to dig every morsel of information out of you that I can."

"I am at your service, madam." He released her hand and stepped back. "I'll say good-night now, Regina. Shall I see you at breakfast in the morning?"

"You will indeed. Good night, Will."

She stood in the doorway for a moment, watching him walk away. His slender figure was erect and moved with precision.

Bemused, Regina went into her cabin and closed the door. Latching it, she stood with her back pressed against the wood. She had thoroughly enjoyed Will's company and was grateful for his generosity in sharing his knowledge of the business with her. She was looking forward to seeing him in New York. However, there was still the matter of her pregnancy. . . .

A knock on the door startled her. Thinking it was Will returning for some reason, she opened the door.

Peter Mondrain stood in the doorway, his look cold and forbidding.

"Peter! What is it?"

"You have spent the evening with the American!"

"I danced with him, yes, and took air on deck."

"It is after two in the morning," he said accusingly.

"We talked business. Will is in the jewelry business, and I asked him a great many questions, as you would have heard if you had remained at the table."

"Will, is it? You think I am a fool, Regina? I could see from the way you looked at him, you are forming a romantic attachment for this fellow."

"And you are being a fool if you think that, Peter! I only met the man this evening."

"You seem to have become very familiar in just one evening, and as I recall, you hardly knew the man Macbride before you set off alone with him."

"It's hardly the same thing, Peter." She was rapidly becoming angry. "Besides, what business is it of yours? I am not obliged to explain my friendships to you."

"I offered to marry you, Regina, and you spurned me. Because I am too old for you. Now you are seeking a younger man to hide your shame."

"You are being ridiculous, Peter. I have no wish to continue this conversation. Good night."

She started to close the door in his face, but he slammed a palm against it. His thin lips curled contemptuously. "And what do you think he will feel when he learns that you are carrying another man's child?"

He stepped back then, letting her close the door. Regina was trembling with anger and indignation. Peter was consumed with jealousy, that much was obvious. Bringing him to America with her was beginning to look like a mistake. Was he going to act this way every time she even looked at another man? Perhaps when they arrived in New York, she should send him back to England. But she needed him badly; even Will had recognized his talents and how valuable he would be to her firm.

DURING THE NEXT TWO DAYS, Regina saw little of Mondrain, except at mealtimes. She tried, by being calm and friendly, to heal the breach; however, it soon became clear that he was not going to meet her halfway. Mondrain's manner was still sullen and cold, and when he did speak to her, it was only to make vague threats with allusions to her unmarried state and her pregnancy.

Now she was as angry as he. How could he sink so low? He had told her that he was her friend and had agreed willingly to come to work for her. She needed him, but what kind of working relationship could they have if he continued to act in such an immature and irresponsible fashion?

And she refused to let him dictate her life or decide who could be her friends!

She continued to spend a great deal of time with Will Logan, and her admiration and affection for him grew. She knew now that she could come to care for this man; she also knew that because of those feelings it was necessary to be honest with him. It would mean risking their developing relationship, yet she realized the strain she was under maintaining a lie. It would be better to tell him of her past now before things went any further, and one or both of them were hurt. If he was shocked and no longer wished to see her, which seemed quite possible, she would at least be left with pleasant memories. If he still wanted to see her after he learned the truth, it would be on an honest basis.

It was on their next to the last day at sea that she told Will the truth. They were strolling on the promenade deck. The breeze was fresh, the sky clear and, despite her nervousness, Regina felt surprisingly relaxed. She knew that whatever happened next between them, she would at least have the satisfaction of knowing that she had done the honorable thing.

As they crossed the afterdeck, she tugged at his arm, guiding him toward the rail. He looked at her in question.

"Let's stand here for a bit. I enjoy watching the wake, and I have something to tell you."

His glance told of his curiosity, but he remained silent.

She took her hand from his arm—she would use no wiles to influence him—and looked at him. "Will, I haven't known you very long, but I feel that we are becoming good friends."

His smile was boyish. "I'm glad to hear you say that. I feel the same way."

Regina gazed out at the wake, white and foamy against the blue. It wasn't easy to get the necessary words out. "You may not feel that way after you hear what I have to say, but I think that I must tell you."

He stared at her without speaking, waiting.

She took a deep breath. "Will, I am not, as I told you, a widow. In fact, I have never been married."

He moved as if to speak, and she held up her hand. "Wait, there is more. I am also carrying a child."

It was difficult to meet his eyes, but she forced herself to do so. She was surprised to see that he showed little reaction.

"The Irishman, Macbride, is the father, I suppose?"

She nodded mutely, trying to read his feelings in his eyes.

"And he refused to do the right thing and marry you?"

She shook her head vehemently. "I would never marry him."

"Methinks the lady doth protest too much," he said dryly. "At any rate, this does not change my feelings for you, Regina. You are hardly the first woman to whom this has happened."

"Then you're not surprised? Not shocked?"

"Surprised, yes. Shocked, no. I've traveled too far and seen too much to be bound by Victorian conventions. We all make mistakes, men and women alike, but women are the ones who have to pay for this particular error in judgment. It is unfair, but then who ever said the world was fair?" He smiled softly, taking her hand.

Regina felt tears of gratitude sting her eyes. "You're an understanding and wise man, William Logan."

"How wise, I'm not sure," he said ruefully. "I suspect that it has more to do with my feelings for you, my dear Regina, than anything else."

He raised her hands to his lips, and Regina felt herself grow weak with relief. She still had Will's friendship!

CHAPTER THIRTEEN

NEW YORK ROARED; or so it seemed to Regina.

Although London was one of the largest cities in the world, it seemed sedate by comparison to New York. In London the streets were not as crowded, and what crowds there were were orderly. Here, disorder and noise was everywhere. Trolley bells clanged; carriages rushed to and fro; and vendors shouted their wares. Regina had seen a few motorcars on the streets of London, but in New York there were many more, engines roaring, horns blaring.

It was intimidating, yet at the same time exhilarating, filling her with a sense of great excitement.

There were other differences also—taller buildings, ablaze with lights in the early evening, and the people. In London, especially in the better business districts, people dressed formally; in New York, within one long block, Regina saw people in every conceivable type of attire. Urchins were underfoot everywhere, playing in the streets, in constant danger of being run down by motorcars, horse-drawn trolleys and lorries.

Theodore Roosevelt was president, having assumed office in 1901 when President McKinley was assassinated. The country was thriving, in the throes of industrial expansion; the byword was

"Bully!" and the song heard everywhere in New York was "There'll Be a Hot Time in the Old Town Tonight." The brassy tune, President Roosevelt's favorite, seemed, to Regina, to express the spirit of the city.

It was autumn now, and the leaves in Central Park were beginning to turn; the nights were chilly.

Regina and Peter Mondrain had settled into a small hotel off Union Square. Matters had calmed down between the two of them, at least temporarily. She recalled the conversation they'd had just before their ship docked.

"If you like, Peter, you may return to England on the first available ship. I will pay your passage. I feel I owe you that."

"You no longer want me to work for you?" Mondrain had been cold and distant since the bitter scene in her cabin, but now he stared at her, obviously hurt—real or pretended, she was not sure.

"Of course, I still wish you to work for me. I need your unique talents. But I will not put up with your jealousy, Peter. I am my own woman, and my private life is my affair. I have no intention of coping with your jealous rages."

He hung his head in dejection, but again she wasn't sure whether or not he was feigning. "It was wrong of me, Regina, I fully realize that. It's just that I do love you...."

"Then you must realize something else. Nothing can ever come of that love."

"Yes, I know that now."

"Then do you believe we can work together, without personal concerns getting in the way?"

He finally looked at her directly, some of his old supercilious manner returning. "If I did not believe that, I would do as you suggested and take the first ship back to England."

"Good! It's settled, then."

Although she was anxious to get started on her project, Regina decided that first she should get a feel for New York. Will had suggested that she visit the other jewelry firms in the city, including Tiffany's.

"Will I see you there?" she had asked.

"Not likely," he said with his boyish grin. "I'm seldom on the floor, and I must write my report on my trip abroad, so I'll be occupied with that for several days. But I shall be free during the evening, and I was hoping we could spend that time together. That way I can at least show you New York at night."

"I would like that."

During the next week, Regina began to get to know the city. Part of each day, usually in the early morning, she roamed New York alone, visiting museums and art galleries and exploring Central Park, which she loved. But she didn't confine her explorations to the better part of the city; she walked through the Lower East Side, where most of the immigrants—much like the ones she had seen in steerage on the ship—lived and worked. It was like being in another city, another world. Traffic barely moved on the streets, since people thronged the sidewalks, spilling out into the streets that were hub-to-hub with wagons and peddlers' carts. She heard dozens of languages spoken, and what little English she heard was so thick that it was almost incomprehensible.

Will understood her curiosity about the city, but he warned her away from certain sections, such as the area under the Elevated that ran along Sixth Avenue, only a block away from the plush Madison Square. But Regina, seldom one to heed good advice, walked along Sixth Avenue and under the Elevated, where hordes of hungry, often dangerous men lived. She was reminded of the dock area in London, except there the rough men had been engaged in useful employment, while the men here were gaunt and unemployed. They stared at her with hungry eyes, but she escaped unmolested.

The evenings belonged to Will Logan. Every night, he called for her in a hack to take her to the theater. On one occasion they saw Ethel Barrymore, the star of *Captain Jinks of the Horse Marines*. They listened to the new opera sensation, Enrico Caruso, at the Metropolitan Opera. They attended the latest rage, vaudeville theater; Will told her that there were well over a thousand vaudeville theaters throughout the United States now, and that it all had begun in New York City. Regina sat enthralled as she watched acrobats, actors, jugglers, talking dogs, singers, dancers and comedians.

Will took her to a tiny storefront theater and they sat in darkness watching the newest addition to the field of entertainment, moving pictures. The picture was *The Great Train Robbery* and Regina was amazed as she watched the images flicker across the screen. She had no idea how such a marvel was accomplished.

All of the various entertainments were exciting, but Regina most enjoyed the places where the wealthy gathered. Will took her to Delmonico's, where they had champagne and dined on pheasant under glass. She watched wide-eyed as grand ladies swept in in their long gowns and spectacular jewelry; and their gentlemen, in evening clothes, also wore diamond studs and huge diamond rings on their fingers.

Will leaned across the table, a twinkle in his eyes. "Regina, you look like you've died and gone to heaven."

She laughed. "Perhaps I have. But actually I'm trying to total the worth of all the jewels in this room."

"I figured that was part of it. That's one reason I brought you here tonight. But wait until tomorrow. I have a surprise for you. I am off tomorrow, so I'm taking you to a place where you'll see jewels that will put these to shame."

"Where?" she asked excitedly.

"No." He waved away her question. "It's a surprise."

"But Will, all this must be very expensive. And you've been spending money on me all week. I feel that I'm taking undue advantage of your generous nature."

"Let me worry about that, Regina. I have earned good money these past few years at Tiffany's, and I have no one, really, to spend it on, except myself."

"You have no family?"

"No immediate family, no. I am an only child. My father died when I was ten years old, and my mother passed away two years ago."

"Then we have something else in common." She reached across the table to touch his hand. "I am an orphan, also." She told him the story of how she had been found in an alley by Adelaide.

"Your adopted mother sounds like she was a wonderful, caring person."

"Yes, she was, and I loved her deeply. I still miss her."

"She certainly brought you up well, with an independence of spirit and self-reliance." He glanced at her dessert plate. "I see you're finished. I'll call for the bill, and we'll go."

THE NEXT AFTERNOON, Will took her to the Waldorf-Astoria Hotel for tea. "This is your surprise?" she asked him as they strolled along Peacock Alley, a corridor almost a block long.

He nodded. "I think you'll be impressed. As you probably know, this is New York's finest and newest hotel," Will said. "It is viewed with respect by the elite the world over. It has one thousand modern bedrooms, I don't know how many fine restaurants, many courts and, of course, Peacock Alley, which runs straight through the double building."

Peacock Alley was a splendid promenade. The walls were honey-colored marble, reflecting rows of electric chandeliers overhead. Interspersed between the palms and doorways were groupings of armchairs and sofas, which were mostly filled, Regina noted as they strolled along. Many of the men wore Prince Albert coats, and the women were brilliantly dressed, and dazzling with jewels.

"Thank you for bringing me, Will." She squeezed his arm. "If I can get only a small percentage of these women to patronize my establishment, I'll have nothing to worry about."

"I thought you'd be impressed. It's said that the cream of New York society frequent Peacock Alley. In fact, it is considered very fashionable to be seen here, on the arm of a gentleman, of course." Will's tone became faintly satirical. "No proper young lady, you understand, would be seen here alone."

"I'll try to remember that."

"It's only a short carriage ride to the section of Fifth Avenue that is now inhabited by what the gentility regard as the vulgar rich. Their newly constructed mansions now line Fifth all the way to Central Park."

"I know, I've seen them on my excursions."

"Do you know the story behind the hotel? Why it is actually a double building with the names of two prominent families attached?"

"No, I don't think I do."

"Well, half of it was built on the spot where Mrs. Astor's house once sat, and the other half on the site of the home of her nephew, William Waldorf Astor."

"What was the reason for that?"

"A family feud. The nephew considered that he was the most important Astor, and that his wife should be *the* Mrs. Astor. But when William's father died, William's aunt let it be known throughout New York's social circles that *she* was *the* Mrs.

Astor. This caused a great deal of confusion, invitations being sent to the wrong Mrs. Astor and the like. William Waldorf declared war. He leveled his house and started construction of a hotel. The hotel shadowed Mrs. Astor's house and garden, so she demanded that her husband tear down their own house and construct another hotel.

"For a time, the feud raged between nephew and uncle, but in the end they realized, both being practical men, that it would be more cost-efficient to combine the two hotels into one. They named it the Waldorf-Astoria."

At the end of the story, Regina was laughing. "What a delightful story! Do you suppose I shall ever understand you Americans?"

"You will, in time. After all, many of us share the same roots as you. We're just a little less formal, perhaps cruder, more direct in our ways. You must remember that the Astor fortune originated with the fur trade, which spawned a great deal of violence and bloodshed. Is it any wonder that feuds and violence still flourish?

"In many parts of the world, blood and violence are a part of the jewelry trade also. Where great sums of money are involved, you are likely to find violence. Many famous gemstones have a bloody history."

Regina shivered slightly. "Thank God our part of the business is free of that."

"Don't be too sure, Regina. Just last year there was a jewel robbery at one of the smaller firms in New York. A clerk was killed, and the robbers got away with quite a bit of swag. You'll have to be security conscious." He glanced around. "Shall we have our tea now?"

She tucked her arm in his, smiling at him. "I think that is a wonderful idea, Will."

DURING THE FOLLOWING afternoons, Regina devoted her time to making a survey of the better jewelry firms in New York. Accompanied by Mondrain, she spent considerable time in each, pretending to be a shopper.

Naturally her first stop was Tiffany's, a large edifice with a cast-iron facade, located on Union Square. She stood with Mondrain before the large display window, admiring the variety and quantity of luxury items shown. Letters on the back wall of the window spelled out Tiffany & Co. New York.

On display was a bewildering assortment of items including: small statuary; vases; cigarette boxes; ornate clocks; a large candelabrum with a carved American Indian motif; and a gold place setting for twelve.

"'The Tiffany Style,'" Mondrain said with a sneer. "It's nothing more than art nouveau, with blatant use of eccentric curves and parabolic arches, insets and lilies, with gilded surfaces. It's vulgar, showing little grace and style."

Regina was forced to agree. "Yet how can you argue with success, Peter? I don't care much for the Tiffany style, either, but it has brought the firm worldwide fame and riches. Will says that the Tiffany motto has always been, 'Good design is good business.' I certainly don't agree that this display shows good design, yet it's a matter of personal taste, I suppose, and it has clearly caught the interest of the public. I happen to think that the buying public is ready to move into a new era of design, and I intend to do just that.'' She took Mondrain's arm. ''Let's venture inside.''

The inside was crowded, and no one took heed of them, so Regina could browse to her heart's content. She stood for a long time before a large, square glass case filled with a dazzling display of diamonds. She took note that all of the cases displaying jewels were designed to be airtight—a fact to remember. None of Slostrum's display cases had been so designed. After a thorough study of the ground floor, she left Mondrain still browsing and went up to the second floor of the five-story building.

It was clear that Tiffany's was much more than a jewelry store. On display were bronze and marble statuary, as well as tasteful furnishings in the Victorian manner.

After two hours, Regina and Mondrain left the store and strolled into the park across the way. They sat on a bench near the fountain, from which they could see the handsome facade of the Tiffany Building as well as other handsome buildings, mostly residences, around Union Square.

''I wonder if I'll ever have a firm as large and as prosperous as Tiffany's?'' she said wistfully. ''I certainly have a long way to go.''

''You must remember that Tiffany's started small, my dear.'' Since their tiff on board the ship, Mondrain had been formal with her. Now he seemed to relax a trifle. ''For what it's worth, I am confident that you shall succeed.''

"Thank you, Peter," she said with a grateful smile, touching his hand briefly. "Soon I'll have to start looking for a suitable building. Will advised me to look along Fifth Avenue. He said that businesses are moving north, and that there has been discussion at Tiffany's about relocating on Fifth, probably somewhere in the Thirties."

Visibly he withdrew. "Do you think it wise to seek advice from a man who is employed by a firm that will be your strongest competitor?"

"Peter!" she said in a warning voice.

He looked off. "I am only thinking of your interests, Regina. In the position he is in, he might deliberately lead you astray."

"I don't believe that for a minute. Will is a dear friend; he would never mislead me."

"You are naive, Regina," Mondrain said heavily. "I should think that your experience with Macbride would have taught you to be more cautious."

"Peter, we agreed not to discuss my private life again," she said, now angry. "Now this is the last time I want to hear you mention my personal affairs."

He bowed his head in acquiescence, but not before she had glimpsed a flash of rancor in his eyes.

AS SHE VISITED other stores in New York—both jewelry firms and the more diversified shops that also sold jewelry—Regina began to feel a sense of urgency. Soon her child would begin to show; she had to start her business before she was too far along or she would have to wait until after the baby was born, and that would never do.

A solution, of sorts, was offered to her.

She located premises that seemed ideal. The two lower floors of a building on Fifth Avenue, in the lower Thirties, were available. Before making a decision, she asked Will to inspect it with her.

"The location is good," he said as they stood before the building. "I predict that this will become the hub of businesses such as ours, and soon. This is in the strictest confidence, but Louis Tiffany has been negotiating for quarters not too far from here. The premises will not be available for a year or two, but I'm sure that he will move into this area eventually."

"But the rent is steep, Will, much higher than I had anticipated having to pay."

"Location is important, Regina, I'm sure you realize that. The extra you pay in rent could well be worth it in the long run. Can you get a long-term lease?"

"Oh, yes, I can get a five-year lease."

He nodded. "That's good. You should be well established at the end of five years."

"Or out of business," she said dolefully.

"Now that's not the Regina I thought I knew. Keep your attitude positive." He took her arm. "Let's go inside and see what it looks like."

Inside the lower floor was one large room, echoing emptily to the sound of their footsteps. They paused, looking around.

"I understand that it's been standing vacant for some time," Regina said. "It badly needs cleaning and fresh paint. The owner promised to do both if I took a lease for five years."

"What was it before?"

"The lower floor was a bank, and they had their offices upstairs."

"You'll need a show window in the front. Did the owner offer to put one in for you?"

"I didn't think to ask."

"If you decide to take it, demand that he install a display window. I'm sure he'll agree to it, with such a long lease, considering it's been vacant for so long. Now let's take a look at the second floor."

The stairs were in the rear. Upstairs was a long corridor, running all the way to the front, with several doors opening off it. The lighting was quite dim.

"Is the building electrified?" Will asked.

"Yes. Some of the offices are quite small, so some of the partitions will have to be taken out to make a large workroom in the front. But the other offices are large enough to serve as workrooms, for Peter Mondrain and others."

"Is the owner willing to stand the cost of the alterations?" Will was walking along the corridor, opening doors and peering into the offices.

"I mentioned it to him and he said he would consider it. Again on a long lease."

"If you take it, make that another stipulation before you sign anything." Turning away from the last office, Will nodded. "I think it would fit your needs nicely."

"Then you think I should take it?"

"I do."

"Will..." She hesitated, choosing her words carefully. "Something has been in my mind. I don't know what you earn at Tiffany's. Quite a bit, I suspect. Would you come to work for me? I really need someone with your experience as a buyer. I would try to match your present salary," she finished in a rush.

"The money is not that important to me," he said with a wave of his hand.

She let her breath go. "Does that mean you'll do it?"

"I might. But I have a condition."

Staring at him, her thoughts flew back to the day Brian had agreed to her financing the expedition to Kashmir, and her condition that she accompany him. "What condition?" she asked warily.

"That you marry me."

Although she supposed that it really shouldn't have been such a surprise, she was staggered by the proposal. "Oh, Will! I don't know what to say."

"I know, you're still in love with this Macbride fellow," he said with a nod.

"That's not true!" she said hotly.

"But I'll take the chance that you'll get over him in time and come to love me. Regina, your child will need a father."

"You're asking me to marry you out of pity."

"Not so. I love you deeply, Regina."

Shaken, she said, "I...I must have time to think about it."

"I realize that."

"There is one thing. If I did marry you and you go to work for me, I must insist. The firm will be called Paxton Jewels. That may not be fair to you, but I want the Paxton name connected to the firm. I feel that I owe my mother that."

He looked back at her steadily. "I have no quarrel with that. It's your dream, I know, and the money is yours, after all."

Regina stared at him; this kind, attractive man was offering her a solution to her most pressing problem. Dare she accept it? If she married him, she would have a father for her child, a place in respectable society and the guidance and help of an expert in the field of gemstones. And what would he receive in exchange? A woman who was not certain that she knew what real love was; a woman who was carrying another man's child; a child to which this man would have to give his name and support. Was it a fair exchange? Could she be a good wife to him?

Looking into his eyes, a wave of affection for him washed over her, and she placed her hand upon his arm. She had made up her mind.

CHAPTER FOURTEEN

BRIAN MACBRIDE could not understand what was happening to him; in several ways he was a changed man, and he blamed it all on Regina. Bloody female!

It had been well over three years since he had last seen her, but she was in his thoughts constantly—and he had been unable to find true satisfaction with any other woman.

That, as bad as it was, was not the worst of it; he had become, if not frugal, at least sensible about money. He had not waited until all the proceeds of their Kashmir venture had been spent before embarking on another expedition, a trip to Australia to search for opals, which had netted him little more than his expenses. Most of the money from his share of their find in Kashmir was still on deposit in a London bank.

It was the first time in his life that Brian had ever had a bank account. Regina's scathing words at their bitter parting about his lack of maturity and improvidence had stung. The words came back to him like a mocking echo every time he began to spend money lavishly.

He also no longer gained his former satisfaction from gem hunting. To be honest with himself, he couldn't really blame Regina for that. Gem hunting wasn't what it once had been. There were no new fields, no new finds; what fields there were had been picked over. Even the gold fields—Deadwood, Leadville, the Yukon—were long past their heyday.

In Australia, he had met a friend, a man who had been a gem hunter for twenty years, but was now a gem trader. "It's all over for us, Macbride," Jim Branton had told him. "Soon we're going to be as extinct as the dodo bird."

"Oh, I think you're being unduly pessimistic, Jim," Brian had said. "It's just a lull. Other fields will open up sooner or later."

"You're dreaming, Irisher. And even if new fields *are* found, they'll do men like us little good. Governments everywhere are tightening down. We'll no longer be able to just walk in, make our find and walk out with the goods. If we do and we're caught, we'll find ourselves in jail."

"Is that why you turned trader, Jim?"

Jim Branton had shrugged. "It was either that or starve. At least I'm still in the trade. Gems is all I know, Irisher. Besides, I'm finding that it's not a bad life. I'm making fair money, I get to travel and I'm not tied down to some job, with some master cracking the whip over me."

"Still, it's *business*, Jim. Bloody hell, I should think you'd be bored to tears."

"Buying and selling gems, Irisher, may not be as exciting as making a good find, but it's far from boring. You have to always have your wits about you. Hell, you already know half of the business, the selling part. To be a good gem trader, you only have to learn how to buy at a low price and sell high."

More out of curiosity than anything else, Brian decided to give it a try. There was nothing else to do at the present time. He could invade the South African preserve of De Beers again, and try to sneak out with a few diamonds, but he had no taste for it anymore. It was not that he was more afraid of the danger than he had once been, but Regina's words, calling him little more than a thief, stuck in his craw.

Withdrawing ten thousand pounds from his bank account, Brian took a ship to the island of Ceylon, which he knew was a good source of sapphires. It wasn't until he got off the ship at Colombo that he remembered that the sapphire was Regina's favorite gemstone. Damn the woman! Was she to haunt him forever?

He was immediately assailed by evil-smelling gem touts when his purpose there was discovered. He thanked the saints for his knowledge of gems, because more than half of what he was offered were fakes; but after a week and the investment of most of his ten thousand pounds, he had purchased a fair number of good stones. To his disgust, he often found himself examining the sapphires closely, looking for a star.

The logical thing to do now was to sail back to London or Amsterdam to sell his parcel of stones. Instead he decided to go to the United States. He rationalized that it was because the United States was becoming a booming market for sapphires, and that he had never been there; but he knew, in his heart of hearts, that he was going because Regina was there.

New York was said to be the best market in the United States, but perversely, when his ship docked in San Francisco, Brian sold the sapphires there. Regina was in New York, he told himself, so he intended to avoid that particular city. There would be too much pain involved in being so close and not being able to visit her.

Brian was pleased at his astuteness as a gem buyer; and was even more pleased when he realized a profit of thirty percent on the sale, which he knew to be substantial for a deal on the West Coast.

It was clear to Brian that he had the makings of a gem trader, but was that what he really wanted to do with his life? It was a good question. No matter how he looked at it, gem trading was a business; and before he had known Regina, Brian had scorned going into business of any kind. He realized, after the fact, that he had secretly hoped that he would fail at gem trading. But he had not failed and now he must decide which direction his life should take.

He went to Montana, hoping that his decision would be made for him. The jeweler to whom he had sold his stones in San Francisco had told him that, just before the turn of the century, sapphires had been discovered there. Most gem dealers did not know that the United States had started mining sapphires, and the value of the Montana gems had yet to be established; but Brian had little interest in their value. He just wanted to make a find.

The month he spent in Montana was a waste of time. The sapphires there were not out in the open for picking, and all of the good claims were already taken. From Montana, he went to Deadwood, South Dakota, in the hope of finding gold. Once again, he came up empty-handed. Deadwood was pretty much a ghost town. He hunted the gullies and streambeds in the area for another month and found only a few grains of color.

Next he dropped farther south, looking along the lower Mississippi River for freshwater pearls, another fairly recent discovery. He found many pearl hunters already there ahead of him, and it didn't take him long to realize that he was, once again, wasting his time.

The irony of his travels hadn't escaped him—for three months he had been drifting closer and closer to New York, and to Regina. Bloody hell, he might as well give in to his secret desire. Wasn't it natural that he should be curious about how she was faring? She might not even be in New York; she might have returned to England, for he was sure that she had failed by this time in her foolish business venture.

He took the train to New York.

It was November when he arrived, and the weather was cold. He found a decent but reasonably inexpensive hotel on lower Broadway. Now that he was settled, how would he find her? he wondered. It was a huge, bustling city of strangers, and one lone lady from England could easily be swallowed up in it.

His search was made easy for him. The next morning, as he left his hotel to go to breakfast at a restaurant across the street, he bought a newspaper, Hearst's *Morning Journal*, from a newsboy. In the restaurant, after he had ordered his breakfast, he leafed through the paper. And there, near the front, he came across a half-page advertisement. The advertisement had the picture of a woman wearing a diamond necklace and a large diamond brooch. The lettering proclaimed, "Jewels for every taste and every occasion—Paxton Jewels," followed by an address on Fifth Avenue.

Stunned, Brian read the advertisement again. It was a simple, understated advertisement, yet very effective. Then, despite himself, he began to grin. By all the saints, the lass had made it! His spirits rose; no matter what he had thought, or what he had told Regina, he was happy for her.

After breakfast, he walked up Fifth to the address given in the paper. And there it was, located in a handsome building, with the name in a tasteful scroll over the entrance: Paxton Jewels.

Brian stopped before the display window, staring in admiration. Unlike many such display windows, it was uncluttered. On a tilted board, covered with rich black velvet, was a simple display: a diamond necklace, and a man's pocket watch, with its lid open, the numerals in small diamonds. There were also several rings: one ruby; one topaz; one diamond; and a large moonstone ringed with tiny sapphires. The settings, like the display, were simple yet elegant. Brian had to smile at another piece—a brooch with a large blue sapphire, surrounded by diamonds. Naturally she would have a piece featuring a sapphire. Next to the brooch was a crystal-and-silver vase, containing one red rose.

On the wall behind the display was a discreetly lettered sign with the same wording he had seen in the advertisement: Jewels for every taste and every occasion—Paxton Jewels.

It was an attractive window, and Brian was certain that Regina had designed and arranged it.

He took a step toward the door, then stopped, fingering his beard. He had not yet shaved it off. He glanced down at his clothes. They were scruffy and worn from all the traveling he had done over the past few months. With Regina prosperous, and it was evident that she was, he could not appear before her dressed like this; he had to look his best. He recalled passing both a barbershop and a men's clothing store on his walk up Fifth Avenue.

Before he faced Regina, he wanted to get rid of the beard and dress himself in a completely new outfit.

FOLLOWING THEIR MARRIAGE, Regina and Will had rented a large flat on 23rd Street, just off Broadway, and they still lived there, in spite of the recent prosperity of the store. The apartment was tastefully furnished, and it was large enough for their present needs.

After breakfast every morning, Will left for the store, but Regina usually lingered awhile at home, spending some time with her son, Michael, who was now three years old.

As she played with the boy in the room they had turned into a nursery, Regina reflected that there could scarcely be any doubt that Michael was Brian's son. He had the same blazing red hair, bright blue-green eyes and forceful disposition.

She had experienced many moments of doubt before the baby was born. Despite his many disclaimers to the contrary, Regina wasn't sure that Will would really accept another man's child as his own. Her fears had proved to be groundless. From the very first, Will had adored the boy, and she had never noticed any reservations in his affection toward her son. He had been very pleased when she named the boy Michael, after Will's own father.

Just a few weeks ago, Will had brought home a kitten, a ball of gray-and-white fur. He had reddened under Regina's quizzical stare and had said defensively, "A boy should have a pet. My father brought me a puppy when I was very little, and I spent many pleasurable hours with that animal. A dog really isn't practical in a flat like this, but I thought a kitten . . ."

Now Regina smiled to herself as she watched Michael playing with the kitten. He loved the little animal but had to be watched constantly when it was near him so that in his enthusiasm he did not do the creature serious harm.

Will was a kind, thoughtful man, a good father and a good husband. Regina had been doubtful at first about the physical side of their marriage, since she did not love him in the way she had loved Brian Macbride. But Will, apparently realizing this, had been patient and considerate, and their love life was . . . well, comfortable and satisfying. Oh, she didn't burn with passion when Will touched her, as she had with Brian, but that was perhaps to the good. Her love for Brian had consumed her, and in the end she had been deeply hurt by it. And to her surprise, she had come to love Will. In addition, she respected him and was grateful for his kindness and sensitivity. If the love did not run as deep and hot as the love she had felt for Brian, she was reasonably content. And she had the business, and little Michael. . . .

Her head came up as she heard the front door open and close. "Nanny," she called, "is that you?"

"Yes, ma'am."

They had been fortunate in finding Bethel Clark, a middle-aged Englishwoman who had come to this country seven years earlier to find work as a nanny. The family she had been with for a number of years had moved to California. Nanny had not wished to leave New York, and she had run an advertisement, which Regina had seen. They had employed her right after Michael was born and had not regretted their decision for a moment—Nanny was a rare treasure.

Regina went into the parlor where Nanny was removing her coat; she had been out shopping for food. She was a tall, thin woman, a spinster, but with none of the sourness often attributed to women of that state. She adored young Michael, yet she could be firm with him and did not spoil him. In addition, she was a splendid housekeeper and a good cook. The flat had servant quarters in the rear.

"It is brisk out today, Mrs. Logan," Nanny informed Regina.

"Yes, autumn is indeed here. I gave Michael his breakfast, Nanny, and he is occupied with the kitten at the moment. I shall get dressed for work now."

As Regina left the room, Nanny called after her, "Dress warmly, Mrs. Logan. There is a nip in the air."

ONE THING REGINA LIKED about the flat was its location. It was only a fifteen-minute walk from the store, and she always walked there unless the weather was foul. A brisk walk always put her in a good mood for a day's work.

She walked rapidly—her stride vigorous, well aware of the admiring glances of the men she met. She had regained her figure without trouble, and according to Will, she was even more beautiful than before her pregnancy.

"Pride of motherhood, no doubt, dear," she had responded.

Now she lengthened her stride and stepped out briskly, enjoying the crisp feel of autumn in the air. She had fallen in love with New York. She loved its energy, its bustle, its brashness and the diversity of its racial mix. She even liked the people who came into the store to shop; although there were exceptions, the rich here were not as haughty as their counterparts in England.

She approached the front of the store now, and as was her habit, she stopped for a moment to study the window display. It was simple, almost stark, unlike the clutter that filled Tiffany's display window. Early on she had decided that simplicity was the key, and she practiced it in the window, the interior of the store and the advertisements she wrote herself.

She smiled at the brooch with the blue sapphire. She had yet to find a star sapphire in its pristine state. The only stars that came into her possession were either already set in a piece, or had already been cleaned, cut and polished. Will knew of her urgent desire for a just-discovered star sapphire that she could make her own and had promised to look for one on his twice-yearly buying trips to Europe. So far he had been unsuccessful in his quest.

It was time, she thought, to change the display, something she did at least once a month.

Looking at the window, she thought back to the day they had opened the shop. They had experienced hard times during that first year of operation, and if she hadn't had funds to fall back on, they would never have made it.

She had to give much of the credit to Will. He was a shrewd gem buyer. They had yet to lose money on any gem he had purchased. The buying was strictly his department. Regina handled the day-to-day administration of the firm, the arrangement of the displays, wrote all of their advertisements and designed many of the basic pieces Mondrain made. She had found that she was very good at all four activities.

Smiling, happy with her life, she went into the store. Three clerks—two men and one woman—snapped to attention, then relaxed when they recognized her. There were only two customers in the store, and they were both browsing. From the beginning, Regina had warned her clerks never to pressure a potential customer; allow them to browse to their heart's content. When and if they expressed an interest in some item, then salesmanship came to bear, but always low-key, never pressure selling.

One of the clerks came to meet her. "Mrs. Logan, your husband had to go uptown on business, but he said to tell you that he should be back in time to take you to lunch."

"Thank you, Bert."

She spoke warmly to the other two clerks, then headed upstairs. On the second floor, she turned right toward the work area. Three women were busy in the big room, cleaning, rough polishing and sorting. Regina and Will tried not to buy any more roughs than necessary to keep production flowing; less time, effort and money were involved if the stones they bought had already gone through the preliminary stages.

Regina spoke pleasant greetings to all three women. She made it a point to speak personally to every employee each morning. She was proud of her employment record. In the three years that Paxton Jewels had been in business, they had not lost a single employee. In the beginning, salaries had been kept small, but as her business flourished, Regina saw to it that every employee received the appropriate raises that their particular skills warranted.

She went down the hall to the open door of the office that Eugene had taken over as his cutting room. Regina had sent for Eugene immediately after opening the store, and he had been well worth her investment of time and money. He was rapidly becoming one of the best gem cutters in the business.

She poked her head in the door. "Good morning, Eugene."

He glanced up from his work and smiled. "Good morning, Regina. How are you this morning?"

"I'm fine. I have been thinking seriously about your request for an assistant. I think it's about time you had one, considering your work load of late. I'll see what I can do about employing one."

"Thank you. I appreciate it."

"Did you have a nice time at the theater last night with May?" Eugene had been courting one of the girls in the sorting room, a shy, gentle girl of Eugene's own age.

Eugene blushed. "How did you learn about that?"

Regina laughed. "There are no secrets from me, Eugene. I won't allow it. Actually May told me about it. How did you two enjoy the play?"

"Well, it was Shakespeare, a play that I had seen a number of times back home. I didn't think the actors were up to snuff."

"Eugene," she said, frowning with mock severity, "you're going to have to start thinking of America as your home."

"I don't know as I'll ever be able to do that."

Regina went on down the hall to another office, one taken over by Peter Mondrain. It was closed and locked, of course; Mondrain was a creature of habit.

Regina hesitated a moment before knocking. She had been certain that he would fly into a cold rage and return to England when she told him that she was marrying Will. Instead he had looked at her distantly and said, "You once told me you would never marry a man unless you loved him. You love this man, then?"

"Yes, I do," she had said defiantly. "At least, I love him enough."

Mondrain had remained in her employ, and she gave him a large share of the credit for their success. If possible, his designs had actually improved; they were innovative, provocative, daring, ahead of their time. Many of his pieces had startled the jewelry trade, and initially she had heard whispers to the effect that his pieces were a disaster, that they would never sell. Well, the trade had been proven wrong in that respect. They still worked well together on the pieces Regina designed, but there was a distance between them similar to that which had existed in the early days of their acquaintance. Where Will was concerned, Mondrain was barely civil. Typically Will didn't resent this, merely commenting that as long as his pieces sold, Mondrain could be as distant as he liked.

Now she knocked on the door. "Just a moment, Regina," came Mondrain's voice.

A key rattled in the lock, and the door swung open.

"Good morning, Peter," she said brightly.

"Good morning, Regina." No more "my dear," or "my very dear."

Her glance went to his worktable. He had been working on a diamond-studded cigarette case, which would be a thing of beauty, and very expensive when complete. Cigarette cases were very popular and Regina knew that she would have no trouble moving it, no matter what the price.

"I see you're about finished with the case."

He nodded. "It will be done by the end of the day."

"That design for a bracelet I showed you yesterday, the one we discussed at length?"

"I remember."

"I worked on it last night, incorporating your suggestions, but I'm still not satisfied with it. Will thought it was very good, but I tore it up. I'm starting over."

"Your husband is a knowledgeable gem buyer, but that knowledge does not extend to design."

She felt a stir of temper. "I value his opinion highly."

"I am sure, but then he is your husband, is he not?"

She sighed, resigned to the fact that she would never reconcile this man with Will. "At any rate, I shall do the design over. I do like the concept, but it needs something." She brightened. "I'm sure that I will accomplish something in the end that will meet with your approval."

"I am confident that you shall, Regina."

"I'll see you later, then, Peter." With a wave, she left him and went along the hall to her own office, leaving the door open, as was her wont. If any employees wished to see her, the door was always open to them.

Her office was large, but incredibly cluttered: old jewelry designs lying around; ledgers open on her desk and on top of file cabinets; invoices scattered here and there; and pages torn from newspapers carrying old advertisements for Paxton Jewels. Regina was neat about her person, and their flat was kept immaculate by Nanny, but that neatness did not apply to her office. She knew that Adelaide would have thrown up her hands in horror. To anyone who dared comment on the clutter, Regina always had the same reply, "This is where I work. At least any visitors will know that I have been busy."

Tomorrow, Friday was payday, and she had to work on the payroll. Behind her old, scarred mahogany desk, she bent to her task, occasionally pushing her hands through her hair when her figures did not come out right.

She had been at work for two hours when she heard a sound in the doorway. "Yes?" she said before she glanced up.

When she did look up, she froze, her mouth open in complete astonishment.

"Hello, lass."

"Brian!" She clapped her hands together. "My God!"

Without thinking, her heart thrashing in her chest, she was on her feet and around the desk, hurrying toward him.

Seeing her there, hair mussed but more beautiful even than he remembered, Brian felt his heart ache. Bloody hell, how he had missed her!

As she stopped before him, Brian took her hands in his, staring hungrily down into her face; and for a brief moment, Regina thought he was going to take her into his arms. Everything else washed from her mind, and she found herself yearning to be held in his arms, to feel his lips on hers.

Then he stepped back slightly, still holding her hands captive. "You haven't changed much, lass."

"Neither have you, you bloody Irishman!" she said, laughing shakily. "But how do you come to be here?"

"I was in New York, and I happened to read an advertisement in the newspaper. And—" he grinned, winking "—here I am." He freed one hand to wave it around. "I must admit that I was wrong, by the saints I was! I'm after thinking that you've done what you set out to do, and more."

"Yes, Brian, I have prospered. And you, what's happened to you?"

"Nothing much has changed. Still roaming the world, rooting out gems . . ."

A cough from the doorway interrupted him. Regina looked past him. "Oh, Will!" She freed her hands from Brian's grip. "Come in, Will, I want you to meet an old friend."

As Will came in, she said, "Brian Macbride, I'd like you to meet my husband, Will Logan."

Brian's face took on a stunned expression. "Your husband . . . ! But the name of the firm is Paxton."

"I did that to honor my mother. And Will, being the nice person he is . . ." She took Will's hand and squeezed hard. "He agreed to let me use my maiden name on the firm."

Brian's face had turned cold and forbidding. "How long have you been married?" he said harshly.

"Over three years now."

"Sure, and you didn't wait very long, did you?" he said in a grating voice.

Then without another word, he wheeled and strode out of the office, limping ever so slightly.

CHAPTER FIFTEEN

REGINA TOOK A STEP after Brian, calling out, "Brian, wait!"

Then Will placed a hand on her arm, gently, and she stopped, still staring at Brian's rapidly retreating back.

"I gather that was your Irishman?" Will said.

"Not *my* Irishman!" she snapped, then softened her tone. "But that was him, yes."

"Michael's father?"

"Yes, Will." She finally looked at him.

His mouth was drawn, revealing his inner tension. "How did he come to be here?"

"I really don't know. He said he was in the city and saw our advertisement in the newspaper. He was only here for a moment or so before you came in."

"I wonder why he came to see you, since you told me that you parted on acrimonious terms."

"I suppose it was out of simple curiosity, to see how I was faring."

Will's stare was penetrating. "If that was the only reason he came to see you, then why did he stalk away in anger when he learned you were married?"

"I don't know, Will." She sighed, running her hand through her hair in a distracted gesture. "I can't read the man's mind."

"How about you, Regina? Do you have any feeling in you for him? Do you still love him?"

"Don't be ridiculous, Will! You know how I feel. Whatever feeling I had for Brian Macbride is long since dead." And yet, even as she spoke the words, she had to wonder if she was being entirely truthful.

BRIAN WAS RAGING as he stormed out of the building. Damn the bloody woman! How could she be so fickle! It seemed she could hardly wait to find a man to marry after their parting of the ways.

A small voice of reason spoke in his mind: How can you fault her for that, Brian Macbride. Weren't you the one who spurned *her*?

He refused to listen to the voice, shutting his mind to it as he strode on. His anger cooled slightly after a few blocks, and he suddenly felt worn and defeated. Not until this moment had he realized— or at least admitted to himself—how much he loved her.

Why couldn't she have waited until they could see and speak to each other again? He was sure that during the electric moment when she had rushed to him across her office, that the old attraction still existed. He could still see it—the anticipation in her eyes, the softening of her mouth. She had expected him to take her into his arms and kiss her. He still didn't know why he hadn't, but something had held him back.

His anger receded as he walked on, at least enough to allow him to think more rationally. He took note of the hurrying people on the street, of the elegant shops along Fifth Avenue, and an idea began to take shape in his mind. Somehow he had to find a way to show Regina that he was not the irresponsible wild man she thought him to be; somehow he had to prove to her that she had made a grave mistake in not waiting for him.

TWO WEEKS LATER Brian was in London, in Andrew Slostrum's office. Slostrum still had a sleek, prosperous look, although his hair was beginning to gray and there were new lines in his face, making Brian realize that the man was growing old.

"It's glad I am to see you, Andrew."

"And I you, Brian. No stones to sell me this time?" Slostrum asked with arched eyebrows. "I did quite well with the stones you brought back from Kashmir."

"Not this time, Andrew. Gem hunting isn't what it once was. But I do have something else to sell you."

"Indeed. What is that?"

"Like I said, gem hunting is not a good trade nowadays. So I'm going into the jewelry business, with a firm of my own."

Slostrum reared back in astonishment. "You, Brian? In business?" He laughed. "You can't be serious!"

"Quite serious."

Slostrum shrugged. "What does that have to do with me?"

Brian took a deep breath. "I have some funds, but not enough to set up the kind of business I want. For that reason . . ." He gestured grandly. "I'm willing to take you in as a partner, Andrew."

Slostrum shook his head pityingly. "I've always known you were a madman, Brian, but you have to be completely insane to believe that I would finance competition for myself, even if I was only a partner. People would wonder what I'm thinking of."

"Not here, Andrew, not in England."

Slostrum stared. "Where, then?"

"In New York."

"Brian, I am a busy man. I don't have the time to idle away listening to such nonsense."

"Why is it nonsense? Other jewelry firms have established New York shops. Cartier's, for one."

"I am well content with my firm here. I have no desire to branch out. Aside from the huge investment, it would necessitate traveling back and forth."

"Sure, and the traveling wouldn't be necessary. I can handle the New York end. As for the money, I happen to know that you are a wealthy man, bucko. Invest some of it. A new venture such as this one would make a new man of you. Surely you're not too old to feel a bit of excitement at the thought?"

"My age has nothing to do with it," Slostrum said in a growling voice. "Why should I risk money in such an endeavor? Indeed. And with you as a partner? You are a wild man, Brian Macbride."

"Sure, but I'm honest and trustworthy," Brian said with a wide grin. "You have told me that yourself."

"That has nothing to do with running a business."

"I've changed," Brian said, suddenly grave. "I'm no longer running around the world hunting gems. For the past year, I've been doing some gem trading, and doing very well at it, if I do say so myself."

Slostrum stared at him narrowly. "You, a gem trader?"

"It's true, I swear." Brian held up one hand.

"That still doesn't mean that you can run a business."

"I know gems as well as any man. Whatever else needs be, I can learn."

"But why America? And why should I become partners with you?"

"The answer to both questions is Regina Paxton." Brian leaned forward, his gaze intent on the other man's face. "She is in New York City, and she has made good on her promise. She is the proud owner of Paxton Jewels, and is doing very well, by all accounts."

Slostrum grunted as though struck, his face reddening.

Ah, the hook is in, Brian thought, now I just have to reel him in. "She did us both harm, Andrew. As soon as she got her share of the sale of our goods, she ran off to America, leaving me without so much as a good-bye. I was ready to marry the woman." The saints forgive me for the small lie, he thought virtuously, I *would* have married the bloody woman if she had given me time. "And you, bucko, you yourself told me how she had wronged you, thinking of setting up here in competition with you, and stealing away your designer."

"Not only that, but a cutter I was nursing along to take Giles's position. But I didn't know she was in the United States."

"Then you see?" Brian spread his hand. "I'm after thinking we both have good reason to show her the error of her ways. You go partners with me in New York, and together we'll drive her to the wall, put her out of business. I'll draw on your knowledge of the business. That, combined with what I know about buying and selling gems, will be too much for her."

Slostrum was finally looking interested. "You think that's possible?"

"I'm confident that we can do it."

"Indeed. God knows I would like to get back at the woman for betraying me." Unconsciously, Slostrum put a hand to his mouth to gnaw on a knuckle. "Still, it would mean a considerable investment, just for vengeance."

"Vengeance would only be a part of it," Brian said in his most beguiling voice. "There's money to be made, Andrew. New York is full of the money-eyed gentry, eager to spend on jewelry. And wouldn't it be a coup for you in the trade to be able to spread the news that Slostrum's is opening a branch in America?"

Still nibbling on his knuckles, Slostrum stared directly at Brian; but from the blank look in his eyes, Brian knew that he didn't really see him.

"I'm thinking that such a chance may never come your way again, Andrew," he urged. "You'll only be investing half of the money necessary, and I'll be doing most of the work. In return, you'll have the prestige of your name on a house in America, and a chance to put Regina in her place."

Slowly Slostrum focused on him. "Indeed. I shall need to give it some thought, Brian. It's a serious decision."

FOR WEEKS, Regina looked up hopefully every time she heard someone approach her office. But it was never Brian. She was torn by two opposite emotions: a desire to see him again; and a wish that he had never reentered her life. She had a good life, she had a kind and loving husband, and if Brian was in New York, there was always the danger that he would see Michael. There was little doubt that he would know immediately that the boy was his son.

She finally concluded that Brian had no intention of ever seeing her again. She determined to put him out of her mind, but she soon found that it wasn't that easy. At odd times of the day or night, she caught herself thinking of him, until finally something happened that disturbed her deeply.

Will, normally an ardent and virile lover, had made love to her only once since Brian had appeared at the store unexpectedly. On this particular evening, Will had several drinks before dinner and two brandies afterward, far more than was normal. When they retired, he turned to her immediately.

Usually gentle and considerate, his manner was rough, but Regina placed the blame on the alcohol he had consumed and endured without complaint. When he entered her, she turned her face away from his alcohol-scented breath and closed her eyes.

Suddenly, across the screen of her mind, she saw Brian's face, his red hair and beard like a flame. He winked at her, and in her almost dreamlike state, the man making love to her became Brian, and she felt arousal and response for the first time. As her passion broke, she rose, clutching Will to her fiercely, crying out, "Brian!"

Will went rigid and immediately disengaged himself from her. He rolled over onto his back, and in the faint light she could see him staring at the ceiling. It was only then that she realized she had spoken Brian's name aloud.

"Will?" She touched him on the shoulder.

He flinched away. "You were thinking of the Irishman, weren't you?"

"Of course not! How could you think such a thing?"

"You spoke his name."

"You must have misunderstood me, darling—" She broke off with an exasperated sigh. "No, I refuse to lie to you, Will. You're right, I did speak his name. The only excuse I can give is that I was greatly upset at seeing him again, and worried that he might return."

His head turned on the pillow. "You haven't heard from him since that day?"

"No, I think the shock of my being married was too much for him. Brian Macbride's pride is easily injured. I'm sure he's gone back to England by this time. The thing that really worries me is that someday he might see Michael. If he does, he'll know immediately that Michael is his son."

"Maybe he should know. He is the boy's father, after all."

"No!" she said vehemently. "I don't want him to ever know. He has no rights to Michael. He walked away from me, and as far as I'm concerned, he walked away from his son as well. Maybe that's wrong of me, but it's the way I feel. You can understand that, can't you, darling?"

"I suppose so, Regina," he said heavily. "But I'm not sure it's the right thing."

"I don't care about that. To Michael, *you* are his father, and I want it to remain that way."

"But is it right for Michael to never know his true paternity?"

"What good would it do for him to know? It would only confuse him. You're all the father he'll ever need."

He fell silent. After a moment, her hand crept across the bed to touch him. "Will, I do love you."

"Do you?" he asked tonelessly.

"I do, Will. Surely you must know that by now."

She leaned over to kiss him, her hair falling across his face. For a moment, he was unresponsive. Then his arms came up to enfold her, and he said huskily, "And I love you, Regina. I love you more than life itself. I would do almost anything to keep your love."

THE CHRISTMAS SEASON, the busiest time of year in the jewelry business, was upon them. Regina immersed herself in work, trying to forget Brian, and for the most part, succeeding.

It was their best holiday season to date; so good, in fact, that she was able to give her employees a nice bonus for Christmas, the first time she had been able to afford such generosity.

Shortly after the New Year, Brian Macbride returned.

Since it was their slack period now, Will hadn't gone into work early as was his habit most of the year. He was in the dining room, dawdling over a cup of coffee and the morning newspaper when Regina came in.

"Good morning, darling," she said cheerfully.

When he didn't look up to greet her, she peered closely at him. His face was cold and forbidding. She said uncertainly, "Will?"

He looked up, his lips tight. Without a word, he handed her the newspaper and tapped a forefinger on the folded page.

Regina took it, mystified. Then as she read what he had indicated, her knees went weak, and she had to sit down.

It was a half-page advertisement: "Grand opening, January 15. Slostrum and Macbride—Fine Jewelry. Free refreshments served. The public is invited."

"Dear God," she whispered. "I don't believe it! Mr. Slostrum and Brian are starting a jewelry firm here!"

"You knew nothing of this?" Will demanded.

She looked across the table at him. "How could I, Will? I only saw Brian for a few minutes, and he certainly said nothing about this."

"It strikes me as rather strange. Why would he choose New York, of all places?"

"For the same reason that I did, I suppose. Because New York offers a good market for gems." She looked at the advertisement again, and a thought came to her. "You know what I think? I think he's doing this to strike back at me."

Will laughed curtly. "A man would have to be foolish to do something like that."

"His pride is wounded, don't you see?"

"And Andrew Slostrum? Why would he go in with him?"

"Two reasons that I can think of. First, Brian probably didn't have the capital of his own to do it. I told you what a spendthrift he is. Secondly, Mr. Slostrum is bitter about my leaving, about my hiring Peter and Eugene away from him...."

He gave her a stormy look, pushed back from the table and left the room without another word.

Regina looked once more at the advertisement. The opening day was one week away.

REGINA SWORE to herself that she would never go near Brian's establishment; and yet on opening day she found herself irresistibly drawn to the place. What harm would a quick peek do? Didn't she owe it to herself to make a quick inspection of the competition?

Will was lunching with a gem trader. The subject of Brian Macbride had not been mentioned between them since Will had shown her the advertisement in the newspaper, and Regina deemed it wise to keep her visit a secret from him.

Slostrum and Macbride was also located on Fifth Avenue, only three short blocks from her own store, and Regina found her heart beating faster as she neared the place.

She wasn't surprised that the store was crowded. Free refreshments and an opportunity to examine fine jewelry would naturally attract people. She was both amused and flattered at the display window; it was as simple and uncluttered as her own. Most store display windows were as crowded as Tiffany's. Here, a few stones were displayed on black velvet, and there was a diamond necklace as a centerpiece. A small sign was fastened to the back wall: Slostrum and Macbride—Fine Jewelers.

The interior of the store carried out the same motif. The crowd was thick before the display cases that were manned by clerks in morning coats, and around a long table in the center. The table was laden with food and drink; there was even a man in a chef's hat carving slices from a huge roast of beef. No women employees in evidence, she noticed; apparently Brian had chosen not to emulate her in that.

She didn't see him anywhere. Feeling relieved, yet vaguely disappointed, she decided to spend a few minutes inspecting the cases. There were few original or daring designs among the finished pieces displayed. Despite the simple way they were exhibited, all were heavy and ornate; some were even what Regina would consider flashy.

She was standing before a case of men's gold, diamond-studded pocket watches, when a voice behind her said, "Sure, and could I interest you in a star sapphire, madam?"

Her heart gave a great leap, and she made herself turn slowly, striving for calm. She said coolly,

"If I were, Mr. Macbride, I would shop for it elsewhere."

He was dressed splendidly, in a stiff-collared shirt and a morning coat. "I'm surprised at the great change, Brian, in a man who once claimed loftily that he would never, never dress like an undertaker and sell jewelry to pampered women."

He flushed darkly. "People do change, Regina."

"Some, perhaps, but it's hard for me to believe that you ever would. How long do you think it will last?"

"Speaking of change, woman, you certainly didn't wait very long after leaving my bed to jump into another."

Regina felt a hot surge of rage. "May I remind you that the bed I share with Will is a marriage bed. Something you never offered! And you might also remember that you walked out on me for good! At least, that was my impression. Why did you start a jewelry business here in New York, Brian, to get back at me because I proved you wrong? You once told me that the Irish always strike back."

"Sure, and you flatter yourself, Regina, if you think that's my reason."

"Then why?"

"Does a man need a reason to start up a business, aside from the hope of becoming a success?"

"But you, of all people!"

"I decided it was time to settle down, and gem hunting isn't what it once was." He relaxed, grinning slightly. "I recall you once telling me that I should grow up."

"Is Mr. Slostrum here?"

Brian shook his head. "No, he remained behind in London. He'll come over, perhaps once a year, but I'm to run the business pretty much on my own. He was to be here for the opening, but he couldn't make it."

She studied him for a moment in silence. Then she said, "I wish you good luck, Brian."

He looked startled. "Why, thank you. I'm thinking you really mean that."

"Oh, I'll do my damndest to beat you at every turn."

"I wouldn't expect less of you, lass." He took her hand. "Then perhaps we can still be friends."

Before she could respond, Regina saw Will halfway across the room, staring at her with a stunned, hurt expression. After a moment, he turned and pushed his way through the crowd to the entrance of the store.

CHAPTER SIXTEEN

WILL DIDN'T RETURN to the store that afternoon, and he wasn't home when Regina arrived there that evening. Such behavior was totally unlike him, and she was concerned.

"Will hasn't been home, Nanny?"

The other woman shook her head. "I haven't seen him, Mrs. Logan."

Regina went into the nursery to check on Michael. He was fast asleep, his thumb in his mouth. She removed the thumb, gently smoothed back his red hair and stood looking down at him for a time. Finally, with a sigh, she went into the master bedroom, undressed and took a bath.

By the time she had dressed again and gone into the dining room, Nanny had dinner on the table. She looked at Regina in question. "Shall I serve, ma'am?"

"You might as well, Nanny," Regina said heavily. She tried to put a bright face on it. "Mr. Logan had an appointment with a gem trader across town. He must have been delayed. Perhaps he's taking the trader out to dinner and had no way of getting in touch with me. We must have one of those new telephones installed."

"Yes, ma'am," Nanny said dutifully.

Regina doubted very much that the woman believed her lie, yet she could think of nothing else to say.

She finished dinner, eating with little appetite, and went to check on Michael. Will still had not put in an appearance.

She settled down in the parlor, trying to read a book but not comprehending a word of it. Her worry mounted as the minutes passed. Finally, shortly after ten o'clock, she heard a key in the lock. She was on her feet and halfway across the room when the door opened to admit Will.

His hair was mussed, his clothing in disarray and his face had a high flush. He stared at her out of glazed eyes. She realized that he was intoxicated.

Striving to keep any disapproval out of her voice, she said, "Where have you been all this time, Will? I've been worried sick!"

"Have you?" he asked with a sneer. "You didn't look very worried when I saw you in Macbride's store at noon."

"I know, darling, I suppose I shouldn't have gone there without telling you first, but you were out of the store. I went on a sudden impulse." She added defiantly, "Why shouldn't I visit his store? It's always worthwhile to check out the competition. I've heard you say that many times."

He turned from her and he mumbled something.

"What did you say, Will? I couldn't understand you."

"I said, it's not only business competition that this Irishman is offering!" His bloodshot eyes glared at her.

His anger was so fierce that Regina recoiled. "I don't understand what you mean."

"Oh, you understand well enough. You're still in love with the man."

"Now you're being ridiculous, Will!" she snapped.

"Am I, indeed? I saw you holding hands. Don't deny it, I saw you as plain as day."

"Well..." She shook her head in despair. "He was offering friendship, he was shaking my hand. What else could I do but accept his handshake? Besides, it was before a roomful of people, for heaven's sake!"

He blinked, gesturing vaguely, and his words became more slurred. "It... hurts me, to see another man touch you, Regina."

"Will, it meant nothing." She went to him then, taking both his hands. She was shocked to realize that he was trembling badly. She said gently, "Will, I married you, not Brian. You're my husband, and I love you. You must believe that."

His gaze softened, and he clutched at her hands desperately. "I do believe you, Regina. Most of the time. But I get to thinking... you were still in love with him when I married you; what assurance do I have that you still aren't?"

She started to deny it vehemently, but she knew, with a sudden, brutal insight into herself, that his charge was true. She had still been in love with Brian when she married Will, and she was no longer sure that that love was completely dead. Instead she said softly, "Darling, I do love you, and you must believe that I will not do anything to shame you. And if it will make you feel any better, I promise not to see Brian Macbride again. That may be somewhat difficult to do, since we are in the same business, but I promise not to seek him out. Will that do?"

"I suppose it will have to," he said, mumbling again.

She stood on tiptoe and kissed him, trying not to grimace at the sour smell of whiskey on his breath.

"Now." She took his hand. "You must get to bed. You'll feel better in the morning."

He laughed shakily. "I wouldn't wager on that. Not with the amount I drank tonight."

As Regina helped Will prepare for bed, she swore to herself that she would keep her promise. Even if there was still some feeling in her for Brian, seeing him, perhaps rekindling the powerful love she had once felt for him, could mean betrayal of Will's love. It would mean destruction of the good life she had made for herself, with Will's unstinting love and support.

WILL WAS STILL SLEEPING the next morning when Regina got up, but she didn't bother him. She knew that he would be dreadfully hung over and needed all the sleep he could get. It wouldn't do any harm if he was late getting to the store. She could have gone in earlier than usual, but she thought he would be hurt even more if she was gone when he wakened.

She had breakfasted and was in the nursery with Michael when she heard Will stirring in their bedroom. She heard him go into the bathroom and then heard water running in the tub. It was close to an hour later when he finally appeared in the nursery, dressed for work. He looked drawn and haggard, his eyes were bloodshot and he had a spot of blood on his cheek where he had cut himself shaving.

"Good morning, Regina," he said in a subdued voice.

She looked at him gravely. "Good morning, darling."

"Regina, I want to apologize for last night . . ."

"Shh." She indicated Michael with a nod of her head. "Later."

"Papa!" Michael squealed and ran at Will, who picked the boy up. Michael wrapped sturdy arms around Will's neck and squeezed.

Will winced, and then gave a shaky laugh. "You're soon going to be as strong as an ox, Michael. Soon you'll be able to squeeze the breath out of me."

"Ahh, Papa!" Michael laughed and pummeled Will around the neck and shoulders with his tiny fists.

Dear God, the same exuberance! Michael was reminding Regina more of Brian every day. Forcing such thoughts out of her mind, she said, "Your father hasn't had his breakfast yet, son. You stay here and play with kitty while Father eats."

Will put Michael down and followed Regina out of the room. "Nanny said she would keep something warm for you," Regina told him.

He groaned. "I don't feel like eating this morning, just some strong coffee."

"If you don't eat something, you'll only feel worse as the day goes along."

Nanny had heard them coming and was placing a warm platter of eggs, kidneys and toast on the table. As Will sat down, she poured him a cup of strong coffee.

"Mrs. Logan?" Nanny gestured with the coffeepot.

"Yes, please."

They sat down, and Will drank half of his coffee in one gulp. Glancing across the table at her, he said abjectly, "How can I ever apologize for last night, Regina? I was a cad. Getting intoxicated was bad enough, but the things I said to you are unforgivable."

"I'm surprised you even remember," she said in a dry voice.

"Oh, I remember, every word." Almost absently, he began to eat and was soon eating heartily.

"You had absolutely no cause to think or say what you did, Will, but I do forgive you. This time. You must stop drinking so much, dear."

"Don't nag, Regina!"

Her temper stirred. "I am not a nagger, Will, you should know that. I'm simply stating a fact. You're an intelligent man; you know you're drinking too much."

His shoulders slumped. "You're right, I know you are. It's just that . . . well, I can't seem to stop thinking about you and Brian Macbride."

"Well, you must stop such thoughts," she said sternly. "Jealousy is like a terrible disease. It eats away at you. I've seen it in Peter Mondrain. And there is absolutely nothing to be jealous about."

"I'll try to remember that." He smiled wanly. "I promise you I'll do better. Now..." He straightened his shoulders. "I must get to the store. I'm late already."

"Since we're both late, wait until I get dressed and we'll go together."

A short time later, they walked together up Fifth Avenue. The weather had been nice for the past week, but now it had suddenly turned cold again, spitting snow. Regina shivered, hugging herself.

"Maybe we should hail a hack, Regina," Will said in concern. "I didn't realize it was so cold out."

"I'll be fine. I like to walk."

He took her hand, almost shyly, as they walked on.

In a bit, he said, "I'm sailing for England on Friday, don't forget."

"Yes, I remember. I wish you didn't have to go, Will. You promised to find a good man to make the buying trips to Europe. It's not only hard on you, but I don't like it when you're away so much. I miss you, and so does Michael."

"I know I promised, but it isn't so easy to find a man I can trust. If he doesn't know what he's doing, he could buy a bad batch of stones, or he could pay so much that the profit margin for us would be nonexistent."

She squeezed his hand. "But you will try?"

"I promise. I'm finding the trips wearing myself."

They turned into the store. While Will went on upstairs to his office, Regina lingered downstairs to speak to each employee in turn.

The last one she spoke to was Bert Downes, the man who helped her arrange the window displays. "It's about time we changed the window, Bert. Do you have any good ideas?"

"Well, it isn't long until St. Valentine's Day, Mrs. Logan. I thought we should use a heart motif. We've never done that."

She smiled. "That's a good thought, Bert. We'll get together after closing this evening and see what we can come up with." She patted his cheek. "What would I ever do without you, Bert?"

She left him basking in the praise and went on upstairs. After speaking to the women in the sorting room, she stuck her head into Eugene's cutting room. "Good morning, Eugene."

He spun around on his stool. "Good morning, Regina." He broke into a wide grin. "I finally proposed to May last night!"

"And what did she say? As if I didn't already know."

"She accepted my proposal! I couldn't believe it!" His voice held a note of awe.

"I don't know why you should think that. May is a very lucky young lady, as I'm sure she already knows. When is the wedding?"

He sobered. "In May, in honor of her name. I have written my parents in London. We have to give them time to come, if they can attend. I just hope they *can* come."

"I'm sure they'll make it, Eugene. And my heartfelt congratulations. I'm certain you both will be very happy."

Regina decided then and there that she would pay for a rousing reception for their wedding; both were her employees and both deserved it.

When she was admitted to Mondrain's workroom, he gave her a quizzical look. "I see that the man Macbride has opened a jewelry firm here."

"I know. I dropped by for the opening yesterday."

Mondrain nodded. "So did I. It is a fine establishment. Since Slostrum is the Irishman's partner, I suppose it is Slostrum's money that financed the firm. Since you went to his place, am I to assume that you are on better terms with him?"

Regina felt her face burn. "I wouldn't go so far as to say that. We're civil with one another, at best."

Mondrain's gaze was keen. "Does he know about the boy?"

"He does not, and he never will!" she snapped, and went out, slamming the door behind her.

ON FRIDAY AFTERNOON, Regina and Michael saw Will off for Europe. Regina experienced a tug of nostalgia when she accompanied Will to his cabin.

"We haven't had a holiday since we opened the business, darling, not even a honeymoon," she said. "Perhaps next year, we can take a delayed honeymoon on board a cruise ship. I shall never forget the one I came over from England on, when I first met you. By next year, Michael will be old enough to enjoy it. And we can take Nanny along, so we'll have some time to ourselves.''

"That sounds wonderful, Regina, but it will be expensive,'' Will said dubiously.

"If we continue to do as well as we've been doing, we can afford it.''

"But who will be in charge of the store while we're away?''

She nodded. "That will indeed be a problem. Bert Downes is very capable. I could familiarize him with most aspects of the business, and a year from now, I think he could manage well enough in our absence. Anyway, give it some thought.''

From up above came the hail, "Thirty minutes until departure time. All visitors please go ashore.''

"Ah, Will,'' she said with a sigh. "We're going to miss you.''

She reached out to him, and they embraced passionately. Regina felt a tug at her dress and looked down into Michael's upturned face.

"Mommy, now me!''

"All right, my love.'' Laughing, Regina stepped back out of Will's arms.

Will reached down, scooped the boy up and tossed him high. Then he kissed him on each cheek. "I have to go away again, son. I'll be gone for a month. Take good care of your mother while I'm gone, you hear?''

"All right, Papa.''

With Will still carrying Michael in his arms, they left the cabin and went up to the main deck, where he accompanied them to the gangplank. He set Michael on his feet, and Regina took the boy's hand firmly and leaned up to kiss Will on the mouth. "Have a good trip, darling. Take care and come back safely."

"How could I do otherwise," he said gravely, his eyes on her intently, "with what I have waiting at home for me?"

Holding Michael by the hand, Regina went down the gangplank. On the wharf, she looked up at the ship until she spotted Will at the railing, waving to them. She threw him a kiss, picked up her son and held him high. "You see Daddy?"

Michael nodded vigorously.

"Wave to him."

Michael waved wildly. As the ship began to swing away from the dock, Regina set Michael down. "Why Papa go away, Mommy?" he asked dolefully.

"It's business, darling. Soon we hope to arrange it so that he can be with us all the time. Would you like that?"

"Yes!"

"So would I, and we're going to work on it."

They watched until the ship had moved out into the channel and they could no longer see Will on the deck, then took a carriage home.

THE PREVIOUS YEAR, Regina had discovered a winter sport that she loved—ice skating in Central Park. The Sunday after Will sailed, she took Michael and Nanny to the lake in the park. It was frozen solid, and many couples were skating, the men bundled up against the cold, wearing tall hats, and the women in their long skirts with muffs and gloves. The temperature was quite cold, but it was a clear day, and the sun was shining brightly.

Sitting down on a bench, Regina fastened on her skates. Although steel blades were becoming quite common, many people still used the old wooden, iron-edged skates, such as Regina owned. Standing, she stepped out onto the ice.

Michael, with Nanny holding his hand, was sliding on the ice, near the edge, his face pink and his eyes bright. "Look at me, Mommy! Look at me! I'm skating!"

Smiling, Regina glided over to him.

"Now you stay close to Nanny and be a good boy. I'll be right out there." She motioned to the center of the lake as Nanny caught Michael's hand and held him still.

Michael nodded and squirmed out of Nanny's grip again. "I skate, too! See!" His chubby legs churned, and he slipped, landing on his well-padded bottom. For a moment, his face darkened, but then he was up again, moving his feet in imitation of the skaters.

"I'll keep a close watch on him, ma'am," said Nanny. "You have your turn now. When the chestnut man comes, I'll buy him some nuts."

As Regina moved out onto the body of the lake, she reveled in the feeling of freedom that skating gave her. This must be how a bird feels, she thought, as the crisp air stung her face.

After a half hour, she reluctantly skated back toward Michael and Nanny. She would have liked to have skated longer, but Michael would soon be growing tired and would be wanting his tea.

As she neared the spot where she had left them, she saw that they were now seated on the bench, and that Michael appeared to have found the chestnut vendor, for he was busily eating something from a cone of paper. Her heart swelled with pleasure, and then she saw the man coming toward them, a tall man with bright red hair.

Brian! For a moment, panic threatened to overwhelm her, and she thought of fleeing, but she knew that she could not remove the skates in time. Skating to a stop before the bench, she called softly, "Nanny, please take Michael and go home!"

Nanny looked taken aback. "What's wrong, Mrs. Logan?"

"Don't ask questions, Nanny, please! Just go. I'll be all right, and I'll be home before too long."

She stood where she was as Nanny hurried off, praying that Brian wouldn't get a good look at his son. Fortunately Michael's head and most of his face were hidden under the woolen cap he wore, and Brian was looking only at her. Regina noticed that he was carrying a pair of skates in his hand. Now he raised a hand in greeting, but she pretended she didn't see him and skated off. She thought of staying on the other side of the lake, yet she realized that would serve no purpose—he had already seen her.

When she skated back to his side of the lake, Brian already had his skates on and was moving toward her. He skated well, his tall body moving with an easy grace.

Damn the man! Was there nothing he could not do well?

He skated to a stop before her, legs bent slightly, the edge of the skates shaving ice. Grinning, he said, "Now isn't this a pleasant coincidence?"

"Brian!" she said in pretended surprise. "Do you skate often?"

"Not since I've been in New York," he said blandly. "But I thought I'd indulge myself when I learned you'd be here."

Now she was surprised. "You *knew* I'd be here?"

"Sure, and I received a little note informing me that Regina Logan skated here on a Sunday."

"A note? Who sent you a note?"

"I have no idea. It was unsigned," he said with a wink. "I'm thinking it was probably a mutual friend, doing us both a favor."

With some asperity, she said, "I don't consider it any favor."

"Well, I do, and now that I'm here, you can't very well avoid me. And since your husband obviously isn't here, who's to know?"

Before she could protest, he had her by the arm and they were gliding across the ice. With an inward sigh, she decided that she might as well go along; if she made a fuss, it would only cause a scene.

Skating with Brian was like dancing—dancing without music. He was a marvelous skater, graceful for such a big man. Regina relaxed, giving herself up to the enjoyment of the sport. However, her awareness of his nearness, his sheer physical presence, was overpowering.

Soon he began more intricate moves she had never tried. Regina pulled back a bit. "Brian, I'm not a good enough skater for this."

"Sure, and you just follow my lead. It's easy, lass. You'll see."

They swooped and dipped and whirled until Regina was dizzy, yet laughing from pure delight. As they finished one intricate maneuver, she clapped her hands together and like an echo, she heard other hands clapping. She glanced around with a start. The other skaters had stopped and now stood around them in a loose circle, watching. Brian winked at her as they came out of a spin, took her hand and bowed with her in all four directions.

The applause rose and voices cried, "Bravo, bravo!"

Flushed with pleasure, she said, "Let's rest for a bit, Brian."

With a nod, still holding her hand, Brian skated with her to the bank. A few feet away was the chestnut vendor's cart. The pungent odor of the roasted nuts tickled Regina's nostrils, and she realized that all the fresh air and exercise had made her hungry.

As though reading her thoughts, he asked, "Would you like some of the nuts, lass?"

She nodded. "That would be nice, Brian."

They sat down on the bank to remove their skates. Regina noticed that Brian's ears were red from the cold. "Aren't you freezing without a hat?"

"Never wear anything on my head." He winked. "As my mother used to say, 'Never cover your head, laddie. It interferes with the blood circulating in the brain pan.'''

"A mother would never say that," she scolded. "I would certainly never say that to—" She chopped the words off, appalled at what she had nearly given away.

His look was curious. "What were you about to say?"

"I would never allow any children of mine out in cold such as this without a head covering." She got up quickly, hoping to forestall further probing.

Brian seemed to accept her explanation at face value. He also got to his feet, and they walked over to the vendor's wagon, where Brian bought two large cones of smoked chestnuts.

They found an empty bench and sat side by side. Regina bit into a nut, relishing the rich flavor.

Brian stretched his legs out full-length. "Sure, and wasn't that a fine time we had on the ice?"

"I must admit that I enjoyed it, yes."

"But then anything we do together is great, I'm thinking," he said with a sly, sidelong look.

"Now, Brian," she said in a warning voice.

"I know, I know, you're a married woman. But the truth is the truth, no matter what."

"What you see as the truth is not necessarily my version of it," she responded.

"Tell me something, Regina. Do you love this man?"

"Of course. I would not have married him, otherwise."

He fell silent, staring off at the skaters, his features cast in melancholy, and she was unexpectedly moved. Perhaps she had been mistaken; perhaps he did love her, in his own way.

After munching on a few chestnuts, she turned to him. "How is your business doing, Brian?" she asked.

He rounded with a start and smiled at her. "Surprisingly well. I say that because I'm surprised to discover that I have a knack for it. It's still early yet, but I'm after thinking you'll have to reckon with us eventually."

"As my husband says, competition is the lifeblood of American business." She stared at him intently. "Tell me the truth now, Brian. Wasn't getting back at me the real reason you went into the jewel business?"

"Aye, I can admit that now," he said with a sheepish grin. "It was small of me, I can see that now. As you told me, you had every right to marry anyone you wished. I treated you rather shabbily. There, I've said it!"

She was somewhat taken aback by his admission. She said slowly, "I do believe you're finally becoming mature, Brian Macbride."

He winked. "Sure, and you must be thinking it's about time." He fell serious and took both her hands in his, gazing into her face. "But as long as I'm being honest, I must say something else. I still love you, lass, and I always will...."

"Brian, no! Don't do this!" She tried to pull her hands out of his grasp, but he held firm.

"I must say it. I didn't realize just how much I loved you until I was here in New York, until I found out that it was too late."

"Brian . . ." She blinked back sudden tears. "If we are to remain friends, you must never mention this again. I am married. I love my husband and would never, under any circumstances, hurt him."

He sighed heavily. "I admire your honesty, Regina. I don't like it, but I must respect it. And I do want your friendship, so I shall never mention it again. You have my solemn word on that." He smiled faintly. "Tell me something, lass. Are you still longing for your virgin sapphire?"

"Yes, Brian, I'm still looking. So far without success."

Again they fell silent, but he still held her hands in a tight grip, and they sat gazing deep into each other's eyes. As much as she wanted to, as much as she knew she should, Regina could not tear her gaze away.

They did not see Peter Mondrain standing in the crowd some distance away, watching them closely, his face a study in malice and pain.

CHAPTER SEVENTEEN

REGINA AND MICHAEL met Will's ship on his return to New York. For days, Regina had debated with herself whether or not she should tell Will about the chance encounter with Brian in Central Park. Of course, it hadn't been a chance encounter, not if Brian was telling the truth about the note he had received, and there was really no reason for him to lie. Once again she wondered about the note. Who could have sent it? And why? Had someone sent it hoping to stir up mischief, or simply out of spite?

In the end, remembering how upset Will had been at seeing her with Brian at the opening of the store, she decided not to tell her husband about meeting Brian in the park. Will might not believe that the meeting had not been arranged, and he was certain to view the story that it had come about because Brian had received a note, with understandable skepticism.

There was no doubt of Will's delight at seeing them on the dock. He set down a satchel he was carrying, swooped Michael up in his arms and kissed and hugged him. Then still holding the boy on his shoulder, he put his other arm around Regina's shoulders and kissed her passionately.

Smiling broadly, he said, "I'm happy to see my family."

"And we're happy to see you, darling. Aren't we, Michael?"

"Yes, yes!" the boy shouted.

There was none of the reserve that she had noticed in Will before he left, and she happily linked arms with him as they waited at the hack for the driver to load Will's luggage. Will kept the satchel with him at all times.

"Was it a good trip, Will?" she asked.

"Fabulous!" He hefted the satchel in his hand. "It was a good diamond sight in Amsterdam. This satchel contains some of the best diamonds I've seen in some years, and I bought a good collection of opals, rubies and emeralds."

She looked at him hopefully. "No star sapphire?"

He laughed and pulled her against him. "No, I'm sorry, my dear. We'll find one for you eventually, I'm sure."

They arrived at the flat just before dark to find that Nanny had dinner ready for them; Will's favorite—steak, boiled potatoes and fresh baked bread. While Nanny fed Michael, Regina and Will discussed his trip as they ate.

It was with some relief that Regina noticed that he only drank a single glass of wine during dinner, and nothing after. They sat in the parlor after the meal while she brought him up-to-date on what had occurred at the store during his absence.

Approximately halfway into her recital, Will laughed abruptly and got to his feet. "In short, the store got along quite well without me."

"Darling, that's not true," she said, distressed. "You are always missed, not only by your family, but by my . . . our employees."

He reached down for her hand. "Then it's time you were showing me how much I was missed."

That night, Will made love to her with a hunger and a passion that stirred Regina's blood. Her response was rich and full; not once during their lovemaking did she think of Brian Macbride.

THREE DAYS LATER, Regina came to regret her decision to keep quiet about her unexpected meeting with Brian.

She had worked late at the store, and Will was already at home when she arrived there. She found him sitting in the parlor, his face set and angry. He was holding a single sheet of paper in his lap. Without a word, he rose and handed it to her.

"What is this, Will?" she asked, puzzled.

"It came in today's mail delivery," he said grimly. "Read it!"

With a sense of dread, she read the short note: "Dear Mr. William Logan, Your wife was observed skating in Central Park with Brian Macbride, and later seen sitting on a park bench with him, holding hands intimately." The note was typewritten, and the first thought that crossed Regina's mind concerned the note Brian had received. Had it been typewritten as well? She hadn't thought to ask him.

Shocked she looked up into Will's angry face. "Who could have sent such a note?"

"That hardly matters, does it? Is it true?"

"Will . . ." She sighed, searching for the proper words. "Yes, it's true. But it wasn't planned. It came about by accident."

"Accident?" he said in disbelief.

"Yes! You know that I often go there with Michael to skate. You've been with us several times."

"Of the million or so people in the city of New York, Macbride just *happened* to be there at the same time."

"Well, there is a little more to it than that. Brian said he also received a note, telling him that I would be there."

"And I'm supposed to believe that?"

She waved the note. "This came to you, didn't it? Obviously the same person wrote both notes." She crumpled it up and threw it onto the floor. "What a contemptible thing for someone to do!"

"Not so contemptible to my way of thinking, since the note only tells the truth."

"But can't you see, Will? Someone is doing this out of malice, trying to cause trouble between us."

"And succeeding very well, I would judge," he said tautly. "Say I accept your story that Macbride received a similar note telling him that you would be in the park. Did that mean that you had to skate with him?"

"Perhaps I shouldn't have, but I couldn't see any real harm in it. He is a good skater."

He glared. "And that is your excuse? What is your excuse for holding hands with him as if you were lovers?"

"Now *that* is not true, Will!" she cried.

"Then you didn't hold hands with him?"

"Well, yes, but not like the note implies, not like lovers, Will. Brian held my hand and told me that he still loved me . . ."

"Then he is still in love with you!"

"He claims to be, but that doesn't mean that I return his love. I told him that, and that I had a husband that I loved, and made him promise to never speak of it again."

He was silent for a moment. "Why didn't you tell me about this when I returned from Europe?"

"Perhaps I should have. I thought long and hard about it, but then I thought it best not to. I remembered how jealous you were after the other two meetings I had with him."

"And with good reason! Fool that I am, I believed you both times."

She felt a prod of temper. "Will, I'm sorry I didn't tell you about the meeting in the park, but I have told you the truth in all else. If you can't trust me, I don't know what else I can say. . . ."

Their voices had been rising, and Nanny chose that moment to come into the parlor to announce dinner. Suspecting that the woman had come in hoping to interrupt a quarrel, Regina gave her a grateful look.

But Will said, "I'm not eating dinner here tonight, Nanny." He reached for his coat and hat where he had thrown them over the sofa.

"Where are you going, Will?"

"Out," he said harshly.

"Please, Will, you're acting childishly. Don't do this."

Ignoring her, he slipped into his coat. As he started out, he said, "Don't bother waiting up for me. I don't know what time I'll be home, and I'll make a bed for myself on the sofa."

Regina watched helplessly as he strode out of the flat. Her pride would not allow her to call him back, to plead with him further. Ordinarily the most reasonable of men, Will was being totally unreasonable now, and be damned if she would cater to his jealousy!

She gave a start as Nanny coughed discreetly. She smiled wanly. "It seems I shall be dining alone tonight, Nanny."

"It has been my experience, Mrs. Logan, that all married people have their little disagreements. I am sure that Mr. Logan will get over his anger and be sorry for it."

"I'm afraid it's a little more than a disagreement, Nanny." Regina suddenly felt the need to confide in someone, and Nanny was the only person to whom she felt close enough to do so. "Please sit down for a minute, I need to talk to someone."

Nanny gestured. "But dinner is on the table, ma'am."

"It can wait."

With obvious reluctance, Nanny sat down, holding herself erect, her expression apprehensive.

Quickly, occasionally fighting back an on-slaught of tears, Regina told the housekeeper the essence of what the quarrel had been about. She refrained from revealing that Michael was Brian's son. At the end, she said, "So you see, I'm at my wit's end. I don't know what to do!"

Nanny looked at her sternly. "Do you love this man, this Macbride?"

"To be honest, I do have some feeling for him. I suppose I always will."

"And your husband?"

"Do you mean do I love him? Yes, I do, al-though I would have to say in a different way. And I would never do anything to hurt him, never!"

"I have never been wed, but I did love a man once, with all my heart and soul. A charming, handsome man. He did to me what your man, Macbride, did, only he left me waiting at the al-tar. A few years later, I met another man, a good and kind man, like Mr. Logan. He asked me to marry him, and I spurned him because I still loved the other man. And I have lived to regret that de-cision. Now I shall never have children of my own, but am doomed to spend my life tending to the children of others." Nanny added severely, "It is not my place to advise you, Mrs. Logan, but I would counsel you not to allow a charmer, even if you still love him, to destroy the happy marriage you already have. And there is Michael. Whatever else, you must consider the boy's welfare." Nanny broke off, looking embarrassed. "I'm sorry, ma'am. It is not my place to say such things."

"Who has a better right, Nanny? I consider you a member of the family." Regina leaned across to take the woman's hand. "And I very much appreciate your advice. It is good counsel, and I shall try to follow it."

BRIAN WAS WORKING late at the store, long after the employees had all gone home. He had found that running a business was much more to his liking than he had ever anticipated, but keeping books was a chore he detested. Arithmetic had always been a weakness of his, and by seven o'clock he was cursing to himself as he struggled to make the bloody figures balance. Yet it was a necessary part of the business, and he had to do it. Despite his boast to Regina, the store was barely breaking even at this point, and Andrew Slostrum would have apoplexy if he, Brian, employed a bookkeeper.

Finally he gave up for the day. He was hungry, ready for his dinner. He poured a glass of whiskey and drank it down quickly, then put on his coat and made a final tour of the store.

A sudden, loud knocking on the front door startled him. Who the bloody hell would be here at this time, he wondered.

The thought of security was always uppermost in the mind of anyone in the jewelry business, and Brian kept a pistol in his desk drawer. He toyed with the idea of fetching it before he answered the door, but surely anyone with the thought of robbery in mind wouldn't be so bold as to come knocking thunderously on the front door.

Brian started for the door as the knocking began again. Angrily he threw it open. "We're closed for the night. Can't you read the sign?"

He blinked at the swaying, disheveled figure in the doorway. Whiskey fumes stung his nostrils. It took him a moment to recognize Will Logan.

"Sure, and it's Mr. Logan." Apprehension seized him. "Is something wrong with Regina?"

"It's you that's wrong with her, you bastard Irishman!"

Brian relaxed, smiling slightly. "Well, now, you'll have to speak plainer than that, bucko."

"I want you to keep away from her! Is that plain enough for you?"

"I'm thinking it's up to the lady to decide, eh?"

"She's my wife, damn you! And if you don't keep away from her, I'll—" Will broke off, seemingly at a loss for words.

"You'll what, Mr. Logan?" Brian said in amusement. "Call me out? Duels are no longer in fashion. Or perhaps you'll beat on me? You're drunk, my friend. Sure, and you're hardly in condition to fight anyone."

"I may be drunk now, but if you come near her again, I'll come hunting for you."

"Now look, Logan, you're upset over nothing." He placed a friendly hand on the man's shoulder. Will knocked it away. "I've seen the woman twice. Once in your store and once in my store."

"How about Central Park?"

"Oh, you know about that, do you?"

"Of course I know!"

Brian shrugged. "That was more or less by accident."

"Not from what I heard. You went there purposely to meet with her. And you were seen holding hands on a park bench."

Brian stiffened. "Seen? By who?"

"What does it matter? You were seen holding hands intimately."

"Intimately?" Brian laughed carelessly. "Nothing like that, Logan. We were just getting to be friends again."

"Regina doesn't want to be friends with you!"

"Told you that, did she?"

"She did. She promised she wouldn't see you again, and I want the same promise from you."

Brian felt his gorge rise, and for a dangerous moment he was tempted to smash his fist into the other man's face. Then he forced his anger back. Will Logan was drunk, and besides, he was right. Regina was a married woman, and he had no right to force his attentions on her, no matter how much he might wish to. He said evenly, "All right, bucko. Now off with you. I don't take much to being threatened, especially by a man in his cups."

Will's face reddened even more. He clenched his fists, and for a moment Brian thought he was going to lash out. He tensed, ready to defend himself, and then Logan turned away and lurched off into the night.

THE TELEPHONE on Regina's desk jangled, startling her. Although the telephone had been installed for some time now, she had yet to become accustomed to the sudden ringing. She picked the receiver off the hook and spoke into the mouthpiece. "Hello?"

"Regina? Brian here."

"Oh, Brian!" She felt a rush of pleasure at the sound of his deep voice, then immediately stifled it. "Brian, you shouldn't be calling me."

"I know, because of your husband."

"Well, yes."

"Is he in the office with you?"

"No, but that doesn't matter."

"It's about him I'm calling, lass."

"What do you mean?"

"He came calling on me last night."

She went tense. "Why did he do that?"

"Apparently he learned about our little outing in the park."

"Yes, someone sent him a note. Probably the same person who wrote you that I'd be in the park. Was your note typewritten?"

"It was."

"Then it was the same mischief maker, I'm sure. If I could find out who it was, I would...well, something drastic, you can be sure!"

He laughed again. "I'm thinking you would indeed."

"What did Will want with you?"

There was a brief silence. "Well, you have to understand that the man was in his cups, and a man in such a condition is apt to talk a little wild."

"Did he *threaten* you?"

"Nothing specific, but he said that if I tried to see you again, he would take action."

Regina sighed. "I'm sorry, Brian. He shouldn't have done a thing like that."

"Sure, and it's I who should be apologizing. I brought this about by going to see you in the park. I've brought you trouble, Regina, and it's sorry I am about that. I'd like to make amends."

"And just how do you hope to do that?" she said a little sharply.

"I have an idea that might help smooth things over. Are you and your husband going to the theater or some other public event any time soon?"

"Why, yes, we have tickets for *Peter Pan* with Maude Adams this coming Saturday night."

"Then I'll see you there, Regina."

"Brian, wait!"

But he had already hung up. Slowly she replaced the earpiece. What did he mean by his last remark? She thought of phoning him back, but she knew that she would be unlikely to change whatever he had in mind. How did he think that seeing them at the theater would help smooth matters?

She had no idea what time Will had gotten home last night. She had gone to bed and was asleep when he finally came in, and he was gone when she got up that morning, a blanket tossed carelessly over the sofa. She knew that he was in his office down the hall, and several times she had considered going down there to try to reason with him. But then why should she? She really had done nothing wrong; it was his place to make the overture.

RELATIONS BETWEEN Regina and Will were strained for the rest of the week, and Will continued to sleep on the sofa in the parlor. Their conversations were civil but kept to a minimum, mostly concerning business matters; certainly the subject of Brian Macbride was not mentioned.

A number of times, Regina thought of asking Will if he would like to cancel their Saturday evening theater; she was fairly certain he would be agreeable. With the bitterness and strain between them, an evening together at the theater did not promise to be particularly pleasant.

In the end, she said nothing. She had to admit to a consuming curiosity as to what Brian had in mind. Whatever it was it could hardly make matters worse.

So on Saturday evening, after eating dinner in silence, she and Will got dressed and took a hack to the theater. Maude Adams was the latest rage of New York, and hacks and carriages were lined up for blocks before the theater, waiting their turn to discharge their passengers.

The lobby was packed with theatergoers, and as they made their way through, Regina looked everywhere for Brian, but he was nowhere to be seen. The inner doors were just opening, and she and Will were escorted to their seats. Until the houselights dimmed, she watched for Brian but did not see him. Had he changed his mind and decided not to come after all? Despite herself, she felt a stab of disappointment.

Finally she put thoughts of Brian out of her mind and settled back to enjoy the play.

AT ABOUT THE TIME the curtain came up on *Peter Pan*, Brian was drawing up in a hack before a brownstone on 35th Street off Lexington. Daisy Carlton lived in a ground-floor flat. A tall, voluptuous brunette with dark brown eyes, she opened the door at once to his knock. Dressed in a long black dress, she tapped her foot in annoyance.

"You're late, Brian Macbride!"

He grinned lazily. "Sure, and don't you know it's fashionable to be late, love?"

"But to the theater? The first act will be over before we get there."

"I'm thinking it doesn't matter," he said with a shrug. "It's all about fairies and children. I saw enough fairies back in Ireland to do me."

She peered at him suspiciously. "Fairies in Ireland? You're making fun of me, Brian."

"Not at all, my dear," he said gravely. "There are many fairies in Ireland. I thought everyone knew that."

He gave her his arm, and they went out to the hack. He had known Daisy for some weeks and had been squiring her around. She was a little slow, but she was decorative, and she was enthusiastic in the bedroom. Best of all, she was a married woman, living apart from her wealthy husband, but had high hopes of worming herself back into his favor. Until that happened, she had told Brian, what was wrong with having a little fun?

They arrived at the theater only a few minutes before intermission. By the time Brian paid the hack driver and they had entered the lobby, the audience was streaming out of the theater, the women gathering in small groups to chat and many of the men going outside to fire up cigars.

"You see, I told you we'd be late," Daisy complained.

"Never mind, love." Brian took her arm and held it close to his side, his gaze scanning the faces of those emerging through the inner doors. "Now no matter what I may say in the next few minutes, just ignore it."

She frowned at him in puzzlement, but before she could respond, Brian spotted Regina and Will Logan across the lobby. He steered Daisy that way, intercepting them. Regina saw him first. Her face lit up, then she frowned as she saw Daisy on his arm.

"Sure, and what a coincidence, Mr. and Mrs. Logan, meeting you like this," Brian said, beaming.

Will visibly stiffened by Regina's side, and a quick glance at his face told Brian that he was seething.

"Daisy, I'd like you to meet Will and Regina Logan, friends of long standing," Brian continued. "And this is Daisy, my betrothed." He threw an arm around Daisy, who looked at him in amazement.

After a flurry of polite hellos was exchanged, Brian said jovially, "And how is the entertainment, Mrs. Logan?"

"We're enjoying it immensely," Regina said with forced cordiality.

"We're finding it an enjoyable evening, yes," Will agreed coolly.

"Too bad we missed the opening act," Brian said. "But I was unavoidably detained. We just arrived. Daisy is always telling me that I'll be late for my own wedding. I'm thinking I must improve my tardy ways."

A bell tinkled, announcing that it was time to return to their seats. Almost rudely, Will took Regina's arm and turned her back toward the theater. Regina went along, resisting a strong urge to look back over her shoulder.

As the Logans disappeared into the theater, Daisy said angrily, "Now what was that all about? I'm your *betrothed*? I already have a husband, you know that! And I wouldn't marry you, Brian Macbride, on a bet!"

"Sure, and I know that," he said cheerfully. "But I told you to just ignore anything I might say."

"What kind of game were you playing with those people, Brian?"

"Nothing that need concern you, love." He took her arm and ushered her out of the theater.

She tried to hold back. "But aren't we staying for the rest of the play?"

"Who wants to see only the last part of a play? Besides, I have dinner reservations for us. I want to avoid the after-theater rush so we can dine at our leisure."

"But you bought tickets for the play! And all for just that little scene in there? Brian, you are mad, utterly mad!"

"Sure, and you wouldn't have so much fun if I wasn't, now, would you?" he said, grinning broadly.

REGINA AND WILL sat through the rest of the play in stony silence. She was so unsettled by the growing rift between them that she didn't enjoy the performance.

Nothing was said until they got home. Once inside the house, Will threw his coat and hat onto the sofa and made for the liquor cabinet. He poured a large brandy and drank half of it in a gulp.

Only then did he look at Regina, his eyes cold as ice. "Now what was that scene with Macbride all about?"

She shrugged helplessly. "You know as much as I do, Will."

"Oh, I think not. You must take me for a complete fool, Regina. The pair of you plotted that little meeting, to make me think Macbride was betrothed to that woman. I saw the look of utter astonishment on her face. It was a complete surprise to her. She was probably some trollop Macbride picked up on the street and paid to accompany him and play out his little charade. Only he should have told her in advance what he intended to say." He tossed down the rest of the brandy.

Regina sank down onto the sofa, clenching her hands together in her lap. In a low voice, she said, "I can only repeat that I knew nothing about it in advance."

"Well, I damned sure don't believe you," he said flatly. "You planned it together."

"That's simply not true, Will...."

He had turned away to splash more brandy into his empty glass.

"Will, please don't drink any more."

He whirled on her. "I shall drink what I damned well please. I intend to drink enough so I'll forget and be able to sleep. Right there!"

He pointed a finger at the sofa where she sat, but in Regina's mind the finger was pointing directly at her, accusing her of many things, not the least of which was infidelity.

CHAPTER EIGHTEEN

"Brian," Regina said into the mouthpiece of the telephone, "just what did you hope to accomplish by that performance last night?"

"Why, I hoped to put your husband's fears to rest. I thought that if he believed that I was thinking of getting married, he would be easier in his mind about us."

"Well, it did not work. It had the opposite effect."

"It did?"

"It most certainly did. Will isn't stupid. He saw that woman's face, and he knew that your statement came as a complete surprise to her."

His sigh came over the line. "Well, I thought it was a good idea at the time."

"Will is more convinced than ever now that something is going on behind his back. He thought we planned that meeting last night together."

"It's sorry I am, lass. I guess it wasn't such a good idea, then. Maybe there's something else I can try?"

"No! Just let it alone, Brian. I hope that Will will calm down in time and start to view this whole business rationally."

"Speaking of business, Regina, I've heard some rather disquieting rumors."

"And what might they be?"

"The story is that some bucko has come up with a means of manufacturing artificial gems."

"Oh, I've heard rumors to that effect before, but it turned out that's all they were, rumors. Many people have tried to make synthetic diamonds, and one man has claimed to have done so. I understand that was enough to shake De Beers to its roots. But nothing more has ever come of the claim."

"Not diamonds this time. It's rubies and sapphires. Some French bloke by the name of Verneuil is said to have developed a surefire method of making them."

"Yes, I've heard of Verneuil, but supposedly he developed this process three or four years ago."

"That may well be, but the way I hear it, a company has now been formed to flood the market with synthetic rubies and sapphires made by his process. Just think what this could mean to jewelers who have fortunes invested in the real thing. Synthetics can be marketed for a fraction of the value of the real stones. I've received several telephone calls from men in the trade, and I received a telegram from Andrew this morning to the effect that all of London is agog with the news. He thinks there may even be some panic selling in rubies and sapphires."

Regina felt a stab of anger and dismay. If the rumors *were* true, it would be a terrible jolt to the jewelry business. Her anger spilled over to Brian, and she said shortly, "Well, thank you for telling me. Meanwhile, Brian, please refrain from doing me any more favors!''

Regina's thoughts returned to Will after she replaced the earpiece on the prongs. Once again, he had slept on the sofa; and he had been uncommunicative and sullen at breakfast.

She knew that he was in his office down the hall now, and again she was tempted to go to him, using the news of the manufactured gemstones as an excuse to speak with him. But then why should she initiate a conversation? She considered herself the wronged party.

Instead she concentrated on Brian's alarming news, thinking back over what she knew about the history of synthetics.

Men had been trying to manufacture gems for years. The earliest experiments she knew of were conducted by Marc Gaudin in France during the 1880s. He had tried to reproduce gem quality corundum—sapphires and rubies. A few years later, rubies appeared on the market, which at first were thought to be natural but were later discovered to be manufactured. They became known as "Geneva rubies," because it was generally thought that they were made in Geneva, Switzerland.

Another Frenchman, Edmund Fremy, had also developed a commercial process for making rubies, but in the form of thin plates. They could be produced cheaply and in large quantities and were now used in watch and instrument bearings. Fortunately they were too thin to make gems.

Then around the beginning of the century, one of Fremy's assistants, August Verneuil, had developed a new process, which he called "flame fusion." The method involved the direct melting of aluminum oxide by allowing the powdered chemical to dribble from a hopper through an intensely hot flame. The powder melted in the flame, falling in the form of tiny droplets onto a rotating ceramic rod. A mass of the material built up, then cooled and crystallized into a single large crystal. Rubies were made by adding a pinch of chromium to the aluminum oxide. Sapphires of different colors were made by adding different combinations of metal oxides.

The Verneuil process had been formally introduced in 1904 and had caused a stir of excitement at the time, yet Regina had heard little of it since. Of course, she realized, it would take some time for people in the trade to accept the fact that the process worked, and for enough of the manufactured gems to flood the market. And if it was true that passable synthetic rubies and sapphires were being manufactured, would synthetic diamonds be far behind?

A number of scientists, especially in France and Russia, had claimed success at synthesizing diamonds in their laboratories by applying heat and pressure to carbon. However, they had not been able to convince gem experts that the microscopic crystals formed by their experiments were actually diamonds.

There was one possible exception that Regina knew of. The story was well-known throughout the gem world.

Only a few months ago, a French inventor by the name of Henri Lemoine claimed that he had discovered a process for mass-producing diamonds from lumps of coal. There had been immediate alarm in the diamond community, especially from De Beers. Sir Julius Wernher, a British banker and one of the four life governors of De Beers Consolidated Mines, realized at once that if the Lemoine process was authentic, it would cause a panic that could easily ruin the diamond industry. Sir Julius decided there was only one prudent course of action—he would demand a demonstration. If the process worked, he would buy it, then keep it a secret.

Henri Lemoine was quite agreeable to conducting a demonstration. He invited Sir Julius to his laboratory in Paris, with the proviso that if it worked, De Beers would either buy the process outright or agree to finance further development.

Lemoine's laboratory was located in the basement of an abandoned warehouse. Sir Julius was accompanied by Francis Oates, the top executive of De Beers. Lemoine seated the men before a large furnace and left the room briefly. When he returned he was naked. He told them that he had removed all of his clothing so that they could see that he was not concealing any diamonds on his person.

Then, with the mysterious flourishes of a medieval alchemist, Lemoine poured a number of substances, all unidentified, into a crucible and mixed them together thoroughly. With another flourish, he showed the mixture to his visitors and then placed the crucible in the furnace and activated a number of switches.

As the furnace rapidly heated, the nude chemist explained to his audience that he was able to synthesize the diamonds using a secret formula known only to him. After a quarter of an hour had passed, he turned off the switches, and using a pair of tongs, removed the white-hot crucible from the furnace and placed it on a table. Allowing it to cool for a time, Lemoine stirred the concoction with a pair of tweezers and then, one by one, he plucked small but well-formed diamonds from the crucible. In total, he removed twenty diamonds and passed them to his guests for their inspection.

Since Francis Oates was the expert, his examination was the most careful. Using a jeweler's loupe, he examined them one by one. He found that they resembled, in both shape and color, diamonds taken from a particular De Beers mine in South Africa. Now highly skeptical of the demonstration that he had seen, he asked Lemoine to repeat it.

Lemoine obliged readily. This time, after the procedure was completed, he extracted over thirty small diamonds from the crucible. Again Oates carefully examined the gems with his loupe and again pronounced them to be authentic diamonds. But when he conferred privately with Sir Julius, he admitted that although the diamonds were real enough, he still had reservations and believed that some sort of hoax was being perpetrated by the Frenchman. Sir Julius respected the man's opinion, yet there was still a lingering fear in his mind that Lemoine had somehow discovered a secret formula for manufacturing diamonds. The possibility was too high to risk, so he offered to advance Lemoine a considerable sum of money to continue his research and further refine his formula, on the condition that the Frenchman would agree to keep his findings secret. In return, De Beers would be given an option to buy the secret formula, which Lemoine deposited in a London bank under seal.

After the first flurry of excitement over the discovery, the majority of people in the jewelry trade openly expressed doubts, scoffing that De Beers had been taken in by a blatant hoax. The rumor mill had it that a Persian jeweler had sold Lemoine a quantity of small, rough diamonds that had been stolen from the De Beers mine in South Africa and smuggled out of the country, and that Lemoine had contrived some way to place the diamonds in his crucible under the very eyes of witnesses.

But regardless of the validity of the Frenchman's claim that diamonds could be manufactured by his process, Regina knew that that particular episode would only serve to add fuel to this fresh story of the synthesization of rubies and sapphires.

Jewelry people were easily panicked; all had large investments in their stock, and even minor fluctuations in price frightened them. Of course, if the story was true, there was ample reason for concern. If manufactured gems flooded the market, it could send the prices of real gems plunging down.

Regina decided to contact a number of her colleagues. A short time later, she hung up the telephone and stared out the window with a grave expression on her face. From what her friends in the business told her, it would seem that the rumors were indeed true.

The question was, what could be done about it? She sat deep in thought for a time, her mind picking at the problem.

Finally she decided to talk to Will. He might not have a solution to offer, but being consulted might soothe his ruffled feathers. Acting on the decision, she left her office and started down the hall toward his. Halfway there, she saw him coming out the door, shrugging into his overcoat.

"Will..." She stopped short as they met, swept by a feeling of dismay. "Will, it isn't even noon yet, and you've been drinking!"

"That is no concern of yours, Regina," he said roughly and started on past her.

"Wait, Will." She stayed him with a hand on his arm. "There's something I need to discuss with you."

He shrugged her hand off. "Not now. I have something to do." He went on past her.

She stood where she was, choking back her anger. Then to her astonishment, she saw him pause to rap on Mondrain's door. The door opened, Mondrain came out and the two men walked together toward the stairs.

Where in heaven's name were they going? Could they be going to lunch together? Could it be that after all this time they had become friends without her knowing it? Then she dismissed the matter from her mind, anger and disgust with Will almost bringing her to tears. How could a good, kind, logical-thinking man allow himself to act in this manner? And all over a tempest in a teapot!

Regina returned to her office and immediately got Brian on the telephone. She had promised Will that she would not contact Brian again, but this was urgent business. Besides, with Will behaving the way he was, why should she hold to her promise?

"Brian, have you had time yet to become acquainted with responsible people in the jewelry business here in New York?"

"I've met and talked with most of them, but I'm thinking I could not call them close acquaintances."

"But they do know and trust you?"

He laughed. "I don't know about trust, but they know me, yes. What's on your mind, Regina?"

"Could you arrange a meeting of as many of them as possible? Say tomorrow, for lunch, at anyplace you choose?"

"Sure, and I can try. It is rather short notice."

"Tell them it's urgent and to the benefit of all. We must do something to stop any possible panic about synthetic stones."

He was silent for a moment. "When we talked before, you didn't seem too concerned. What's changed your mind?"

"I made some inquiries and you may be right. Now about the meeting. I think it's more likely they will turn up if it's called by a man, instead of a woman."

"You have a plan, then?"

"I'm working on one. Again I wouldn't mention anything about me. Let them be surprised!"

Regina got busy, working right through lunch and well past closing time. By the time she was ready to go home, she was confident of her course of action. Whether she could convince the male members of the jewel fraternity that it was workable was another matter.

By closing time, to the best of her knowledge, Will had not returned to the store; but before she left, she checked his office—it was empty. On her way out, she knocked on Mondrain's door. There was no answer.

Will was not at home, either, and Nanny had not seen him all day. Regina ate the supper Nanny had kept warm for her, tucked Michael into bed and sat down in the parlor to go over her plans once more. When she retired at ten o'clock, Will still had not come home.

The next morning there was no sign that Will had spent the night on the sofa, and when Regina went into the kitchen where Nanny was preparing breakfast, the housekeeper shook her head to the unvoiced question. Regina could only conclude that Will had spent the night somewhere else. Furious at him, yet saddened, she dismissed her husband from her mind and prepared for her noon meeting.

THE MEETING TOOK PLACE in a conference room in a popular restaurant a block off Fifth Avenue.

Regina was purposely late, wanting everyone to be present when she arrived.

She came in briskly, carrying a folio of papers. There were eight men seated around the table. Brian, at the head of the table, got to his feet with a broad smile. "Regina! We thought you weren't going to make it."

"Sorry, gentlemen," she said crisply. "I was unavoidably detained."

She received several glowering looks, all of which she ignored. She sat down on Brian's right.

"Since you were tardy, and the waiters were becoming a wee bit grumpy, we have already ordered lunch," he said. "We're having fish. Does that meet with your approval?"

"That's fine, Brian."

As though her arrival were a signal, two waiters came in just then, carrying trays. As they bustled about, Brian used the opportunity to say in a low voice, "Can you give me the gist of what you have in mind, Regina?"

"Let's wait until they've all eaten," she said with a shake of her head. "If they overhear us, they may bolt. I see wine carafes. Hopefully they'll be in a more mellow frame of mind with full stomachs and enough wine."

A half hour later, they were finished. A couple of the men took out cigars, then hesitated, looking at her askance.

"You may smoke with my blessing, gentlemen," she said affably.

When the cigars were lit, a cloud of blue smoke hovering near the ceiling, Brian rose, tapping on the table with his knuckles. "It's time, gentlemen, to get down to business. Mrs. Logan has something to say to you."

One of the cigar smokers almost choked on a mouthful of smoke. When he got his breath back, he said angrily, "What is this, Macbride? We didn't come here to listen to a woman!"

Brian stared at him with icy contempt. "This woman you're talking about knows the jewelry business better than most. She started from scratch and now has one of the most prestigious firms in New York."

"That's as may be," said another man, "but women have no place in business, certainly not in the jewelry business. It's always been that way, and it always will be."

Regina had been listening calmly. "Businesses *and* times change. As Mr. Macbride says, gentlemen, I am successful. I don't think any of you can deny that."

"But you have a husband. If you have something to say that will help us over this hump, why isn't he here speaking for you? That would be the proper way to go about it."

"My husband buys all the gemstones for my firm, and is very good at it. But I run the rest of the business."

Brian said harshly, "You buckos are scared out of your breeches that a panic will hit the jewelry business. Now Regina here has a solution to offer, and by the saints, you're going to listen to her!" He doubled his fist and thumped it on the table. "If one of you tries to go out that door before you've heard her out, you'll have me to go through. Is that clear?''

Regina noticed that Brian seemed to have lost much of his brogue. ''Gentlemen, there is no need for harsh words,'' she said. ''It appears to me that we're all here for the same reason. What harm can it do to listen? It will only mean a few minutes of your time, and you're under no obligation to follow my suggestions, although I do think it will be to your advantage to do so.''

One man Regina recognized as representing Tiffany's spoke for the first time. ''The young lady is right. Common courtesy demands that we listen.''

Some of the men nodded in agreement, and the grumbles subsided. Regina opened her folio on the table and took out a sheet of paper.

''Now Mr. Macbride has told me that in conversation with some or all of you, you have expressed alarm at the news that rubies and sapphires can now be produced synthetically. That appears to be true, but there is certainly no cause for panic. That would be the worst thing you *could* do.''

''Then what do you suggest?'' one man asked.

Regina looked at him levelly. ''I am coming to that, sir. Firstly, I have no doubt that there will be some initial interest in synthetics, simply because they are new and relatively inexpensive. But no matter what can be said of them, they are fake. In the long run, there is little for us to fear. Our gems are real, and the people with money to invest want real gems. Suppose we compare the situation to paintings. You know very well that people will not knowingly buy a fake Van Gogh, or a fake Rembrandt..."

The cigar smoker interrupted. "The comparison doesn't hold water, lady. From what I've seen of the synthetics, it takes a real expert to tell the difference between manufactured and real gems."

"It also takes an expert to tell a fake painting from the real masterpiece, sir. And it is a criminal offense to sell a fake painting, and so it will be to sell a manufactured gem as the real thing. People do not knowingly buy fake paintings. Some will, of course, buy synthetic stones, but not people desiring the real thing."

The room was silent for a moment before one of the men said, "You still haven't told us what you have in mind."

"First, I again suggest that we do not panic. Our businesses may suffer for a time, but people who want value for their money, the customers who have the money to spend, will continue to purchase the real stones. I'm sure that some of your firms will stock the manufactured gems, but will label them as such. In the long run, this may even mean increased business. In addition, I suggest an advertisement, a statement published in all the newspapers." She picked up the piece of paper she had taken from her folio and gave it to Brian. "I roughed this out last night, and I intend to run it."

Brian read aloud from the sheet. "Do not be misled into purchasing manufactured gems, such as the rubies and sapphires soon to be on the market. The wonder of a natural gemstone lies in its individuality, its natural beauty and the craft of nature and man in shaping and refining the stone until it comes to you, the customer. Invest your money in natural stones. Authentic gems last forever, and their value will only increase with time. While imitation stones will be cheaper initially, their value will increase little, if any, over a period of time. Come to Paxton Jewels for the real thing!''

At the end of the reading, Brian glanced around the table. "I think this is an excellent statement! Gentlemen?''

Many of the faces wore skeptical expressions.

"As Regina said, what harm can it do?'' Brian urged. "I'm certainly all for it.''

"It will be expensive running an advertisement in all the papers,'' one man said. "My firm doesn't much believe in advertising.''

"Personally I think it may be worthwhile, but I can't make a decision on my own,'' another said. "I'll have to talk to the owner.''

"We'll all have to talk it over first,'' another said.

"We can't fiddle around too long,'' Brian said. "I saw an item in a newspaper just this morning about this new process. The other papers will pick it up and run it tomorrow, you can be sure.''

"I agree. It should be done immediately,'' Regina said. "I have already reserved space in all the newspapers for mine. Actually, to make a really strong statement, I think we should run another, a joint advertisement, with the names of all firms attached. It will be less expensive and more effective. In any case, mine will run two days from today.''

The men were getting to their feet now. Most of them passed her without so much as a glance, but two men lingered to express their approval and their admiration for her cleverness.

"You argue a good case, Mrs. Logan," one of the remaining men said. "Since I own my own store, the decision is mine alone, and you have my full support. I definitely agree to a cooperative statement, if enough of the others go along to make it worthwhile."

The other said, "My sentiments exactly. And I wish to congratulate you on the success of your store, Mrs. Logan. This is the first opportunity I've had to tell you so. You are a good example to all of us."

As the two men made their exit, Brian, beaming, took her hands. "You were marvelous, lass! You have my admiration." He winked. "Someday, I may have enough sense to stop underestimating you."

Regina felt a current as strong as electricity running through her from the touch of his hands. Flustered, she said, "Why, thank you, Mr. Macbride. Also, I wish to thank you for your support. But for you, I think they may have all gotten up and walked out before I had a chance to say a word."

They fell silent, staring deeply into each other's eyes. His lips were so close, and she yearned to feel them on hers. She swayed slightly toward him, and his mouth moved toward hers. At the first touch of his lips, she wrenched herself free of his grip.

"No, Brian! Nothing has changed."

He smiled beguilingly. "Sure, and what harm can a friendly kiss do?"

"You know very well what it can lead to. I'll have none of your Irish wiles, Brian Macbride!"

He sighed theatrically. "Ah, well, you can't blame a man for trying, now can you?"

"Oh, I'm sure you'll never stop trying." She tucked her folio under her arm. "Good day to you, Mr. Macbride."

Watching her walk away, her back straight as a ruler, Brian muttered, "Aye, a shame it is, a real shame. You love me and you know it. What a waste!"

REGINA'S ADVERTISEMENT appeared in all the New York newspapers, and the day after that, a similar statement, signed by all the prominent jewelers in the city, appeared.

Two days later there was a small item in a morning newspaper: "Yesterday, a customer purchased what was purported to be an authentic sapphire. The customer, a Mr. Jeremy Foster of Boston, had the sapphire appraised by a reputable expert and learned that the sapphire was, in fact, a manufactured gem.

"The sapphire was purchased at Paxton Jewels. The owner of the store, Mrs. Regina Logan, took out an advertisement only two days prior in all the New York papers, warning people not to be misled into buying the synthetic gems. She declared that Paxton Jewels would sell only authentic gems, not the imitations."

CHAPTER NINETEEN

THE TELEPHONE on Regina's desk jangled. She took the earpiece from the hook and spoke into the mouthpiece. "Hello?"

"Regina, did you read the piece in the newspaper this morning?" It was Brian at the other end.

"I read it, yes," she said tightly.

"How did it happen?"

"I don't know yet, but I'm certainly going to find out, and quickly."

"Bloody hell! After your advertisement, you're going to be in trouble. Not only that, but the other jewelers are going to be mightily upset with you, I'm thinking, after you signed that joint statement. They'll figure it's going to rub off on them."

"Right now," she said grimly, "I'm too worried about what effect this will have on my own business to be concerned about theirs."

"What do you plan to do, lass?"

"I've hardly had time to give much thought to it. I only saw the item an hour ago."

"Well, Regina, knowing you as I do, I'm thinking you'll come up with something."

"I wish I could be as sure."

"If there is anything that I can do, don't hesitate to call on me."

"Thank you, Brian."

As Regina hung up the earpiece, she saw Bert Downes in the doorway. He had been busy with a customer when she entered the store, and she had left word for him to come to her office the minute he was free.

"Come in, Bert." As he stopped before her desk, she threw the newspaper, open to the damning item, down before him. "Have you seen this yet?" She tapped the story with her forefinger.

Downes picked up the paper. "I haven't read a newspaper this morning." He read it quickly, taking on a stricken look. "Why, this is terrible, Mrs. Logan!"

"You don't have to tell me that. Did you sell the sapphire to Mr. Foster?"

"Yes, ma'am, I did. But I had no idea that the gem was a synthetic."

"There's no reason why you should. I'm not blaming you. Did the sapphire come from the stones Will brought back on his last buying trip to Europe?"

"No, ma'am," Downes said, his glance sliding away.

"It didn't? Then where *did* it come from?"

Downes hesitated, still not looking at her.

"Bert, tell me!"

His shoulders slumped, and he said slowly, "Mr. Logan, he . . . he bought six sapphires a few days ago."

"He bought them here, in New York?"

Downes nodded. "I would assume so."

Regina closed her eyes for a moment, her mind in a turmoil. After a moment, she opened her eyes again. "Have you sold any of the others?"

"Not yet."

"Then I don't have to tell you not to sell them. Collect the other five and give them to Eugene. Now about this customer, Jeremy Foster. Did you get his address?'

Downes was nodding. "Yes, Mrs. Logan."

"Then I want you to go to Boston today and—" Abruptly she changed her mind. "Never mind, I'll handle it. Just leave the address on my desk." With a nod, she dismissed him.

After Downes left, Regina sat for a moment, as both anger and sadness swept over her. In a bit, she got to her feet and went down the hall to Will's office, her steps dragging. She pushed the door open without knocking. As she had expected, the office was empty.

As she went back down the hall, she saw Bert Downes coming out of Eugene's workroom. Seeing her, he waved a piece of paper in his hand. "This is Jeremy Foster's home address, Mrs. Logan."

She took it from him and folded it into her pocket. "Thank you, Bert."

"Are you going up to Boston to see him?"

"I am. Probably this afternoon, after Eugene and I examine the other sapphires."

"But maybe a man should handle it," he said hesitantly.

She shook her head. "No, it's my responsibility to deal with this matter."

Inside Eugene's workroom, she saw that he was already examining the sapphires. He glanced up at her. "Bert told me what happened, Regina. It's a bad thing for the store."

She sat down beside him. "What do you think?"

"I haven't had time yet to tell anything for sure."

Eugene had a powerful light aimed at the stones, and he held a strong magnifying glass in his hand. Regina also picked up a magnifying glass and one of the stones. She knew that synthetic corundum had distinguishing characteristics. For one thing, the manufacturing process produced curved growth lines that were visible under strong light and magnification. These curved lines were called striae and never appeared in natural gemstones, since all their growth lines were straight. Another characteristic of synthetics was the presence of perfectly round bubbles, which often had small tails, similar to a tadpole's. The appearance of the stone after cutting also indicated its origins.

A single glance was enough to tell Regina that all of the five stones were well proportioned. A close examination under magnification showed the telltale curved lines in the stones, as well as the round bubbles.

She sat back with a sigh. "I don't think there is any doubt, Eugene. They are all manufactured stones."

"I'm afraid so, Regina." He glanced at her in sympathy. "What are you going to do?"

"I haven't thought it all out yet. Several things, you can be sure," she said forcefully. "One thing

I certainly do not want is those stones downstairs on sale. So why don't you wrap them in a separate package and keep them in your safe, where no one but you can get their hands on them.''

''All right, Regina.''

She stood. She was tired and felt as though she had not had proper rest in days. At the same time, anger was growing in her, a strong sense of outrage that she knew would fuel her for all the things she had to do.

''Eugene, if anyone asks you about those sapphires, either inside the store or out, tell them nothing. Refer them to me.''

Leaving his workroom, she once again started down the hall toward Will's office. At Mondrain's door, she hesitated, raised her hand to knock and then changed her mind and went on. Will still was not in his office. Perhaps it was just as well, she thought. She already suspected how the sapphires had come to be in Will's possession, and she was just as happy to postpone any confrontation with him.

In her own office, she checked the railroad station to learn what time she could get a train to Boston and found that one left early that afternoon. After the call, she got busy with paper and pen, sketching out another statement to publish in the newspapers, if she was able to get what she wanted from the man in Boston.

Finished, she placed her papers in a folio and went downstairs. Bert Downes met her at the bottom of the stairs.

"I'm leaving for Boston shortly, Bert, and I'll have to stay overnight. You're to be in charge while I'm gone. I should be back sometime tomorrow afternoon. Now I want you to get something for me . . ."

JEREMY FOSTER LIVED in an affluent section of Boston, in a large brick house on a lot that was screened from the neighbors by shrubbery and trees. Regina, after finding a hotel room for the night, had taken a hack directly to the Foster residence. It was after nine, but she wanted to be sure he was home and not at work when she called.

He was a small, jovial-looking man of middle age, with thinning hair and faded blue eyes. He peered at her suspiciously when he answered the door. "Yes? Can I help you?"

"Mr. Foster, I am Regina Logan."

He frowned. "Logan? I don't . . ."

"I own Paxton Jewels."

His eyes opened wide, and he took a step back. "Your store sold me that sapphire!"

"We did, yes. That is why I'm here. I want to make amends. May I come in?"

With some reluctance, he stepped back to allow her to enter, then motioned her to the right into a lighted room off the entryway. It was a sitting room with a cheerful fire burning in a fireplace. A pleasant-looking woman got to her feet.

"This is my wife, Bessie. Bessie, this is Regina Logan, who owns the store where I bought the sapphire to celebrate our anniversary."

Regina looked at the woman with interest. "Is the sapphire also your birthstone, Mrs. Foster?"

"Yes, it is," the woman said with a nod.

"Mine, as well. And I can't tell you how sorry I am that this happened. But that's the reason I'm here, to make restitution." She opened the folio she was carrying. "Mr. Foster, this is a check for the exact amount that you paid for the synthetic stone." She held the check out, and he took it with a look of stunned surprise. "And here..." Also from the folio she took a small box and held it out to his wife. "This is for you, Mrs. Foster. The finest sapphire in our store, and at no cost to you. Happy birthday, Mrs. Foster, even though it may be a little late."

Mrs. Foster accepted the box, opened it and gasped. She removed the sapphire and held it up. Light glinted off the stone. "Why, how lovely! Look, Jeremy!"

Foster took the stone, glanced at it, then looked at Regina warily. "This is the real thing?"

"Absolutely. You may take it to any jeweler for appraisal." She waited for a moment while he examined it. "I'm curious, Mr. Foster. When you found out that the stone you bought from us wasn't natural, why didn't you bring it back to the store?"

"Well, I didn't learn that it was a synthetic until I got back here to Boston. I was going to have it set in a locket for Bessie. I took it to a jeweler I know and he told me that it was manufactured." His voice hardened. "He advised me to consult an attorney."

"And have you done so?"

"Not yet, no. As a matter of fact, I was going to see one tomorrow."

Regina tried not to show her relief. "Well, there's no need for that now, is there? Unless you think the check and the sapphire aren't enough restitution?"

She held her breath while Foster glanced over at his wife, saying, "Bessie?"

His wife took the sapphire from him and again held it up to the light. "Oh, Jeremy, this is so beautiful," she breathed. "I think Mrs. Logan is being very generous."

"There is one more thing I should add," Regina said quickly. "I don't as yet know for sure how a synthetic sapphire got mixed in with our real ones, but I certainly intend to find out and see that it never happens again."

Foster relaxed, grinning widely. "Very well, Mrs. Logan. I agree with Bessie. I don't see why there should be any more trouble about this matter, since you have been so kind as to come all the way up here to make good."

"Thank you, Mr. Foster. And now, there is one small favor I'd like to ask of you in return...."

REGINA TOOK THE EARLIEST train back to New York. Instead of going home or to the store, she made quick stops at all the newspapers, to arrange for an advertisement to run in the next day's editions.

Only then did she direct the hack to take her home. When she opened the door, Michael came running across the room on chubby legs to fling himself against her. "Mommy, Mommy, you've been gone!"

Regina picked him up and looked over his head into the concerned eyes of the housekeeper. Nanny shook her head mutely.

After spending some time with Michael, Regina took a bath, put on fresh clothing and hurried to the store. The floor clerks, even Bert Downes, avoided her gaze, and she knew that Will was in his office and probably not in the best of shape.

She headed immediately for Will's office. He got up from behind his desk as she entered. His clothing was rumpled, he was unshaven and she was saddened to see that he looked dissipated.

"How dare you go away overnight without letting me know first?" he demanded harshly.

"How could I?" she retorted. "I didn't know where you were!"

"For what possible reason did you go to Boston?"

"I think you know, Will. I went up there to try to undo the damage to the store's reputation."

"What damage?" he blustered.

"You know very well. You bought those synthetic sapphires, didn't you?"

He sank down into his chair, mumbling something she couldn't hear.

"What did you say, Will?"

He raised his eyes to meet hers. "Yes, I bought them, but I didn't even suspect they were synthetic, Regina. I swear to you! They looked authentic, and they were such a bargain, I couldn't resist.''

''Yes, a great bargain,'' she said caustically. ''Selling that one as a real stone came close to ruining our reputation forever, especially after those two statements published in the newspapers. Didn't you know about all the manufactured sapphires flooding the market?''

''No, I hadn't heard,'' he said miserably. ''If I had known, don't you think I would have been more careful?''

''I don't know, Will, I truly don't, not after the way you've been acting of late.''

''And whose fault is that?'' he flared up.

''Yours, Will,'' she said harshly. ''Everything you've accused me of is purely a product of your imagination. How could you have bought those stones, Will? You're the most astute gem buyer I know. How could you be so easily fooled?''

''I wasn't myself, Regina. I'm sorry.''

''You mean you were drinking?''

He nodded, looking away again. ''It was a bad mistake, I can see that now. At the time, I thought you'd be proud of me, buying such fine sapphires at such a bargain price.''

''Didn't it even occur to you to wonder why they were such a bargain?''

''I thought they were stolen.''

''Stolen! Will, you know that one of the first decisions we made on opening the store was to never buy stolen merchandise.''

"I know, but I wanted to accomplish something that would make you proud of me, to show you that I still knew my trade."

"I have always been proud of you, Will, until lately. The only way to make me proud of you again is to stop drinking, stop clouding your judgment with alcohol and become the man I loved and married."

"I promise to try, Regina. I have made a terrible mistake, and I'll try not to repeat it."

She hardened herself against his plea. "That's not good enough, Will. You're going to have to prove yourself first. Until you stop drinking and straighten yourself up, you'll buy no more stones for us."

He looked stricken. "Don't do this to me! What will people think?"

"I've overlooked your behavior too long. I cannot afford to risk the chance that you will make another mistake. However, no one will know that you are not buying gems, certainly not from me."

"But what will we do for stones?"

"There are enough left from your last European trip to last us for some time. If you are recovered by the time your next trip is scheduled, fine. If not, I will go, or send someone else."

"I suppose you'll send the Irishman?" he said with a sudden flash of anger.

"Is that an example of how you're going to keep your promise?" She sighed. "I doubt that Mr. Macbride would be interested. He has his own business to attend to."

"I'm sorry, Regina," he said wretchedly. "I shouldn't have said that."

She was moved by pity, but she allowed none of it to show. "How did you learn about the synthetic sapphires you bought? I suppose Peter steered you to them."

He got a startled look. "How did you . . . ?"

"I'm not stupid, Will. I saw you leave here with him the other day."

He looked even more miserable. "He came to me and told me that he had located a bargain in sapphires, and it seemed to me that it was a good chance to make money. Mondrain should know a bargain, since he has been around gems most of his life."

"Didn't it occur to you to wonder why he was doing you a favor, since he's hardly been civil to you?"

"He said that he had decided that we should be on better terms since we worked together, and that he thought this was a good way for a new beginning."

"Well, he lied to you, that's obvious." She started out of his office.

"What are you going to do, Regina?"

"I'm going to discharge him, right now."

"But what will you do for a designer?"

"I'll find one, somehow. I'll not have a dishonest employee working for me."

As she reached the door, he said, "Regina?"

"Yes, Will?"

"I'm sorry for all that's happened."

"Sorry won't do, Will. You're going to have to change, or it's over between us, as much as it hurts me to say that."

She went on out and down the hall to Mondrain's workroom. She tried the knob before knocking and was surprised to find the door unlocked.

Mondrain was packing his things into two satchels. He looked at Regina with a wry smile. "I have been expecting you, Regina."

"Is that the reason you're packing your things?" She nodded at the satchels.

"Yes. I saw you go into your husband's office earlier, and I knew that he, weak-spined creature that he is, would tell you how and where he got the sapphires."

"Will may be weak in some ways, but at least he is honest!" she said angrily. "Why, Peter?"

"Do you need to ask?" He snapped one satchel closed. "I offered my love, I offered to marry you, and you spurned me. Then you married a man like Will Logan."

She stared at him narrowly. "You also wrote the two notes, didn't you? I should have guessed as much. In fact, I suppose I knew, in some part of my mind, but didn't want to face up to it, to confront the fact that a man could be so spiteful. Whatever else you might be, Peter, I would have judged you to be too much of a gentleman to stoop so low."

"A gentleman has feelings, too." His face twisted into a mask of hate and despair, and his voice was filled with anguish. "You hurt me, Regina, and the more I brooded on it, the more it ate away at me. I had to make you pay for that."

"I could file criminal charges against you. . . ."

"For what cause? I did nothing criminal."

"The sapphires were synthetic."

"I did not tell your husband that they were natural stones. I simply took him to the man who had them to sell. Your husband has dealt in gemstones for years. Am I to blame if he could not tell the real from the false? And I did not sell the sapphire, your clerk did."

"But Will was drinking heavily when you took him to buy the stones. His judgment was impaired."

"Neither am I in any way to blame for that. Face the truth, Regina. Your husband is weak."

"Perhaps you're right. However, that does not mitigate your culpability. I might not be able to file a criminal charge against you, Peter, but I can certainly see to it that no other jewelry firm in New York will employ you."

He shrugged, closing the other satchel. "That does not concern me. I realized that you would find out and discharge me. I have booked passage on a ship departing tomorrow. I am returning to London. I should never have left."

She turned away but stopped before she reached the door. "I am curious about one thing, Peter. As full of spite and malice as you seem to be, why didn't you tell Brian that Michael is his son?"

"I have nothing against your bastard son." His eyes glittered. "Besides, I am sure that the more time that elapses before Macbride learns about his son, the angrier he will be with you.''

REGINA'S statement-advertisement appeared in all the newspapers the following day. She clipped one from a paper and fastened it to the front window of the store.

This is an apology to all of my customers, present and future. A mistake was made. Paxton Jewels sold a synthetic sapphire as a genuine stone. The matter has been rectified, and I give my personal guarantee that this will never happen again. The following affidavit is self-explanatory. Regina Logan.

Below this was another short paragraph:

Of her own accord, Mrs. Regina Logan, the proprietor of Paxton Jewels, came to me and not only paid me the full price of the manufactured sapphire I purchased in her store, but also replaced it with a beautiful, authentic sapphire. My wife and I are most grateful for this generous gesture. I shall feel no reservations whatsoever in the future about purchasing jewels in her store. I swear that all the above is true.

Jeremy Foster.

That evening when Regina entered the flat, Nanny was waiting for her, her eyes red from weeping. ''Your husband is gone, Mrs. Logan. He packed his suitcases and left. He gave me this to give to you.''

With a sinking heart, Regina accepted the folded sheet of paper from Nanny. She opened it and read, ''My darling Regina: I am sorrier than I can ever put into words for all the trouble I have caused you by my reprehensible behavior. Knowing how much you have longed for a virgin star sapphire, I am going abroad in search of one, and I shall not return until I can do so with my head held high. Perhaps then you will find it in you to forgive me. And always remember this; no matter how I have acted, I love you more than life itself, and I always will. Farewell for now, my love, and keep well. Please kiss Michael for me and tell him that he can be proud of his father when once again he sees him. Will.''

CHAPTER TWENTY

"REGINA!" It was Brian on the telephone. "I just had to call to tell you that I think that piece in the newspapers yesterday was a stroke of genius! That should not only reassure your customers but should also soothe the ruffled feathers of your competitors. I've already heard from several, and they're pleased."

"Thank you, Brian," she said in a choked voice. She had wept off and on all night and had determined that she would weep no more; but now her eyes flooded with tears.

"Regina? Lass, what is it? You sound like you're weeping."

"Will has left, Brian."

Brian was silent for so long that Regina finally said, "Brian? Are you there?"

"Aye, lass, I'm here. I am shocked, is all."

"Well, if you are shocked, imagine how I feel!"

"Maybe he just left for a day or two," Brian said carefully. "Sure, and he may come walking back any minute."

"No, he packed his bags, and he apparently left on a ship."

"Then he's left for good?"

"Not exactly."

"For how long, then?"

"It's a little difficult to explain on the telephone, Brian. . . ." She had to stop for a moment, battling another onslaught of tears.

"I'm coming right over."

"No, Brian!" she said hurriedly. "It would not look right for you to come rushing over here the moment Will has left."

"But you need a friend, Regina, someone to talk to. Why don't you join me for lunch, and we can talk it out?"

She said hesitantly, "I suppose there's nothing wrong with that."

"Then let's meet at that little restaurant around the corner from you. It's quiet there, and we won't be bothered. I'll meet you at one o'clock."

"All right. One o'clock."

Regina sat for a long time after talking to Brian, her thoughts dreary. Why had Will done such a foolish thing? She could not help feeling a certain measure of guilt. In effect, she had driven him away.

Her thought stream was broken as Bert Downes stepped into the doorway. "Mrs. Logan," he said uncertainly, "I understand that Peter Mondrain is no longer employed with us."

"You understand correctly, Bert," she said, sitting up straight, her voice laced with anger. "I learned that he was the one responsible for Will buying those synthetic sapphires, and I discharged him."

Downes was frowning. "Then we're going to need a new jewelry designer."

"I'll find a replacement somewhere."

"I know a man who I think would fit the bill. He's a Russian, only recently arrived in New York. He worked for Fabergé for many years. He was in the store only yesterday. Neither you nor Mr. Logan was in, but he did leave an address where I can get in touch with him."

"Have him come see me." As Downes started out of the office, Regina said, "Bert, there's something else you should know. Mr. Logan has left."

He stared. "Left? You mean for good?"

"I'm not sure as to that, but he won't be in the store for a while."

"I'm sorry, Mrs. Logan."

"So am I. The thing is, I will also be needing a buyer. I can probably handle what buys we make here, but the trips to Europe, to the diamond sights, are a different matter. Do you think you could handle it?"

"I would certainly like to try," he said eagerly. "I know I'm not the expert Mr. Logan is, but gems have been my life, and I believe I can handle the job." Then he looked abashed. "But maybe you wouldn't care to trust me, after the fiasco with the synthetic sapphire."

"You had absolutely no reason to suspect that it wasn't a natural gem. Anyway, we'll talk about this further."

With a nod, Downes went back downstairs. Regina washed her face and began getting ready for the luncheon appointment with Brian. No matter what she did, she could not erase the signs of recent weeping.

When she entered the restaurant, he was already there, at a table relatively isolated in the back. He stood as she approached, his face grave.

"Ah, Regina, it's sorry I am for your troubles," he said, taking her hands, his gaze raking her face. "Even sorrier because I am the cause of them."

He held a chair out for her. "You're not wholly to blame, Brian," she said sadly. "It wasn't only because of his jealousy of you that Will left."

"It's not?" he said, sitting down.

She had debated with herself whether or not she should tell Brian about Will buying the manufactured sapphires and had finally concluded that he should know the truth. She didn't want the whole city of New York to know, but she had learned that, despite Brian's faults, telling secrets was not one of them. "No. Will bought the synthetic sapphires."

He stared at her in astonishment. "Your husband did that? How could a man with all of his buying experience make such a mistake?"

"He was not himself, Brian," she said. "The night he confronted you? That wasn't the first time he'd had too much to drink. He has been drinking heavily of late, and his judgment was not of the best that day. In all fairness, he didn't know that the synthetics had come on the market, and Peter Mondrain lured him into buying them."

"Now why would the bloke do that?"

"I never told you this, but Peter asked me to marry him back in London, before we sailed for America. I refused him, and he never forgave me for that. Peter wrote both the note you received about me being in Central Park that day, and the note sent to Will telling him of our meeting.''

''Why, the bloody sod!'' His big hands opened and closed on the table. ''Wait till I get my hands on him! By the saints, I'll wring his neck!''

She smiled slightly. ''It's a little late for that, Brian. He's on board a ship bound for England.'' She shook her head. ''I knew he was a bitter man, but I never once thought he would try to ruin my life and my business.''

Watching the play of emotions across her face, Brian's heart ached for her. He longed to hold her, to comfort her in any way he could, yet he knew that he had to tread carefully. Now was not the time to do anything that might upset her further. ''At least that piece in the newspapers should halt any further damage to your business,'' he said.

''I can only hope so.''

''And you still can't be sure that your husband won't come back, after he's had time to think about it.''

''He won't be coming back for some time, at any rate.''

''Why do you think that?''

''You remember how much I've always wanted an uncut star sapphire, a virgin sapphire, as you call it?''

''Aye, I well remember.''

''Well, that's where he's gone, looking for one for me. That's what he said in a note he left for me.'' Her short laugh was wry. ''It seems that my long-held desire has turned on me, and may very well cost me my husband.''

"Your husband has gone gem hunting?" Brian said in disbelief.

"That's what he said in his farewell note, and I have no reason to doubt him."

"Sure, then he'll be back before too long," he said reassuringly. "As you very well know, lass, gem hunting is not for the inexperienced. He'll soon find out it's not so easy."

"I'm not so sure. Will is a stubborn man, and I have a feeling he won't come home until he finds a star for me."

"They're not so easy to find these days. I looked myself on my last expedition and didn't find one—" He broke off, realizing what he was giving away.

She stared at him, her eyes suddenly warm. "You mean, after our bitter parting, you still hunted for a star for me?"

"Sure, and did I say it was for you?" he said in a blustery voice.

"Brian, how sweet of you." She reached across to touch his hand, then jerked hers away, making a fist of it and pounding it on the table. "Why would he do such a foolish thing, Brian? Certainly I've always yearned for a virgin star, but not to this extent. It can be dangerous, we both know that, and he could easily lose his life. If that happens, I'll never forgive myself!"

"He loves you, Regina," he said gently. "And men have been known to do foolish things in the name of love, as my old mother used to say."

She smiled through sudden tears. "A font of wisdom, your mother was."

He nodded solemnly. "Sure, and that's the pure truth! I have never gone wrong following her advice."

"Brian Macbride, you have never followed good advice in your whole life, I'll wager."

He assumed a look of hurt. "You wrong me grievously, lass."

They were almost finished with their lunch now, and the rest of their conversation was mostly devoted to business matters. By the time they left the restaurant, Regina was wondering about Brian. She had had some trepidation about meeting him, fearful that he would once again declare his love for her, knowing that Will was out of the way. But despite her concern, she had been acutely aware of his vitality and strong physical presence. She felt flushed and nervous as Brian walked her back to her store. Yet he never once hinted at intimacy, and he could not have been gentler or more considerate of her.

It was only at the entrance to the store that he broached more personal matters. He took her hand and stood looking down into her face. "I fully realize your state of mind, Regina, but I must speak of this. I enjoyed our luncheon, and I sincerely hope that we may do it again. After all, we are friends of long-standing, and you need friendship to help you through your time of trouble."

"I appreciate your friendship, Brian, truly I do. God knows, I need friends now. Ever since I've been in New York, I've been so occupied with establishing my business that I've had little time to cultivate close relationships. But..." She looked at him in suspicion. "Just as long as you understand that friendship is all I have to offer."

He smiled guilelessly and winked. "What sort of a bucko do you think I am, lass, to take advantage of your present situation?"

ALEXIS FEDEROV was flamboyant, given to extravagant gestures and much hyperbole. He was also handsome and charming. In his early forties, he was well over six feet, with bright blue eyes, hair the color of ripe wheat and the long, sensitive fingers of an artist. He was dressed in clothing cut in the European fashion and carried a small satchel in his right hand.

When Bert Downes ushered him into Regina's office and she came around her desk to greet him, the Russian took her hand and bowed over it. "Charmed, dear lady, charmed."

Regina flushed slightly and retrieved her hand quickly. As Downes left them alone, she gestured Federov to a chair and went around behind her desk.

"Tell me about yourself, Mr. Federov. Why did you leave Russia and Fabergé? Fabergé is the most illustrious jewelry firm in the world."

Federov arranged his long legs in an elegant sprawl and said, "Mother Russia is not...how you say...what it once was. Revolution is coming."

"But how will that affect Fabergé?"

Federov shrugged expressively. "Communists will confiscate all jewelry." His smile was contemptuous. "They not believe in jewelry, claim it is a weakness of the aristocrats."

Regina was surprised at his command of English. Except for being slightly stilted and free of articles, it was excellent. "Your English, Mr. Federov, is quite good."

He grinned charmingly. "Federov had been thinking of leaving Mother Russia for two years, more, and began to learn English. Federov had a good teacher."

"You did indeed. What made you decide to come to America?"

"A wealthy country. Federov is best designer, and he thought this be a good country for his work. And..." He grinned again. "Revolution here long over."

"Have you tried other firms?"

"Yes. But all have designers. I heard that you are needing a designer. Federov is best."

"That much is true, about my needing a good designer, but how do I know that you are the best? Aside from the fact that you have worked for the house of Fabergé."

"Ah! Federov show you." He stood, opened the satchel and removed three pieces of jewelry, proudly placing them on the desk before her.

Regina leaned over to study them. They were samples of exquisite workmanship. It occurred to her to wonder how he came by them. Had he stolen them, taken them with him when he left Russia?"

As if reading her thoughts, Federov said, "Federov did not steal pieces, dear lady. I made them, yes, but I was given them as reward of my long years of devoted service to Fabergé."

Regina nodded and examined the pieces closely. One was a gold brooch made in the form of a knotted bow of broad ribbon. Enameled a translucent pink, each ribbon was bordered with rose diamonds set in silver. The second piece was what she knew was called a *minaudière*, done in an art nouveau design. The exterior was of green gold, with four thumb pieces made of cabochon sapphires. She pressed the thumb pieces, and the *minaudière* opened to show compartments for powder and rouge on one side and a clip for notes on the other, as well as a tiny mirror backed by an ivory writing pad. The interior was decorated with an elaborate pattern of leaves in green gold and brilliant, small diamonds. There was also a gold chain attached so that it could be suspended around a lady's neck.

"This is a beautiful piece, Mr. Federov," she said. "But it is done in art nouveau. Art nouveau has lost much of its popularity in America and is becoming difficult to sell."

Federov shrugged, spreading his hands expressively. "Federov is aware of this, but is of no consequence. Federov can design any fashion or style."

Regina frowned over the third piece, puzzled as to exactly what it was. It was fairly large and had the look of an elongated bowl with a chased foliate border, set with rose diamonds. There was a two-inch handle, set with rubies and sapphires. The piece was supported by a crimson enameled base.

She picked it up and looked under the base, which had Federov's designer mark—AF. She turned it over and over in her hands.

"I must confess to some puzzlement, Mr. Federov. What is this supposed to be, and what purpose does it serve, if any?"

"That is *bourdalou*, dear lady."

"All right, that may be its name, but what is it for?"

Federov squirmed a little, showing some signs of embarrassment. "Is receptacle for relief of ladies forced to sit for long periods of time at opera or ballet, or when suffering discomfort at lengthy sermons by windy priests. In fact, receptacle is named after just such a priest, a Jesuit priest of seventeenth century."

Regina stared at the object, then at Federov, and she began to laugh. "You mean, ladies relieve themselves in this?"

He nodded, his color high.

"Dear God, it must cost a small fortune! And for such a purpose!"

Her laughter grew until it threatened to get out of control. It seemed to her that she hadn't laughed for weeks. She had been feeling composed this morning, her weeping done, finally accepting Will's abrupt departure. She was still saddened that he had been so foolish; but she could only hope that Brian was right and Will would give up his quest before long and return.

Her laughter finally under control, she felt cleansed of sorrow, her spirits renewed. "Mr. Federov, I very much doubt that any ladies in

America will be interested in such an item, unless as a curiosity piece.''

Again he gave an expressive shrug with the spreading of his hands. ''Federov did not know this.'' He brightened. ''Perhaps, dear lady, you will accept *bourdalou* as gift, as 'curiosity piece,' as you so quaintly put it.'' Then, as her expression hardened, he held up his hands, palms toward her. ''Please not to misunderstand. Federov not making offer in exchange for employment.''

She let her breath go, relaxing. ''Well, I should hope not. But I do like your work, Mr. Federov, and I think you will fill the position nicely.''

He smiled brilliantly. ''Thank you, dear lady. Federov was becoming concerned.''

She leaned forward and said briskly, ''Now let's discuss the terms of your employment....''

THE DAYS PASSED QUICKLY now. Some of the pain of Will's leave-taking was eased for Regina. It took only a few days for her to realize that she had made a wise decision in employing the Russian designer. Unlike Mondrain, he was soon fast friends with everyone in the store, and she was more than satisfied with his work. He was a brilliant designer, and he worked much faster than Mondrain. He was innovative, daring and quite amenable to any suggested designs Regina presented to him. His pieces sold almost as fast as they were finished and placed on sale downstairs.

Regina had lunch with Brian two or three times a week, and she began looking forward to their times together. He was always the proper gentleman, never once making advances toward her. He was great fun, regaling her with tales of his adventures during various gem hunts throughout the world; she was sure that most of the tales were greatly embellished, if not outright falsehoods, but the stories were amusing. They also talked business; his store was doing very well.

"At least Andrew is happy," Brian said with a laugh.

"Doesn't he ever come to New York?"

"He made one trip, a month after the opening. He said he didn't care for the ocean voyage; it made him seasick. He told me he wasn't visiting again, as long as his share of the profits kept coming his way."

That reminded Regina of something she had forgotten—Will's predisposition to seasickness. Poor man! Not only was he braving unknown dangers, but he must be enduring dreadful sickness if he was traveling from country to country by ship.

Brian leaned forward. "You suddenly look sad, lass. Are you thinking of your husband?"

They had carefully avoided the subject of Will during their lunches. Now she said, "Yes, I was just remembering something. Will once told me that he could get seasick in a bathtub."

"Sure, and perhaps that will bring him scooting home before long."

"Well, he can choose his own time, just as he chose to leave," she said stiffly. "Not that I won't be glad to see him come back."

Brian tried several times to talk her into going to the theater or to dinner, but she resisted all such offers, realizing the danger inherent in going out in the evening with him. The strong physical attraction between them was still there—if anything, more intense. She was afraid that she would give in to Brian if she spent an evening with him.

Although he didn't put it into words, he seemed to sense her fears. With a wink, he said, "Sure, and I'll keep asking. You'll give in sooner or later, colleen."

The date for Eugene's wedding was growing near, and Regina began making plans for the big reception following the ceremony. Wanting it to be a surprise, she told Eugene that she wished to give the newlyweds a small party. Eugene protested that it wasn't necessary, but she could see by his smile that he was pleased.

There was a new restaurant just off Times Square, which was modeled after an English pub. It had a large private room for parties and even a small dance floor. Regina thought that Eugene would like the familiar atmosphere, especially since his parents were coming over from England for the nuptials. She hired a small orchestra, arranged for an elaborate dinner and had engraved invitations sent to everyone she knew, including Brian.

The day of the wedding was a pleasant spring day; the trees in Central Park and along the avenues were just coming into bud. Since she wanted the fancy reception to be a complete surprise to Eugene and his bride, most of the guests were not invited to the actual wedding. Only May's father—her mother was dead—Eugene's parents, the employees of the store and Brian were present.

Eugene's parents were in their late fifties, a little stodgy and seemingly bewildered by these strange, boisterous Americans. Typically British, Regina thought, and had to laugh at herself.

Eugene waited before the altar as the "Wedding March" began and May, radiant in her white wedding gown, came down the aisle on her father's arm.

Sitting beside Brian, Regina felt tears mist her eyes. It was no time to be thinking of Will, yet she couldn't help herself. Theirs had been a civil ceremony, performed before a justice of the peace; there had been no one to give her away, and the only other people present had been paid witnesses. In fact, this was the first real wedding she had ever attended.

Brian's hand took hers, and he squeezed gently. He leaned over to whisper in her ear, "You know what I'm thinking, lass? If I hadn't been such a great, blundering fool, I'm thinking we could have had a wedding like this."

She blinked away the tears and whispered back, "It's a little late for such thoughts, isn't it, Brian Macbride?"

"As my old mother used to say, hope springs eternal," he said, a chuckle in his voice.

She took her hand from his and moved a few inches away, refusing to look at him again as the ceremony began.

Then it was over, as Eugene lifted the veil and kissed the bride. Regina and Brian moved in close.

Regina hugged May fiercely, then turned to kiss Eugene.

"Congratulations to both of you!" she cried. "I know you'll be very happy, and I'm delighted for you, even if I do lose a gem sorter in the bargain."

"Oh, May wants to continue working," Eugene blurted. "At least until..." He turned red in the face, unable to continue.

May kissed him on the cheek and said serenely, "He means until I have children, Mrs. Logan. We intend to have at least four children, don't we, darling?"

Eugene could only nod, still blushing furiously.

Brian took Eugene's hand, saying heartily, "Sure, and it's a grand day for you, laddie. And you, too, lass. Now I'll go round up some hacks for us."

A few minutes later, they had all piled into two hackneys and were on their way to the restaurant. As Eugene handed his bride out of the hack, he turned to look at the pub, which had a swinging wooden sign, The Queen's Tavern.

His face lit up, and then he frowned, glancing over at Regina. "Regina, I've heard of this place. They say the food is very good, just like back in London. But isn't it terribly expensive?"

"Now don't you worry about it." She took his arm and urged him toward the entrance. "You're not only a highly valued employee, but one of my dearest friends, Eugene. I want to do this for you and May."

She led the way into the restaurant. The owner, whom Regina had met while making the arrangements, strode forward to greet her. An Englishman with a beefy, flushed face and a large stomach attesting his love of food and drink, he said jovially, "Ah, Madam Logan! The arrangements are as you ordered. And this is the bride and groom, I take it?"

Regina introduced Eugene and May, and the restaurateur offered his heartiest congratulations, then ushered the small party toward a door in the rear. He threw it open with a flourish.

The guests had already gathered and were waiting with glasses of champagne. An immediate toast to the bride and groom was proposed, and then Regina went around the room with Eugene and May, introducing them to those guests they did not already know.

Regina had sent invitations to most of the jewelry firms in the city, and almost all were represented. Respect for her business acumen had risen since her adroit handling of the synthetic gem crisis; and most especially after the manner in which she had handled the near disaster at her own store.

After the introductions, Eugene and May were seated together at the head of the long table, with their parents to their right and left.

Eugene said embarrassedly, "We weren't expecting anything like this, Regina, but it's a wonderful thing for you to do."

She squeezed his shoulder. "It's my pleasure, and no more than you deserve, Eugene. Now enjoy yourselves."

Regina and Brian sat down together at the table. Service began immediately, and the orchestra began playing recent hits from the London music halls.

The food, as well, was British. Brian leaned toward her. "Aye, lass, you're after doing it up grand. I could swear that I was back in London this very minute."

She looked at him curiously. "Do you miss London, Brian?"

"Not really," he said with a shrug. "You must remember that London wasn't actually my home, merely an operating base. I'm already a confirmed New Yorker, thinking of becoming a citizen. And you?"

"I missed London in the beginning, but I've settled in now and consider this my home. By marrying Will, of course, I automatically became an American citizen."

Brian lowered his voice, speaking next to her ear. "Tell me, Regina, who is that bucko across the table in the funny clothes?"

Smiling, Regina gazed across the table at Alexis Federov. He was in full Russian regalia—loose, ruffled blouse, trousers stuffed into high, polished boots, a short cape and a tall fur hat. When Regina had asked him about his costume, Federov had replied, "Is a wedding, is it not? Federov wears typical Russian costume for the dancing."

Laughing, Regina had said, "I doubt that there will be the kind of dancing you have in mind, Alexis."

"Dear Lady, Federov will show wedding guests how to dance at wedding celebration."

"That's Alexis Federov, my new jewelry designer," she told Brian. "I'm sorry, I thought I had introduced you to him."

"The bloke looks like he's ready to ride across the Russian steppes, swinging his sword."

"Alexis is a little strange to our ways, I must admit, but he is a brilliant jewelry designer, Brian, a great asset to my store."

"Is he better than Peter Mondrain?"

"In many ways, yes. He is equally as good a designer, and he works much faster. He is also well liked by everyone in the store. The women all adore him...."

They were interrupted by the waiters coming around to clear the tables of dishes. Then a several-tiered wedding cake was brought in. At Regina's instructions, the decorations on the cake were made in the form of various gemstones, except for the figures of the bride and groom. Eugene and May, holding the knife together, cut into the cake, taking the first slice for themselves. Then the rest of the cake was cut and distributed around the table.

As soon as the newlyweds had eaten their cake, the orchestra struck up a waltz. Eugene took May into his arms, and they moved around the floor to great applause. Soon, others joined them.

Brian stood, holding out his hand. "May I have this dance, colleen?"

For a big man, he was light on his feet and very graceful. They glided across the floor as one. Regina grew a little breathless at his nearness.

He put his lips close to her ear, his breath warm. "Do you realize this is the first dance for us?"

"Yes, I know," she murmured and tried to put a small distance between them, but Brian would have none of it, pulling her close against him as they danced. His nearness, his touch and the champagne she had consumed made Regina slightly giddy, and she determined to take it easy on the wine.

But the wine kept flowing, and she accepted a glass now and then. Everyone was enjoying themselves, and for the first time in a long while there was nothing on her mind but the present moment. She danced with Brian until she was exhausted, laughing at his stories and reveling in his nearness, his touch on her shoulder, the occasional brush of his mouth across her cheek.

She begged off for one dance, while Brian danced with the bride. Her glance drifting around the room, she saw Alexis Federov talking to the orchestra leader.

When the number was finished, the conductor clapped his hands for silence. As the room quieted, he said, "Mr. Federov has asked that the floor be cleared, that the next dance be his alone. He has also asked us to play a Russian tune. I'm not sure how well we can comply, but we shall do our very best."

The orchestra struck up a lively, foreign-sounding tune, and Alexis Federov took up a stance in the middle of the empty dance floor. Then he began a wild, uninhibited dance, with a rhythmic stamping of his booted feet and loud cries in accompaniment to the music. All at once he squatted on his haunches, his arms crossed over his chest, and began a leg-kicking step such as Regina had never seen.

She watched as he went around the floor, never standing erect, kicking out first one leg, then the other. She didn't understand how he could possibly retain his balance, but he seemed to manage without difficulty.

When the dance was finished, he sprang to his feet, arms thrown wide and high, his face flushed, his eyes blazing. He turned slowly in a circle, clapping his hands together, and the crowd joined in, applauding wildly.

As the band struck up another melody, Federov, breathing heavily, came over to where Regina was standing. His face dripped perspiration. Removing a voluminous kerchief from his pocket, he wiped at the sweat dripping down his forehead.

"That was spectacular, Alexis!" Regina exclaimed.

He beamed with her praise. "Federov not dance like that since leaving Mother Russia. Is hard work, much harder than making jewelry pieces."

Shortly the group began to dwindle. The bride and groom left at eight; they were to take a week's honeymoon at Niagara Falls.

The remaining guests took this as a signal to depart. Regina and Brian were the last to leave, as Regina had to settle the bill with the restaurant owner. Brian had a hack waiting when she emerged from the restaurant. He helped her into the vehicle, then climbed in after her. "'Tis early yet. Shall we go for a wee ride in Central Park?"

She hesitated only briefly. "I would like that."

As the hack started off, the horses' hooves clattering along the street, Brian said, "Sure, and that was a grand thing you did for the young ones."

"It was the least I could do. Eugene has been a faithful, valuable employee."

"I'm thinking it's a fine woman you are, Regina."

"Flattery, Mr. Macbride?" she said with a sideways look at him.

"Sure, and you're prickly as a hedgehog these days, Regina. Every time a fellow tries to compliment you, you rear back and spit."

"I'm sorry, Brian," she said with a sigh. "I suppose I am rather touchy."

"Just relax, lass," he said soothingly. He put an arm around her and drew her close.

Regina didn't fight it. She relaxed against him, feeling warm, secure and cared for. The long day and the excitement and emotion of the wedding began to have its effect; by the time the hack entered the park, she was dozing on Brian's shoulder. He held her gently as she drifted in and out of sleep. After some time had passed, she heard Brian say something to the driver. The hackney changed directions, but she was too drowsy, too comfortable, to look around.

Then they were still, and Brian was helping her out. He handed the driver some money and guided a half-awake Regina toward a building.

She roused, looking around at unfamiliar surroundings. "Where are we? This isn't my building."

"No, lass, it's mine. This is a flat I rented two months ago and have been working hard at fixing up. I thought you might like to see it."

Regina knew what was going to happen. Later, she might feel like blaming her dazed state, her consumption of wine; but now, she wanted it to happen. Her whole being yearned for Brian, for love and the surcease of pain that it offered. And why should she feel guilt? Will was the one who had deserted *her*. Even before that, he had withdrawn himself from her, physically as well as emotionally.

Just inside the door to Brian's flat, Regina turned into his arms, her lips eagerly seeking his. Their kiss fed the fire already banked inside her, and all else was swept from her mind.

She never did get a good look at his flat; Brian didn't even have time to turn on a light. Locked together, they moved into his bedroom, which was dimly illuminated by the glow of the streetlights below.

With hurried yet gentle hands, he removed her clothing, item by item. Naked, she shivered as the cool air brushed across her fevered flesh. She fell across the bed, mindlessly waiting for him, her senses further inflamed by the faint rustling sounds as he undressed.

Her arms went up to embrace him as he joined her on the bed.

She murmured deep in her throat as their lips met again. His hands roamed over her body.

"I love you, colleen," he muttered against her throat. "I have never stopped loving you."

Mutely she urged him to her. At their joining, she cried out, rising to meet his thrusting. They moved together into a rage of passion and shared need.

At the height of that passion, she cried his name aloud in the dimness, her body convulsing in almost unendurable ecstasy.

After a little, Brian, lying on his side, his breath hot against her cheek, said huskily, "So much time we have wasted, darlin'. So bloody much time."

"Hush, don't talk, Brian. You'll spoil it." She placed her fingers across his lips.

As he quieted, Regina lay with her eyes closed. She groped for his hand and held it tightly. She must leave soon; she had to get home before it grew too late. But she was relaxed, comfortable, and she was so tired.

Gradually her grip on Brian's hand relaxed, and she drifted into a deep slumber.

CHAPTER TWENTY-ONE

THROUGH A FOG of sleep, Regina heard, somewhere in the distance, a bell tolling midnight. Instantly she sat upright, fully awake.

At her side, Brian stirred, reaching out for her. "What is it, darlin'?"

She evaded his grasp and slipped out of bed. "It's midnight! I must get home!"

He sat up, yawning. "Why? There's no one waiting at home for you."

"But there is..." She stopped, realizing how dangerously close she had come to mentioning Michael.

"Who, then?"

"The housekeeper. She sleeps in the flat."

"The housekeeper?" He laughed. "It's a fine day when a mistress has to account to her housekeeper!"

Regina was already getting dressed. "She could gossip if I stayed out all night. That could hurt my reputation."

"This is the modern age, lass. I'm thinking no one pays heed to backstairs gossip."

"I'm a respectable businesswoman, Brian. I've just run one risk to my reputation. I don't care to run another."

"Darlin'," he said in his most cajoling voice, "I want you to stay the night with me." Sitting up on the edge of the bed, he reached out for her hand.

She pulled away. "No, Brian! I'm going home. Now will you get dressed, go down to the street and hail a hackney for me? If you don't, I'll go down by myself."

"Bloody hell!" he grumbled. "All right, all right, if you insist."

It was long after midnight when Regina let herself into the flat, halfway expecting a disapproving Nanny to be waiting up for her; but the flat was quiet. Regina tiptoed her way down the hall and into Michael's bedroom. He was sleeping peacefully. With a feeling of great relief, she bent to kiss him gently on the forehead, then made her way down to her own room and into bed.

She lay sleepless for a time, reliving the pleasurable moments in Brian's arms. Gradually, in spite of her determination, guilt crept into her thoughts. No matter how much she might rationalize, she had been unfaithful to Will, to her marriage vows. The irony of it struck forcibly. Will had been right to feel jealousy. Would she have been unfaithful if Will had not left her in such a manner? Search her soul as she might, she honestly didn't know the answer.

BRIAN CALLED HER in midmorning the next day. "And how are you this morning, colleen?"

"I'm fine, Brian," she said crisply.

"Aye, and the same goes for me. I'm in fine fettle this fine morning," he said with a rich chuckle.

"There seem to be too many fines in there," she said in a dry voice.

"Don't be telling me you're having regrets now?"

"I haven't quite decided about that. But I *am* a married woman, Brian, there is no getting around that."

"A mere technicality, woman," he scoffed. "The man has gone from your life and you're the better for it."

"You were very clever about the whole thing, weren't you, Brian?"

"I don't catch your meaning."

"I think you do. You bided your time, waiting to catch me off guard. You knew I would back away if you moved too early."

"Sure, and you misjudge me sorely, lass," he said in a wounded voice. "Be that as it may, how about having lunch with me today?"

"Not today, Brian. I am going to be very busy today; for the next few days, as a matter of fact."

"You wouldn't be trying to avoid me, now, would you?"

"No, Brian. Alexis and I have a great deal of work to accomplish." Excitement crept into her voice. "We may have a commission to design a trophy for Walter Tremayne, said by many to be the most astute breeder of thoroughbreds next to August Belmont. He has informed me that he wishes to have a cup made that is more expensive, more lavish, than any of the various Belmont trophies.''

''Am I correct in believing that Tiffany's made the Belmont cups?''

''That's right! So think what this means. This is my chance to gain real recognition. If we can get this commission, we'll earn as much respect as Tiffany's, who make most of the boating and racing trophies in the country.''

''It would indeed be a feather in your cap, darlin'.''

''Alexis and I have been invited out to the Tremayne stables on Long Island. We're to stay there for a few days, while we sketch some of the Tremayne thoroughbreds. Their pictures will be incorporated into the design of the cup, which is to be called the Walter Tremayne Memorial Cup. It all hinges on whether Mr. Tremayne likes our design, but we're going to do such a fabulous job that he can't help but like it!''

''I'm thinking you'll do just fine, Regina. All the best of luck to you. Give Tiffany's a run for their money. And we'll have lunch when you get back.''

REGINA KNEW most people would find it hard to believe, but she had never seen a racing horse. The only type of horses she was familiar with were those used to pull carriages and hackneys, and the ones the police rode in New York City. She had never been on a horse in her life.

The Tremayne estate on Long Island was extensive, with a fine white house on the water. She and Federov never saw Walter Tremayne during the three days they spent on the estate, nor anyone else from the big house. They occupied small guest cottages near the stables, which were located a good quarter of a mile from the main house.

"So fine gentry will not have to smell horse manure," Federov said, grinning. "Guests do not matter. Is that not so, dear lady?"

"Perhaps," Regina said with a laugh. "But it's just as well we're staying out here. This is a working visit, not a social one."

The stablemaster, one Jonas Welch, a dour, taciturn individual of indeterminate age, showed them to their quarters and escorted them through the stables. The thoroughbreds were lovely animals, with long, graceful necks and slender legs; their coats were burnished until they shone like satin.

Each morning, shortly after daybreak, Regina and Federov stationed themselves at the railing of the exercise track and watched the horses being put through their paces.

"They're beautiful, aren't they, Alexis?"

"Seeing them makes Federov long for Mother Russia," he said wistfully. "In Russia, we have many beautiful horses." He gave her a flashing grin. "But Federov not long too much."

After the exercises, they studied the animals as they were rubbed down, and later in their stalls. All the while, Federov was making charcoal drawings. Regina had learned to sketch a little when she became interested in jewelry design, but her drawings were clumsy and amateurish in comparison to Federov's. His sketches were lifelike, catching the essence of the animals' grace and beauty. He could have been a painter, she thought.

After three days, they returned to New York with a folio of sketches, and they worked long hours making a model of the proposed trophy.

Finally it was done. Regina stood back to study it. In its final form, the cup would stand eighteen inches high from the base to the cover. The cover would be fastened with tiny roses set with small diamonds. On the base of the eighteen carat gold cup would be the figures of two thoroughbreds made of silver, and another, wearing bridle and racing saddle, would stand on the cover. The animals, of course, were made to conform to the sketches Federov had made.

Regina clapped her hands in delight. "I think you have done a marvelous job, Alexis. You are indeed a true artist. If Mr. Tremayne doesn't approve, there has to be something wrong with him!"

"This man Tremayne will approve," Federov said with maddening complacency.

"Well, we'll soon see."

She sent Walter Tremayne a message, and he came to the store the following day. A tall, thin man with a stern countenance and piercing gray eyes, he studied the model for a long time in silence, walking around it twice. Then he stared down at it again, chin propped on one hand, while Regina waited with bated breath.

Finally he nodded and looked at her without even a trace of a smile. "My congratulations, Mrs. Logan. And Mr. Federov. It is precisely what I had in mind. You have the commission."

DURING THE NEXT SIX WEEKS, Regina and Federov worked long, exhausting hours on the trophy. Although the Russian was a fast worker, he agreed with Regina that they should work slowly, since Tremayne had imposed no time limit.

"I want this to be a true work of art, Alexis," Regina exclaimed.

"So it shall be, dear lady, so it shall be."

Actually there was little Regina could do, except serve as his assistant and voice an opinion now and then. But Federov had no objection to her hovering over him constantly; in fact, he seemed quite pleased. Regina suspected that he welcomed the chance to show his artistry.

Brian was upset with her. For the first few days after she had received the commission, he had called repeatedly, asking her out to lunch or to dinner, first because he thought she owed herself a celebration, then just because he wanted them to be together.

Regina pleaded the press of work. "I'm working practically around the clock, Brian. This is very important to me, you must see that. I'm so tired at night, I just fall into bed."

In a huff, he had finally stopped calling her. She could have taken time to be with him without any harm being done to the project, and she finally realized that she was using the trophy as an excuse. She wanted to be with Brian; she longed to feel his lips on hers, to revel in his passionate embrace, but she refused to give in to her traitorous longings. She dimly realized that her self-denial was a means of punishment, yet she steadfastly refused to see him, promising that they would be together when the cup was completed.

And finally she was satisfied with it. To Regina, it was an object of great beauty.

Again she sent a message to Walter Tremayne, and he came into the city at once.

He took one look at the finished trophy and smiled for the first time since she had known him. His words echoed her own thoughts. "It is a thing of rare beauty, Mrs. Logan. It shall be my great pleasure to see it awarded each year to one of the country's greatest racing thoroughbreds!"

An hour later, Regina gazed at the retreating back of Walter Tremayne as he left her office, carrying the trophy in a padded box. She transferred her glance to the check in her hand.

She wanted to jump up and down and shout out her elation, but she forced herself to remain seated. This was her first real triumph and she knew that word would soon spread throughout the jewel community. Soon others would follow Tremayne's lead and come to Paxton Jewels when they wished something of real quality such as the Tremayne Memorial Trophy.

It was well into July now, and it was hot and muggy in New York. The faint breeze coming through the open window behind her did little to cool the room. She doubted that she would ever become accustomed to the hot summers here. She could feel perspiration running down her back, and her shirtwaist stuck to her like flypaper.

Yet the discomfort was nothing, compared to the delight she felt over the coup she had just carried off—she and Alexis. She must not forget his part in it. Without his artistry, her store would not be the success it had become.

Her hand strayed toward the telephone stand. She had to call Brian; she had to share the good news with someone. She stopped as her fingers touched the earpiece. If she called Brian now, he would want to have a celebration dinner; and she knew very well what would happen.

But why should she hesitate? This was her moment of triumph, so why should she not share it with Brian?

She started to pick up the earpiece when a discreet cough coming from the open door stayed her.

It was Bert Downes, wearing a grave face. As their glances met, he came into the room. "This was delivered a few minutes ago, Mrs. Logan."

He held out a small, square package wrapped in brown paper and bound with a cord. Regina took it, a strong sense of foreboding sweeping over her.

With a nod, Downes went out, and Regina sat staring at the package, afraid to open it. It was postmarked Sydney, Australia.

Finally her inertia broke and she took a pair of scissors from her desk and snipped the cord. Inside the wrapping was a small box and two sealed envelopes. Both envelopes had her name written on them. With trembling fingers, she opened the larger envelope first. Inside was a single sheet of paper embossed with the seal of the American consulate in Sydney, Australia.

My dear Mrs. Logan,
I sincerely regret to inform you that your . . .

She stopped reading, closing her eyes tightly. It was several moments before she could force herself to start reading again,

My dear Mrs. Logan,
I sincerely regret to inform you that your husband, William Logan, is dead.

Your husband expired on June 14. From the scanty information I can gather, he was taken ill of some tropical fever. He was forced to leave the ship here in Sydney, but instead of checking into a hospital, he took up quarters in a rooming house. Within the week, his illness had progressed to the point where medical treatment was useless.

When the authorities went through his effects, it was learned that he was an American citizen, and I was called in. Having no alternative, I ordered his burial. Among his effects was the enclosed box addressed to you, along with the sealed envelope that I have enclosed without opening.

His other personal effects, which are pitifully few in number, are also being shipped to you, by slower passage. May I extend my sympathy, Mrs. Logan, for your grievous loss. If I can be of any further assistance, please do not hesitate to contact me.

The letter was signed by the American consul general in Australia.

Feeling too numb even for tears, Regina read the letter again, postponing opening the second envelope. Finally she could delay it no longer. Picking it up, she slit open the white paper. The writing on the enclosed sheets was in Will's familiar hand.

My dearest Regina,

If you receive this letter, you will know that I am dead. On my travels, I have contracted some exotic tropical disease and the doctor tells me that I have waited too long to seek medical attention. He can do nothing for me. That seems to sum up the story of my life; always too little or too late.

Do not grieve for me, my dearest. I am not worthy of your grief. Go about making a new life for yourself. My only regret is the trouble I have caused you, through my stupidity and jealousy. Please believe that I have never stopped loving you. Knowing and loving you have made my life worthwhile.

I did accomplish one thing of which I am proud, as you shall see when you open the box. Accept it in the manner in which it is given; a measure of my love and devotion.

I shall leave it to you as to what to tell Michael. If you choose to tell him that I am not his real father, I would be most gratified should you also tell him that I could not have loved him more had he been my natural son.

Do not blame yourself for what has happened. You are in no way at fault. I mean that with all my heart. Farewell, my dear Regina. All my love, and best wishes for the life that is yet ahead of you.

Will.

Regina put the letter down, smoothing it with trembling fingers. Grief burned in her, but still the tears did not come.

She picked up the small box, hesitating for a long moment before opening it, certain that she knew what was inside. When she lifted the lid of the box and pushed aside the crumpled tissue, she saw that she was right—it was a sapphire. It had been cleaned, but was still in a rough state.

Picking up the stone, she went down the hall to Eugene's workroom. It was the lunch hour and he was out. Placing the sapphire under a strong light on his worktable, she took up a magnifying glass and scrutinized the stone closely. She knew that a star's asterism, or six-ray star pattern, was not readily detectable until it was properly cleaned and cut, but a few minutes of study told her that this was a true star. An asterism was caused by a hexagonal growth pattern, which in turn was caused by needlelike silk inclusions within the stone. These silk inclusions react to form a six-ray star pattern when the light enters the top of the stone.

Not only was this a star sapphire, but it was what was called a black star, the rarest of all stars. In truth, a black star could be brown, blue, purple or green in color. This one was blue, and the more blue color a star possessed, the more valuable and expensive it was. This was indeed a rare gem!

Without feeling the delight she had always thought she would experience when possessing an uncut star, Regina trudged back down the hall to her office. Her first inclination was to dispose of it, to throw it away without anyone ever knowing of it. This stone had cost Will his life. But for that very reason, shouldn't she keep it, cherish it for the rest of *her* life?

She placed the sapphire in the exact center of her desk and reached for the telephone. When that familiar, deep voice answered on the other end, she said in a choked voice, "Brian..."

"Regina, is that you?"

"Brian, Will is dead!"

"I'll be right there, darlin'," he said instantly. "Just hold on."

He hung up, and she sat for a few minutes with the dead earpiece in her hand. The tears came then. It seemed that putting the fact of Will's death into words had finally brought it home to her. She wept bitterly, her body racked by sobs. Through the blinding tears, she managed to hang up the earpiece.

When Brian arrived a half hour later, she had found a measure of control, but the sight of his concerned face threatened to bring on fresh tears.

His own eyes wet, he plucked her out of the chair and held her close. "It's sorry I am, darlin'. Sorrier than I can ever say."

After a bit, he held her away from him and gazed down into her face. "How did it happen?"

She gestured wordlessly to the letters and the sapphire on her desk. She sat back down while he read the two letters quickly.

"Poor fellow," he murmured. "Sure, and he had bad luck all the way round." He picked up the sapphire and examined it at length, then whistled softly. "This is the finest grade sapphire I have ever seen. When it's properly cut and mounted in a brooch, you'll be the envy of all."

She shook her head vehemently. "No, I'll never wear it and I'll never sell it. I'll keep it just like it is, to remind me of what it cost. My husband's life!"

"Regina, you shouldn't think of it like that." He squatted beside her chair and took her hands. "You mustn't blame yourself. Will said as much in his letter and I find myself respecting him the more for that. The sapphire was only an excuse. He was a weak man in many ways, yet he had the sense to realize that about himself. Darlin'..." He took a deep breath, looking directly into her eyes. "I'm sure you will think this a terrible time for me to be asking, but I think it *is* the right time. I don't want to lose you again. Marry me, Regina."

"Oh, Brian!" She tried to wrestle her hands away, "I have just learned that my husband is dead!"

"I know," he said gravely. "And I know you'll need time to mourn for the man. But when the proper time has passed... Besides, that was what he was saying in the letter, I'm thinking. 'Go about making a new life for yourself.' Sure, and he didn't mention my name, but I believe that was his meaning." He frowned suddenly. "He mentioned the name Michael, and something about loving him as much as if he was the real father. What did he mean by that?"

Regina experienced a moment of panic. She had forgotten that Will had mentioned Michael in the letter. Then she knew what she had to do; the time had come.

She got up from her chair. "Come with me, Brian. I want you to meet someone."

FIFTEEN MINUTES LATER, she keyed open the door to the flat and went in, Brian right behind her. All the way over, he had tried to quiz her, but Regina had refused to satisfy his curiosity.

At the sound of the door closing, Michael came running in from the other room. He skidded to a stop at the sight of a strange man, his eyes going wide.

"Brian, this is my son, Michael," she said quietly.

Brian didn't answer, his glance fastened on the boy. Then his mouth fell open, and he took on a look of consternation such as she had never seen before. Finally he turned on her, his eyes alight. "He's my son, isn't he?"

"Yes, Brian," she said simply.

"Then that's the reason you married Will Logan?"

"That was one of the reasons, yes."

"But why didn't you tell me, back in London?"

"By the time I knew, you were gone, or so I thought. I also didn't think you deserved to know."

For a moment, his eyes blazed in anger, and he took a short step toward her. Regina thought that he was going to strike her, but she refused to give ground.

Then he stopped, pivoting around to drop to one knee. He held his arms out. "Come here, lad."

Michael hesitated for a moment, looking at his mother, who nodded, smiling. The boy ran into Brian's arms. Brian embraced him for a moment, then stood lifting the boy with him. When he turned to face Regina, she saw that his eyes were glistening, but he was smiling.

"By all the saints!" he crowed. "Sure, and I can't believe it. Now it's time I put something right. You must marry me darlin'."

She returned his look composedly. "First, I must mourn Will. But if I marry you, there is one thing that must be understood. Paxton Jewels is mine. Besides, I have the strong feeling that we would never get along running it together."

"I have no objection." He winked. "I'm after thinking there's no reason why a husband and wife can't be friendly competitors. My old mother used to say that a man and wife can never work together in the same business and hope to keep harmony in the household."

He shifted Michael to the crook of his left arm and beckoned to Regina with the other. She moved to him and he put his arm around her shoulders, pulling her against him.

At that moment, Nanny came into the room. She stopped short, her eyes going wide at the tableau greeting her.

"Nanny, this is Brian Macbride," Regina said calmly. "We shall be having a guest for dinner."

Patricia Matthews, ''America's First Lady of Romance,'' will delight her fans with these spellbinding sagas of passion and romance, glamour and intrigue.

Thursday and the Lady	$4.50	☐
A story of a proud and passionate love set during America's most unforgettable era—as suffragettes waged their struggle for the vote, the gold rush spurred glorious optimism and the Civil War loomed on the horizon.		
Mirrors	$4.50	☐
Intrigue, passion and murder surround a young woman when she learns that she is to inherit an enormous family fortune.		
Enchanted	$3.95	☐
Caught in the steamy heat of America's New South, a young woman finds herself torn between two brothers—she yearns for one but a dark, foreboding secret binds her to the other.		
Oasis	$4.50	☐
A spellbinding story chronicling the lives of the movie stars, politicians and rock celebrities who converge at the world-famous addiction clinic in Oasis.		

Total Amount	$	
Plus 75¢ Postage		.75
Payment enclosed		

Please send a check or money order payable to Worldwide Library.

In U.S.A.	In Canada
Worldwide Library	Worldwide Library
901 Fuhrmann Blvd.	P.O. Box 609
Box 1325	Fort Erie, Ontario
Buffalo, NY 14269-1325	L2A 5X3

Please Print

Name: _____

Address: _____

City: _____

State/Prov: _____

Zip/Postal Code: _____

WORLDWIDE LIBRARY

PAM-1

Worldwide Library provides the best in historical romance—magnificent sagas of passion, romance, adventure, and suspense set during some of the most turbulent and dazzling periods in history.

		Quantity
SPRING WILL COME—Sherry DeBorde A young Southern woman is left alone to face overwhelming odds during the tumultuous years leading up to and including the Civil War.	$3.95	☐
THE BARGAIN—Veronica Sattler A young woman accepts a position as ''governess'' to the Duke's grandson but discovers that he is not a small child but a handsome young man.	$4.50	☐
UNTIL I RETURN—Laura Simon A novel of love and adventure in nineteenth-century Nantucket.	$3.95	☐
DEFY THE EAGLE—Lynn Bartlett An enthralling saga of love set during the dramatic period of the Roman Empire in Britain.	$4.95	☐

Total Amount	$ _____
Plus 75¢ Postage	.75
Payment enclosed	_____

Please send a check or money order payable to Worldwide Library.

In the U.S.A.	In Canada
Worldwide Library 901 Fuhrmann Blvd. Box 1325 Buffalo, NY 14269-1325	Worldwide Library P.O. Box 609 Fort Erie, Ontario L2A 5X3

Please Print

Name: _____

Address: _____

City: _____

State/Prov: _____

Zip/Postal Code: _____

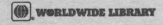 **WORLDWIDE LIBRARY**

HSR-2

Worldwide Library provides the best in historical romance—magnificent sagas of passion, romance, adventure and suspense set during some of the most turbulent and dazzling periods in history.

Breathtaking sagas of romance and passion set during some of the most captivating periods in history

		Quantity
MADAWASKA—Willo Davis Roberts	$3.95 U.S.	☐
A riveting love story spanning several generations set against the eighteenth-century backdrop of the tumultuous plight of Acadians fighting to keep their land.	$4.50 Canada	☐
THE DEFIANT—Mary Canon	$3.95 U.S.	☐
Set in Ireland during the turbulent sixteenth century, a powerful story of love between a highborn Englishwoman and a fiery Irish rebel.	$4.50 Canada	☐
TURNING POINT—Shannon OCork	$4.50	☐
A young woman discovers love after a painful relationship, only to be drawn into the golden world of nineteenth-century Newport where beautiful faces hide daring lies . . . and perhaps even murder.		
ICE FALL—Shannon OCork	4.50	☐
The captivating saga begun in the TURNING POINT continues with ICE FALL, where fate, love and destiny meet on the tragic voyage of the *Titanic*.		

Total Amount	$	_____
Plus 75¢ Postage		.75
Payment enclosed	$	_____

Please send a check or money order payable to Worldwide Library.

In the U.S.A.	In Canada
Worldwide Library	Worldwide Library
901 Fuhrmann Blvd.	P.O. Box 609
Box 1325	Fort Erie, Ontario
Buffalo, NY 14269-1325	L2A 5X3

Please Print

Name: _____

Address: _____

City: _____

State/Prov: _____

Zip/Postal Code: _____

(()) **WORLDWIDE LIBRARY**

HSR-3

From the *New York Times* bestselling author
Patricia Matthews, a sensuous story of hope
and passion

Rich in adventure and vivid with authentic detail, this
captivating novel tells the story of a courageous woman
banished to Australia who vows to build a new life for
herself and her two daughters.

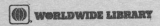 **WORLDWIDE LIBRARY**